To Sleep with Reindeer

Acclaim for Justine Saracen's Novels

Sniper's Kiss

"If you've read Saracen before, she's at her finest here. Her action sequences pop, her plots are twisty, and she loves to put her heroines in the most dire of circumstances and extract them slowly."—*Out in Print*

"*Sniper's Kiss* is an epic tale of one woman's love for another and what she is willing to go through to be with her. It is a beautiful love story between two characters that pulled at my heart strings…Justine Saracen has researched this period so well and her writing made me feel as if I was there amongst the noises, smells and tragedies of war. A truly fantastic book that I highly recommend."—*Kitty Kat's Book Review Blog*

"Justine Saracen's writing is very in-depth. You know going into them they are superbly well researched and you most likely will be a bit smarter by the time you finish. Saracen's attention to detail and an inclusion of historical facts in her novels help make the stories and characters riveting…This book is a fascinating tale of history and relationship's born out of horrifying circumstances. A historical fiction with just a hint of romance…overall this was a fantastic read."—*Romantic Reader Blog*

The Witch of Stalingrad

"[O]ne of the best lesbian historical novels I've read…on the Eastern Front (not just) the night bombers, which Saracen more than excelled at portraying (but also) the conditions of POW camps, citizens who were affected by Stalin's purges that left thousands dead, and the camaraderie between strangers in terrifying situations."—*The Lesbrary*

"This book is full of amazing, admirable women and I was pleased with each one, from the war correspondent who must fly a plane in battle...to the medics who carry the wounded under fire, to the POWs in camp who huddle around their tied-up comrade to prevent her from freezing to death, this story honors them all."—*Book Babe*

"*The Witch of Stalingrad* is way more than just a wartime romance. At first, I didn't expect such depth and historical accuracy, but I was delighted to find it. This book is gritty, a realistic look at life in a war zone...I'll just say it's fantastic."
—Leeanna.ME Mostly a Book Blog

Waiting for the Violins

"A thrilling, charming, and heartrending trip back in time to the early years of World War II and the active resistance enclaves... Stunning and eye-opening!"—*Rainbow Book Reviews*

Beloved Gomorrah

"I can't think of anything more incongruous than ancient Biblical texts, scuba diving, Hollywood lesbians, and international art installations, but I do know that there's only one author talented and savvy enough to make it all work. That's just what the incomparable Justine Saracen does in her latest, *Beloved Gomorrah*."—*Out In Print*

Tyger Tyger Burning Bright

"Saracen blends historical and fictional characters seamlessly and brings authenticity to the story, focusing on the impacts of this time on 'regular, normal people'...*Tyger Tyger Burning Bright* [is]a brilliantly written historical novel that has elements of romance, suspense, horror, pathos and it gives the reader quite a bit to think about...fast-paced...difficult to put down... an excellent book that easily blurs the line between lesfic and mainstream."—*C-Spot Reviews*

Sarah, Son of God

"*Sarah, Son of God* can lightly be described as the 'The Lesbian's Da Vinci Code' because of the somewhat common themes. At its roots, it's part mystery and part thriller. *Sarah, Son of God* is an engaging and exciting story about searching for the truth within each of us. Ms. Saracen considers the sacrifices of those who came before us, challenges us to open ourselves to a different reality than what we've been told we can have, and reminds us to be true to ourselves. Her prose and pacing rhythmically rise and fall like the tides in Venice; and her reimagined life and death of Jesus allows thoughtful readers to consider 'what if?'"
—*Rainbow Reader*

Mephisto Aria

"*Mephisto Aria* could well stand as a classic among gay and lesbian readers."—*ForeWord Reviews*

"Saracen's wonderfully descriptive writing is a joy to the eye and the ear, as scenes play out on the page, and almost audibly as well. The characters are extremely well drawn, with suave villains, and lovely heroines. There are also wonderful romances, a heart-stopping plot, and wonderful love scenes. *Mephisto Aria* is a great read."—*Just About Write*

"Justine Saracen's latest thriller, *Mephisto Aria*, brims with delights for every sort of reader…delight at love's triumph, and at Saracen's queer reworkings of the Faust legend, are not this novel's only pleasures. Saracen's understanding of the world around opera is profound. She captures the sweat, fierce intelligence, terror and exultation that characterize singers' daily lives, in rehearsal and performance, she evokes well the camaraderie that a production's cast and crew share, and she brings to literary life

the curious passions that bind people who make music together. Brilliantly fusing the insights of twenty years' worth of feminist and queer opera criticism to lesbian fantasy fiction, Saracen has written a passionate, action-packed thriller that sings—indeed, that sings the triumph of Rosenkavalier's trio of lovers over Dr. Faustus' joyless composer. Brava! Brava! Brava!"
— *Suzanne G Cusick, Professor of Music, New York University*

Sistine Heresy

"Justine Saracen's *Sistine Heresy* is a well-written and surprisingly poignant romp through Renaissance Rome in the age of Michelangelo...The novel entertains and titillates while it challenges, warning of the mortal dangers of trespass in any theocracy (past or present) that polices same-sex desire."
— *Professor Frederick Roden, University of Connecticut, Author, Same-Sex Desire in Victorian Religious Culture*

"Historical fiction [is] a genre that must artfully blend historical accuracy with fanciful conjecture in order to succeed. And succeed Saracen does. Casting such an iconic artistic and historic figure as Michelangelo in a controversial new light is risky business—some would say a heresy unto itself. But Saracen portrays Michelangelo and his cohorts as anything but corrupt, endowing them with an absolute sensitivity and absolute humanity."—*ForeWord Reviews*

The 100th Generation

"*The 100th Generation* is a fast-paced, complex battle of good and evil, where the author dabbles in religions both old and modern in an exploration of what happens when everyday people are involved in world-changing events."—*Just About Write*

By the Author

Visit us at www.boldstrokesbooks.com

TO SLEEP
WITH REINDEER

by
Justine Saracen

2020

ISBN 13: 978-1-63555-735-0

This Trade Paperback Original Is Published By
Bold Strokes Books, Inc.
P.O. Box 249
Valley Falls, NY 12185

First Edition: October 2020

CREDITS
Editor: Shelley Thrasher
Production Design: Stacia Seaman
Cover Design by Sheri (HINDSIGHTGRAPHICS@GMAIL.COM)

Acknowledgments

To longtime friend and editor Shelley Thrasher; and cover designer Sheri; to Cindy Cresap, Sandy Lowe, Stacia Seaman, Ruth Sternglantz, invisible BSB staff, and above all, to Radclyffe, here we are at historical novel number thirteen. I never imagined it would come so far. (Removes hat, nods humbly.)

It's been an honor and a pleasure.

Prelude

Nazi-Occupied Norway
November 1942

Far from the war and the occupation, on the wild Norwegian plateau, nature took its own brutal course. A reindeer had given birth out of season to a white calf. Only two weeks old when migration to the winter pasture began, the tiny calf lurched through the deep snow, laboring to follow its mother. But its spindly legs tired quickly, and it lagged far behind.

Though snow had been falling all day, the sky began to clear, and a white-tailed eagle spotted the exhausted creature separated from the others. The large male raptor was also out of season, having failed, due to a damaged wing, to migrate toward the coast with its flock, and had fed thus far on carrion. But the new snow had rendered such meals nearly invisible, and it was starving. The struggling calf presented an opportunity.

The eagle swooped down and seized the infant deer by its withers, lifting it off its feet. The calf thrashed and bleated in pain and terror as the predator strained its wings to gain height. But it managed to rise only a few meters before the struggling calf wrenched itself free and dropped to the ground, where it lay motionless and bleeding.

The raptor made a wide circle preparing for another strike, but now an adult deer stood over the calf. Worse, another creature on two legs approached, waving threateningly. Shrieking, the eagle banked away and flew off toward the rest of the herd, searching for easier prey.

Chapter One

July 1942

Drenched and shivering, Kirsten Brun gripped the gunwale of the transport boat as it heaved over the waves of the North Atlantic.

The seaman coiling rope next to her seemed to balance unaided. "Don't you worry, miss. These cutters are slow in a head sea, but they'll stand up to any storm. Why don't you go below decks and lie down?"

She weighed the benefit of warmth against the thought of the tiny cabin, where the lurching would be just as bad, but the smell of the diesel exhaust from the engine would be worse. And lying down would do nothing for her seasickness.

"Thanks. I'll stay aboveboard for now." To avoid looking at the terrifying gray waves, she focused on the wheelhouse and the exhaust pipe jutting from the top. It emitted a solemn tonk-tonk-tonk that she could hear even above the roar of the wind.

They had slipped out of Bergen Harbor at nightfall, and now it was daylight—such as it was. At least they were in the open sea, far enough away from the Norwegian coast that meeting a German ship was unlikely, and the wind and cloud cover protected them from German aircraft.

"When do you expect us to arrive in Shetland?"

"Can't really say, miss. In good weather, we can make the crossing in twenty-four hours, but in this headwind, we're barely doing seven knots. Could take a day and a half."

They dropped again into the trough of a wave with a sickening thud, and a cloud of spray struck her. She wiped salt water out of her eyes with a wet hand.

"I see. Do you suppose I can go into the wheelhouse?"

"Long as you don't bother the skipper."

Grateful, she lurched toward the wheelhouse and let herself in. The pilot at the wheel ignored her as she entered, so she groped her way to a corner bench and held fast to a bar on the wall. The mission was turning out to be more hazardous than she'd expected, and she had only a vague idea of what it was. That was policy, of course. If captured and interrogated—which she understood meant tortured—she could reveal only what she knew, and that was rather little.

She'd never been in Shetland and recalled only that it was a cluster of islands whose only virtue was their location midway between Scotland and Norway. Until the war, traffic between the two countries was sparse, and now she knew why.

Her code name was Chemist, and she carried letters from the Norwegian resistance leaders to the exiled Norwegian government in London. But upon leaving, her father had given her a rucksack of personal items—dry socks, toothpaste, a block of chocolate, and a folding knife. At the last moment, her stepmother, Johanna Brun, had also handed her a small cloth purse, saying, "A woman should not need to worry about feminine hygiene when she's on a mission." Seeing Kirsten add the purse to the other items, Jomar Brun ordered cryptically, "If you encounter Germans, you must throw everything overboard. Everything, even that." She'd agreed without questioning.

She closed her eyes, and to calm her stomach she tried to imagine her childhood home in Rjukan before the arrival of the Nazis. It was a lovely town, deep in a gorge flanked by luscious green in summer and bluish snow-light in the long dark winters. But they were the vague emotional memories of a child, for her parents' divorce had taken her away at the age of twelve. The ten years in London with her mother thereafter had dulled her Norwegian patriotism, but never her nostalgia.

"Looks like the sea's calming a little," the pilot said, rousing her from her reverie. "Well done to you, miss, for holding up. There's them that don't." He scratched his cheek through a three-day beard. He had a friendly, wizened look, but his skin lacked the dark, weathered look of the other seamen and suggested he hadn't been a fisherman for long. He wore a well-stained jacket and a knitted cap, but the hair that peered out from under it was gray.

"You're from Rjukan, aren't you? I recognize the accent."

"Yes, indeed. Born and raised, miss. You've got a good ear. I moved north a few years ago. I was at Tromsø when the British rescued King Haakon."

"Really? That must have been exciting. How'd he look?"

The pilot leaned forward and peered through the window of the wheelhouse, obviously calculating the weather conditions, then seemed satisfied and returned his attention to her.

"Well, you know that in 1940, the king and the prince and the ministers fled north through the woods to the coast. The British collected them at Tromsø. I was on the docks when he boarded, and you never saw a more broken-spirited man. It was a grim day, but the king and the government got away, and that gave us hope."

"I hear his broadcasts from time to time on the BBC. Inspiring."

"You held on to a radio, eh? Lucky, but dangerous. Since that slimy Nazi Terboven took power, you risk your life listening." He mimed spitting on the deck. "A pox on the Germans and their Norwegian ass-kissers. Haakon is my king, and I wear this to show it."

He held open his jacket so she could see the "H7" monogram of Haakon the Seventh woven on his vest. "The Germans don't recognize it, but Norwegian patriots do."

"Ah, then I'm in good hands."

"Yes, miss. You are."

❖

A day and a half later, after a harrowing trip over the North Atlantic and another ferry ride from the Shetlands to Scotland, Kirsten finally sat on the train to London. The precious letters to the king and other leaders were in a thin leather folder inside her jacket, and her rucksack lay safely under her feet. She was beyond weary, sensed the vague cramping and nausea that signaled that her "days" would start soon, and was grateful for the protection Johanna Brun had given her.

The thought of her father and stepmother gave her a slight pang of guilt. They appreciated her independence, which she clearly got from her English mother, but she had long ago reached marriageable age. They obviously wondered why she didn't settle down like other women. But how could she explain that the thought of being some man's faithful wife filled her with revulsion?

With a background in chemistry, she'd applied for a position at the Vemork Hydro Plant in 1939, where her father was chief engineer. "Go back and finish your chemistry exams," he'd said. "Then we'll talk."

She'd agreed, but a year later, in 1940, the Germans occupied Norway, and everything changed. Two years after that, a veritable war had developed at the university as Reichskommisar Josef Terboven tried to nazify both students and faculty. Both had resisted, and Kirsten herself became radicalized. She winced, remembering the fire in the Great Hall and Terboven's use of it to close the university. She'd even been briefly arrested, for vague political reasons, but then released, with even less explanation.

In limbo, she once again applied to work at Vemork with her father, but the job Jomar finally offered her was as a courier to London and had nothing to do with chemistry.

An outburst of male laughter shook her back to the present. Her railcar was packed full of troops, and though their noise and smoking at first irritated her, her complete exhaustion and the clatter of the train wheels rocked her to sleep.

By the time she reached King's Cross station in London, she was dazed, ravenous, and craved a bath. It was therefore a relief to discover that an agent waited with a car. He offered to carry her rucksack, but she refused. "I'm to deliver everything directly to Mr. Tronstad, and until then, I'll hang on to it, if you don't mind."

Half an hour later, they arrived at the Special Operations Executive offices, abbreviated by everyone simply as SOE. The second floor held the Norwegian High Command, and at the end of a long hall, the agent led her to a door marked SECTION IV. After a brief knock, he ushered her into the office.

A man in the uniform of a major in the Norwegian Army, whom she recognized as Leif Tronstad, stood up from his desk. A slender, attractive man with long legs and short upper body, his large, warm eyes were at odds with his reputation as a hardheaded resistor and activist. She could more easily imagine him in an easy chair smoking a pipe and with a dog at his feet. Another man stood to his right, light-haired, balding, somewhat corpulent.

"Welcome to London, Miss Brun." Tronstad offered his hand, and as she shook it, he glanced toward his portly colleague. "This is Colonel Wilson, head of the Norwegian SOE. He has a great interest in our undertaking."

"We hear good things about you from your father," Wilson said, requiring another handshake. "He told us you had a close call with the Germans while at university."

"Oh, that. It seems they were giving us the opportunity to be Aryan masters in the new Reich. When blandishments didn't work, they gave us our own Reichstag fire in the university auditorium. That, in turn, provided them with the excuse to close the university and arrest more than a thousand of us. Students and professors alike."

"And you escaped?" Wilson seemed impressed.

She smiled weakly. "Nothing so heroic. They released the women students and about half of the men. The other half, which I guess seemed more promising, were sent to German camps for indoctrination. It remains to be seen what will come of that. In any case, I'd had it with the 'master race.' I'd have signed up for Milorg, but as it happens, my father needed me for this delivery."

"Norway's clandestine military organization has its uses for local resistance, but we feel we can accomplish more from over here. So, welcome to Britain and the Free Norwegians," Tronstad said and gestured toward the chair in front of his desk. When she was seated, he asked, "How was the crossing?"

"Ghastly, but at least we weren't intercepted or bombarded. Something to be thankful for, I suppose." Getting to the point of the meeting, she drew the leather folder from her shoulder bag and held it out to him.

Tronstad took it with curiously little interest and laid it on his desk. "Actually, it's the personal items I need to see."

"My personal items? Uh, yes, sir." Puzzled, she rummaged in her rucksack until her fingers found the soft purse her stepmother had given her. Fortunately, her normal "schedule" had been late, and she hadn't needed any of the intimate products. But what the hell did Tronstad want with them?

She handed the package to him and watched, embarrassed and slightly affronted, as he drew out her spare undergarment and shook out the several unused tampons and pads.

"Is that necessary, sir?"

"It's the whole purpose of your mission," he replied, inserting a pencil into one of the precious Tampax tubes and forcing the cotton plug out the bottom. He pulled apart the wad of cotton, exposing a tightly rolled paper at its core, which, unrolled, revealed a diagram. He passed it over to Colonel Wilson, who sat across from him.

She watched, slack-jawed, as he emptied two more of the tampon tubes and then squeezed out the contents of the toothpaste tube. Each ejection produced a tiny roll containing a photograph or diagram. What would have happened if she'd needed to actually use the products? It seemed a major slip-up no one had considered.

"So, the letters were just window dressing," she remarked, bemused.

"Not completely. King Haakon will be pleased to get them, of course. But these items..." He held up one of the still-half-curled diagrams. "These reveal the layout and design of the Norsk Hydroelectric Plant at Vemork. If you'd been caught with these, we would have had to cancel our whole operation. Congratulations for making it through."

"Diagrams of the plant? Very interesting. I can probably supplement them from my memory of the place. I visited it once, a few years ago."

Tronstad nodded, obviously pleased. "Another reason Jomar chose you for the delivery."

"Can you tell me why you need to know about the workings at Vemork?"

"I'm afraid that's a military secret," Wilson interjected. "Let's just say it has considerable interest for the British War Cabinet."

"Is it about the deuterium? They're producing quite a lot of it these days."

Wilson looked taken aback, but Tronstad replied, "Ah, yes. We should have assumed you'd know about the heavy water."

"Of course I would. My father is very proud of it and even showed me around the laboratory. This was before the Nazis took over, of course. Why is it suddenly so important to Britain?"

It was clearly a question she wasn't permitted to ask, and in the silence that followed, she drew the obvious conclusion. "Has it some value as a weapon?"

Tronstad looked uncomfortable. "I'm afraid that's also secret, as you can imagine."

She wasn't having it. "Well, it doesn't take a genius to see that the Germans control what the plant is producing, and the British want it. Or at least want to prevent the Germans from having it."

More silence, which was beginning to annoy her. "Do you want Norsk Hydro to smuggle some of its heavy water to you? It looks just like normal water. I could have brought some in a bottle."

Wilson shook his head. "No. The US has not asked for that." Then he added with sudden candor, "Actually, we're not sure what the Germans are doing with it, but the fact that they're demanding mass production suggests it has a military use. Perhaps you can appreciate that it's not your concern."

"Well, it *is* a good medium to use for controlling atomic fission," she observed lightly, and their renewed expressions of surprise annoyed her even more. She was essential to their surveillance, or could be, yet they were keeping her ignorant, no better than a packhorse.

"I have a degree in chemistry, after all, and have as much an idea as anyone of the difference between H_2O, and D_2O. I'm guessing the Germans want to use it for some sort of fission experiments, either for power or for a bomb. And that the West wants to stop them. Am I right?"

Caught off guard, Wilson winced. "I can't reveal any information relating to military strategy. But you can help us by describing the facilities you say you've seen."

"They're in the lower basement, very well protected. So, if you're considering, say, bombardment, you'd have to obliterate the whole power plant before you got to them. Vemork supplies power to all southern Norway, so it would be a very destructive act to an occupied nation. You wouldn't reach the deuterium cells, but you might hit the liquid-ammonia tanks at the bottom of the valley, which would endanger all of Rjukan."

Tronstad stared into space for a moment, then seemed to gradually accept her in the strategic conversation. "Landing a plane nearby and sending in troops is also under discussion."

She glanced toward the same part of the ceiling where he looked, visualizing the terrain. "Well, you could land a plane on one of the frozen lakes near the plant, but you couldn't be sure the ice would be thick enough to support aircraft."

Wilson leaned back and crossed his arms. "What about dropping the men off in gliders? After the operation, they could escape through Sweden."

"Gliders? All the way across the North Sea? Hmm. That's a very long distance to tow an aircraft. You'd arrive on the Hardangervidda."

"Vidda?" Wilson apparently didn't recognize the term.

"Hardanger Plateau. We treat it as one word. Anyhow, it's not really suitable for glider landings. Violent winds come up suddenly and blow sideways, and the ground is full of bogs, fissures, boulders hidden by the snow. Not to mention the Swedish border is four hundred miles away."

Tronstad chewed his lip. "Yeah. That's what we told them, but it seems the least awful of several bad plans."

"So that *is* the plan. You're going to send in gliders. To the Hardangervidda. In spite of the hazards."

"That's what the war cabinet has decided. I'm telling you this because you've already risked your life for the operation. But it goes without saying, revealing any of the plan to anyone would be a capital offense."

"Understood. But does the war cabinet have any idea what they're up against? How do they plan to move the men from the landing site to the target or even find it?"

"Those details are currently being worked out," Tronstad replied vaguely. "But the order has come from the highest levels, that the plant has to be taken out, no matter what. It's called Operation Freshman, and the men have already been chosen."

She nodded, blinking, absorbing the dubious plan. "So, based on the diagrams I've brought, you're sending British soldiers who speak no Norwegian to find a place to land on the Norwegian tundra all on their own, then travel to the Norsk Hydro plant, all on their own, and then to ski over four hundred miles to Sweden. All on their own." She heard the sarcasm creeping into her voice.

Wilson looked slightly offended. "The sappers won't be on their own. We're sending a team of Norwegians to prepare the landing site and then guide them to the Vemork plant."

She pressed a knuckle against her lips, weighing the possibility of success against the overall folly of the undertaking. The chances were about 70–30, heavily weighted toward failure. If that was the optimum plan, what were the worse ones?

At that moment, she heard a brisk rap on the door. Before anyone replied, an orderly stepped inside and held the door open. "His Majesty would like to have a few words with Miss Brun."

"Certainly, come in," Wilson said belatedly and stood up.

King Haakon VII was an angular, balding man with a full walrus moustache. Such a growth would have made an ordinary man, particularly such a slender one, look foolish, but it seemed to suit a monarch. His courage in refusing to name Nazi Vidkun Quisling to head the government and in enduring bombardment of the village where he had taken refuge gave him all the gravitas he needed, no matter his facial hair. That he had escaped Norway alive was due to widespread assistance from subjects who loved him. Once established in London, he became the symbol, if not the active head, of Norwegian resistance and encouraged it with regular radio broadcasts.

"Ah. This must be Jomar's daughter." He offered Kirsten his hand, and she took it with pleasure.

"Your Majesty."

His narrow face radiated genuine interest as he spoke with a convincing sincerity. "We are very grateful for your service. With so many brave British lads sent to fight for us, I'm happy to see a Norwegian volunteering as well, though I would not have expected anything less from Jomar Brun's family."

"Thank you, Your Majesty, but all I did was deliver documents."

"Critical ones," Tronstad interjected, pointing with his chin to the diagrams still lying curled on the table. "We could not even begin this operation without them. In any case, Miss Brun has also carried letters for you." Tronstad drew the envelope from the leather folder she'd delivered and handed it over.

The king took the envelope and tucked it under his arm. "Each of us does our part," he said, which seemed to exhaust the conversation. But kings are nothing if not diplomats, and so he bent slightly at the waist in the hint of a military bow and offered his hand again. "A pleasure to meet a patriot, and now I will let you all get on with your very important work."

Kirsten watched as they stepped through the doorway and the adjutant closed the door behind them. Half a dozen thoughts crossed her mind: remaining shock at the ill-conceived mission, admiration for the lads who had volunteered for it, and brief, intense loyalty to the Norwegian king. She turned to Jack Wilson.

"The mission to the Hardangervidda. I want to join it."

CHAPTER TWO

July 1942

Kirsten knocked at the door of the apartment she remembered with a mix of bitterness and homesickness. The spacious Brixton flat had been her home for nearly a decade, before she'd returned to Norway, but her military stepfather, whose status and income had secured the apartment, had ended the familial warmth.

The door opened, and she stood in front of the image of herself, twenty years older, the ex-Eleanor Brun, currently Eleanor Wallace. Eleanor's hair, once gorgeously red, was now peppered with gray, but her narrow nose and sharp chin had remained unsoftened by age. Her face brightened as if a light suddenly had gone on inside her.

"Oh, my Lord! It's you!" She embraced Kirsten lightly the moment she entered. "I thought you were still in Norway." She coughed from excitement, then led Kirsten to the sofa. A cigarette lay in the groove of a crystal ashtray, sending off a thin stream of smoke, and as they sat down, knee to knee, she claimed it and took another puff. She exhaled from the side of her mouth, giving a token wave to waft away the smoke.

"I was worried when the newspaper ran the story of the Germans closing the university and arresting so many of the students. Fortunately, they listed the names of the people released, and I saw yours. That was a relief, but then I heard nothing more."

"I'm sorry. But I couldn't write, of course. And if I'd been in any real trouble, Dad would have gotten word to you."

"I see, but that was months ago. What have you been doing in the meantime?" Eleanor leaned back and drew up her legs, and Kirsten noticed that she'd lost weight. Well, so had most people since rationing began.

"Well, I went back to Rjukan and tried to convince Dad to let me work for him."

"That's where you've been? Up in Rjukan?"

"Uh, no. Not exactly. I can't tell you very much. Suffice it to say that he sent me back here to do war work for Norway. But please don't ask for any more details."

"You and your father always did have your secrets. So now he's involved you in espionage." She pressed out the stub of her cigarette in the ashtray. "Will I see more of you, now you're back home?"

Kirsten glanced away. "Uh, no. I'm doing work that takes me out of London. I'll be off training."

"Training? Blimey." Eleanor took another cigarette from a porcelain holder and ignited it with a lighter in the shape of an Aladdin's lamp. She took a deep inhalation, coughed into her fist, and finished her thought. "What are they going to teach you? Boxing, rifle practice, jujitsu?"

"Nothing so masculine. Closer to administrative work." She was lying again, but lying was now part of her job. "You don't have to worry. But let's not talk about me. How are you? You're looking good." Another lie.

Eleanor shrugged. "As good as can be expected. No bombs have dropped in our street. But it hasn't been easy being married to a career officer. It was bad enough before, but since the war, Harry's never here, and I'm alone when I'm not working at the newspaper. Now that he's been promoted to captain, he's gone for days at a time. Your father was a much more attentive husband, even if he was dull. I guess I've jumped from the frying pan into the fire."

"You may be counting too much on your husbands to make life meaningful." Kirsten leaned back and appraised her mother gently. "You know, it was possibly as much a curse as a blessing that you were so beautiful. Sorry, *are* so beautiful. It made you a bit of a coquette."

"Coquette? Me? Don't be silly." She took another puff, then held the cigarette up between two slender fingers. "You really think I'm still beautiful?"

"Of course I do. You definitely are." She patted her mother's shoulder. "Anyhow, I just stopped by to check up on you and let you know I'm alive and well. I probably won't be able to stay in contact with you in the coming months, but if anything bad happens, Dad'll let you know." Kirsten stood up.

"More of your secrets. Well, that's the way it is, I suppose." Eleanor stood up as well and followed her to the door. "At least give your mother a hug." They embraced warmly, which felt strange to Kirsten. The last maternal embrace was when she left Britain to return to Norway, years before.

"Take care of yourself, Mother." She placed an awkward kiss on Eleanor's cheek.

"You too, dear. Don't hurt yourself boxing."

"I promise."

❖

July 1942

In the late July afternoon, the SOE training camp STS 26 in Aviemore, Scotland, was shrouded in fog as Kirsten stepped off the bus from the train station and made her way alone to the main lodge. A heavy wooden door opened to a small anteroom where a corporal sat at a tiny desk. He looked up as she entered and strode toward him.

"Good afternoon. I'm Kirsten Brun, and I'm assigned here starting tomorrow." She handed over her orders.

He glanced through the papers with marginal interest. "Welcome to Camp 26." He read a few more lines. "It says here you'll be training with the RAF engineers."

"That is my understanding."

He pursed his lips. "Yes. Not many women train here, so we don't have a women's barracks." He paused, frowning, as if to imply that her arrival indicated a mistake from someone in the planning hierarchy, which presented him with a dilemma. She waited for the "but..." and it finally came.

"However, we've adapted the gardener's cottage for the odd female."

Did he expect her to express gratitude? She only continued to smile.

"Well then, I'll show you to your quarters," he said. He stepped toward the door without offering to carry any of her baggage, which she took as a sign of victory. It marked her as an equal.

It had been hard enough to convince Tronstad and Wilson to add her to the otherwise all-male team of sappers. SOE, to which she now officially belonged, had plenty of women, but none had been included in this operation. "Women just don't have the physical endurance," Tronstad had insisted, with some justification. But her own argument was even stronger. The men would need her. She was a local and knew the terrain, having skied on the Hardangervidda more than once. She spoke Norwegian and, most importantly, she knew the layout of the Norsk Hydroelectric plant.

Finally, he had capitulated, and here she was in the Cairngorm mountains.

They arrived at a tiny cottage that, as they entered, presented a spare and slightly depressing space for minimum habitation. Two sets of bunk beds stood against adjoining walls, each with a sheet and blanket folded up at the foot. Clearly, she would have no roommates. A well-battered cabinet on the opposite side was obviously for clothing. One corner held a small sink with exposed pipes running sideways into one of the walls. Devoid of curtains, the windows could be darkened only by closing the outside shutters, and it was clear that the cottage had been a service outbuilding rather than housing. She could still see the hooks where picks and shovels had hung.

"The toilet is outside in the rear, and supper will be at 18:00 hours in the main building," the corporal said, then stepped outside, closing the door behind him.

Checking her watch and noting the time until supper, she began to unpack her baggage, a process that took all of ten minutes. Aside from toiletries, she'd brought only a single change of clothes, four pairs of underwear, a heavy jacket, and military boots from Norway, assuming she would be issued a training uniform.

She studied her spartan surroundings, which might have counted as depressing had she come from cozier circumstances, but her recent residences—her cabin on the transport boat, her room at Vemork, and before that, her student quarters in Oslo—had all been similarly cheerless. For that matter, she couldn't remember the last time she'd been cheerful.

She brushed off the thought, tied her shoes, and headed toward the canteen.

The open door of the mess showed four tables with roughly ten men at each, and when she entered, she felt as if all forty of them looked up at her. Their expressions seemed neither hostile nor friendly, merely puzzled, as if the burden of their acceptance rested fully on her.

To hell with that, she thought, joining the line where a man in a white apron was serving food. Closer inspection revealed a playing-card sized piece of meatloaf, three slices of carrots, and a glob of mashed potatoes. She stood for a moment with tray in hand, searching for a place to sit, but every table seemed full. Was this how it was going to be? It was a bad start.

"Come over here," someone said, and she searched for a moment to spot where the invitation came from. At a table on her right, a man sitting at the corner beckoned her over. Relieved, she hurried over as his companion stood up with an empty tray and vacated a seat.

"Thank you," she said, sitting down. "I was afraid I'd have to eat standing."

The invitation came from a wiry, thin-haired man with a prominent nose and sharp chin. "Don't take offense if the men look at you like a ghost," he said as she sat down. "They're nice chaps, most of them, and just didn't expect a woman to show up. We're training all day long, each of us trying to outdo the others. Some of the men might be a little grumpy at having a woman added to the competition."

"I thought SOE had a lot of female agents." She scooped up a forkful of meatloaf. It was mealy and lukewarm, but tasty enough.

"Not in mountain rescue and survival. Oh, by the way, I'm Reggie Tomlinson." He held out his hand. "Are you in administration, or are you actually going to train with us?"

"Kirsten Brun. Definitely not administration. Nope. I'm afraid I'll be out there in the mud, or rather the snow, with all of you." Another bite of the rapidly cooling loaf and a dollop of potato went into her mouth.

"Snow's right. We're headed up into the Cairngorms tomorrow.

Do you think you're tough enough? I'm not mocking you, only asking an honest question."

She chewed and swallowed. "And my honest answer is that I don't know. I'm not afraid of snow. I grew up in Norway and can ski as well as any man. But whether I have the strength and stamina for all the rest, I've yet to find out."

He shoved his tray away from himself. "Well, in the end, none of us knows what we're capable of. We don't even know what they're actually training us for. Something to do with mountain climbing and demolition, obviously. Are they putting you in the classes with dynamite and TNT?"

She tried the official coffee and found it significantly better than the substitute she'd been drinking at home. That was something to be thankful for. "As far as I know, I'll be going through everything you are. Arctic survival, ice-climbing, parachuting, radio operating. We Norwegians are pretty tough."

"I'm sure you are. Your countrymen, too. Do you know those chaps over there?" He indicated with his chin a group of men seated at the end of the far table. They wore rough shirts instead of uniforms and looked like fisherman. One of them leaned against the wall smoking a pipe.

"No, but they certainly look Norwegian."

"They're from Company Linge. They keep to themselves, mostly, but I have the feeling they'll be working with us on the next operation."

She debated joining the Norwegians at their table but decided against it. She'd have had to barge in on their conversation, and so far, with the exception of Reggie, no one on the mess had shown the slightest interest in meeting her.

He collected his tray and stood up. "Jolly nice meeting you. See you on the mountain."

❖

In the days and weeks that followed, Kirsten skied as well as, if not better than any of the men, and even held her own in ice-climbing. To be sure, she lacked the arm strength of the men, but she had both agility and long practice to put her on a par with them. The only task she did poorly in was the physical rescue, which required her to carry a man on her back. In the deep snow, she managed only some hundred feet before her knees buckled. But four of the men didn't do any better, so she felt no shame.

Reggie caught up with her on the descent from the slope on Cairngorm mountain. He halted next to her as she unbuckled her skis. "Well done, old girl. I have to tell you, I never imagined you'd last this long. But now I can trust having you along on the mission."

"Only if I don't have to carry you." She laughed, her warm breath sending out a cloud of steam. "But I could drag you by your feet any distance. If you didn't mind your head bumping over the rocks."

He snickered. "I'll try not to need carrying. How do you feel about parachutes?"

"Oh, right. We have to do that, too. I'd put off thinking about it."

"Parachuting is easy-peasy. You'll do fine." He lifted his skis onto his shoulder, then marched ahead of her to join a group of his mates.

Reggie's encouragement notwithstanding, parachuting got off to a bad start. She did manage to conceal her fear and drop through the hole in the platform without hesitation, but on the practice flights she had little control of direction and was blown far off the target zone, where she dropped with jarring impact. As if to humiliate her further, a bubble of wind stayed in the parachute canopy and dragged her aching body a long way before she wrested control.

"Don't worry, Brun," the training sergeant said. "We'll work out the problem in the next two jumps."

Two more jumps? Oh, joy. Her mood improved that evening back at Station 26. After supper, she was on her way back to her cottage, when one of the Norwegian members of Company Linge crossed her path. She recognized him immediately.

With his square, open face, slightly protruding ears, and a hairline that extended in a smooth horizontal across the top of his forehead, he suggested a peasant simplicity that his reputation belied. He held out one hand in greeting, and with the other he removed his pipe from his mouth. "Jens-Anton Poulsson," he said. "I understand you're Jomar's daughter."

"Nice to meet you, Lieutenant Poulsson. Yes, I am. Though I haven't heard from him in a while."

"Then you'll be happy to learn we prevailed upon him and his wife to flee Norway. Shortly after you, in fact, though by way of Sweden. They'll make it over here eventually. After our team leaves, unfortunately."

She processed the new information. "Did someone denounce him?" Rjukan was filled with collaborators.

"No, but he couldn't have worked much longer without falling under suspicion, especially in the coming weeks."

"Thank you for letting me know he's safe, Lieutenant Poulsson. Your team will be leaving soon?"

"Yes, in just a few days. Groundwork. Well, hope to see you again soon." With a casual and unnecessary salute, he continued into the mess.

SOE kept a firm need-to-know policy, and she was sure the men she trained with had no idea what they were training for. She herself had more or less pieced together the operation, and now she knew the timing. Poulsson and the other Norwegians would be dropped in first, to choose the landing spot. Presumably, in the coming weeks, when all the details were worked out, the manpower would be sent over and the operation would take place. Would they parachute out of planes or land in their gliders? They were trained for the former, but she would prefer the latter. Jumping out of planes was not her strong suit.

She felt a certain comfort in knowing someone of Poulsson's abilities was on the team to prepare the landing and to lead the sappers to Vemork. Still, the entire operation felt very vague. She knew the Hardangervidda better than anyone at the training station, and she was well aware of how deadly it could be, even if they all managed to land in the right spot and without injury.

A sudden image of her mother came to her, complete with cigarette and disdainful remark. "Blimey."

❖

November 1942

The engines of the Halifax bomber roared for a few moments—just long enough to set Kirsten's heart pounding—and then the Horsa glider was jerked forward. It rolled along on its towline behind the Halifax for a few hundred meters, then was hauled upward, swinging wildly from side to side. After two or three minutes, the aircraft stabilized, and Kirsten's fear subsided.

Though the glider carried only fifteen men beside herself, it was packed full, transporting their food, weapons, equipment, and explosives. Nonetheless, the atmosphere was cheerful, the tense cheer of solidarity of a band of soldiers leaping into the unknown.

Operation Freshman, it was called now, and Kirsten found the name unnerving because it suggested amateurism. Though she'd known what the target would be for weeks, the young volunteers had learned just that morning, but if any of them were anxious, it wasn't apparent.

The interior of the glider was dark in any case. The Horsa had tiny porthole windows along the fuselage, which were virtually useless. They provided no light, and even when she pressed her face against the glass, she could see only a gray wall of fog.

Kirsten reminded herself that Poulsson and the others waited for them. They'd have laid out a landing strip with lights and would ensure that the sappers were uninjured and well fed before they led them south to Vemork. With a little luck, well, with a lot of luck, they would succeed, she reassured herself.

She'd made sure she sat next to Reggie and the others she liked, and their banter kept her from brooding about the odds against them. He bumped her with his heavily padded elbow.

"Hey. What do you call a grumpy German?" he asked.

"I give up."

"Sauerkraut!" he said, and snickered.

"Okay. Think you're so smart." She bumped him back. "How do Germans tie their shoelaces?"

"Umm...I give up."

"With little knotsies."

The man who sat on the other side of Reggie snorted laughter. "I've got one," he said. "Why are streets in Paris lined with trees?"

"We give up," everyone said in unison.

"Because the Germans like to march in the shade."

Another man farther down the line called out, "How did the Germans conquer Poland so fast?"

"We don't know" came the ritual response.

"They marched in backward, and the Polish thought they were leaving."

Kirsten shook her head. "Oh, that one was naughty."

The anti-German one-liners gave way to a series of knock-knock jokes, but the men wearied of these as well, and after a few hours, a general silence fell over them, broken only by occasional murmurs.

Kirsten twisted around to peer again through the tiny porthole window behind her. At one point, she thought she could see the other plane-and-glider pair, two vague shadows in the mist, but it could have been her imagination. She fervently hoped it was, for the two shapes suddenly broke apart, and the smaller one dropped precipitously out of sight.

She convinced herself it was just clouds, for it was her worst nightmare—to be cut loose too soon and float helplessly and blindly, not knowing whether they would land on water and drown or crash on a mountainside. She shook her head to dispel the images.

"I thought we would get reports from our Halifax pilot. We've been flying for hours, and I'd really like to know if we've made landfall yet."

"Nope. Nary a peep since we took off," one of the men close by groused. "The telephone cable attached to the towline must have broken." He snorted. "We're flying blind *and* deaf.

The sappers fell silent again as another hour passed, and Kirsten felt a mix of boredom, anxiety, and annoyance. Something must have gone wrong, and nobody was telling them. Then she sensed the glider rise suddenly and abruptly fall again, as if the Halifax itself was searching for something at different altitudes. Better visibility, perhaps? Did it mean they were near the drop zone, or were they lost?

She resisted the urge to grab Reggie's hand and instead peered again through the porthole. When she realized the gray blur she was looking at was a layer of ice, a shot of fear effaced her other emotions. If the porthole was iced, so was the entire glider, and the Halifax, too.

Abruptly, as if to confirm her worst fear, a sudden violent jerk that threw them all forward told her the towline had parted. A moment later, the glider began a nosedive. It pulled up and, with the towline no longer dragging them in a straight line, swerved from side to side, buffeted by wind. The glider banked, began to drop fast, and she prayed the pilot could see more than she could.

She was thrown violently to the side as the air filled with the sickening sound of splintering wood and cries of alarm. With closed eyes, she sensed only sudden violent pain in her foot, her side, and her head, and everything went black.

Chapter Three

Maarit Ragnar stood on a rock on the Hardangervidda and watched the long strands of reindeer as they migrated eastward. She'd herded the reindeer often enough in her youth, but this time it was different. Now she was an orphan, though she wasn't sure you could call yourself that at the age of twenty-seven. If not orphaned, then defeated. She'd had such laudable aspirations and achievements—a solid pre-medical education at the Norwegian College of Teaching and a student apprenticeship at the New Trondheim Hospital. It hadn't even mattered that she was half Sami.

Then, the Germans had arrived, which set off a string of disasters.

First, her Norwegian father, who'd convinced her to educate herself rather than herd reindeer, had fallen at Narvik, trying to keep the Germans out. That loss had already shattered her. But more hardship followed. German victory and a change in the political atmosphere had forced her out of her position at the hospital. Sami, according to the new mentality that swept over Norway, were no better than Jews.

But when she returned to her mother's village, she learned she'd lost her brother Karrel and her mother Anik to the Germans as well. Her father, Erik Ragnar, had died courageously, and the battle that killed him could be counted as having held off the Nazis long enough to let the king escape. But Anik Ragnar and her son had died for nothing.

And here she was, herding again, with her grandparents, Jova and Alof, wondering what to do next.

"Hoi!" she called out, helping the dog turn one of the stray reindeer back toward the scattered mass that drifted slowly eastward. The herd was spread out in lines over half a kilometer, alternately feeding off the lichen they uncovered under the snow and rambling on, following the tame härk reindeer with its bell. It was enough to ski along the northern periphery, together with herders from two other families, while Grandfather and Gaiju skied along the south, keeping an eye out for stragglers or calves too weak to keep up with their mothers. In the distance, slightly ahead of the herd, Jova skied next to another tame härk that towed a sled holding the poles and cloth for the *lavvu* tent. Behind the first sled, a second härk pulled another one full of bedding and provisions, and dragging a sapling they would cut for firewood.

Alof would choose a place to stop wherever he spotted a supply of lichen for the deer, and there they could make supper and rest for the night.

But that was hours away. She couldn't gauge time from the sky, since it had grown dark already at three, but she could measure by the pain in her legs, which was still only unpleasant. When it became excruciating, she figured Alof would be tired too, and they'd stop.

Her family had come that way last year, and the year before, and the year before that. Her ancestors—well, her mother's ancestors at least—had moved for thousands of years along the same stone-age trails across the vidda. Their destination, the winter feeding-grounds close to Sweden, would keep them nourished until the following spring, when they would reverse course.

In the long twilight, the snow radiated a blue-gray light, and although the vidda was largely featureless, her grandparents and Gaiju were familiar with every boulder and crevasse. The herd dog panted toward her and brushed briefly against her leg, confirming their teamwork. He belonged to the Tuovo family but knew and answered to most of the herders.

"Hey, Chammo," she said, admiring the bright spots over his eyes that legend said gave him the power to see the wind. "How are things in the spirit world? Any sign of them showing interest in getting rid of the Germans?"

The dog glanced up at her balefully through bright-blue eyes.

She bent and patted him on the side. "Not really their area of expertise, is it?" Chammo trotted off to bring in another cluster of reindeer that was edging toward the north.

She strode along on her skis, hearing the soothing *shish shish*, her own breath, and the distant tinkling of bells on the lead deer. From time to time she could hear Gaiju call to one of the dogs. Grandfather's brother, widowed and childless, Gaiju had made the migration almost as many years as he was old.

She followed the ridge that gradually emerged, and when she reached its highest point, she swept her gaze over a mass of some eight hundred and fifty deer, herded by three families. When they marked the new calves in their ears later in the year, Maarit reckoned her family would gain another thirty. Not a large herd, but respectable, though if the damned Germans kept shooting them to feed their troops, that number could decline rapidly.

So far, the deer looked good. Many had lost their antlers, and some of them looked a bit comical with a single antler that had not yet fallen off. They would migrate, Sami or no Sami, as they had done for thousands of years, northwest in the spring and southeast in the fall. All that she and her kin did was supplement their food in the sparse patches and guard them from predators.

Something caught her eye, and she recognized an eagle swooping toward one of the calves. It was a rare white calf, a small female that had fallen behind its mother. She was surprised to see an eagle so late in the season, but there it was, enormous and hungry. The powerful raptor even managed to lift the poor creature off the ground for a moment. But the calf was simply too heavy, and it thrashed until it freed itself from the eagle's grasp.

Its mother turned and galloped toward her baby that lay now in the snow. Angry at herself for not noticing the stray calf sooner, Maarit rushed toward it, focused on the blood staining its white coat. She helped the calf to its feet, but it collapsed again, trembling.

Overhead, the thwarted raptor shrieked outrage and flew past a row of boulders out of sight.

The other reindeer, spooked by the attack, had increased their pace, and Maarit had no choice but to carry the wounded beast. Taking both ski poles in one hand, she hauled the calf up and draped it over her shoulders.

"Oof!" she groaned, as the full weight of the calf dropped like a yoke. It would slow her, but she was determined not to lose a single deer on this trip, least of all the precious white one.

She plodded on, straining her muscles, for two more hours, the mother trotting alongside her. With exhaustion creeping in, she slowed her pace and fell behind. She was in little danger of losing sight of the herd, since they kicked up a mist of powdered snow she could see for kilometers.

But the herd itself had begun to gather in denser masses. A bright whistle drew her glance over the bobbing sea of reindeer backs, to the spot where Grandfather stood. He pointed with his arm toward a cluster of boulders. Grandmother was already unloading the tent poles from the first sled.

She waved back, and at both their whistles, the dogs galloped to the front of the herd to stop its forward motion. The lichen were abundant under the snow here, so the reindeer were already slowing to graze. They would have enough to feed on through the night, and guarded by the dogs, they would soon lie down in the snow to rest.

Her burden and her aching muscles delayed her, and when she arrived at the campsite, Gaiju stood in front of it. "So that's what held you up." He lifted the lame calf from her shoulders so she could bend down to remove her skis.

The tent poles were already tied together in tepee fashion, so all that remained was to pull the canvas covering around the frame and lash the tent down. She knew the order of construction, and while Alof chopped wood and Gaiju unloaded their provisions, Maarit tramped down the snow inside and laid out the twigs they'd brought for flooring. Moments later, Alof bent through the opening with an armload of wood and lit a fire, while Jova tied a branch crosswise between the support poles and hung the kettle on its chain. With the lavvu fully erected, Maarit fetched in the calf and laid it down.

"What's wrong with the calf?" Jova dropped handfuls of snow into the kettle. "You been carrying her long?" She unpacked yesterday's bread and the dried meat that would be their supper.

Maarit was about to unwrap the woven cloth from around her leg and tug off her deerskin shoes when she realized she had to go out again. "Attacked by an eagle. Lucky calf was too heavy, and it let her go, but she seems to be injured."

"You can leave her there while we eat, but the tent's too small for all of us to sleep and keep her, too. You'll have to put her in the sled."

"Well, we could make a stew out of her," Gaiju said, half serious. If the calf turned out to be lame, slaughtering it made the most sense. But a female calf was doubly valuable because she could have her own calves, and her white coat gave her an almost mystical aura. "Let's give her a chance tonight. I'll carry her out to let her suckle."

"Suit yourself, dear."

Maarit stepped back outside to search for the vaja. As she'd hoped, the mother stood close by, obviously anxious for her calf. Alof followed her out and grasped the deer by her antlers while Maarit held the calf against the mother's warm belly. To her relief the injured animal still had an appetite. But immediately after suckling, the calf collapsed again in the snow, so she carried it back to the sled and covered it with a deerskin.

Inside the lavvu again, Maarit sat down to remove her shoes with a sigh of relief. Even though her shoe-grass lining kept her feet warm enough, it didn't prevent the ache of a ten-hour forced march. She hung shoes, leg-cloths, and damp shoe-grass overhead on the crossbeam that held the cooking-pot chain. Grandmother's shoe-grass was already there. Everything gave off a sour odor of unwashed body and damp wool.

"I'd forgotten how hard the migration is on the feet," she remarked, drawing up her legs.

Across from her Alof lit his pipe with a cinder from the fire. "Living in Trondheim has made you soft, child."

"I'm sure it has, Grandfather. But it has also made me smart. If I can ever finish my medical studies, I can help the Sami as a doctor."

"You're just like your mother, Maarit. Stubborn. Determined. Reckless." He blew out a puff of smoke. "Never satisfied with the life up here. She had to go into Trondheim and take care of the white people's children. Look what became of her."

Maarit massaged her toes. "Yes, but that's how she met my father and made me and Karrel. She was very happy with a Norwegian husband. And she did come back to the Sami. She died because she was a good Sami mother trying to save her son from the Germans, not because she married a Norwegian."

Ignoring the conversation, Grandmother set about melting the frozen meat over the flames.

Gaiju lit his own pipe. "Germans!" He spat toward the fire. "Without our help, they wouldn't last one week in their shiny boots. They know that, so they steal our reindeer and grab our young men for guides."

Maarit stared into the fire, brooding over what had after all brought her back to her mother's people. The Sami tried to stay out of the conflict, but their ability to find their way across the barren, featureless arctic landscape rendered them useful. And the seizure of the young men meant that women and the elderly bore the burden of the migration.

The conversation stopped when Jova poured coffee powder into the kettle of boiling water. A few moments later, she passed around the steaming cups. There were only three—an enameled tin cup shared by her grandparents, a wooden one used by Gaiju, and a ceramic one Maarit had been wise enough to save from her student days. A private cup was a luxury.

The lavvu did little to keep out the creeping frost, but Maarit warmed her hands around the cup, then sipped its contents and winced. She appreciated the warmth, but it was even more bitter than normal.

Without looking up, Jova poked at the heating deer meat. "It's all they had at the trader's. Because of the war. Here, try it this way." She cut chips of now-warmed reindeer meat and handed them around.

Soaking in the scalding coffee, the reindeer cooked slightly and added a saltiness to the drink. Maarit sipped and nodded at the familiarity. Salted Sami coffee that she would forever associate with the migration.

Finally, the bread had also heated, and they tore off steaming shreds of it to dip into the coffee stew. The long, comfortable silence that was essentially Sami fell over them and gave her time for introspection. What was she going to do? Although Sami only through her mother, she was fully accepted into the family. And besides, they obviously needed her.

But she was also her father's child, and she felt guilty withdrawing into the tundra while the Germans installed themselves all over Norway. Wilderness and civilization had equal claim on her. She hated the invader but had no idea what to do about it.

Finally, Grandfather knocked the ashes from his pipe into the fire, signaling the end of the evening. The tiny lavvu scarcely allowed room for four, and when one person lay down to sleep, all had to do so. Without commentary, Jova began to put order in her tiny kitchen to make space for her own bed. Gaiju tapped out his pipe as well and slid over next to Alof, then wrapped up in one of the deerskins.

With her head directly under Jova's feet, Maarit adjusted the hides around herself and wondered again about the calf that lay curled up in the sled. If it could still not walk the next morning, she would have to surrender the poor creature to the natural order and let it be butchered.

Drowsiness was already overtaking her, and she submitted to it, vaguely sensing one of the men who had begun to snore.

CHAPTER FOUR

Kirsten sensed stinging cold on her face and pain in her jaw. Worse, when she tried to lift herself up on her elbows, the jolt of pain in her side suggested broken ribs. She heard moaning and forced herself up again to assess what had happened.

Obviously, they had crashed. The glider lay at the end of a long trough with both wings broken off. She'd apparently been thrown some distance from the wreck, as had most of the others. Some of them lay motionless, while a few were on their knees and struggling to stand.

She lay next to a mound of churned-up snow, and as she tried to clear her head, she heard groaning behind her. With effort, she turned to look over her shoulder. Reggie was nearby, higher on the mound, alive, though one leg was bent grotesquely to the side.

Before she could help him, she had to assess her own injuries. Her left side hurt with every deep breath. Her head ached, but her vision was good. Mild concussion. She clenched her hands inside her gloves and moved her arms slightly. No broken bones there. Both legs could bend at the knee and pivot at the hip, but as she tried to rotate her left foot, pain shot up her leg.

Sudden activity among the staggering men near the wreck drew her attention. A shot rang out and one of them fell, the reason for their panic soon becoming clear. A German ski patrol had spotted the gliders as they crashed and was arriving to capture them. Shit.

"Hide!" Reggie called down to her from his exposed position. "Under the snow. You've got a chance."

She hesitated for only a moment, wanting to save him as well, then grasped the impossibility. Instinct for survival, and the memory of all the times she'd hunted with her father in the woods, urged her to claw a sort of tunnel into the mound she lay next to. Desperation gave her strength, and just as she heard the first German voice call out, she had excavated enough space to roll into, gritting her teeth against the pain in her foot and side. She swept down handfuls of snow over her, leaving a hole the size of her forearm at the side for air.

Panting from exertion and fear, she listened to the sounds of capture only a few meters away. German voices shouted, while the surrendering British sappers were mostly quiet. What would they do with the injured, she wondered, but the answer came immediately. Gunshots. Unhurried. One sounded right next to her. "*Noch einer*," a soldier said.

Reggie's voice above her, clear and unmistakable, "Fuck you, bloody murderers!" followed by another gunshot.

Grasping her sidearm, which she knew would be useless against a whole platoon, she waited for them to discover her. But after agonizing long minutes, their distant voices told her they'd overlooked her. They seemed to be leaving—with prisoners or without, she couldn't tell. But either way, they'd surely seen that the glider was full of supplies and would soon return with a sled to collect them.

She waited until every sound had stopped. No voices of the soldiers, no moaning from the wounded. She began to shiver from the cold and knew she had to emerge soon or freeze to death. Taking a deep breath, she raised both arms to push off the snow that covered her upper body and sat up.

It was an appalling sight. Men lay scattered around her, unmoving. Reggie, too, had been executed. Of the other dead men, she counted eight. Five men had been taken prisoner. She hoped their British uniforms would give them POW status but had no way of knowing, and she had her own life to worry about. She had to get away from the glider before the patrol returned, but could she walk? Or even stand up?

Laboriously, she drew herself up, first to her knees, and then, supporting herself on her good leg, she tried to take a step. The sharp pain in her left ankle caused her leg to buckle, and she fell back onto the snow. She crouched for a moment, gathering determination, then hauled herself up again. She could stand but not walk.

Crawling, she dragged herself over to the largest man she could see. It was Fitzsimmons. Turning him over was a struggle and wrenched her rib muscles, but she finally managed to remove his overcoat. After taking off her backpack, she drew the coat on over her own. Its greater size allowed her to button it across her chest, making a double layer against the cold, although the thickness in her armpits made it difficult to move her arms.

Gathering her strength and dragging her pack, she crawled turtle-like with splayed arms from corpse to corpse, trying to avoid looking at their faces. Each one still wore a backpack, and each one contained a field-ration kit. She could stuff no more than seven into her own pack, which, with her own, made eight. If she couldn't find help in eight days, she was doomed. But for now, her main concern was her foot. How bad was the damage, and would it support her well enough to flee?

Another arduous trek brought her back to the wrecked glider, where she located the emergency kit. It held a wide roll of bandage, scissors, iodine, and morphine syringes, but nothing to serve as a splint. The only object remotely useful was a spade she slid out from under a seat. It was fortunately a short one, so the handle came no higher than mid-thigh. Gritting her teeth, she laid the spade head against her foot and wrapped her lower leg from ankle to knee with a strip of bandage. The splint was ridiculously primitive and did nothing to reduce the pain, but would at least allow her to take a step. She considered using one of the morphine syrettes but feared it would make her groggy and slow her down. Instead, she dropped one into her pocket.

What else would she need? The tents were too heavy, and so were the tommy guns. The radio transmitter, which she might have tried to drag away, was smashed. A metal box carried ration cards, useless until she reached civilization, but she slid a couple into a pocket. A zippered wallet held Norwegian cash, which she folded and shoved in next to them.

She labored, panting, for another twenty minutes to locate maps, a tarp, and snowshoes, and she managed to force her feet into them, even with the spade head. Finally, dizzy with pain and exhaustion, she inhaled long and deep, and, with a loud groan, set out.

Getting away from the site was the hardest, since the wreck had thrown up mounds of snow, and each deep step left her breathless. Only the simple knowledge that to stay meant capture kept her moving.

Once she'd made it onto smooth snow, she set off in a shuffle, bending under the weight of her two coats and bulging backpack and checking her compass for direction.

The patrol's ski tracks showed they'd gone west, so she traveled east. After what seemed like an hour, she glanced back, shocked at how little ground she'd covered. In the eerie blue light of the polar twilight, the wreck was still visible.

"Shit," she muttered, and lumbered on, unwilling to expose her wrist long enough to check her watch. Time was irrelevant at that moment anyhow. She snorted softly as her weary mind played with the idea. Didn't Einstein say time and space were on the same continuum? Fancy that. Would he say that if he were trudging with a bad foot across bloody nowhere to escape the bloody Nazis?

She wasn't yet cold, but she worried now about being lost. She tried to recall the map they'd all been shown, of where they expected to land relative to where both the Vemork plant and Poulsson's cabin were located. The plant was south and the cabin vaguely east. But they had crash-landed far short of the target zone. Should she travel southeast, southwest, or due east?

Then she recalled her snowshoe tracks, which made it child's play to locate her. The patrol had only to follow them. "Shit!" she muttered again. Well, she wouldn't give up without a struggle, and she did still have the sidearm they'd all been issued. She staggered on, trying to minimize the fear and pain by murmuring folksongs in Norwegian. When she could think of no more, she began "God Save the King" under her breath, all the lines she'd been forced to learn in school.

She'd just reached "Not in this land alone, but be God's mercies known," when she became aware of the snowfall. It began as a soft sprinkling but soon increased in volume and flake-size, until she could no longer see where she was going. That would at least take care of the snowshoe-tracks problem.

She stopped. Now that she was safe from pursuit, what were her choices? Clearly she had only two: to continue either southeastward or to rest. Rest sounded very attractive, but was that the same as surrendering to the cold? Would she die in the wilderness?

It didn't seem so. The second coat had warmed her, almost too much, in fact, and the only danger was frostbite where she was less covered. Her brain said, *Keep going until daylight, when you might see signs of life*, but her body rebelled, and the pain in her foot was almost unbearable. Moreover, the wind had increased, lowering the already-frigid temperature, and the snow was blowing sideways.

She nodded agreement with her body. She'd park. In training, they'd taught her how to build a snow shelter. As long as she stayed dry and well-fed, she could keep her body temperature up. And she had morphine and eight ration packs.

She mentally reviewed the steps. In principle, she had merely to hollow out a minimum of space and insulate it. Fine. She could do that. She dropped down where she stood, first wrestled off her backpack, then untied the shovel-splint. Her ankle still radiated pain, but it had supported her weight for hours, so perhaps it was strained but not broken. Using the spade, she gathered loose snow into a mound. The swinging motion caused her injured side to hurt like hell, but she persisted until the mound was slightly longer than her body length and high enough to allow her to sit up. Exhaling relief, she tamped it all down by lying on the top and pounding it with the spade.

After sliding down on one side, she began excavating the mound from a hole on the side. Ironically, the damaged foot that had forced her to create a splint might have saved her life, for the spade allowed her to dig far more effectively than she could have done with her hands. But she worked blindly, barely making out the form of the exterior under the snowfall and unable to see the interior at all.

She scooped out shovels-full of snow to a depth a bit longer than the spade handle, then turned to hollow out the mound in the other direction of about the same depth. At the spot where she'd begun, she scraped out snow from the roof to make a slight dome, where she could sit upright. Theoretically, this would also help any condensation run down the walls rather than drip onto her head.

Her whole body ached now with the exertion, but she felt a certain satisfaction in completing the shelter. Now she just needed to unfold the tarp from her pack and drag herself, and it, into the tiny cave.

Once inside, she lay for a moment on her side, catching her breath. With a careful shifting, she found a suitable position leaning diagonally against the back wall. It seemed unlikely she'd sleep much. But she could rest and eat.

She also determined that if she withdrew her arms from the sleeves of the outer oversized coat and used it more like a cape, she was still sufficiently warm but had greater arm mobility.

She had to remove her gloves to fish the morphine syrette from her pocket, and before her fingers froze, she yanked up the left leg of her trouser, exposing her swollen ankle. She snapped off the needle guard, which at the same time broke the seal to the tube containing the morphine. Taking a breath, she inserted the hollow needle at a shallow angle under the skin of her ankle and pressed on the tube, forcing its contents into her foot. The pain of insertion made her cry out, but within moments, the morphine took effect, and she exhaled with relief, sliding her pant leg down and tucking it into her boot.

Her fingers were becoming numb, so she slid on her gloves and rummaged in her pack until she located one of the survival ration boxes. It was well sealed, and she had to tear it with her teeth to open it, but, she remembered, it contained matches.

Quickly she scooped out a hollow right at the entrance and piled up the cardboard scraps of the ration box. The fire would last only a few moments, but the thought of it made her euphoric.

She emptied the contents of the box at her side and examined each part as much by feel as by sight. First she identified the folding metal gadget that made up a tiny spoon, fork, and can opener. She snorted to herself. The opener would have been useful to open the pack in the first place. Next she felt the various cellophane packs of oatmeal, sugar, gum, hard and sweet biscuits, and four paper-wrapped cubes. Two of them, she knew, were bouillon, and two were a hard-packed mixture of tea and sugar. Beneath those were packets of biscuits, both hard and soft. Several tube-type items, she recalled, were tightly rolled toilet paper and cigarettes. Best of all, at the bottom, she found a tin, which she knew contained meat, and a block of chocolate. And below those, the precious matches.

With everything laid out within reach, she unhooked her mess tin from her backpack and set it down for the foundation of her micro-bonfire. Then she gathered the cardboard packaging, the cigarettes, and one of the toilet-paper rolls into a tight bundle and set it onto the empty tin.

She struggled to open the meat tin using the attached key, though, with her gloved fingers, it took several long, infuriating minutes to pry the key from the top of the can. She had only a few minutes of flame and so readied both the open meat tin and her metal cup of snow.

Then, praying that the matches were dry, she scratched one of them against the abrasive strip. It lit with a small, intense flame that made her squint, and she held it to the bundle of paper and cardboard.

In the few moments the fire lasted, she held the meat tin and cup of snow over the flames. It was just enough to melt the snow and render it lukewarm, and she dropped one of the tea cubes into it. The meat tin had heated on the outside, but the meat, which she determined now was ham, was still ice cold. She spooned it out with the round end of the metal gadget and swallowed chunks of it along with bites of the dry biscuits. The lukewarm tea, which was at least pre-sweetened, washed it all down.

She nibbled at the sweets, watching the embers of tobacco that still glowed, giving off a sooty odor. Then all was darkness again. Only one task remained before she could try to sleep, and it was going to be a struggle.

She didn't dare remove her woolen trousers, so simply unbuttoned them and inched them halfway down her hips. Lying on her stomach, she removed one glove, held the empty meat tin under her pubis and slowly relieved herself. It was messy business, but the warmth of her urine heated her legs slightly, and she lay for several moments over the heated tin re-absorbing her own warmth. Then she carefully slid the tin up out of her trousers and tossed it through the hole that was her door. She had no plan for when the other part of her digestive system did its work but would solve that dilemma when the time came.

Bodily needs taken care of, she wiggled back into a sort of fetal position, using the second coat as a blanket and its sleeves as a pillow. In the nearly complete darkness, she pressed snow up against the cave opening, leaving only a small hole for air. Every part of her was chilled or ached, but she was no longer famished, and it was good to lie down. Tightening the earflaps on her sheepskin cap, she made herself as small as possible and attempted to sleep.

It seemed impossible that she'd slept, for she recalled only shivering in various painful positions, but patches of a nightmare of being on a boat lost in a vast dark sea on heaving waves suggested she had in fact dropped off for brief periods.

After what seemed like hours, she punched a hole in the wall of snow, and a soft light poured in. When she widened it, she saw the snowing had stopped and the sun was just above the horizon. The temptation was great to stay longer in her little snow-cave, but she had to trek onward in the few hours of daylight available.

First, she needed another meal, and she repeated the entire procedure of the previous evening, crumpling the cardboard box into a ball and using the tiny bonfire to melt snow for two morning drinks, one of bouillon and the second of the delicious sugary tea. This time she was able to see the meat tin as she opened it, which saved her the use of a match for light. It held tuna fish, but the biscuits and the block of chocolate were the same. She could chew the chocolate while on the move.

Fortified, she packed her rucksack and swung it onto her back again, noting that the lack of two ration packs made no difference in its weight.

She checked her map and her compass and decided arbitrarily to head southwest. Eventually, she should reach some sort of habitation, and if not…she chuckled bleakly to herself, Sweden was only a few hundred kilometers east.

Strapping on the snowshoes was no easier than on the day before, for the morphine had worn off, and her foot hurt again terribly. It seemed now a mistake to not have taken off her boots to sleep, for she could feel nothing in her feet and couldn't move her toes.

She set off again, southwestward, grateful at least for the temporary light and clear skies. The wind had died down, and she checked the time. After four hours, she sat down, made a low wall around her from piled snow, and spread out her tarp. Meal preparation had become a smooth operation by now, and she quickly consumed ration pack number three.

It began to snow again as she resumed her trek, and she was glad she'd eaten. It had grown dark, and though she tried to continue in the chosen direction, she could no longer orient herself on the distant mountains and had to rely on her compass. But soon, heading into the wind that threw walls of snow against her, she could make no headway.

On a flat, open plateau, devoid of trees, buildings, and visible boulders, she had nothing to measure movement against. No matter how long she plodded, the mountains, when she could see them, seemed exactly as distant as they had two hours before. Twice she bumped into a snow-covered rock, and once she toppled down a slope into a gully, both causing violent jolts of pain to her side and her foot.

The wind increased, and the ground seemed to boil, sending up snow powder like a vapor. Soon her front became coated with a layer of frost, and she was just another white-covered object on an endless white landscape.

As she had done the day before, she piled up snow and made another shelter, but the fresh snow was too light to pack down. She could construct a wall around her, but had to use the tarp as a cover, and the wind wouldn't let her build a fire, so she ate the fourth ration pack freezing cold. In the hours that followed, she couldn't sleep at all, but simply squatted, shivering in her hidey-hole, waiting for the storm to stop.

But it didn't stop, and all she could do was eat. Under her tarp, which had accumulated snow and so sagged in on her head, she managed to create another tiny fire, but it lasted only long enough to partially melt a cup of snow, and then the wind blew it out. Her fifth and then sixth meal were cold.

❖

Was it the third day? With so many hours of darkness, punctuated by only a hint of daylight, she couldn't be sure. It seemed like she'd been trudging for days, weeks. Life before snowshoes became a blur. Her rational brain asserted itself momentarily. How many ration packs were left? Two, she thought. Matches? Several packs of them, but nothing to burn.

Crap. The mission she'd been on. Operation Freshman? Yeah, that was it. Damn. They'd sent advance gliders with canisters of fuel and other supplies, but they lay somewhere far behind her.

And she was so tired. She'd plodded step after step, moved by the sheer urge to live, but her muscles were giving out. *The spirit is willing, but the flesh is weak.* Her dazed mind meandered. Spirit, flesh. Did she have a spirit? If so, how had it gotten her into this? Obviously, it hadn't reckoned with the spirits of the Arctic. She hadn't seen any living thing on her trek, but she was pretty sure the blizzard had a spirit, and that it hated her.

Tired, so tired, and finally she collapsed. She fell sideways, one snowshoe lying on the snow, the other one jutting up vertically. She relaxed inside her double coat. Her muscles stopped aching, and she was no longer even cold. Images of ghosts dancing in the snow flashed in front of her, and then she surrendered to delicious sleep.

CHAPTER FIVE

Was she sleeping? Was she dead? Something wet and fetid touched her face. Slightly delirious, Kirsten opened her eyes, bewildered. An animal snout sniffed at her hair, her brow. She flinched and the snout pulled away, revealing several other snouts with light-brown fur leading up to widely spaced eyes. They made a sound, something between a throaty snort and an oink. Slowly she made sense of them. Reindeer.

She thought vaguely of her pistol. Should she shoot one? Whatever for? Then something shooed them apart, and a human face bent over her. Wide, troll-like, with a short, unkempt beard, thick lips, and a flat nose. But the brightly embroidered band around his head, topped by a red pompom, and the banded, blue smock, identified him to her half-conscious brain. Sami.

"Help me," she croaked weakly, but he disappeared.

Something poked Kirsten in the chest, and she opened her eyes again. This time it was a woman, wearing the same blue, banded tunic as the man, but younger, less threatening. The woman brushed the snow from Kirsten's chest.

"Can you hear me? Are you hurt?"

Kirsten worked to find her voice and managed only a weak sound. "Can't feel my legs."

The stranger patted her arm. "You'll be all right. We have sleds. Just a few minutes and I'll come back. Don't worry."

The curious reindeer re-formed around her as the woman

disappeared, and roused now by the realization of being saved, Kirsten stared up at them. Their nostrils sent out a cloud of steam with each snort, as if they cleared their throats. A strangely comforting sight.

When the woman returned, shooing away the deer, it was with two elderly Sami, bulky in their heavy tunics, who brought a sled right up next to where she lay. She glanced up hopefully at the wooden contraption and the tame deer that was hitched to it.

Unlike the flat snow toys of her childhood, the Sami sled was built to carry cargo. Slightly longer than a man, the boat-like body consisted of a high back and sides that sloped toward the foot. It stood on runners that curved upward in the front and extended beyond the back.

"We're going to lift you now," the young woman said as she knelt behind Kirsten's head and reached down to grasp her under the arms. One of the old men lifted her at the knees, and together, they swung her into the sled, covering her with reindeer hides.

While Kirsten relaxed into the increasing warmth of her new bed, she became aware of something bony and fidgety next to her, and when it honked into her ear, she grasped it was a young calf. Someone loaded her rucksack and snowshoes on top of her, and with a jerk, the sled took off.

Her sheer sense of relief seemed to enliven her, and she turned her head toward the woman skiing alongside the sled. She seemed a little tall and fair-skinned for a Sami, but her clothing was identical to theirs. Catching her glance, the woman skied closer.

"Don't worry. You're safe now. In a couple of hours, we'll stop to make camp. Once we've set up, we'll make some food and coffee and warm you up."

The Sami woman spoke good Norwegian, which Kirsten hadn't expected. She wanted to talk and express thanks, but her face was so cold, and her lips wouldn't move. Then the calf bent its little head and snorted into her neck, warming both itself and her.

She fell into a half-sleep, faintly conscious of the rocking of the sled over the swells of snow. When she opened her eyes, the nameless woman was still within sight, as well as an older woman, who led the reindeer drawing the sled. She recalled seeing two men also, but noticed no sign of them.

The sky overhead was dark and relatively clear, a few stars visible. Kirsten savored the comforting *shish shish* of the sled over the snow, the tinkling of the bell on the reindeer that pulled her, and the dull mix of grunting, honking, and snorting from the beasts that seemed to be all around them. The dark form of a single reindeer had detached itself from the main herd and remained close to the sled. The tiny calf at her shoulder kept raising its head, so perhaps it was the mother.

Abruptly, the sled stopped, and Kirsten's rescuer skied up to her side. "Ah, you're awake. How do you feel?"

Kirsten's body felt divided. Her lower part was numb, while her arms, face, and shoulders tingled painfully. Perhaps the reindeer calf had added just enough warmth to save her. "My chest hurts, broken ribs, I think. My legs ache, but I can't feel my feet."

The woman nodded, solicitously. "Unfortunately, I can't do anything for you just yet, but we're stopping now, and in a few minutes, we can at least put something warm inside you."

The sled edged a bit farther along, and Kirsten could finally make out another sled next to a circle of tall poles tied at the top. Two other Sami were covering it with something, and a third one was unloading sacks from the sled.

Her heart sank. She could already see that the shelter was tiny, barely large enough for all four of the Sami. They would certainly have no room for her. "We'll stay here?" she asked weakly.

"Only for a few hours to sleep. My grandparents have to rest, and so do I."

The flap that served as the entrance to the tent was open, and from her position, Kirsten could see an old woman apparently preparing a fire inside. While she watched, it ignited, sending out a spot of blinding yellow light. In the middle of the wasteland, the flames caused the tent itself to glow and offered deeply satisfying comfort. With her fire started, the old woman stepped out of the tent, and all four Sami approached the sled.

"Anyhow, I'm Maarit. This is Jova, my grandmother, my grandfather, Alof, and Gaiju, my grandfather's brother."

They all nodded but didn't reply. Did they not understand Norwegian? Then the whole family seemed to lose interest in her as they busied themselves preparing for a temporary rest.

A moment later, Maarit appeared next to the sled again, holding a ceramic cup of something that steamed. "Here, drink this, slowly. It should warm you." She handed the cup to Kirsten and helped lift her head to reach it. "It's not exactly coffee, but it's hot, and you need it. You'll also get some smoked meat in a couple of minutes."

Finally able to move her lips, Kirsten sipped the steaming brew and winced. "Hot, yes, but tastes like tree bark."

Maarit chuckled. "I think that's what it is. Impossible for us to get coffee these days. Not up here, anyhow."

Thirst trumped taste, and when the brew had cooled below scalding, Kirsten took several more gulps. It warmed her throat and chest, which was a relief, but as the warmth spread to her legs, she felt the awful tingling of nerves that began to function again. She had to move her legs, massage them, do something.

"I…have to move," she grunted. "My legs…awful pain. My chest, too."

Can you sit up if I help you?" She slid an arm around Kirsten's back.

"I'll try." Pushing with her good leg and gripping the sides of the sled, she was able to haul herself up to a sitting position, though the tug on her ribs caused a pain to shoot through her. The reindeer calf also slid farther down under the cover and bleated. The change of position did little to stop the excruciating sensations of electric shock in both legs or the ache in her side. She finished her tree-bark coffee, determined to wait out the pain.

"You've been asleep off and on for hours. Do you need to relieve yourself?"

Damn, there was that, too. "I guess so. But how? I don't think I can stand up."

"Let's try to get you out of the sled first. I can hold you from one side. Moving will warm you more than anything." She waved over the one called Gaiju, who seemed a bit sturdier than the other two, and he took up position at her feet.

Maarit pulled off the several reindeer skins that had served as covers. "Do you need to wear two coats?"

"As long as I'm in the sled, no. Can you help me out of one of them?"

Maarit slid the outer coat over Kirsten's shoulders and managed to yank her arms out of the tight sleeves. Rolling out of the outer coat, Kirsten took a breath and hauled herself up. Gaiju lifted her legs over the edge of the sled. With another swing, they raised her fully from the sled and stood her upright on the snow. She wobbled, pain shooting up under her left arm and through both legs, her left one especially, and she could barely put weight on it.

"What do you think? Can you take a step?"

"Only if you support me on my right side."

"Sure. I can do that. We have no formalities here. The area behind that rock is our...uh...family toilet."

Kirsten held her breath so as not to cry out and leaned hard on Maarit to keep from collapsing. With a series of grunts, she limped her first painful steps. The pain in her legs was bad, but the numbness in her feet worried her more. With her arm slung along the small of Kirsten's back, Maarit half led, half carried her behind one of the massive rocks that protected the shelter from the wind.

Behind the snow-covered rock, Maarit stopped and turned to face her. "Now it gets serious. I'll hold you up while you slide down your trousers. Then you bend forward and let go."

Kirsten's humiliation was diminished only by the persistent pain and the knowledge that the only alternative was to soil herself inside her clothing, which would freeze and turn to ice. "All right," she managed to say. Supporting her weight largely on her right leg, Kirsten opened her coat, unbelted her trousers, and undid the row of buttons in the front. "Now is good."

Maarit stepped in close and embraced her from the front, sliding her hands under Kirsten's shoulders and around her back. Bracing herself on a wide stance, she pulled Kirsten's upper body close and allowed her to bend just enough to avoid drenching her trousers.

The sudden rush of icy air on her bare buttocks nearly stifled the urge, but with concentration, she was able to release. Hearing the hiss of urine pouring onto the snow, she felt simultaneous relief and excruciating embarrassment. "Thank you," she murmured into Maarit's shoulder.

"Sure, any time." Maarit lifted her upright again and helped her pull up her trousers.

As if executing an awkward dance step, the two of them took their original position, and Kirsten pivoted on her good leg. They started off back to the sled, while two reindeer approached and sniffed the new patch of yellow snow.

It was no easier climbing back into the sled than it was getting out of it, and Kirsten breathed through clenched teeth as she folded herself into it. The calf hadn't moved, and she noticed for the first time that it was white. She pulled the warm creature toward her while Maarit rearranged the deerskins around them both. Jova appeared with another cup of bark coffee and turned away. It tasted just as bad as the one before, but this time it had slices of what appeared to be smoked reindeer meat in it. She told herself it was not coffee, but a bitter meat stew, and hunger made it tolerable.

"I'm grateful you found me," she said. "I didn't even know the Sami were still herding during the war. And this far south. All those reindeer are yours?"

Maarit glanced out at the herd. "No. This herd belongs to my grandparents and two other families. They're camped just ahead of us. This route is ancient, but it's made up of lots of trails, not just one. You're lucky you were lying along the path they took this time. Otherwise you'd have frozen, and someone would have found you in the spring. Or your bones."

"Oh, now you've really cheered me up."

Gaiju was back at the sled again, a cup of hot bark coffee in one hand and a pipe in the other. He said something in Sami.

"He's asking what you were doing on the vidda," Maarit said in Norwegian.

Kirsten dropped her glance. What to tell them? The last thing she wanted, or was even allowed to do, was involve these innocent people in a war mission, even if it had failed.

"It's a long story. I'll tell it later, when I'm back on my feet again." It was a rude answer but all she could think of at the moment.

The old man scowled, took a long pull on his pipe, and returned to the lavvu.

Maarit was not so easily put off. "I'm guessing you parachuted in for some reason and got lost. Am I right?"

SOE training had not prepared her for friendly interrogation by rescuers. She relented slightly. "Half right. No parachutes. We came by glider but crashed. Most of the crew died, and the ones who could walk were captured. I was the only one to get away, but then I got lost. So where am I, exactly?"

"Somewhere midway between Hainefjørd and Udsek where we—and the reindeer—will spend the winter. But I'm not finished asking.

Why did you come in the first place? You speak Norwegian, but your coats are British military. You were on a mission, but I can't imagine for what? What were you looking for on the Hardangervidda?"

"Really, it's better I don't tell you. If the Germans capture you, the less you know, the less they can hurt you. Just help me recover, and I'll try to get out of your life as soon as possible."

"That serious, eh?" Maarit shrugged. "All right. We'll leave it for now." She gestured with her chin toward Kirsten's feet. "You've got a bad foot, maybe frostbitten, which needs to be looked at. Unfortunately, we can't take off your boot until we reach our *goahti* about a day away from here. You can come inside and warm up, and we'll take a look at everything then. Do you think you can hold out?"

"Now that I'm warm, and fed, I'm pretty sure I can. Is that coffee thing your main meal?

Maarit chuckled. "Salty coffee not your favorite, eh? Fortunately, we have other food to offer." Just then, the grandmother came up beside her and handed her another steaming bowl. "This should be more to your liking." Maarit exchanged the bowl for Kirsten's coffee cup. "I'll be back in a minute, and we'll eat together."

While she stepped away, the three other Sami remained staring at her for a moment, but then left her to squat by the tent. Moments later, Maarit returned with her own soup and sat on the edge of the sled. "How do you like our Sami food?"

Kirsten held the bowl in her gloved hands and sipped the liquid from the edge. It was fish soup. "This one's actually quite good."

"We'll try not to shock your palate too much at first. No reindeer brains yet."

Realizing Maarit was serious, Kirsten thought it wise not to ask more about the Sami diet. They ate in silence, and when they finished, Maarit took the empty bowls to Jova, where they wiped them clean with snow. Kirsten studied the two Sami women.

Jova seemed ancient, though she could have been any age over fifty. Her skin was weathered and deeply lined, and the hair that hung outside of her red and blue woolen cap was gray. She wore thick trousers, as did the others, tucked into high rubber boots, but her outer coat, similar to the others in its blue color, hung below her knees with oddly incongruous red ruffles at the bottom. She laughed quickly at something Gaiju said, with a sort of infectious cackle. Kirsten assumed she was part of the joke.

Maarit's dress was more interesting. The blue tunic, with red and yellow embroidered bands on the cuff, collar, and shoulder seam, was almost identical to those of the others, but sat better on her slender form. Around her hips, she wore a belt from which hung a coil of rope and a knife in a leather sheath.

Like the men, she wore thick trousers that bulged at the knee over a patterned band that wound like a puttee down her shin to her shoes. Sami shoes, made of reindeer fur, with an upward curve at the toe.

Only her hair was anomalous. Like the old woman, she wore a felt cap with a border, but, unusually for a Sami, her hair was a light brown.

Kirsten glanced away as Maarit returned and lifted the reindeer calf from Kirsten's side. "Dinnertime for her, too," she said, carrying the calf to the mother that had waited close by the whole time.

The calf nursed greedily, and when she dropped her head, sated, the mother took a few steps away, as if urging her infant to follow her. But all it did was stand in place, wobbling and honking mournfully. Sighing audibly, Maarit swept the animal into her arms and carried her back to the sled.

"I hope you don't mind sharing your bed again with the calf. She was injured by an eagle yesterday and still refuses to walk. Gaiju keeps pressuring me to slaughter her for dinner, and any other family would have done it by now, but I've grown sentimental."

Kirsten shifted to the side to offer more space. "I don't mind at all. She'll help keep me warm."

Maarit tucked the calf in at Kirsten's shoulder. "Let's hope that, by tomorrow, you'll both be walking again." She patted its head. "Will you be okay, you think?"

"I'm fine. We're fine." Kirsten brushed her chin over the top of the calf's head.

"By the way, if the mother becomes a nuisance, give her some of this." Maarit untied a burlap sack from behind the sled and dropped it onto Kirsten's chest. "It's lichen, their winter food. There's plenty under the snow, but they love it when you serve it to them personally, warm and dry."

The mother reindeer trotted a step closer.

Maarit lifted out an armload of firewood from the foot of the sled and turned away. "Good night, then. Call out if you need anything."

"Good night, yourself. And thank you for saving me."

Maarit glanced back over her shoulder. "Actually, the reindeer saved you."

Kirsten watched the grandparents as they crawled into the lavvu, which still glowed amber, from the fire at its center. Gaiju and then Maarit followed them, pulling the entrance closed. The bulges in the walls of the structure made it clear that it was full. To ensure her own comfort while she slept, Kirsten pulled on her second coat and felt the increased warmth immediately.

As if she'd been waiting for Maarit to leave, the mother reindeer crept closer and laid her long head over the edge of the sled. Amused, Kirsten handed over one, then another and another handful of lichen.

Other reindeer obviously took note of the offered snacks and trotted close. Three, then four, reindeer heads hung over the edge of the sled, surrounding her with a protective wall of antlers, and smiling, she fed them all. As soon as the sack was empty, the visitors lost interest and trotted away.

She lay back and took stock of her situation. She was, if not quite warm, at least not shivering, and now reasonably well-fed. A significant improvement over lying unconscious and dying in the snow. Her various pains had dulled to simple aches, and her injuries would probably heal.

But the failed mission…ah. The thought of the men who had died or been murdered in the disaster made her wince inwardly, out of both sorrow and guilt for being the only one to escape. She had to report to London, of course. But to do that, she had to get off the vidda and find a radio. That was not going to happen in the immediate future.

Shifting position slightly, she tilted her head back and gazed at the stars—pristine, indifferent, eternal. They made her anxieties seem trivial. Even the war seemed trivial. At that moment, there was no war, no enemy, no mission. There was only herself and four Sami in the frozen wilderness, trying, like all creatures, to stay alive.

The mother reindeer nuzzled her white infant, whose head lay against Kirsten's neck. She felt an overwhelming affection for the calf, its mother, the reindeer who clustered around her, bumping against the sled, for the Sami family that had hauled her along during their own arduous migration; and for Maarit, who'd held her while she peed in the snow.

Smiling to herself, she murmured to the calf, "I'm going to name you *Lykke,* for the luck you brought me." Then she dropped off into shallow sleep and wasn't sure whether she dreamed or actually caressed the reindeer.

CHAPTER SIX

It was still dark when a hand drawing the deerskin cover from Kirstin's head woke her. Lifting her chin from her cocoon, she saw a face that instantly cheered her. She sniffed to clear her nostrils and suddenly smelled cooked fish.

"Drink this," Maarit ordered. "Grandmother heated last night's soup. It'll warm you up."

Kirsten sipped from the steaming cup through cold lips, letting the salty brew warm her mouth and throat. Slowly the sensation spread to the rest of her, awakening her fully.

"How do you feel?" Maarit leaned against the sled.

"Better, I think. It was strange to sleep surrounded by reindeer, like I was part of the herd. I probably smell like them now."

Maarit chuckled. "We all smell like reindeer, which is why they trust us." She reached into the sled. "I'm putting the calf out to suckle now." She lifted the animal gently and stood her on the ground. The calf honked mournfully, then staggered the few meters toward its waiting mother, where it suckled energetically.

"That's a good sign," Kirsten said.

"Well, it saves her from the stew pot. But she's still too weak to follow the herd." She turned back to the sled. "What about you? Can you walk yet?"

"Or risk the stew pot? I sure hope so. If you could just help me out of the sled." Hanging onto Maarit with one arm, Kirsten threw her right leg over the edge of the sled and rolled the rest of her weight after it, arriving on two feet. A single step told her she still couldn't put much weight on her damaged foot, although the leg seemed strong. She cursed quietly, not wanting to repeat the humiliation of the day before.

"If you can move me around to the rear of the sled, I think I can manage to take care of business alone this time."

"I don't mind helping you again, but sure. Let's try." Maarit stepped under her left shoulder, acting as a crutch, and pivoted Kirsten around to the high rear of the Sami sled, then stepped back. "Call me if it doesn't work," she said, then turned away discreetly.

Mercifully, Kirsten succeeded, though only just. Supporting herself on one leg and with her right hand on the sled, she used her left to execute the complicated maneuver of dropping her trousers just long enough to relieve herself and then yanking them back up again.

While she rebuttoned, the two reindeer who had remained near the sled once again exhibited interest in the apparently flavorful yellow snow.

"Congratulations." Maarit approached the sled with an armload of hides and other objects that made up their moveable household. She loaded everything into the foot end of the sled and helped Kirsten back into the passenger seat. "Glad you're stronger, because we're taking off now, before daylight, to make the most of the light when it arrives."

In fact, as the draft reindeer was harnessed onto the sled and the family spread out to monitor the herd from both sides, the night sky was just beginning to lighten. The calf was back at her side but apparently recovering, and so was she.

She watched the stars disappear as the light increased, brooding once again about the mission that had so spectacularly failed. She had survived, but instead of being a hero to the nation, she was dead weight being towed by noncombatants, as useless as the reindeer calf. Only the sight of the draft reindeer's amusing hindquarters saved her from depression. It trotted along, seemingly unstressed by the weight of the sled, and every so often defecated onto the snow behind it, a comment, perhaps, on its indifference to her plight.

As the sky began to lighten, Maarit appeared again, skiing beside the sled, and it seemed a good moment to ask questions. "Why are some of the reindeer tame and the others aren't? Or maybe I mean, how do you tame them?"

"They're a bit like horses. They start off wild, especially the uncastrated males, which we call *sarvs,* and they're always skittish. But the females, called *vajas,* are usually calmer, and the castrated ones, the *härks,* are the ones we use as draft animals. They usually wear the bells and do all the work. When the ground's bare, like in summer, we can't use the sleds, so the härks serve as pack animals. The males in general follow the vajas with the bells, even when they're not in season." She laughed lightly. "They'll even 'follow empty,' as we say, when a Sami carries the bells instead of a deer."

"You really know the deer. Have you always lived with them?"

"No. Not at all. Before the war, I was a student in Trondheim. Medicine. I was doing a sort of apprenticeship at the hospital. But when the Germans came, well, everything changed, so for now, I'm up here full time."

"I'm sure your grandparents are happy to have you. And your parents?"

"No parents. Both gone." Maarit glanced away.

"Sorry if I'm prying."

"No. It's all right. My father was Norwegian."

"Was? Sorry," she repeated. "That's probably prying, too."

"He was killed at Narvik."

"Oh, I'm…She was about to say "sorry" but realized she'd said it already twice. "That's why you left your studies?"

"That and the fact that the quisling Nazis in Trondheim didn't like having a Sami, even a half Sami, taking a place of a Norwegian. We're inferior, you see, like Jews."

"Ah, of course. That nonsense was in the air when I was studying in Oslo. Jews, Slavs, Gypsies, Sami. Anyone not Aryan." She thought for another moment. "So your mother is Sami."

"Was. But again, it's a long story. Just like yours."

"Oh. I was prying. I apologize. But a non-personal question: what do the Sami think of the Germans and the war?"

"Most of them…us…are basically just waiting for it to be over. If the Germans left the Sami alone, we'd have no interest, but they come up here and shoot our reindeer to feed their troops. And sometimes kidnap our men to serve as guides in the north."

"Can't you appeal to your own government to stop that?"

"Our government is completely under the authority of Reichs-kommissar Josef Terboven, and he hates us."

"Isn't there anything people can do? Sabotage? Resistance?"

"Resistance is not in the Sami mindset. They're as political as the reindeer or the forest. Outside forces will be the ones to fight, and win, the war."

The sun emerged at the horizon as if in a sudden leap, illuminating the snow-covered landscape in blinding yellow-orange light. Kirsten squinted into it, imagining its warmth on her face and feeling a wave of optimism. Something about early morning light went right to the soul. "I guess that's where I come in. Or *came* in, but I failed. Yet I'm sorry to involve you, and endanger you, without your agreement."

Maarit continued to ski wordlessly beside the sled, each of her exhalations visible, like those of the reindeer. But when a distant shout drew her attention, she said, "I'll come back later," and rushed on ahead.

Kirsten's sled deer plodded onward, following those in front, and soon she passed Maarit and Jova tugging small bushes from the ground. Presumably for firewood, though Gaiju was cutting longer stems. To build another sled, perhaps?

A short while later, Maarit caught up with her and loaded the wood into the foot of the sled. "Hope you don't mind the crowding. But this will cook our dinner tonight." Kirsten drew up her knees, which caused a sudden pain in her ankle but no sensation in either of her feet. Alarm shot through her. She had frostbite.

The sled jerked forward and moved on, hour after hour. She must have dozed off, for when she awoke again it was dark, and something prickled her face. It was snowing.

What had awakened her was the sled stopping, and when she drew herself up on her elbows she saw why. Atop a small rise was a mound. She would have assumed it was a snow-covered rock but for the door on one side. Directly behind it, another smaller structure, also covered with snow, was visible, and behind that, a sort of platform on stilts. Beyond those, some dozen similar "hills" of various sizes dotted the landscape, one or two of them emitting a thin stream of smoke from their peaks. Apparently, they had arrived.

Maarit suddenly appeared with her skis over her shoulder. "Udsek. Our winter home." She swept her hand in an arc. "We even have an outhouse and storage facilities. No more traveling now for the next few months." She laid her skis on the ground, unharnessed the draft reindeer, and brushed snow from her mittens.

"Let's see if our baby is doing any better," she said, lifting the calf out of the sled and setting it on the ground. It stood bleating for a moment, then lurched awkwardly toward its waiting mother.

"So far, so good," Maarit said, then turned toward Kirsten. "How are you feeling?"

"No different, actually. I'm afraid I'm still pretty useless."

"We'll get you inside in a minute." She waved over Gaiju to help her lift Kirsten out of the sled. They repeated the same technique they'd used hours before and helped her again to a standing position. Using Maarit as a crutch as before, Kirsten got as far as the entrance of the hut.

"You go inside first," Maarit instructed her, and Kirsten staggered painfully through the entrance. Once inside, she dropped to the floor and glanced around.

She knew from school days that the structure was called a goahti. It was surprisingly roomy, four times the size of the lavvu, and she could already see the functional layout. Behind the central hearth, at the back of the hut, Jova sat in what was presumably the kitchen. Flanked by sacks of utensils and cardboard boxes, she had just lit a fire in the hearth and hung a cauldron filled with snow on a chain directly over it.

She waved Kirsten over to the left side of the fire, where several deerskins were laid over a bedding of twigs. Insulation, Kirsten thought, and slid closer. Maarit sat down beside her.

"I've seen pictures of these places from the outside, but never inside. I'm amazed at how comfortable they are. If you have enough food and firewood, you can last the winter here."

"The Sami have, for thousands of years."

Kirsten swept her gaze around the interior walls, long wooden poles rising side by side to a smoke hole at the top. She could make out the rows of bark that encircled them on the outside and knew that outside of those was a layer of sod. Jova's kindling had caught, and a fire burned now, sending up smoke through the hole overhead. A rifle leaned against the rear wall, an old model from the First World War. For hunting, she supposed.

Alof stepped through the doorway and took his place next to Jova, and Gauji followed him in, dragging his two poles. The three of them occupied the space on the right side of the fire pit. The other "sitting room," she concluded. Maarit removed her cap, and long, light-brown hair tumbled out.

They all unwound strips of woven "puttees" from their ankles and tugged off their curved reindeer-hide shoes, scraped out the grass inside, and hung the wads here and there to dry. Unnervingly taciturn, the Sami men lay back to rest, apparently indifferent to her. Only Jova was active, preparing food.

Maarit dropped down next to her. "All right. First, let's take off those coats you have on. Maybe someday you'll tell me why you're wearing two." She slid behind her and pulled on the sleeves while Kirsten shrugged out of the shoulders. Under the coats she had on a simple high-neck sweater, which needed no explaining.

"Yes, some day."

Unperturbed, Maarit came around in front of her again. "Let's take a look at your feet now," she said, and helped Kirsten unlace her boots. They managed to tug off the right one, but the left one refused to move at all.

"It's frostbite, isn't it?" Kirsten grimaced. It was the most likely explanation for the loss of feeling in her feet. If so, she might be facing disaster.

"Probably, but let's worry about it after we've seen it." She unlaced the boot completely, then gripped both sides, peeling them away from the foot. Inch by inch, she managed to draw the foot out of its confinement. "Does that hurt?"

"No, and that's what worries me." Wincing, Kirsten slid off her woolen sock and was shocked at what she saw. No wonder she couldn't take off her boot. The entire lower part of her foot was swollen and yellowish, and all her toes were blistered. The worst were the two center ones, which looked like yellow balloons, while the big toe was merely red.

"Try moving your foot in a circle, from the ankle."

Clenching her teeth, Kirsten tried. The swollen foot didn't have much mobility, but limited movement was still possible. Maarit massaged her heel and halfway down to the damaged toes. "Does any special place hurt more than any other?"

"Just the ankle. It's strange that my ankle hurts so much, but my foot feels nothing."

"Probably because you have two different injuries. Anyhow, it seems to me, being able to walk at all after the crash means your ankle isn't broken. You can walk with a broken toe, or with a fracture in one of the foot bones, but not with a broken ankle. And since that's where the pain is, I'd guess you have a bad sprain. Your toes are the big problem."

"They look terrible. Frightening that I can't even feel them."

"I saw a few cases in the clinic where I worked in Trondheim, and of course Sami freeze their toes all the time. This looks like second-degree frostbite. If the blisters were bloody, or the whole area blue, I'd worry about gangrene, but I think this can all heal. We'll warm your feet, of course, which will probably hurt a lot, but you should recover."

"How long will it take to heal? I've never had anything like this."

"A few weeks. The skin will slowly dry, turn black, and peel off. Looks nasty, but the muscle underneath should heal with no damage."

"And this one?" She slid the sock from her right foot, which looked like a milder version of the left one.

"Same thing, I'd say." Maarit gently grasped the toes in her palm and warmed them, though Kirsten felt nothing. "Considering how deadly frostbite can get, it looks like you got off lightly."

"So that means I'll have to—"

Before she could finish her sentence, Jova reached past Maarit with a metal pan.

"Warm water. Jova knew right away what you needed. Let's get this over with." She set the pan by Kirsten's feet and placed each foot gently in the water. "This will undo the freezing, but of course it won't reverse the damage."

The warmth was pleasant on Kirsten's heels, but as the frostbitten flesh began to thaw, she sensed a combination of prickling and burning. Within minutes, the pain was excruciating, and she moaned through clenched teeth.

Maarit grimaced in clear sympathy. "Hold on, and try to remember that the pain is a good sign. It shows that the flesh underneath is still viable. And now that your toes are unfrozen, you have to be especially vigilant that they don't freeze again."

"Yes, they...warned us about that...in training." Kirsten forced the words between pants.

"Training? Who trained you? For what?"

"Sorry. Shouldn't have said that." She changed the subject. "What about my ribs? Can we do anything about them?"

"If you were trained to deal with injuries, you know you don't do anything for ribs. We don't have an X-ray machine, of course, but we can assume the fracture, or fractures, are simple. If they were compound, with bone splinters puncturing the lung or the pleura, you'd be in much worse shape. Pneumonia is still a problem, and the only way to avoid that is to breathe as deeply as you can, even if it hurts."

"Yes." Kirsten grunted. "I actually knew that already, too. I was just hoping you had some magic Sami cure."

"No magic cure, but some good Sami soap." Maarit held up a clay pot containing an unappealing gray-brown substance.

Kirsten sniffed it. "Not bad. A bit piney."

"Birchwood ashes, pine-tree sap, and crushed juniper. It's the reindeer fat that holds it all together. It will take away some of the grime while your feet heal." Maarit gently massaged Kirsten's feet, spending a few more minutes on the one with the sprained ankle. "Is the pain any better?"

"A little, I suppose. A notch down from 'kill me please' to simply unbearable. How am I going to walk? It was better when I couldn't feel anything at all."

"It should ease off in a while. With any luck, you'll be able to stand by tomorrow."

"But I'll never get my boots back on."

Maarit turned to Jova, who was preparing food over the fire. The two spoke for several minutes in Sami, and all Kirsten could do was try to interpret their tones and facial expressions. Jova seemed initially affronted, resistant, but then her expression softened. Maarit must have said something funny, for the old woman cackled and nodded. She reached into one of the wooden chests that backed up what was obviously her domain. After some fumbling, she drew out a pair of deerskin shoes, made in the Sami style, with high backs and a toe that curved upward. She murmured a few more remarks, then handed the shoes to Maarit.

"Of course you can't fit into your own boots now. Maybe not for weeks. But in the meantime, my grandmother has agreed to lend you these." She placed the shoes beside Kirsten. "They're my brother's dress-up shoes. Jova made them for him, but he wore them only once.

He had large feet, so even with shoe-grass for padding, your swollen feet will have plenty of room."

"Your brother? *Had* large feet? You mean he's…"

"He was killed last year."

Suddenly the pain in her feet seemed trivial. No wonder Jova had been reluctant. "Please tell her I'm deeply grateful. I promise to take good care of them and to return them as good as new."

Jova obviously understood Kirsten's remark because she cackled agreeably, while she poured some mysterious chopped substance into a coffee pot. Kirsten lifted her feet from the pan of water, which had grown cold, and Maarit wiped them with a dishcloth. The diminishing pain allowed her to notice that she was hungry.

"My pack, is it still on the sled?"

"No. It's here." Maarit reached toward the jumble of sacks and bundles piled by the door, then tugged it out by its strap. "Something you need?"

Kirsten rummaged through the sack, feeling socks, utility knife, her side arm, and the crumpled remnants of the final food kit. "Ah, this is what I was looking for. At the end, I was too weak to eat anything." She held up a packet of oatmeal, then turned toward Jova. "You can add this to the larder," she said, with no idea whether the old woman spoke Norwegian.

Jova took the proffered packet and shook the dry oats into the coffee pot. After a few moments of waiting until it softened, she poured the lumpy mix into everyone's dinner bowl. Though it was chewy, it was softer and more appealing than dried reindeer chips, and the slight sweetness of the oatmeal offset the bitterness of the "coffee." For Kirsten's palate, it made a decent meal.

When all had finished, Jova gathered the cups and bowls and scrubbed them clean with snow that she clawed through the ventilation hole behind her. With both medical treatment and meal finished, everyone fell silent.

Kirsten took the moment to study the faces of her rescuers. She hadn't seen many Sami up close before, as they were rare in Oslo, but the grandparents seemed to fit the image she had of them.

Alof and his brother Gaiju had round, somewhat flat faces with leathery skin a shade darker than most Norwegians, a look that hinted slightly of Siberia. Gaiju, who was missing several lower front teeth, looked slightly more savage than his brother, and she was a bit afraid of him.

Jova's face was also wide, though her eyes were large, deep pools of dark brown. Her expression was severe until she laughed, when it seemed to burst open with a high-pitched laughter completely at odds with her usual demeanor. All three had dark, almost black, hair.

Maarit bore little resemblance to them. Only her eyes were the same, chocolate brown under thick black eyelashes.

Maarit glanced over at her and, caught staring, Kirsten blurted out, "The calf. Is it all right?"

"With the vaja," Alof said from the other side of the fire. Drawing his knees up, he pulled a pipe from a leather pouch on his belt.

So, the old scoundrel spoke Norwegian after all, she thought. As if the three words had exhausted him, he busied himself with packing his pipe with something flaky and brown.

"Good the Germans did not find you," he finally continued, starting a new subject. Curious, his ability to speak Norwegian suddenly rendered him less alien, more attractive even. But the subject was a dangerous one. Soon he might ask what she was doing on the plateau in the first place. She deflected.

"Yes. A lucky thing the reindeer were passing. Are all your neighbors herders, too?"

Alof stared into space, in no hurry to speak again.

"Some are." Maarit filled in the silence. "Five other families live here, and three have herds of different sizes—Tuovo, Paaval, and Aavik. The reindeer that are scattered all over the valley belong to all of us. They'll stay together until we need to round them up later in the winter."

"It's safe to leave them alone?"

"The deer? Yes and no. They've kept the same feeding habits for centuries, but we do check on them and watch for predators, injuries, or a frost that freezes the snow so they can't get to their food."

"Or Germans," Jova said unexpectedly. It seemed the whole family spoke Norwegian.

"Yes, the Germans." Kirsten nodded, calculating ways to keep the discussion away from herself. "Has the occupation been difficult for the Sami? Have the Germans taken much?"

Jova looked away, almost bitterly, it seemed, leaving the answer to the others. Alof took one of the glowing coals from the fire to light his pipe. When he puffed on it and blew out smoke, it became obvious it was not tobacco. It smelled rather of burning wood.

Gaiju also glanced up at the question, and she thought he would comment, but he seemed engrossed in some carving of the branches he'd collected and remained silent.

Alof puffed a few more times, as if marshaling his thoughts, then spoke. "It was already difficult. The Norwegians have been pushing us out of our grazing lands forever. Every year they take more reindeer, and our herds grow smaller and smaller. Taxes, they call it. The Germans don't call it anything. They just shoot the reindeer for meat or try to harness them for work, but they don't know how to treat the animals."

He paused, staring into the flames, his pipe adding smoke to that of the dwindling fire. Kirsten wondered what kept the hut from filling up with clouds of it, then detected a stream of cold air behind her. A vent for just that purpose. Clever. She waited to hear more from the others.

But Alof had no more to say and simply tapped the ashes from his pipe and lay down on his deerskin, using his brightly colored cap as a pillow. It seemed a signal to the household.

Jova leaned up against a sort of backrest with her deer hide over one shoulder, and Gaiju also set aside his work and lay down.

Kirsten turned to study Maarit's face, bronze in the light of the smoldering fire, then lowered her voice to a murmur so as not to disturb the others. "I'd like to hear more about you. Is it strange living in two worlds?"

Maarit drew closer and also spoke quietly. "I told you my father was Norwegian and my mother Sami. When they were both alive, we moved back and forth, between Oslo and the Hardangervidda. My brother came up every autumn and spring to help during the migrations. Sometimes I did, too, but mainly I wanted to have a life outside the Sami. So I finished school and went to study medicine in Trondheim."

Kirsten studied Maarit's face while she spoke.

She had a narrow, authoritative nose that arched slightly at the top and bore no rememblance to that of her relatives. The Norwegian father explained her pale coloring and her light brown hair. Like Jova, Maarit's lips were robust, earthy. Fuller at the center where they formed a soft double bow, they tapered off at the sides into thin lines that curved up a millimeter at the end. The effect was an almost-smile, even when she stared, expressionless, into the dying fire.

Maarit tossed another bit of firewood onto the embers. "Time to sleep," she said definitively and lay down with her feet to the fire. "Unless you prefer the sled and your little reindeer."

"No, this is fine. Thank you." Kirsten lay down back-to-back with Maarit, drawing up her larger coat as a blanket and sensing an extra warmth on her shoulders. It was fine, indeed. Her feet and ribs still ached, but her stomach was full, and the war was distant—and so for the moment was guilt. She would return to duty as soon as she could walk again, and that was that. Faintly aware of the wind whistling around the hut, the first snores of the men, and the comfort of Maarit's back, she was at peace. She thought of the little reindeer she'd slept with until now. "By the way, I've named her Lykke."

❖

Kirsten awoke, as before, bleary-eyed and alone, with all the others already up and working. Embarrassed to be useless, she sat up and forced her swollen feet into her new Sami reindeer shoes. Then, with some effort, and no little pain, she crawled to the hut entrance.

Outside, the snow and wind had let up, and once she had pulled herself up to a standing position, she had a clear view of the valley where they had arrived. In the distance, she could make out five other goahtis of various sizes, scattered over the hillside, as well as a dozen or so platforms and outbuildings. Smoke rose gently from most of the households.

The reindeer had moved away, though they were still visible in a loose herd grazing in the snow off to her right. Alof and Jova were nowhere in sight, but she spotted Maarit talking to someone at one of the neighboring goahtis.

Suddenly aware of her early morning physical needs, she glanced down at her feet and wondered both where to take care of business and how she was going to get there. At that moment, Gaiju came from around the rear of the goahti carrying his two poles on his shoulder.

He said something in Sami, though it could have been Norwegian, but his missing teeth made it unintelligible. However, the tilt of his head toward a smaller structure some twenty yards away suggested he was pointing out the outhouse. "Thank you," she replied but did not move.

Gaiju chuckled and swung the poles from his shoulder, planting them in the ground in front of her. Kirsten squinted, confused, at the three-foot-long objects he had constructed. Each one bore a smaller branch tied at a diagonal to create a Y shape, with the tops joined by a crosspiece. All was held together with twisted root-cord, and the crosspiece was padded with a patch of reindeer hide. Surprise and delight rose in her like a bubble. He had made her crutches.

"Oh, my heavens, thank you, Gaiju," she said with warmth, but he had already turned and walked away.

She admired the crutches for a long moment, then fitted them under her arms. They were a bit low and awkward, but allowed her to limp slowly toward the narrow shed, which, upon arriving in front of it, she confirmed was, indeed, an outhouse.

She emerged some ten minutes later, pleased with her reclaimed toilet autonomy, and glanced around, looking for something useful to do. Gaiju must have had a similar thought, for at that moment, he stepped forward and handed her two Sami coats. The sleeve of one had been torn wide open, perhaps by a reindeer antler, and the other coat had holes in both elbows.

"I'll need some thread and a needle," she said, miming the act of sewing, in case he didn't speak Norwegian like the others. He grunted and detached a small leather sack from his belt, then pressed it into her palm. Opening it, she saw it contained several bone needles and a card with a large steel needle, as well as spools of coarse black thread.

"All right, then," she said. "Mending it is." She'd been assigned women's work, but that was all she was up to anyhow. After throwing the coats over her shoulder, she limped back to the main hut, leaned the crutches against the door frame, and limped inside. The fire had gone to ashes, so she took the liberty of stoking it with more wood, and the air soon warmed enough to allow her to remove her mittens.

She felt a certain amusing connection with her English mother. Had Eleanor Wallace ever mended her husband Jomar's coat? It seemed unlikely. Kirsten suspected none of the women in her lineage had mended coats, and if Eleanor could see her daughter doing it now, she'd have snorted contempt.

Nonetheless, the act of stitching up torn clothing was oddly satisfying, for she was finally earning her keep.

As she set aside the first finished coat, Maarit appeared in the entryway. "Ah. I see they've put you to work."

"Yes, and I walked by myself, all the way to the outhouse and back. With the crutches Gaiju made for me."

"I noticed them outside. You see? The old grump has a heart, after all. How's the ankle?"

"A little better each day. But the frostbite hasn't healed yet, of course."

"No. It won't for a long while."

"At least I don't feel helpless any longer, and I'm beginning to think about my own responsibilities. I have to contact the people I work for some time soon. Any villages within reach that might have a radio?"

"Not the short-wave kind you mean. For that we'd have to go into Rjukan, and even then, we'd have to ask around discreetly. They're illegal, of course, and only people in the resistance would have one. But when you're more mobile, in a week or so, I'll go with you."

"I don't want to endanger you."

"Too late for that. If the Germans are looking for you, you've already endangered us by being here. You should at least let us know why."

Kirsten tried to think of an evasion, but the Sami had saved her life, and if she wanted them to help her get back in contact with headquarters, she had to reveal at least a minimum.

Although they were alone, she leaned in close. "I'll tell you as much as I dare, but you must keep it from the others. Bad enough I've involved you at all, but if your grandparents also actually know anything, the Germans will be on them with full force."

"I'll make up some story or other. They won't press for details. But you have to tell me the truth, or I won't help you."

Kirsten gave a long exhalation. "All right. I was on a British operation that came in on gliders, but we crashed."

"That explains the British coats. But you speak Norwegian without an accent. Are you British or Norwegian?"

"Norwegian, but I lived for a long time in England. As for this mission, I was part of a team that was to attack…an important installation, but it failed when we crashed. Obviously, I have to report to headquarters to tell what happened and to say I escaped. Some of the others were captured."

"The only installations I know of anywhere near the vidda are the Møsvatn dam and the power plant at Vemork. I assume the workers at both places are all Norwegian, but the Germans have control of them. Were you planning to attack one of those? Whatever for?"

"Those are the kind of details I'm not allowed to reveal. The important thing is, we failed, and at the moment, London has no idea what happened to us. Do you have any contact with Milorg, for example? They would certainly have a radio."

"The Sami have no connections to Milorg. Most don't even know what it is. The only thing we…that is…I could do is guide you to Rjukan, where you could put out feelers yourself. That is, when you can walk again."

"You're willing to accompany me that far? That would be a start. How far are we from there?"

"It's about 120 kilometers from here if you cross the vidda, longer if you go around. In any case, you're not going anywhere for the next few weeks, months maybe. I have serious work ahead and can't get away anyhow."

"I thought the migration was over now." The promise of a guide to Rjukan cheered Kirsten, but the mention of months alarmed her.

Maarit ran her fingers through her hair, a gesture that caused her to raise her chin. It was a very attractive chin. "Herding is only the first part of it. Right now, our reindeer are mixed in with deer from three other families. We've got to separate out our vajas and sarvs to butcher or castrate, mark our calves, repair our sleds and houses. Any number of things we couldn't do on migration. My grandparents have no one to help them now except me. I'm afraid you're stuck here with us for a while."

Kirsten considered her choices and realized she had none. Until she could walk or ski long distances alone, she was helpless. Maarit's offer of assistance after a few weeks of recuperation had more and more appeal.

"Fair enough. We'll make our move when I'm back on my feet, and I'll be as useful as possible, in the meantime."

"Agreed." Maarit patted her softly on the face. "Now finish your mending, Grandma."

❖

Kirsten had no idea how Maarit explained her to her family and the others in the settlement. Perhaps she didn't explain her at all. If the other Sami families viewed her as an interloper and foreigner, their taciturn nature gave no evidence of it. On the rare occasion she hobbled beyond the perimeter of Alof's goahti, they greeted her with a nod, and when they stopped by to exchange fish for bread—for Jova was an excellent baker—they revealed no special curiosity.

It was, after all, winter, and concerns for warmth, food, and the welfare of the reindeer trumped all. Jova accepted her without comment and demonstrated as much by handing over the rest of the mending. When there were no more rips to repair, the scraping clean of hides became the next task she could accomplish sitting down.

Then, in the second week of Kirsten's confinement, Jova entrusted her with the sewing of a blue wool over-garment for Alof, which she learned was called a *gakti*. To be entrusted with such a task was clearly meant as a compliment, and Kirsten took pains to get it right. She had to first learn the colors and patterns of stripes that ornamented the heavy tunic and to stitch them carefully by firelight, so they would hold up for years. She was therefore pleased when he finally tried it on and smiled approval.

Every day, though designating "day" was arbitrary in the dark arctic winter, Maarit and the men would work outside for six or eight hours, while Kirsten and Jova tended the household, such as it was. They talked little, and the main sound, other than the wind outside, was Jova's soft humming in a string of sounds in which Kirsten could never identify a melody.

Kirsten's next assignment was bread-making, which proved to require more skill than mending. But under Jova's alternating scolding and snickering, she managed to form and bake the unleavened cakes on the stone without burning one side and leaving the other one gummy.

Bread and reindeer meat were the mainstay, with vegetation a rarity, though Jova introduced her to mountain sorrel, which, when pounded and boiled, made a tolerable, if somewhat bitter, dish called *jobmo*. She ate it out of courtesy, assuming it would also help her avoid scurvy.

With her increasing mobility, Kirsten began to plan her departure. Maarit had promised to return with her to Rjukan once the frostbite had healed, and to perhaps wait around until she had contacted Milorg. At that point, the decent thing to do was to send her back to her people with as little knowledge of Milorg as possible.

She checked her feet daily but found little change other than reduced swelling. She could stand, even walk, though both were painful, and she never ventured more than a few steps. But soon she was able to assist in the weekly milking of the vaja, while the calves were slowly being weaned. The harvest of milk was sparse compared with cows and goats, but they had enough to lighten their coffee and stews.

"I must be getting used to the Sami life," she remarked to Maarit. "I don't even mind all the reindeer hairs I've inhaled and ingested in everything I consume."

"Good for you." Maarit laughed. "You'll make some Sami herder a good wife."

The thought horrified her. "Um, do you have any non-wife tasks I can do?"

"In fact, I do. Alof just hauled in a long branch at the back of his sled. We need to cut it up for the fire."

"Let me give it a try. After three weeks of baking and spinning, I'm willing to do anything."

"I'm sure you are. But let's not hurt those ribs. Why don't I do the chopping while you set up the wood and gather the pieces? That way you only have to bend a little."

Outside the goahti it was the familiar polar dusk, which it seemed to be most of the time, but the bluish ambient light was sufficient for most work, even without firelight.

Kirsten set the first block of wood upright on a hard-packed snow mound. "Over to you, my dear."

"My pleasure." Maarit took up the axe. Taking a wide stance, she swung it over her head and then downward in a smooth arc onto the center of the block. It split cleanly down the middle with a satisfying *CHOCK*.

Collecting the firewood from the ground, Kirsten had to admire Maarit's grace and prowess. She didn't mind being the lowly assistant. They were doing something together, and it was a step up from being an invalid and mender of clothing.

Maarit piled the cut wood just before the entrance but showed no interest in going inside again. Kirsten stopped as well, simply enjoying the pleasure of accomplishment and of being in the open air. They were, after all, five people hunkered around the fire inside, day after day. Perhaps Maarit, too, found the confinement stifling.

She gazed up at the overcast winter sky and took a deep breath. "What other fun things do the men do that the women don't?"

Maarit crossed her arms and stared at the same empty part of the sky. "Well, they castrate and slaughter the deer, though I guess that's not what you meant by 'fun things.' But men also do the spiritual things. Women can be healers, but the shaman is always a man."

"Shaman? I thought the Sami were all Christian."

"They are, for the most part. Jova and Alof will tell you that in a second. But when there's illness, an unexpected death, a difficult pregnancy, they turn to magic. The old religion still lurks in the backroads of every Sami's mind." She chuckled. "Except for Gaiju. For him the old gods are right at the front. Ask him to tell you the story of Aigi."

With the wood already stacked, Kirsten bent down to help collect the chips for kindling. "Speaking of reindeer, whatever happened to the white calf you saved? The one I named Lykke."

"She's fine. She's right over there with her mother, in fact." She pointed toward a cluster of deer that nibbled in the snow on the periphery of the settlement. "They both seem fond of staying close by. She's yours, if you want her. Gaiju has already carved her ear with a special mark for you."

"My own deer? I'm touched, but I think she'll have to stay here. As long as you promise not to eat her."

"Don't worry. White reindeer are rare, and nobody likes to slaughter them."

It had been calm while they chopped wood, but now the wind picked up. Hugging her wood chips to her chest, Kirsten bent through the hut opening and deposited them by the entrance. Alof and Gaiju arrived at the goahti just behind them, driven in by the wind. Jova had hot food waiting, reindeer-meat stew and blood dumplings, and this time Kirsten felt she'd earned her share.

When the dinner bowls were empty, each person began their private evening occupation: Alof his pipe, Gaiju some handcraft, Jova her weaving. Sami domestic tranquility. Kirsten turned to Maarit. "You have a wonderful family, you know. You're very lucky."

Maarit stared into the fire and seemed to have something more to say, but it was unlike the Sami to share private details. "Not so lucky. I lost my mother and my brother in one week."

"Oh, I'm sorry," Kirsten said, hearing the triteness of her reply. "Would it be rude to ask what happened?"

"I'll tell you what happened." To Kirsten's surprise, it was Jova who spoke. "Germans took her brother. We never saw him again."

"They simply kidnapped him? How awful."

Jova's expression grew hard. "Two Germans. But one was worse. Ugly, a head big on top and small on the bottom. A big mouth that went from ear to ear." She ran her thumb from one of her own ears to the other, to illustrate. "He liked to spit. He pointed his gun at Karrel and took him away. Then my daughter went to look for him, and she never came back either. We found her in the snow."

She fell silent, and Maarit remarked, "So, that left me, their other half-breed." She drew up one knee and began to unwind her leg band. Its colors were similar to those on the band Jova was currently weaving.

Half-breed. Strange remark, for Maarit's people had shown no sign of resenting her. But perhaps the tragedy lay in the other direction, that not only the reindeer were reduced in number, but also the full Sami. It was at least a change of subject. "Has it been difficult to live in two cultures?"

"It has its challenges. On my best days, I feel doubly enriched, but on the bad ones, I sense I don't quite belong in either."

"Like Aigi," Alof remarked suddenly, and both heads turned toward him. He puffed his pipe leisurely, as if he hadn't just heard the story of the death of his daughter and grandson.

"How is it like Aigi?" Maarit asked.

"He took the pipe stem from between his teeth. "Aigi was the unwanted child of two lands, but he was a hero."

Kirsten shifted her position to hear him, relieved that the evening's conversation had shifted from lament to storytelling.

"He was a witch's son, with tainted blood, but chosen to challenge Hahtezan, goddess of dark things, and Stallu, eater of children."

"Stallu is the Sami boogyman," Maarit explained softly. "Parents threaten children that if they wander off from the village, he'll catch them and eat them."

Alof took a long puff on his pipe and continued.

"It happened that Hahtezan, the fae who ruled the winter night, seized the magical waters of the six springs. She sent ghosts to guard them and to kill anyone who came near."

Kirsten threw a side glance at Maarit at the unfamiliar names, but Maarit seemed intent on the story. Perhaps there would be some character development.

"Aigi was summoned to take back the magical water for Njavezan, the fae of light and summer. The boy was able to approach the ghosts because he was the son of a witch and knew some of the dark spells. But the brute Stallu captured him and tried to eat him. Stallu got only as far as eating one foot before the golden Arctic fox saved Aigi. But then Aigi was lame and had to rely on the golden Arctic fox to fulfill his calling, so together they found a strong reindeer to carry them toward the sun bridge formed by the first beam of spring."

"And he succeeded, didn't he? The hero always succeeds," Maarit remarked.

Alof shook his head as he tapped out the ashes from his pipe and packed in fresh spruce bark. "Victory is momentary, but time is long. An old man knows this."

"So what happened?" Kirsten couldn't help asking. The plot was already pretty complicated, and she couldn't see its message.

"Aigi freed the waters from Hahtezan and Stallu. Stallu was an eater of children, but time is the eater of all things, both defeat and victory. The six springs began to produce more magic water."

Mythology meets science, Kirsten thought. "So what did he do then?" she asked out loud. "Does the story end with the victory of Hahtezan and Stallu?" Myths were generally not so cynical.

"No, my child. You were not listening. Time eats all victories, even that one. The waters became so coveted that Stallu poured them into a great vessel and tried to carry it away in a boat."

Waters in a boat. That's a good one. It was beginning to sound like a fairy tale again.

"But Aigi and the golden Arctic fox found the boat and dug a hole in its bottom, and it sank, and all its water flowed into the lake. The magic caused the lake to become beautiful, but the magic was never strong enough to be of any use to Stallu and Hahtezan."

"And the six springs? What happened to them?"

"The legend does not say." Alof relit his pipe and puffed at it, apparently terminating his narration. Jova had already packed up her kitchen and curled up on the woman's side of the goahti, an additional signal that the day was over. Kirsten and Maarit exchanged glances that amounted to a shared shrug, then also lay down for the night.

Kirsten dreamed about Aigi, but the waters didn't belong to gods with impossible names. They belonged to her father Jomar, and the Germans had stolen them. And it was her task, like Aigi, to win them back. But that was the anguish that made the dream a nightmare. How could one rescue water? You couldn't lift it in your arms and run away. And she couldn't even approach the water anyhow, since she could barely walk.

When she awoke the next morning, she lay for a few moments, recalling her failure and frustration.

❖

In the second month of her sojourn, as shuffling became walking, and the pain in her ribs disappeared, she felt increasing shame and guilt. While she was injured, she was, in a manner, excused from service, but as soon as she was fit, she was duty-bound to return. Besides, Maarit had promised.

While Maarit and Alof were away with the men on a wolf hunt, she examined her feet, as she did almost every day. They were still unnaturally pink but no longer swollen. On an impulse, she rummaged in her rucksack and pulled out her boots and tried to slide her feet into them. Her right foot fit easily inside, though the left one, that had suffered the sprain and the more severe frostbite, required a bit of force. Nonetheless, she stared triumphantly down at her feet, once again shod with her own boots. One more week, she thought. Seven more days for the left foot to recover, and it will be time to go.

She glanced up to see if anyone had noticed her achievement, but Jova had dozed off over her weaving, and Gaiju was carving something. He often carved bowls and utensils for the family, but today he fashioned something on an antler, and she watched him with curiosity. When he finally noticed her gaze, he beckoned her to him. Intrigued, she stepped over to his side of the goahti and sat down next to him.

He smelled strongly of burnt birch tobacco, but as she leaned away from him, he drew her back and placed a small knife in her hand.

She stared at the knife, puzzled, until he added a three-inch length of reindeer antler that forked at one end. He'd already taken a slice from one side, creating a flat surface on the round antler, obviously for some marking. He showed her first the way to tilt the knife just slightly to achieve a narrow, barely perceptible groove. Then he pressed his thumb on one of the charred logs and smeared it over the cut. A brief wipe of the image with his palm revealed the soot-filled groove as the first line of a drawing.

"Ah, so that's how you do it." Closing her hand over the antler fragment, she stepped back to her own side of the fire to work. Maarit wore such an antler amulet, and Kirsten liked the idea of having one. She already knew the image she wanted.

Intent on her carving, she lost track of time and so was surprised when the wolf hunters returned. Intrigued, she stepped out to see if they'd succeeded.

Two of them dragged a hand-sled bearing the carcass of the wolf. It was a large male, and she could see how he would have had the power to pull down a reindeer, even without the rest of his pack. It was a splendid beast; she couldn't help but regret its death.

Maarit must have noticed her glance. "Don't worry. It took only one shot. Well, two. One to stop him and the other to finish him off. It was a more merciful death than his deer suffered."

"I know," Kirsten said dully, as the hunters unloaded the carcass for skinning and butchering. That night, everyone ate wolf meat. It was tougher than deer meat, and eating it made her feel more detached than ever from civilization. Another reason to go home.

As the evening wore on and the family began to doze, Kirsten leaned toward Maarit and spoke under her breath. "You know, I can walk again. We need to talk about going to Rjukan." The thought of the trip across the wild vidda frightened her, but she had said the words, and now she was committed. It would test her to her limits, but she was in charge of her own life again.

Maarit was silent, and Kirsten feared she would object. Without Maarit's help, she was all but trapped. But Maarit nodded. "This is a good time. The reindeer have enough food for a while, and we won't round them up for castration and slaughter for a couple of months. But can you travel? You can play brave to me, but not to the wind and cold. You'll have to ski for a day and a half and spend a night on the ice."

"It sounds ominous, I admit, but really, I've already pushed the boundary of cowardice by remaining here, coddled by the Sami for nearly two months. If I stay any longer, it's desertion."

"I understand. Well, all right. I'll tell Jova and Alof tomorrow. I've got loose ends to tie up, and we'll have to adapt some Sami skis for you, but we should be able to leave in a couple of days."

"Well, then. It's settled. By the way, while you were out hunting, Gaiju showed me how to carve on antler bone. It's my first try and it's pretty primitive, but…you'll see." She reached inside her jacket and pulled out an object, then dropped it onto Maarit's palm. A piece of antler in the shape of a Y. On the surface, just at the bifurcation, she had scratched out a stick figure with four legs and two protrusions on its head.

Maarit studied it for a moment, obviously pleased. "Well done! A reindeer. How appropriate."

"It couldn't be anything else. The reindeer found me, after all."

"It's beautiful. Now all you need is a cord to wear it." Maarit crawled a few feet toward Jova's "kitchen" and began pulling things from a box of household items: wooden utensils, a hammer and nails, knife handles. Finally, she found a length of leather cord. Tying it around the antler, she made a necklace of it and draped it over Kirsten's head. Kirsten fingered it for a moment as it hung over her chest, then dropped it under her sweater. "I saw that you had one and wondered what's carved on yours. I've been meaning to ask."

Maarit drew her amulet out from under her gakti and ran her thumb over the image. "It's a fox. It's supposed to make me clever."

"Well, it must be working. You managed to heal my feet, both the sprain and the frostbite. And without benefit of medication."

"You don't need medication for those things. They heal by themselves."

"Don't brush off a compliment. I'm trying to tell you, because of you, I can wear my own boots again."

"I'm so glad. Now, get some sleep, and tomorrow I'll tell Jova she can have her shoes back."

CHAPTER SEVEN

A search around the settlement produced a pair of old skis, and Gaiju's wood skills made them serviceable again. Some days later, by the first light of the winter sun, they set out with a hand-drawn sled carrying supplies. In consideration of Kirsten's limitations, they set up a rhythm they could sustain, skiing for two hours, interspersed with fifteen minutes' rest.

Because it would have been suicide to appear in Rjukan in British clothing, Kirsten had relinquished her two coats and exchanged them for an old Sami gakti. Like her shoes, it had belonged to Karrel in his younger days, and he had long outgrown it when he disappeared. Unlike his shoes, it was worn, and the ornamental braid was frayed and stained. It made her look like just another Sami woman used to sitting on the ground. All she had to do was take care to cover her red hair.

She was energetic and optimistic, even a bit smug, until, during the sixth hour, the sky began to fill with clouds, and the wind increased. When the snow began, and the wind blew it into their faces, Maarit finally stopped. "I'd hoped we could reach the rock outcroppings just east of here, but we can't make it. We'll just have to shelter here."

Kirsten surveilled their surroundings, but all she could see was an endless expanse of snow and distant—very distant—mountains. She recalled her own largely successful efforts at shelter-building two months earlier, but her training in the Cairngorms had shown her other methods as well. "What do you think, a snow wall, a ditch?"

"A little of both. I'll give you the easier job, digging the pit. About two feet should do it. I'll tackle the wall."

They'd had the foresight to carry along the small shovel that had been Kirsten's splint, and once again, it proved useful. Under the heavy snowfall, she scooped frantically while Maarit rolled up large snowballs, as if for a line of snowmen. Three adjacent balls with snow packed into the crevices worked well as a wind block. Three more balls made an L shape, curving inward, that provided protection from the east. By then, Kirsten had managed a shallow pit some three feet wide and five feet long.

"What about the other side wall?"

"You'll see. Help me unload the supplies," Maarit shouted over the sound of the wind. "Lay the deerskins on the bottom, quickly."

Kirsten obeyed, and when the sled was empty, Maarit hauled it up on its side, forming the third wall of a loose triangle. By the last bit of visibility, she stretched the tarp over the top of the two snow walls and the sled, anchoring it with packed snow. Brushing flakes from her arms and shoulders, she clambered into the pit next to Kirsten. A third deerskin was left, and Maarit pulled it over their heads.

Within moments, Kirsten felt the tarp sag as snow accumulated on it. But the narrow "roof" held and sheltered them against the wind in their triangular igloo.

Satisfied with their construction, they lay down back-to-back on their deerskin flooring. On a whim, Kirsten turned onto her other side and pressed her forehead against Maarit's back, which provided a soft place for her head and reflected back her warm exhalations onto her face.

"Better?"

"Yes, much. What about you? Isn't your face cold?"

"No. I'm breathing on my glove. Relax now. Let the warmth spread."

They weren't exactly warm, but the reindeer skins and the thick gaktis they wore insulated them to the point where they didn't shiver. Exhaustion helped them both sleep.

As always, when she slept on snow, Kirsten was sure she hadn't slept at all. But when she lifted the deerskin from her head, both wind and snow had stopped, and it was full night.

Maarit turned to face her. "Ah, you're awake. How are you doing?"

"I'm all right. Though I can't tell if I still have feet. How about you?"

"Fine. It looks like the storm's cleared up, so we should start out again." She rose to a sitting position, throwing off the hide that had covered them. "I've packed enough kindling for one fire. After you've found your feet, why don't you make a little fire and heat some water while I load the sled." She hauled herself up from their sleep niche and stomped in a circle to warm herself.

Kirsten rummaged through their sacks for kettle and twigs. Her hand brushed against their flint, which was just as important as the wood, and she gathered the wood scrap and moss into a small bundle. A single swipe on the flint ignited it, and she set the snow-filled kettle over the flames. The fire lasted just long enough to warm the snow water so that she could add a handful of ersatz coffee. By the time she'd thrown in a few chips of frozen meat, the brew was lukewarm, but against the bitterly cold air, it seemed luxurious.

When they started off again eastward, the land looked much the same as before, only that the featureless surface that stretched out in front of them now held waves, like a frozen sea.

Kirsten checked her compass. "Southeast is in that direction." She pointed with her mittened hand.

"I know the way. It's right between those two ridges over there." Maarit nodded toward a spot more toward the right.

"If you say so," Kirsten conceded. What was a compass against Sami geography?

Both her feet ached now, as well as her knees and her buttocks and her shoulders. Upon consideration, she realized no part of her didn't hurt. Even her teeth ached slightly from clenching her jaw. Staring down at her feet and sliding them one after another, she didn't complain. She would have fallen down dead in her tracks before she would admit that her insistence on the journey was a mistake. But when she'd just begun to formulate a way to beg for a rest, Maarit stopped.

Puzzled, Kirsten thought the landscape was unchanged, and then she saw the new feature. In front of them, the vidda continued, unbroken, for another two hundred meters, but at that line, the white stopped, and a dull gray-green strip crossed the horizon. They were looking at the edge of the plateau, and the strip of color was the tree-studded land on the other side of a great gorge.

"That's it! We're here," she exclaimed. "Rjukan is just below us."

"Don't get too excited. It's a long climb down." They skied to where they could see over the sloping rim and down into the valley below. Some hundred tiny lights were scattered more or less along the bank of the Måna River. They were houses, seemingly forlorn in the dismal valley.

"It's just as I remember it. Dark all autumn, winter, and spring, even when there was light up on the plateau. The sun could never reach into the valley."

"Ah, so you know this place. And you never climbed up to the top?"

"No. I was about ten when my mother moved us back to London. I saw Rjukan from halfway up the mountain for the first time when I returned in 1935, to study in Oslo. My father invited me to see the new hydroelectric plant." She nodded toward another cluster of tiny lights from buildings on a rocky cliff on the other side of the gorge.

"Your father worked for the Norsk Hydro Plant? You never mentioned that."

"I never mentioned a lot of things. Yes, he was chief chemical engineer."

Maarit studied her for a moment. "You have ties to the hydroelectric plant. It's under the control of the Germans now. Everyone knows that." She squinted as if that helped her think. "Your coming here, before you crashed, had something to do with the plant and the Germans, didn't it? What do the British want to do with the plant? Use it? Destroy it?"

"It's better not to ask all those questions. Even if I were allowed to tell you, it would simply endanger you even more than you are."

"I believe we've had this conversation before. I appreciate your wanting to protect us, but I've brought you this far, so I'm already involved. Fatally perhaps. So tell me. Do the British want to destroy the hydro plant?"

Kirsten stared across the gorge, then down at the houses below. "I don't know the details, of course. But it has something to do with what the Germans are able to produce at the plant. Heavy water, they call it, with deuterium in place of simple hydrogen. It's an isotope of hydrogen, with a neutron attached to the proton."

"So why do we care about this water?"

"It's used in research and experimentation for atomic power. The Allies are afraid the Germans want it to make a bomb."

"And you were supposed to stop them."

"I and thirty-four good men. I told you, some of them were killed in the crash, and others were captured. The British have no idea what happened to them, or me, so I need to inform them and to essentially report for duty."

"I see. Well then, let's stop chatting and start the climb down."

They transferred the deerskins and other essentials into backpacks and abandoned the sled. With their skis now on their shoulders, they needed more than two hours to negotiate the slippery path from the plateau to the outskirts of Rjukan. Only the final kilometer was smooth enough to permit skiing.

The town was darker and more dismal than she remembered. No wonder she'd been so thrilled to arrive in London in the spring of 1920 when the entire day was light-filled.

"Do you suppose anyone will recognize you?" Maarit asked.

"Unlikely, after twenty years. And I won't recognize them. Even if I did, I have no way to separate patriot from quisling."

They dropped their voices as they passed a local policeman, who nodded perfunctorily, and again, when two German soldiers strode past them.

"Two Sami women in town to shop. I guess we're convincing, which reminds me. What will you use for cash? We need to buy food and pay for a place to sleep. I don't fancy curling up in the snow again."

"Don't worry." Kirsten pointed with her thumb at her backpack. "I still have the cash they issued us for the initial operation. That should cover us for the first day or two. After that, I don't know."

"Where did you live?"

"In a nice house near the town hall. My father continued to live there after the divorce with his new wife, but now he's fled. I'm sure the house was thoroughly investigated, maybe even seized. In any case, showing up there would get us into trouble immediately."

"All right, then. So, what's the next step?"

"The intelligence we received before our glider mission was that Milorg was active in Rjukan. They didn't give us any names, though, since we weren't supposed to be anywhere near here."

"Finding them will be tricky, especially since you don't want to approach anyone from the old days. Any ideas on how we can ask around without getting in trouble?"

"A few. A little farther along this street, we'll find a public house.

An old man called Torwald used to own it, though I'm sure he's died by now. But he was a patriot, flew the Norwegian flag every Sunday and holiday. If anyone in the family is still running the place, I'm betting they're patriots, too."

Some hundred meters farther on, they passed a high stone wall, the rear of some sort of storage building. Hastily splashed on the gray stone, presumably in secret, the royal monogram stood four feet high in black paint. The tall capital *H*, with the number seven slashed diagonally down its center.

"For King Haaken the Seventh, head of the Free Norwegian resistance," Maarit muttered. "Obviously, there's at least one resistor here."

"More than one, I'd say." Kirsten pointed with her chin toward a fence post, where the same monogram appeared in miniature. "That's good news. We just have to find one and work our way up to someone who has a radio transmitter."

"First things first. Let's find that public house and see what happened to Torwald. We might also have a good meal." Maarit started off.

"Couldn't agree more. Anything but reindeer chips in bark soup."

"Oh, suddenly picky, are we?"

They arrived at the public house they were looking for, and Maarit glanced up at the sign over the door that read *Varm Mat*. "Warm food. Sounds promising," she said as they unbuckled their skis, stepped out of them, and stood them against the wall.

The interior in unpainted pine held an iron stove at one end. Five small wooden tables revealed a very limited clientele, and the shelves behind the narrow bar held only bottles of beer and two kinds of aquavit. Of the five tables, the one closest to the stove was occupied by two old men playing cards. The men glanced up when they entered but seemed to lose interest quickly and returned to their game.

As they sat down, a woman, presumably the owner, approached them. She was tall and bony, but with the wiry musculature of a man. Her narrow skull, ice-blue eyes, and long, straight nose marked her as a perfect Nordic Aryan. But gray hair pulled back in a tight bun and a severe expression gave her the air of a schoolteacher, the kind that instilled terror in her pupils.

Wiping her hands on her apron, she asked, "What will you have?"

"What's available?" Kirsten asked, trying to recall the flavors of all the meats she hadn't tasted in months.

"Fish stew."

"Is that all?"

"'Fraid so."

"Then we'll have two bowls of that."

"And to drink? Coffee, tea, beer?"

"Do you have real coffee?" Kirsten asked hopefully.

The woman frowned, as if resenting the question."Not unless you're at least a major. For you, coffee and tea are ersatz. The beer and akvavit are the real thing."

"Coffee," Maarit said. Kirsten nodded.

While they waited, the door opened again, sending a blast of frigid air into the room. Kirsten turned to look at the cause, and her heart sank. Two German soldiers. From what she could remember, they looked like sergeants. She glanced away, trying to avoid drawing their attention.

Useless, for the Germans had no interest in the old card players so had nothing to look at but the two of them. The soldiers swaggered toward them.

"The skis outside. They belong to you two?" one of them asked in patchy Norwegian.

"Yes. They're mine."

"They're really shit, you know. How do you get around on those things?" He chuckled at his own wit.

The representative of the master race had a strangely shaped head, wide at the top and narrow at the bottom, like a half-filled balloon. His mouth was much too wide and seemed to run from ear to ear. She thought suddenly of Josef Goebbels, and then of the man Jova had described. Was this the same one, or did the Germans have an entire subspecies of such men?

"They've worked pretty well for a few hundred years," Maarit said pleasantly. "It was the Sami who invented skis, back when Germans still plodded through snow up to their hips."

The sergeant squinted, as if trying to determine if his race had been insulted, and went on the offensive. "Yeah, but we had houses while your lot lived in piles of dirt and crapped on the ground."

Kirsten's heart began to pound. Had Maarit's boast started a confrontation, which could end in disaster?

But the other man, who hadn't spoken, suddenly seemed annoyed. "*Lass sie doch in Ruhe, Debus.*" He stepped away toward one of the tables near the iron stove. With a look of contempt for them, the one called Debus sucked air through his front teeth and followed him.

When the soldiers were seated a few tables away, the owner quickly set two cups of coffee and a plate of dark bread in front of them. The soldiers seemed pleased at the rapid service and smiled up at her. As she strode back to her kitchen, her sideward glance toward Kirsten seemed to say, *I've calmed them down, so don't start any more trouble.*

But the only sounds were the slurping of hot coffee and the murmurs of the old men playing cards, and in a few moments, the owner returned with their soups. As she bent over to set the bowls on their table, something hanging on her neck caught Kirsten's attention. A single krone, that bore the monogram of the king.

She raised her eyes and caught the woman's glance. "I like your necklace. A patriot's necklace," she added softly.

The woman touched the coin at her throat and shot a quick look toward the Germans.

Kirsten pressed on. "We're patriots, too, and need help."

"Sorry. All I do is cook."

"That's too bad. A good man named Torwald used to own this place, and he would have helped us."

The mention of Torwald seemed to change everything. The woman gave another glance over her shoulder at the soldiers, who were engrossed in their own conversation. The two old men were still playing cards. "Finish your soup and come back again in two hours? To the storeroom entrance in the alley." She turned away abruptly and returned to her bar.

Having achieved both a hot meal and a possible contact, they placed a few kroner on the table and left. Outside, they buckled on their skis again and, during the two-hour wait, explored the town. Kirsten remembered it from early childhood, but under the occupation, it seemed quieter, more cowed. While German soldiers patrolled here and there, it was as if the town had drawn into its dark self and was waiting for it all to be over.

At the designated time, they arrived at the alley door and knocked. It opened immediately, and they stepped inside.

The storeroom was a spare, functional room with shelves on two sides, a narrow table with a bench on a third, and a small cast-iron stove in the corner. The shelves held several crates of beer and miscellaneous boxes marked as dry produce, but the café itself didn't seem well supplied.

The woman closed the door behind them and locked it. "How do you know my father?" she asked coldly.

Kirsten had guessed correctly. "Ah, so you're Torwald's daughter. I'm glad to see that patriotism stayed in the family. But maybe you could tell us your name."

She squinted at Kirsten, ignoring the question. "Your friend might be Sami, but you aren't. Not with hair like that." She gestured to the few loose strands that hung below Kirsten's hat. "What are you doing showing up here dressed that way?"

"I'll be glad to explain everything if you'll let us warm up." Kirsten nodded toward the bench in front of the iron stove. The warmth of the room indicated the stove held a fire.

"Sure. Go ahead, but then start talking."

Kirsten and Maarit slid their rucksacks from their shoulders and sat on the bench with their backs to the stove. Kirsten savored the warmth for a moment, then faced their interlocutor.

"Good observation. My friend is Sami, but I'm Norwegian, and I lived here as a child. I remember your father, in fact, though not very well. My own father brought me here once, and I saw him. He had an odd white beard that was divided in the middle, which I found comical. And as I recall, he walked with a limp."

"Yes, that was him, but just because you lived here twenty years ago still doesn't prove I can trust you."

Kirsten winced in frustration. "Look, the only newer reference I can give you is Leif Tronstad. I work indirectly for him and need to get word to him of my whereabouts. He doesn't even know I'm alive."

"Professor Tronstad? He left for London a year ago. Some people call him a traitor."

"But we know he's a patriot, don't we?" She waited for the woman's scowl to soften. "Anyhow, he thinks I'm dead. We're hoping you can connect us with someone with a radio transmitter."

The woman seemed to reminisce. "He was in here once. A handsome man, before he got that scar that he tries to hide with his beard."

Kirsten frowned. "We're not talking about the same man. Leif Tronstad has no scar on his face, and he doesn't have a beard. Not when I saw him. And by the way, you still haven't told us your name."

The woman chuckled for the first time. "It's Birgit. And you're right, he doesn't. I was testing you. You never know who to trust. Just last week the Germans put out a false air raid and forced the entire town of Rjukan into the shelters for fifteen hours so that they could search every house for radios. They found one of ours and arrested one of our men, Torstein Skinnarland. Everyone is nervous they'll do it again."

"Skinnarland. That was one of the men who was supposed to join up with us. And now the Germans have him. Damn. Obviously, it's all the more important that I contact headquarters. We were hoping to track down someone who could send a message to London."

Birgit frowned and shook her head. "London already knows about Torstein. As for your message, I'll give it to our radio man, but it'll have to be short. He won't broadcast for more than a minute from any one place. Here, write it down." She took a scrap of wrapping paper and a pencil from one of the shelves.

Kirsten thought for a moment, trying to reduce their situation to the minimum of words, then wrote.

Operation Freshman crashed. Others dead or captured.
I escaped injured but now recovered. In Rjukan and await
instruction. Chemist.

She handed the scrap to Birgit, who glanced at it, seeming puzzled. "Chemist?"

"That's my code name. It's best if that's all you know. Don't you agree?"

Birgit muttered agreement and shoved the paper into a pocket. "I'll deliver it, but it's already late. Come back tomorrow or the next day if you want a reply."

Kirsten rubbed her neck as if to signal apology for asking. "Um, we've traveled a long way and don't actually have a place to stay. Do you think you could put us up for the night?"

"I'd rather not. This is a public place, and the Germans barge through the door all the time."

"I appreciate the danger, but we don't have any other place."

Birgit glanced with what might have been disdain toward Maarit. "Don't your people camp out in the snow all the time?"

Maarit was quick to reply. "Yes, with a tent and a bonfire. Do you suggest we set that up in the square?"

Birgit lowered her eyes. "Oh, sorry. Didn't mean to sound so heartless. It's just that—" She interrupted herself. "All right. You can bed down here for the night." She frowned again, evidently considering details, ramifications. "You'll find horse blankets in a sack under the table. The outhouse is at the end of the alley. I store bread and a cheese in the cupboard so you can take some, but not too much. Our stock of beer is also there on the shelves, but please take only two. It's damned hard to get these days. Make sure you keep the storeroom locked, and don't go into the public room. Too easy to see inside through the window on the street." She wiped her hands on her apron, ending the conversation, then turned away abruptly and left them to themselves.

Weary, they smiled at each other at their success. Then Maarit tugged off her heavy gakti. "I'd say we were damned lucky you remembered her father. We might not have convinced her to trust us otherwise."

Kirsten did the same, then bent to untie her snow boots. "Yes, and lucky too that the old man had that funny beard. I might not have remembered him otherwise."

Maarit laid out their reindeer skins near the stove and collected the food from the cabinet. "Not as cozy as our goahti," she observed, laying out a small portion of cheese and slightly dry bread from the cupboard, together with their remaining travel rations. "But certainly warmer than our snow pit."

Kirsten leaned against the wall and opened both bottles, handing one to Maarit. "Beer's a nice touch," she said, taking a long drink. She nibbled on some of the hard cheese. "It'll be a relief to reconnect with headquarters." She took another swallow of the beer and felt a wave of well-being. "I owe it all to you, of course. You saved my life, and I'll be sure to inform London of what you've done."

"Mmm," Maarit murmured coolly, then leaned back on her elbow and stared at her beer bottle.

"Have I said something wrong?"

"No. Of course not. You shouldn't treat me like a patriot. Really, I'm just being swept along by it all. The war took away my most of my family, but it gave me you. That was something I didn't expect."

Kirsten's face warmed. "Me? An invalid you had to take care of for months, who in the beginning couldn't even pee without your assistance? Not exactly a gift."

Maarit chuckled. "I forgot about that pee-moment. Yes, you brought some problems with you, but also something new. A sort of branch that falls in a stream and changes its course."

"You being the stream? Sounds poetic, but I don't see how I could have changed the course of anything. What did I do, other than your mending?"

"From your perspective, I was just another Sami, but I'm not at all. A Sami woman my age would already have married, had her own reindeer herd and a couple of babies by now. I'd already ventured outside the community, with a plan to study medicine. Your arrival reminded me of what I'd almost achieved before the occupation and my own cowardice beat me down."

"Beat you down? How?"

"The Norwegians have no great love for the Sami. They're not as bad as the Germans, but there are plenty of Norwegian nationalists, not to say quislings and collaborators, in Trondheim. In the hospital where I was a student, they made it clear that I, a Sami and a woman, was taking a place that should have gone to some Norwegian man. They more or less threw me out, or at least they made life so unpleasant that I left."

Kirsten set aside the empty beer bottle and finished off the rest of the crumbs. "And you see me as a reason to go back and try again?"

"I…I don't know. Maybe."

Kirsten studied Maarit's face, neither Sami nor Norwegian, but slightly triangular, with deep, dark, intelligent eyes that penetrated when they looked at you. It was hard to imagine her giving up anything. "Assuming the Germans are forced out, how do you envision life after that?"

"I have trouble envisioning anything. I love the reindeer and the purity of the Arctic, but I can't see myself as a young Jova, crisscrossing the vidda year after year, endlessly baking bread. But maybe, if the

Germans are forced out, along with the quislings and Sami-haters, I might finish studying medicine. The Sami do need doctors, so I'd have a foot in both worlds. What about you?"

Kirsten shifted to a more comfortable position. "I was forced out of my studies, too, when the Germans closed down Oslo University. I was already sympathetic with the resistance, and then, being arrested with so many other students for nothing pushed me over the edge. I was studying chemistry, so after the war, I suppose I'll look for work as a chemist. Science runs in the family."

"But no husband or children?"

"Not in the cards for me. If I'd been married, I would never have volunteered for the mission I was on, which brought me to the Sami. I'd be somewhere in Britain, maybe working as a fire warden, waiting for my hubby to come back from the war."

Maarit half smiled. "Instead you got me."

"Yes. And that very nice oversized Sami coat that will serve very well as a pillow." She folded up her gakti, placed it at the top of the deerskin, and lay down on it.

Maarit did the same, then slid down back-to-back with her. She lay that way for an awkward moment, until she turned on her other side and threw her arm over Kirsten's waist. "Like we slept under the snow, up on the plateau. I liked that," she murmured.

Kirsten relaxed against her. The warmth and contentment of close contact was familiar, but something new emerged. Perhaps it was the pride of achievement and return to duty, of the growth from invalid to fighter, that brought the new sensation. For now, unmistakably, what coursed through her was arousal.

"Yes. Me, too."

A banging on the door awakened them, and Birgit's head appeared in the opening. "The stove in the public room is lit, and I've just made coffee. The café's still closed, so come in, when you're ready."

They both clambered up from their deerskin bed into the icy air of the storeroom where their fire had long gone out. Hurredly, they pulled on their gaktis, tied up their boots, and shuffled into the café.

Birgit handed them their cups. "Our radio man took your message and will send it today to his own contact with instructions to pass it on to Leif Tronstad. With any luck, you'll have a reply tomorrow."

Kirsten held her coffee against her chest, the aroma and steam underscoring the pleasure of the news. "That's fine. After two months in the wilderness, I can wait one more day."

"I'd prefer it if you didn't spend it here in the café." She slid a plate toward them that held the hard bread from the previous evening. "Germans come in all the time, and I'd have trouble explaining your presence here a second day."

Kirsten dipped a slice of bread into the coffee and found the taste combination agreeable. "No. Of course not. Anyhow, we've got a job to do outside that will take most of the day. But I need to know. How do people get up to the plant at Vemork these days? Do they still have the rail line?"

"The one that runs directly from Rjukan? Yes. The workers ride up on it every day and use it to transport materials. There's also a footpath that leads to a suspension bridge across the gorge."

"Those routes have been there for decades. Is there any other way up?"

"Not that I know of, short of climbing down one side of the gorge and then up the other side, which no one would be crazy enough to do." She rose from the counter and turned back toward the cooking stove. "The café got a ration of goat meat that will go into a stew today. I'll save some for you."

"We can pay," Kirsten said. "We actually have some money."

"Good to hear. The café is rationed the same as individuals are, and I have to account for everything. The beer and the overnight are on the house."

"We're very grateful. The British government will be, too."

Birgit shrugged indifference. "Just get the damned Germans out of Norway, and we'll call it even."

❖

Maarit and Kirsten skied westward along the Måna River in the murky, sunless light of the Rjukan morning.

"Do you think Tronstad and the SOE are still interested in the hydro plant?"

"Since they were willing to risk the lives of thirty-four of us to attack it, it's obviously valuable. If I'm wrong, and they're onto something altogether different, that's fine. But I'm guessing they're still planning an attack, and a good description of alternative routes will be valuable."

Keeping as much as possible out of sight, they pushed on along the road that ran parallel to the gorge and the Måna River below. After leaving Rjukan, it snaked in a wide, half-mile-long curve down the mountain to a village.

"That must be Vaer," Kirsten said over her shoulder. "We should take a shortcut down this way to avoid getting near it." They left the road and removed their skis, hiding them in the snow behind some bushes. Then they began the steep descent, anchoring each step on the slippery snow by kicking holes in the crust. At the bottom of the gorge, near the frozen Måna River, they stared upward, scrutinizing the brush that grew between the rocks. It had furnished enough handholds to permit them to descend safely. It could hold others as well.

"There's the suspension bridge." Maarit pointed toward the bridge that swung across the gorge about a quarter of a mile away. "Now we just need to cross the river and find the same kind of route up to the plant."

They hiked along the water's edge for a short distance, until Maarit pointed toward a slope slightly less steep than the one they'd come down on the other side. "Plenty of growth, too. I think we have our route."

Kirsten noted the distances and landmarks before they crossed the river again and hiked back to the location of their descent. At the top, as they latched on their skis, Maarit glanced back at the trail they had left behind them in the snow.

"You're not worried that this might all be wasted effort? You could have simply reported in again before undertaking all this."

"But if the Vemork mission was so important back in November, I'm guessing it's still on. When I report in again for duty, I'd like to have something to offer."

Maarit nodded understanding, and in the growing darkness, they began to ski back to Birgit's café.

Chapter Eight

Once again in Birgit's storeroom, Kirsten was too nervous to relax. What would London's response be, and would they consider her derelict for the time she was absent?

But at the end of the day, after Birgit had locked up the café, she entered the storeroom with a comrade. "This is Arne," she said, nodding toward the stocky man who'd followed her in. "Not his real name, but he doesn't know yours either." She turned toward the man. "Tell them what London said, Arne."

He tugged off his knit cap, revealing a thick head of black hair. That, together with his square head and bushy eyebrows, made him look vaguely troll-like. But his message, which he'd memorized, was altogether welcome.

"Two radio reports came. One from Tronstad said, 'Glad you're alive. JB is here. Have notified local team head, who will contact you for ongoing operation.'"

"I'm assuming you know who JB is," Birgit remarked coolly.

"Yes. That would be my father," Kirsten said. "He talked about heading to Sweden when I left. What's the second message?"

"It was from the local Milorg head that said, 'Someone will meet you Saturday at Center.'"

"Very good, but where is 'Center'?"

Birgit frowned. She seemed to always frown before speaking, as if reluctant to reveal information. "This is Center. Right here." Then she laid a hand on Arne's back and led him toward the storeroom door.

Kirsten turned to Maarit, smiling. "Looks like, starting tomorrow, we're back on duty."

❖

As promised, Saturday night, after the café shut down, someone appeared at the storeroom door.

"Einar Skinnarland," he said, holding out his hand first to Kirsten, then to Maarit. At Kirsten's puzzled expression, he added, "I'm Torstein's brother. Let's sit down, because you have a lot to catch up on."

She was struck both by his good looks and the shape of his face. The impression started at his hair. Long, thick, and combed straight back from a high forehead, it flattened out at the sides, creating corners to his head. But his wide lips, straight eyebrows, and square chin also added horizontal lines, culminating in an almost perfect square. It gave him an aura of superficial masculine glamor.

Birgit went back to brew coffee for everyone, and Einar began. "Tronstad knows about the Freshman disaster, but SOE is still targeting the Vemork plant. The new operation is called Gunnerside and involves much the same sabotage strategy, but with an all-Norwegian team trained in Scotland."

"Is Jomar Brun involved?"

"Yes. He was one of those in charge of training the men, since he knows what the place looks like inside and out. London has sent five men in by parachute: Poulsson, Helberg, Kjelstrup, Haugland, and Strømheim."

Birgit had returned with mugs of coffee and passed them around. "Are you allowed to tell me what they want to sabotage?"

Skinnarland blew over the top of his scalding cup, looking very boyish. "Last month, word got around that the Americans had made some kind of breakthrough in their atomic research. In Chicago, I think. Anyhow, the Germans put their own atomic program into high speed. Part of what they need is up at the Vemork plant. When they learned about the gliders headed toward the plant, they put two and two together."

"They learned about the sabotage by capturing the men who didn't die in the crash. Do we know what happened to them?"

"We think they were all shot eventually. But they must have given *some* information, and the Germans found explosive material on the gliders, so they know Vemork was a target. Reichskommissar Terboven drove up personally to Vemork to inspect the factory. Right away, they strengthened the garrison of soldiers in Rjukan and laid mines around the plant."

"How is Operation Gunnerside going to deal with that?" Birgit asked.

"By demolishing the research facilities, just as we'd planned during Operation Freshman, only this time with a smaller team and no gliders." He glanced with apparent disapproval at Kirsten. "London has ordered me to put you on the team, but I have to tell you, the men didn't like the idea of adding a woman." Suddenly his boyishness wasn't so charming.

"Women," Maarit interjected coolly. "There are two of us."

"Women," Skinnarland echoed. "Even worse. In any case, their objections were overruled since, according to Jomar Brun, you've been inside the plant and know the layout. That makes you indispensable."

"So we'll be eight altogether," Maarit concluded, refusing to respond to his annoyance. "And where will we meet the others? Will they be coming here?"

"No. Too dangerous. The others are in a cabin at the northwest part of the Hardanger, about eighteen miles northwest of Rjukan, near the lake. Torstein was in charge of bringing them food, but he's been arrested, so they must be pretty hungry by now. I'm taking the food in his place, and now you as well. The supplies are ready, so we can leave right away."

Kirsten stood up. "All right, then. Let's get to it."

❖

Climbing from Rjukan up onto the plateau hauling a fully loaded sled took over two hours of hard labor. But once they reached the top, they made good progress on their skis, drawing the sled behind them.

Several hours later, Skinnarland pointed with his pole toward a black dot on the side of a distant hill. "There it is."

Thank God, Kirsten thought. For the second time, she'd pushed herself to her limit. But, having cajoled her way into both the original and the new mission, she could not admit weakness.

When they reached the cabin and one of the men opened up,

Skinnarland greeted him with, "Hello, Jens." Kirsten was shocked. The haggard man in front of them wasn't the Jens Poulsson she'd met in training three months earlier. His long, unkempt beard did little to hide an emaciated face, and his bloodshot eyes were ringed in dark circles.

"I hope you brought food," he said as they filed into the hut.

"Don't worry. We're loaded. You can already set water on to boil."

"Thank God. We've been living on oatmeal and lichen for weeks." He finally seemed to notice her and Maarit. "And Jomar's daughter. Kirsten, is it?"

"That's me, sir. And this is Maarit. She knows the terrain better than anyone." She spoke all in one breath, to ensure acceptance at the outset. The last thing she, or the team needed, was resentment.

"Fine," Poulsson said indifferently. "This is Knut Haugland, Kaspar Idland, Birger Strømsheim, Fredrik Kayser, Arne Kjelstrup, Joachim Rønneberg, and Claus Helberg. You might remember Claus from training in Scotland." He reeled off the names too quickly for her to remember any of them, but all showed the effects of hunger and exposure. Names, for the moment, didn't seem important.

After unloading the desperately needed food, the men sat or squatted where they could in the crowded cabin and filled their stomachs. At the end of the meal, Poulsson cleared away the table and laid out a map and diagram. "This is where we are," he said, pointing to a spot northwest of Rjukan. "And the hydro plant is over here on the other side of the river. We need to find a way to get there without being detected. That leaves out crossing the suspension bridge, at least on the way in."

"We *could* cross it," one of the men said. "With Skinnarland staying back as radio operator, we're nine people, and they never post more than four guards. We could storm them. I don't mind being right in front. They might get one or two of us, but the rest would make it in to do the job."

Poulsson shook his head. "Thank you for your zeal. I think most of us share it. But the people of Rjukan don't. If any Germans are killed, reprisals will follow immediately."

Haugland scratched his hairy neck. "The only alternative is going down into the gorge and climbing back up again on the other side. That will cost us a couple of days to look for a route down and up through the rocks that won't kill us. We'll be carrying heavy loads, and none of us are rock climbers."

Kirsten glanced around at the haggard faces and took a breath. "We found a way."

All heads turned. "While we were waiting for our message to go through to London, Maarit and I explored along the river. We discovered a place where you can get down into the gorge pretty safely. It's steep, but we found enough handholds between the rocks to break any fall. Better still, we located another route, farther along the river, where we could climb up toward the plant. Not with skis, of course. Only by foot."

Haugland shook his head. "That's fine going in, but not for the retreat. We'll be exhausted, with the Germans on our heels, and it will take far too long to climb down and then back up to where we've left our skis. We'll be trapped in the gorge."

Poulsson lit his pipe and took a long pull on it, blowing smoke from the side of his mouth. It quickly filled the cabin, though no one seemed to mind. "So we're agreed that Kirsten's route works for going in. Now all we have to worry about is getting out. Once we set off our explosives, the whole detachment will be after us, not to mention the forces stationed in Rjukan itself."

Poulsson thought for a moment. "It might not be as bad as that." He raised a finger. "Hear me out. According to Jomar's diagrams, the heavy-water extraction is limited to the basement laboratory. Our best entry point, according to him, will be the cable conduit. Once we're inside the laboratory, it won't take a massive explosion to demolish it, but only a series of small connected explosions."

Kirsten nodded. "That's true. When I was there, I saw a long row of canisters, all in a single hall. With all the noise from the turbines and the water flow, small explosions won't be heard very far."

"Yes. That's my point," Poulsson said. "If the reaction is restricted to a handful of confused guards *inside* the plant, we have a good chance to get down without interference and then start back up the gorge on the north side. If we leave our skis close to the road, we can manage after maybe two hours of climbing. And remember, darkness and the bushes will hide us."

Idland spoke for the first time. "You know, they'll be expecting us to head westward. If we head east, back toward Rjukan, we could use the construction path under the old cable-car lift. The lift's been shut down for years, and the abandoned path will be covered with growth, but it's still there."

Poulsson tapped the ashes out of his pipe into a can. "All right, then. I think we have our approach and escape strategy. Now we just need to agree on how to handle the demolition."

Kayser raised his hand as if in school. "I propose Idland, Strømsheim, Rønneberg, and myself for the demolition party. We're all good with explosives."

"I should be part of it, too," Kirsten interjected. "I know the layout of the plant better than anyone here."

"Agreed," Poulsson said. "And the rest of us will be the covering party. And Maarit," he added, as if just noticing her. "But we'll all carry explosive material, so if anything happens to the demolition group, the covering group will go in and do the job. We'll try for no fatalities, neither ours nor theirs," Poulsson elaborated. "But if they attack before the job's done, every man…and woman…has the task of completing the mission. And if you're caught or wounded, you have to take the bullet yourself. We know the Germans torture, so we can't have anyone fall into their hands. Are we all in agreement?"

All murmured consent without hesitation.

"Any questions?"

"The explosive material," Kirsten said. "It came in by parachute?"

"Yes, everything did. It's all piled up outside the cabin. Camouflage suits, detonators, sidearms." He nodded toward several crates partially covered with snow and just visible through the window.

"And by the way, you'll have to give up your Sami coats. If we're spotted, we don't want the German army invading Sami villages looking for you or taking revenge." Poulsson reached into a cabinet and pulled out two old sweaters. "Wear these under your camouflage. It should be enough."

Kirsten set hers aside for the morning. It smelled like pipe tobacco. "You know what else would be good, if you have any extras? Socks for both of us. Mine wore out, and our shoe grass is no good anymore."

Poulsson chuckled. "Lucky for you, SOE sent us a supply. I'll have them for you tomorrow. If that's it, then I suggest you all try to get some sleep."

❖

Kirsten and Maarit curled up together in one corner. "I'm sorry now that I dragged you into this," Kirsten whispered. "These guys seem pretty competent, but it could still turn out to be a suicide mission. I'm willing to take the risk, but you shouldn't. No one expects you to fight to the death over some esoteric weapon the enemy may or may not have."

Maarit snorted. "It's a little late in the game to suggest I leave, isn't it? You forget. My father died fighting at Narvik, and my mother and brother died because of the Germans, so I have more to avenge than you do."

"What happened, exactly? You never told me the whole story."

"The Germans forced my brother to act as a guide on the Hardanger. For weeks my mother heard nothing about where he was or what was happening to him. My father was already dead, I was away in Trondheim, and she couldn't bear to lose her remaining child. She simply put on skis and went out looking for him. It turned out my brother was shot trying to run away, and she was injured somehow before she ever got to him. A herder found her body in the snow. No one has found my brother's body."

She took a breath, and her expression became hard. "For months I've felt helpless and bitter, but tomorrow, finally, I'll have some revenge. What's more, I want a code name."

Kirsten took her hand, pleased. "What name do you want? Something strong, like Eagle?"

"No. Reindeer will do."

"Reindeer. Yes. I like it."

CHAPTER NINE

Kirsten wakened to the sound of men coughing and the clatter of the kettle on the stove. Next to her, Maarit was rubbing life back into her face, and they smiled encouragement at each other. This was the day.

Poulsson lit his ever-present pipe, even before taking a sip of coffee, then knocked on the table to get everyone's attention. "Let's do a final check. Skinnarland stays behind to radio London of the result. First team, Idland, Kayser, Strømsheim, Rønneberg, Brun—you have the detonators and explosives?"

Kirsten smiled to herself. He'd called her by her last name, like one of the men. She was accepted. Even better, two pairs of thick winter socks lay folded up beside them, and she drew one pair on, savoring the luxury of warm feet.

Rønneberg replied, "Packed and ready. Both teams have a set."

"We have a couple of hours before we need to leave, so everyone should eat a good breakfast and make sure to pack enough food to get where you need to go once the mission's done."

The men grunted assent, though everyone knew escape was the weakest part of an already rather vague plan. Sweden was hundreds of kilometers away, and it was February.

In the afternoon, they reached the slope that led down into Rjukan. Eight men and two women in winter camouflage, they skied in a line along the highway running parallel to the river, dull-gray shapes against the white snow. They passed the settlement of Vaer, keeping their distance, then turned away from the road onto the steep slope down into the gorge. Tying their now-useless skis to their backs, they scrambled down the wooded part of the descent, gripping the surrounding growth to keep from slipping.

Arriving at slightly more level ground, Poulsson signaled halt. This was where they'd agreed to hide their skis before the final descent. In the growing darkness, camouflage was no longer necessary, and Kirsten was relieved to be rid of the wide flapping material that kept catching on shrubbery. All the men wore British uniforms in an attempt to spare the Norwegians reprisals if they were captured, though it was a flimsy attempt. Kirsten was the only one who spoke unaccented English, and any serious interrogation would soon reveal they were all Norwegians.

The descent became hazardous as they careened with their heavy packs over the slippery rocks and ice-encrusted snow, and only kicking a hole in the crust from time to time could slow them down.

Finally, they arrived at the bottom of the gorge, at the edge of the Måna. Unexpectedly, and alarmingly, the river was no longer fully frozen. Several inches of meltwater covered the surface, and everywhere, even in the dim light, she could see dark spots that suggested the ice had melted through. What the hell would they do now?

Poulsson waved them to follow along the stream to search for a spot that still held. Luck brought them to a narrow ice bridge, and they filed over it one by one. The chill of icy water on Kirsten's ankles made her shiver, not only at the water, but at the thought that it might be even worse later when they had to cross back.

Shielding the beam with his hand to prevent an upward glow, Poulsson swept his light along the bank until they located the spot planned for the ascent. Only intermittent cracks and low growth broke a steep slope of bare rock. Kirsten winced inwardly. It had held her and Maarit a few days earlier, but now they'd all be climbing weighted with explosives, detonating hardware, and tools.

Once again, iron determination propelled them upward, even as some of the men lost their grip and fell several meters before catching hold again. All but Maarit had trained in rock-climbing in Scotland, and Kirsten worried. But a glance over her shoulder told her that Maarit was holding her own.

Every muscle straining, Kirsten forced herself up, propelled in part by a sense of responsibility. She had identified this route, and if any of the men lost their lives, it would be her fault.

All arrived at the ridge panting. Taking deep, cold breaths, Kirsten leaned toward Maarit. "You okay?"

"Still here." Maarit peered upward, and Kirsten followed her glance. The plant was clearly visible now, and she studied its two main buildings, the seven-story electric-generator building and the power plant behind it. They were positioned on a rocky ledge midway up the mountain. Several smaller sheds and outbuildings were part of the complex, but the most impressive sight were the twelve huge pipes, each one some six feet in diameter, that lay side by side and carried water down from the plateau hundreds of feet above the plant.

The plant's engines thrummed as if the mountain itself vibrated, while the rush of water through the enormous feeder pipes added a tone at a higher pitch. It was so loud they could talk without fear of guards hearing them. The thunderous industrial noise seemed at odds with the peaceful moonlit arctic landscape around them.

Thin clouds slid over the moon, but toward the south, Kirsten could see stars. Unfathomably distant and unfathomably old, they gave a brief sense of triviality to the mission. She smiled to herself at the thought of suggesting to Poulsson, "The stars say we shouldn't bother." She doubted he'd be amused.

Poulsson risked a second-long shine of his flashlight onto his watch. "Right on schedule. Now, when we reach the rail line outside the plant, the demolition team goes straight in. If the steel door won't open, move on to the cable tunnel. You've all memorized the layout, but Brun will act as guide."

At Poulsson's signal, they began the final ascent toward the single rail line, and in just a few minutes, they all crouched together in the moon-shadow of a shed. As Kirsten recalled, it held some sort of transformer.

They rested again, waiting through the final countdown, and Kirsten felt Maarit at her shoulder. "Look. You can see lights down in the valley on the other side." The roar of the plant engines and the rush of tons of water drowned her voice.

"It must be Vaer. Farmers sitting by their fires, with no idea we're up here risking our lives for the war, for them."

"I guess that's the point of a secret mission, isn't it?" Maarit was silent for a moment. "However it turns out, I want you to know I'm happy to be doing this with you."

Kirsten leaned toward her. "Me, too. No matter what happens, I'm grateful you stayed with me. If we make it back, we should…I don't know…stay friends somehow, don't you think?"

Maarit pressed toward her, cushioned by their bulky clothing. "We're more than friends. I helped you pee, remember?"

"Listen, you can't tell that story to *anyone*. Understand?"

Poulsson's order to move forward cut off Maarit's reply. Kjelstrup started out first, carrying heavy shears. With a smooth, efficient motion, he severed the chain on the gate and tossed the shears to the side. A single sudden kick caused the gate to swing open.

With a tommy gun at the ready, Poulsson led the covering party. Haugland followed with the more optimistic weapon of two tubes of chloroform. Maarit pressed a sudden kiss on Kirsten's cheek and rose to join them.

Idland signaled the demolition party to follow him, and they scuttled toward the steel door of the electric-generator building. It was locked, of course. After only the briefest hesitation, he led them to the spot Kirsten remembered from the diagram Jomar had sent with her to Shetland. She grasped the full importance of the diagram, since the entryway was almost invisible. Only the top rung of the ladder showed above the deep snow. Glancing briefly over his shoulder to make sure they followed, he scrambled down the ladder to the dark spot that was the opening of the cable conduit.

Oh, shit. Kirsten was sure the others thought the same. They had all memorized the spot designated CABLE CONDUIT ENTRY, assuming it was a pipe tall enough for them to crawl through with ease. It was not.

The cement conduit was perhaps five feet in diameter, stuffed with a dozen crisscrossing steel lines and pipes. They could pass through them only on their stomachs, dragging themselves over and around the lines, foot by foot, pushing their packs ahead of them.

And she was in front. Once in, if she met an obstacle, she couldn't turn around. The last man would have to wiggle back out again, feeling his way along with his feet, with everyone forward following him. In the freezing, wet, thundering dark. It was the stuff of nightmares.

The pride she'd felt at being the guide of the demolition team crashed against sheer claustrophobia. Nonetheless, she took a breath and started in, shoving the flashlight into her collar to free up both of her hands. Foot by foot she crawled, slid, wiggled, and pulled herself along over cables slippery with oil, and her gloves kept slipping off them.

As distraction, she thought of Maarit outside in the yard protecting her: Maarit, who had joined the mission out of friendship; Maarit, who had just kissed her.

Behind her, Idland grunted and cursed, and in spite of her own misery, she worried about him. He was bulkier than she was. All of them were. And all of them pushed or dragged sacks filled with explosive charges. They carried sidearms as well, just as she did, in canvas holsters, and the damned things kept catching on cables, yanking her to a sudden halt.

She lost any sense of time, and all existence seemed to shrink to the single task of inching along the conduit. Then, almost by surprise, they reached the first aperture. According to the diagram, it led to the room adjacent to the high-concentration laboratory. Mercifully, they could fit through it.

Removing the cover screen, they dropped in, one by one, their boots thudding on the tile floor. Only the ongoing din of the factory machinery covered the sound.

The door at the end of the room led to the concentration laboratory, and it opened from Kayser's first push. She exhaled with relief. They had arrived at the target and, so far, not a drop of blood had been shed.

Peering through the doorway, Kirsten saw what, in fact, she had only poorly remembered—a long hall with rows of glass cylinders running along both sides. Each cylinder was connected to a maze of pipes and wires and was jacketed in stainless steel. There could be no mistake; these were the precious heavy-water cells. They were rather beautiful.

Curious. The bit of fluid she could see through the glass seemed in no way different from ordinary water. But, she reminded herself, so did gin.

At the near end, a man hunched over a table writing in some sort of ledger under the light of a goosenecked lamp. At their entry, he turned and lurched to his feet.

Kayser raised his pistol with one hand and signaled silence with the other. "Just be quiet, and nothing will happen to you. British soldiers don't kill civilians." The man blinked, stupefied, hearing perfect Norwegian from a man in a British uniform, then sat down again, his hands still raised.

Rønneberg stepped past him and stood for a moment of admiration before the cells. "Amazing," he said. "They're identical to the drawings Brun sent us." Kirsten felt a sense of pride that she'd been the one to carry them to Shetland. The cold and seasickness had been worth it.

They went to work, placing the soft-plastic explosive coils around each one, and they fit perfectly. The planning of the demolition at least had been extraordinarily precise, compensating to a certain degree for the catastrophic misjudgments of the glider operation.

After all eighteen cells were enclosed in their explosive "sausages," Rønneberg and Kayser attached the long fuse to a series of short fuses, and Kayser signaled for the others to gather at the steel door. With pistol in hand, he led the Norwegian overseer toward the door and ordered him to unlock it.

Fumbling with his keys, the man obeyed, docile, but when Rønneberg flicked open his stainless-steel lighter to light the fuse, he became animated. "Wait! Wait. Please!" he pleaded. "My glasses are at the table, and with the war, they are impossible to replace. Please!"

Kirsten was sure Rønneberg would refuse the delay over such a trivial thing. They'd tempted fate all along and were within seconds of fulfilling a mission that men had already died for. A delay of even a minute could mean the arrival of guards to yank the fuses and thus bring the project crashing down.

But for reasons known only to him, Rønneberg clicked the lighter closed and nodded to the overseer, who ran back to the table. He rummaged frantically though his papers searching for the glasses, while Kirsten and the others gritted their teeth. Finally, he found them and rushed back to grip Rønneberg's hand in gratitude.

The tension seemed broken when suddenly footsteps on the stairs sounded, and all of them drew their sidearms. They were going to have to kill someone after all.

"No! Don't shoot!" the overseer called out. "It's the night foreman. He's Norwegian."

Another terrified civilian halted at the foot of the stairs. Obviously bewildered at seeing his colleague with hands held high, surrounded by British soldiers, he raised his hands as well.

"Enough," Rønneberg muttered, clicked his lighter open again, and lit the fuse. He turned to the two civilians. "Now run for your lives up the stairs."

The men took flight instantly, and the team of saboteurs flung themselves through the open doorway into the yard.

Outside the steel door Kirsten could see several of the others emerge from the half-light of the yard. As she reached the fence, the sound of the detonations reached her, and she glanced over her shoulder. The flashes of light in the basement windows showed the explosives had all gone off, but the series of dull thuds they produced seemed too weak.

She had expected elation at the completion of the mission, but felt only confusion and disappointment. Even escaping lacked drama, for no guards seemed to have been alerted, and, astonishingly, no one pursued them.

Only when they'd thrown themselves into the descent, slipping and scrabbling over the icy rocks, did they hear the sirens. Someone had finally discovered the damage, whatever its extent, and at least they had reached the bottom of the gorge. But now they faced an obstacle just as frightening as a squadron of armed guards.

The ominous rise in temperature they'd sensed on their way to the target had grown worse during the action itself. The Måna was now in that terrifying middle stage between frozen and liquid. Sheets of white ice, separated by inch-wide lines of black water, jostled against one another, forming a deadly moving mosaic. A new sound mixed with the sirens—the cracking of ice and the gurgling of water as it was forced up between the slabs.

They had no choice. Sheer, life-threatening necessity drove them across, sometimes stepping upon a floe wide enough to hold them, but just as often dropping to their knees when it broke in half and they had to clamber to the next block. Kirsten lost her balance as the slab supporting her tilted suddenly, and one leg slid into the freezing water. She drew it up, shocked by the burning cold, and struggled on hands and knees from one ice floe to the next one. Maarit was nowhere in sight.

At the back of her panicking mind, she grasped that the searchlights had not yet gone on. At least none shone down into the gorge, where the light would have made them easy targets. And she heard no cracking of rifle fire. Poulsson had been right. The sheer audacity, not to say insanity, of an attack down one cliff and up another had delayed discovery of their whereabouts.

But the two Norwegian workers who had seen them would have to report the five intruders, and it was only a question of how long it would take the chain of command to operate and call out the remaining guard, both in the plant, and in Rjukan, where the garrison was based. She only hoped the two men identified them as British.

The dark shape beside her revealed itself as Maarit. "Are you all right?"

"Bloody freezing, but otherwise fine. You?"

"Soaked, but I'll make it."

The highway, when they finally reached it, was streaming with snowmelt, and they splashed through it, already half numb. Reaching the spot where they'd hidden their skis, they heard the German trucks racing along the flooded highway on the way to the plant. After pulling on their white camouflage again, they stood in a circle around Poulsson for a final debriefing.

Poulsson laid a hand on the shoulder of the man standing next to him. "This is where we spread out before the German command realizes what we've done and mobilizes across the whole territory. Haugland, Kjelstrup, and I will go to headquarters near Lake Skrykken to report in, then head down to Oslo. Does everyone else know their route?"

"Sweden, for us." Rønneberg nodded toward Idland, Kayser, and Strömsheim.

"What about you, Brun?" Poulsson looked toward her, but his question obviously included Maarit. "The Germans won't be looking for women."

"I think you're right. We'll go back to Rjukan, to dry out. Birgit can pass on the message of our success. After that, I don't know."

"Then we're going back together to my village," Maarit added firmly, ignoring Kirsten's surprise. "No one will connect the sabotage with the Sami, and we'll be safe there."

"All right, then. The men will come with me along the cable-car road up to the plateau. Godspeed to you." Poulsson gave her and Maarit a brief hug and turned away, while the other men waved and fell in behind him.

Kirsten watched them, dark forms moving amongst the low foliage of the path until they disappeared. Good men, and true, striking a blow with no blood shed. This was the way to fight a war.

CHAPTER TEN

It was early morning and not yet light when they arrived at the rear of Birgit's café.

"You two are a sorry sight," she said as she closed the storeroom door behind them.

"Yes, but we did the job, and we're still alive. So is everyone else. That's all that counts." Maarit threw off her mittens, dropped onto the bench, and labored with stiff fingers to unlace her boots. Beside her, Kirsten did the same and together they slid off their drenched socks.

"You can hang them over the woodstove," Birgit said begrudgingly. "So, everyone's gotten away safely?"

"Everything went off more or less as planned. We just hadn't reckoned with the river thawing. That's why we're so wet."

"The Germans have every man out searching houses, cabins, and storehouses. They've already been here this morning, so we're safe for today."

"We should be safe anyhow, if we can make up a good reason to be here. They won't be looking for any women. Only two workers saw my face, and I'm sure no one recognized I was female. Maarit was hidden with the team outside."

Maarit massaged her toes, trying to bring sensation back. "Least of all, two Sami women." She dragged the bench closer to the heat and placed their boots on the stove to dry.

Standing in the doorway, Birgit seemed unconvinced. "What do you want me to report to Milorg?"

"Just that the operation was a success, with no fatalities on either side. Skinnarland will contact London with the details. In the meantime, can we rest here for a while?"

Birgit glanced toward the café. "I suppose so, but people will be coming and going all day. I'll lock the storeroom door, but you must stay quiet. You know where the blankets are." She nodded toward the table and the sack underneath it. "I'll check on you in a few hours."

Kirsten nodded gratefully. "We'll be out of your way as soon as we can. Thanks for your help."

Birgit smiled faintly. "Thanks for your sabotage."

The hot soup and the woodstove had warmed them nicely, and after they'd spread out the blankets, Kirsten lay on her back in what seemed like luxury.

"I'm sorry we had to give up our gaktis. I know that Karrel's was precious to your family."

"It's not important compared to the operation we just accomplished."

Kirsten rolled onto her side and rested her head on one hand. With the other, she tapped Maarit's shoulder through the blanket. "And we did it together."

"Yes. This feels very good. Though a bath would feel even better. One of the things I missed during winter herding with the Sami—being in a place warm and safe enough to take off all my clothes and lie in hot, soapy water."

"Mmm. It would be luxurious. First a thorough shampoo, to wash weeks of grit off my scalp. Then a good scrub of everything else from the chin down. Then, finally, my feet."

"Yes. Feet. Between every toe. And afterward, I'd just want to fall asleep that way—clean, damp, naked."

"That's not the first thing that comes to mind if I were clean, damp, and naked." Kirsten lay back down to avoid looking directly at Maarit.

"What would you do? Dance?"

"No. I would make love to you."

Maarit was silent.

Kirsten's face warmed. "I'm sorry. I shouldn't have said that." Her throat felt tight.

Maarit looked away. "No. It's a nice thing to say. Just not possible. Anyhow, I'm really tired. We should go to sleep."

"Yes, of course. Sure." Kirsten stared at the dark ceiling and couldn't fall asleep. Maarit, too, seemed to lie awake, silent, though at some point, both succumbed to exhaustion.

In the evening, after Birgit brought them a final meal and they pulled on dry socks, they prepared to leave. The subjects of bathing, or nudity, or lovemaking didn't come up.

❖

Nor did they come up during the three days it took them to reach the Sami settlement. During the two nights they camped on the snow, wrapped again in their reindeer skins, they slept back-to-back, without reminiscing.

They arrived at the settlement during the long afternoon dusk, to both welcome and agitation. "Germans," Gaiju complained, his grimace revealing the wide gap where his front lower teeth were missing. He spoke a mix of Sami and Norwegian, which she'd learned he understood but rarely used. "Patrols, little planes flying low over the plateau."

"Reconnaissance planes?" Kirsten frowned. "Odd. Did they land?"

"No, nothing. But men came this morning. With guns, watching us." He mimed them hunched over, clutching their rifles, scowling.

Jova had joined them, and Gaiju backed up a step, leaving her to make explanations.

"How many were there?" Maarit asked.

"About twenty, but only two of them talked. An officer and an ugly man with a big mouth. They spoke bad Norwegian, but we understood. We told them 'No British! No British. Only Sami.' They took a couple of our deer and then left."

"Did they seem satisfied?"

"What does a satisfied German look like?" Jova said bitterly. "I have never seen one."

Comforted by the fact that the Germans had already been to the settlement and found nothing, Kirsten sat down to one of Jova's reindeer-stew suppers and rested from the long ski-march. The subject of Karrel's missing gakti didn't arise, though Jova's disappointment was obvious.

Otherwise none of Maarit's family inquired as to their whereabouts for the last ten days. Was it diplomacy and the suspicion that they engaged in resistance, or simply general Sami indifference to political events? She'd have to ask Maarit later.

"How is the herd?" Maarit asked between chews.

"Well enough. We had to slaughter a lame calf."

"Oh, no. Not Lykke!"

"No. She's still with the others," Alof reported between puffs.

"That's a relief." Kirsten wanted to ask to see the calf, but everyone was already settling in for the night. Alof had thrown a final block of wood on the fire, and she became aware of her own sore muscles. Maarit, as she had the past few nights, lay down and turned her back, signaling it was time to sleep. Kirsten lay down next to her and relaxed into the springy cushion of soft twigs under her deerskin.

She couldn't tell how long she'd slept, but it couldn't have been more than an hour, for the embers still glowed. The sound of boots kicking on the goahti door woke them all. Alof, who was closest to the door, pushed it open.

Befuddled, Kirsten saw a hand snatch him by his shoulder and haul him outside. She was on her knees when the muzzle of a rifle poked through the door opening, and she heard the command "*Alle 'raus!*"

Fully awake, Maarit leapt out in front of her, then Gaiju. Alarmed, Kirsten followed, noting briefly that Jova hadn't stirred. Was she sleeping so deeply she didn't hear, or simply petrified?

Outside she faced two German soldiers and a slowly growing number of Sami neighbors. Both soldiers held rifles, and the one in front spoke to her directly. "I knew you were here and everyone was lying," he said in his clumsy Norwegian. "All I had to do was come back and force one to point you out." It was the Goebbels-head with the wide mouth they'd faced in the café in Rjukan. She even remembered his name. Debus. His colleague held a terrified young boy by his collar, obviously the poor lad they'd forced to identify her goahti.

"Why are you looking for us? We haven't done anything."

He spat onto the snow. "Shut up and put on your shoes."

Her mind buzzing with thoughts of how to argue their way free, Kirsten bent down through the hut opening to fetch out her and Maarit's boots. Strangely, Jova still slumped, immobile, eyes closed, at the back of the hut, barely visible in the murky darkness of the last embers.

Kirsten handed Maarit her boots and knelt to tie on her own. Their Sami neighbors murmured among themselves, anger and helplessness in their voices. When Kirsten stood up again, the two soldiers grasped them by the arms and urged them forward.

The Sami stepped to both sides, creating a wide alley for the four to march past them, and the soldiers, smug in their success, lowered their rifles.

Kirsten glanced to the side at Maarit, searching for some sign of what they should do, but she had nothing to offer.

"We haven't done anything," she repeated, helplessly.

"They told us to look for anything that wasn't normal. And two Sami women showing up in Rjukan just before the attack. That wasn't normal. And with that hair…" He pointed to Kirsten's exposed red hair. "That's not normal for a Sami."

He was right, of course. They were trapped. How was she going to get them away from the village?

A shot rang out, and Debus's hand suddenly dropped from her arm. The second soldier spun around just as another shot sounded, and then both men lay at her feet. She turned to see Jova standing at the entrance of their goahti with her hunting rifle. "That's for my daughter and my grandson," she said.

Alof stepped beside her as the murmurs of fear among the other Samis grew louder. He raised his hands and spoke to his neighbors in Sami, clearly to reassure them everything would be all right. The men and women nodded in apparent agreement, and two men approached him. She recognized Paaval and Aavik. "Don't worry," Paaval said to her in passing. "We've seen nothing. Now let's move their bodies."

Alof touched Jova's arm reassuringly and turned to Maarit. "Prepare the sled."

Laying aside the rifles they'd seized from the dead men, Maarit and Kirsten set off to fetch one of the tame härks and hitch him to a sled. When they arrived at the front of the goahti, the two men grasped the bodies of Debus and his nameless comrade and laid them on the sled.

"Should we bury them in the snow?" Maarit asked, sliding their rifles beside them. "They'll be invisible until spring."

"No. The Germans have dogs, and they'll smell them."

Now clearly in charge of the disposal mission, Alof thanked the men for their help, then turned to Kirsten and his family. "Fetch your skis and the ice axes," he commanded with quiet authority. Everyone obeyed and skied alongside the sled together for some two hours. The vidda landscape never appeared to change, but Alof, who had spent his life there, seemed to know exactly where they were.

Finally, the rocky undulating terrain changed abruptly to smooth ice. Since, by her reckoning, they had traveled almost due south, she was pretty sure she recognized the lake. "This is Lake Skrykken, isn't it?" she asked.

"That's what the Norwegians call it," Alof answered. "It's deep in the center, and the ice will be thinner."

Kirsten grasped now what he intended to do with the bodies. But just how thin was the ice in February? The river below Rjukan was melting, but Skryrkken was farther north, and the wind kept it frigid. At least in theory.

They halted, and without further explanation, Alof handed one of the two axes to Maarit. Stepping away from the sled, he marked out a circle about a meter and a half in diameter with the tip of his axe and began to hack.

Maarit chipped along the other side of the circumference, handing the axe over to Kirsten when she tired. Gaiju relieved Alof until they heard the satisfying sound of the disk of ice breaking away. The two men hooked it with the sharp corners of the axes and slid it up to the side, like a lid, exposing a circle of black water.

In the meantime, Jova had dragged the bodies from the sled to the edge of the ring, and, at a signal from Alof, shoved the first one—it was Debus—into the hole. Though Kirsten knew the man was already dead, the sight of him sliding headfirst into the icy blackness slightly horrified her. This final act seemed somehow more barbaric than simply burying him.

With the man's shoulders already underwater, Gaiju fetched stones from the sled and slid them into his pocket. Smart, she thought. They would keep the body submerged even as it decomposed and became gaseous. Then, from both sides, they stuffed him in completely. Finally, only the bottoms of his boots were visible, and Gaiju poked those to the side under the ice to make room for the next one.

The nameless soldier followed more quickly, since all were impatient now to finish the job. Kirsten gave the final shove to his boot, propelling it downward, and when it bobbed up again, they shoved him sideways under the uncut ice.

All that remained was to dispose of the rifles. Jova lifted them from the sled and dropped them into the hole, and Alof slid the ice disk back into place. All stood for a moment of grim satisfaction, before turning back to the sled for the return journey. They followed the ski tracks they'd left, and Kirsten worried. "Won't the Germans simply track us down the same way?"

"Yes. They will start to look tomorrow," Alof said. "But in a few hours, the hole will freeze closed, and tomorrow, our tracks will be covered." He tilted his head upward and smiled at the flakes of snow that had begun falling. "Maybe sooner."

It had grown dark, but as they came within about a kilometer of the settlement, they could see a tiny spark of light in the distance. Someone had made a beacon fire for them.

"Hahtezan, goddess of dark things, is helping us tonight," Gaiju said, and for once, Kirsten was inclined to believe him.

CHAPTER ELEVEN

For the first few days, though no one spoke of it, the entire village was apprehensive. If the Germans returned demanding to know what happened to their men, not all could remain silent. And if the truth was revealed, the reprisals would be grave.

But the Sami gods did indeed seem to be looking after them, for no new patrol came, and the reconnaissance flights overhead suggested the Germans were searching for a large British force rather than two or three saboteurs. It began to look like Debus and his comrade, who'd arrived in the middle of the night, had been acting on their own.

A week passed, then two, filled with the normal winter labors. Knowing SOE had put her on standby for an indefinite period, Kirsten enjoyed a sort of vacation from the war.

The gradual return to normalcy, such as it was for the Alof family, also meant a change in Maarit. She was once again the amiable person who had saved Kirsten. Her glance was open, warm, and at night, when they slept side by side in the goahti, her embrace was spontaneous. Whether that meant sisterly affection or the reopening of negotiations wasn't clear.

With Karrel's gakti lying still in Skinnarland's cabin, Kirsten reclaimed one of the two British coats she'd worn when she was first rescued. Jova had kept both, though, as she pointed out sheepishly, she had remade the larger one into trousers for Alof.

On the last day of February, when Kirsten was just beginning to waken, and Jova was stirring up the embers, someone rapped on their door. Alof opened to the leaders of the three other herding families—

Tuovo, Paaval, and Aavik. Standing at the front, Paaval announced, "It's time for the separation."

"Why do you separate them?" Kirsten asked Maarit. "I thought they remained together all the time."

Maarit tied on her shoes. "At the moment, all four herds are scattered throughout the valley. Reindeer don't know who they belong to, so we have to collect them in the corral from time to time."

"For what purpose?"

"To identify them and to mark the ears of any of the calves who slipped by last time. Sometimes they only have a spot of paint on them that's beginning to wear off. But we also have to check them for sickness, especially the vajas who are carrying this year's calves. If they show signs of malnourishment, we supplement with fodder we've collected ourselves. Best of all, or worst of all, if you're sentimental, each family slaughters a couple of fat ox-deer to stock up for the next few months."

"I see. So, how can I help?"

"You can either stay with the women and help shore up the corral and the side pens to hold the separated deer, or you can join the men who are rounding them up."

"Oh, the roundup sounds much more exciting. Count me in for that."

❖

The roundup team, which amounted to most of the able-bodied men and their dogs, was already setting out. They marched in a long line, with Alof and Gaiju close to the end and Maarit and Kirsten following at a distance behind them. After about two hours of hiking, they'd made a wide loop around the entire range. When the loose— very loose—circle was completed, Kirsten heard the whistles signaling that everyone should move inward.

The herders were careful to avoid sudden movements and to keep the dogs from barking, for any of those disruptions could set the reindeer in panic. If they did, they could scatter in all directions, and it would take days to collect them again.

Hour after hour of continuous gentle urging caused the dispersed deer to slowly edge together. At the end of the long and exhausting day, the circle was still wide and porous, but the herd at last looked like a single mass. In order to prevent the deer from scattering again, the herders lit bonfires around the periphery and kept watch with the dogs against predators. Leaving a few sturdy souls on guard, the others returned to their goahtis for a few hours' sleep, and on the second day, the circling began in earnest.

Alof drove the deer inward now, by harnessing one of the sled härks and skiing along the flank of the herd dragging a line of clattering wooden objects.

Finally, the herd formed a vague teardrop shape, its narrow end pointing toward the corral. Now, even the children of the village came out to join the labor, waving and shouting encouragement.

They opened the gate wide, and the first several reindeer hurtled in. Driven by momentum, they continued to gallop in a circle along the fence line. More poured in behind them, sustaining the flow, until hundreds of deer were captured and the corral roiled in a gray-brown gyroscope of antlers.

Someone shouted the command, and dozens of hands shoved the gate closed.

Kirsten skied to the corral fence and leaned against it, enchanted by the sight. The hooves of the swirling mass of animals had stirred up powdered snow and dust. Together with the steam of their own breath, they produced a cloud that engulfed them in an otherworldly haze. The steaming sphere seemed a symbol of the thousand-year-long equilibrium between the Sami and the arctic.

The deer were allowed to circle until they tired and it was safe to go among them without being trampled. Tuovo and two of his sons entered first, followed quickly by the other families, all wielding coils of rope.

"This is the skillful part," Maarit remarked. "You see right away who the experts are." Just then lassos shot out left and right, slender, quivering serpents that fell on passing antlers.

"How do they know which deer belong to them?" Kirsten asked.

"Some do, some don't. The ones who've done it for years can spot the earmarks of their own animals, even in the mist. Then they have only a few seconds to toss their lassos over them as they trot past."

In front of them, Alof swung his rope high over the head of one of the large males and brought it to a halt. It bucked and twisted, almost yanking him off his feet. Maarit ran to help him, and together they tugged it from the herd toward the fence and into the family pen.

By then, Gaiju had caught one as well, and Kirsten lunged toward the beast to shove him along from the rear. After that success, she became cocky, and as Alof's next lasso landed, she took the rope from his hand. "I've got him," she called out, and moments later she was yanked off her feet and dragged facedown through the snow. As the lasso slipped from her hands, she heard someone above her laughing.

Struggling to her knees, she saw it was one of the Tuovo men—Miko, the oldest son. He patted her shoulder. "Good try," he said, and marched away.

The separation took the rest of the day and the next two as well, and when the main corral was empty of reindeer and the family pens all full, the next stage began.

"Give me a hand here," Alof ordered Kirsten, seizing one of the calves and pressing it to the ground. The patch of green paint on its side that indicated it was his property had almost worn away.

Alof lifted the female calf and dropped it on its side. "Hold her legs so she doesn't hurt herself." Kirsten obeyed and watched as he threw one leg over the calf's neck to immobilize her and, with a deft movement, snatched a clipper from his belt and cut two quick slices in the animal's ear. A moment later the deer was on her feet again, shaking her head as if in annoyance, and Alof was reaching for the next one.

Marking the calves, of which there were only about twenty, was easy, and Kirsten was feeling rather proud of herself. But some minutes later, Alof and Gaiju together wrestled the first *sarv* to the ground for a less amusing side of the herding.

Maarit had already explained that the males were good for replenishing the herd but useless as pack or sled animals. They had to be castrated or slaughtered in mid-winter, before the next mating season, when the hormones racing through them would make their meat inedible.

She watched, horrified, as Alof used a large pair of metal tongs to crush the area just above the testicles. The poor beast was obviously in shock and pain, and she winced as he let out a hoarse shriek. But the crushing of the ducts lasted only a second, and the newly castrated animal was allowed to stagger to his feet again.

Some fifteen sarvs were neutered in this way, and though Kirsten cringed at each one, she had to acknowledge that as long as she ate reindeer meat, she had to accept the necessary brutality. That realization was brought home the following day during the slaughter.

"We choose the härks, mostly, especially the ones who've gotten fat," Maarit pointed out as Alof lassoed the first sacrifice.

Kirsten watched nervously as Alof dragged the härk to the corner of the pen. As it bucked, lifting its rear hooves into the air, Maarit looped a rope around one of them and held it off the ground. Gaiju stepped in and seized the deer's antlers, then turned them sharply to the side. With only three legs to stand on, the creature fell to the ground, and Gaiju sat on him.

The animal was allowed to calm down for a moment, until he stopped thrashing. Then Gaiju drew a knife from his belt and thrust it deeply into the base of the deer's skull. The deer's sudden collapse suggested that the blow had severed its spinal cord, cutting off sensation. A second later, Gaiju raised one of its front legs and plunged the knife again, into its heart. With a final twitch, the reindeer gave up its life. The entire slaughter had lasted less than a minute.

More shocking, in fact, was the sight of its butchering, though that too was executed quickly. Alof made a long cut along the deer's belly to remove the viscera. He flung them to the side, where they lay in a pile, steaming in the winter air.

The first slaughter was the beginning of an assembly-line process, during which one of the boys dragged each dressed carcass out of the pen for skinning, while Gaiju lassoed the second deer to go.

By the third deer, Kirsten had recovered from the shock enough to take over the task of tying up the rear hoof, allowing the others to deal with the bloodier work. Mercifully, Alof had decided that six deer would be sufficient to provide meat for the family for the remainder of the winter, so the entire process took less than two hours. But the grounds of both the corral and all the family pens were now a morass of melted snow and blood.

Exhausted and gory, Kirsten staggered to the fence of the main corral just as someone opened the gates to all the pens. Tuova led one of the härks wearing a bell to the gate to draw the captured animals out, but the newly ear-marked and castrated reindeer were slow to grasp that they were free. A few trotted after the härk, then a few more, and finally the collective heard bustled toward the opening and streamed back up to their grazing grounds as if nothing had happened.

❖

Though Kirsten still winced inwardly at the thought of the innocent creature that had trotted across the Hardangervidda only to be slaughtered, she did enjoy the meal of fresh reindeer meat. Afterward, Maarit and the men left to meet with the other herders for cleanup chores. Only Jova remained, wiping out the eating bowls with snow.

Familiar now with the taciturn Sami, Kirsten picked her teeth with a sliver of wood, prepared for a long, comfortable silence. Jova's sudden question came as a surprise.

"What have you done to my granddaughter?"

Taken aback, Kirsten was at first defensive. "Do you mean that I convinced her to join a military mission? That was her own decision. I believe she did it, in part, for you."

Jova gazed at her across the fire, deep sorrow in her eyes. "I know that. Remember, I was the one who shot those soldiers for the deaths of my daughter and my grandson. All that's left to me is Maarit, but now you've taken the Sami out of her. She was a good herder and was soon to marry, bring more children into the family. Now all she talks about is being with you."

Kirsten began to grasp the tug-of-war between her and Jova. One of them would lose Maarit. "Please believe me. I don't want to take her away from her family or her people. If she wants to marry, she can still do that."

Jova's large, soft brown eyes remained fixed on her, drawing her in. "I know she will choose you. And when she leaves us, I want her to be happy. Please do not be careless with her."

Kirsten felt a twinge of guilt. Maarit wasn't "hers" to begin with, let alone to take care of, and all she'd done thus far was endanger her. How could it be otherwise? She wanted to make some sort of pledge to Jova, but their plans seemed to change from day to day, and anything she could say would be false.

Maarit's head appearing in the opening of the goahti door interrupted the morbid conversation. "Hey, come outside. The lights are quite nice tonight."

Reprieved, Kirsten slid her feet into her boots and bent through the doorway. "Ooh, you're right," she murmured, gazing upward. She stared, hypnotized, as curtains of neon chartreuse undulated slowly across the night sky, like gently fluttering drapery. A strip of bright red quivered along one edge, and flashes of blue and purple flickered and faded along the other.

They stood side by side, brushing shoulders. "Like a vast cloak, and on the far end, just out of sight, is a goddess," Kirsten remarked.

"Now you see where Sami religion comes from." Maarit slid her arm along Kirsten's back. Through the layers of Kirsten's coat and sweater, her touch was barely perceptible, but it was nonetheless like an electric shock. She stood, immobile, willing the arm to stay, and it did.

She pressed close to Maarit. "Sometimes I don't know whether to sorrow for the world or rejoice. The war, the men we shoved into the lake, and the slaughter today leave me despondent. And then I stand here with you and see such magnificent splendor. I can't quite get my mind around it."

"I know what you mean. The lights are always sort of miraculous."

Kirsten laid her head on Maarit's shoulder. "I've seen the northern lights in Rjukan and once in Oslo, but up here, they seem to belong to you."

"That's a sweet thing to say."

"I mean it. Everything you've given me here makes me feel richer."

Maarit hesitated before replying. "Strange. For me, it's almost the opposite. You draw me away from this." She extended a hand to suggest the entire landscape.

Kirsten felt as if she'd been struck. It was what Jova feared. "I don't want to ever take you away from the Sami."

"I don't mean it as simply as that. But you must know, you've changed me. Before you, I cared about everything equally—my family, the herd, the Sami. Everything was the same color, and I gave it all the same loyalty. Then you arrived with all your complexities, other colors, ideas, responsibilities."

"You mean, I brought the war. Those two soldiers came because they'd seen us in Rjukan, and we were in Rjukan because of me."

"No. The war was already here. You just reminded me that we

have to fight it. You pulled me out of the grayness I was in. I think about your courage, and you make me courageous, too. I think about how weak you were when we found you and how you dragged yourself back, then joined a nearly impossible mission. I think about your mind, your conscience, and…even your body, which I've never seen." She paused again and took a breath. "And I think all the time about what you said when we slept in Birgit's storeroom, that you wanted to take a bath so you could make love to me."

Maarit's hand was still on her back, and now the conversation was about love. "You never said what you thought that night."

"I think…I wouldn't know what to do."

"You don't have to know what to do. Things happen by themselves if you let them." Kirsten pivoted around until they were face-to-face. The night was clear, and the shimmering light of the aurora borealis cast a faint green on the snow, as if touching it with celestial color.

Maarit's arm had slipped away, but Kirsten now grasped her around her heavily padded waist and pulled her close. She waited for Maarit's smile, then pressed her lips on it, warming a small place on their cold faces.

Scarcely had the joy of their kiss begun to stir her when something thudded in the distance. Maarit broke away. "What's that sound?" She glanced toward the south.

Kirsten listened and could make out only a dull rumbling far away. Was it thunder? Impossible. The night sky was crystal clear. "Could it be artillery?"

"No. Too difficult to bring the cannons up here."

"It's bombardment, then."

"By the Germans or the Allies?" Maarit asked, stepping out of the embrace. "Though it makes no difference, I suppose? It's still Norwegians being killed."

"I have to go back to Rjukan," Kirsten announced. "If there was ever a sign that I needed to report for duty, that was it. I'm leaving tomorrow, by first light. I have a compass, and I've made the trek twice now. I'm sure I can find my way."

"Don't be ridiculous. I'm going with you."

❖

Maarit took on the disagreeable task of informing her family that she was leaving again, while Kirsten busied herself taking all British markings off her winter coat and avoided eye contact with Jova. Leaving Udsek for the war was the very opposite of taking care of someone.

She stood off to the side the next morning as Maarit embraced her grandparents, and they set off. For a day and a half, they skied south past Mår and Grytefjord, then curved west toward Rjukan. They traveled with large backpacks containing equipment for the two nights out on the snow and were adept by now. Though they arrived early in the evening, the arctic sun had long set as they worked their way down into the valley and through the streets of the town.

Birgit opened the door to the storeroom, obviously surprised to see them. "I thought you two would be long gone. Come in quickly."

They both stood their skis upright against the wall, stepped inside, and dropped their packs and heavy outer clothing onto the floor. "What happened two days ago? We heard what sounded like bombardment."

At that moment, Kirsten perceived another figure in the storeroom, a tall man with bristly gray hair and a beard that covered both chin and neck. "Oh, sorry," she said. "We've interrupted something."

"This is our radio man. In the organization, he's called Odin."

He held out his hand to greet them.

As Kirsten took it, she realized with a shock that he was one of the two men she'd seen in Birgit's café the day she and Maarit had arrived. One of the card players, who had seemed utterly indifferent to them.

"Radio man. I'll be damned. Well, it's our good fortune, since we need to report in to Tronstad. I'm sure he's already heard from Skinnarland that our operation was a success. I just want to tell him that we're still here and await further orders. You can sign it Chemist and Reindeer."

Odin crossed his arms and stared down at them. "I'll send it, but you should know that whatever you did in Vemork wasn't enough. Word came from our people up at the plant that the Germans simply rebuilt the installation and resumed production."

"What the hell?" Maarit said what both of them were thinking. "All that labor for nothing?"

Odin sniffed, indicating his disdain for their whole operation. "Worse than that. We're assuming that's the reason for the bombardment two days ago. By the Allies."

Kirsten's voice weakened. "Did they accomplish anything?"

"Accomplish? It was a stinking disaster," Odin all but snarled. "The bombers must have been targeting the plant, but the whole mountainside was fogged in, and they let loose bombs everywhere. The top floors took a few hits, but the production in the basement was untouched."

"Christ," Kirsten muttered. "So no damage to the electrolysis plant?"

"No, but they did knock out the suspension bridge. And your genius pilots managed to destroy some of the pipes carrying water down the mountainside. If the sluice gates hadn't closed automatically, the water would have flooded the whole shelf that holds the plant, and dozens of Norwegians would have been killed."

"Oh, hell." She swore again, at a loss for anything better.

"And there's more." Odin scratched the back of his neck, obviously wanting to get a lot of anger off his chest. "They hit our nitrate plant and filled the air with poison for a whole day."

"Any fatalities?" she asked, almost timidly. The raid had nothing to do with her, of course, but she understood that, to the local people, she represented the British.

Birgit replied, and this time her constant frown seemed justified. "About twenty, including everyone in a new air-raid shelter we'd just built. We've radioed protest to the Norwegian government in London."

"Dear God," Kirsten murmured. "I hope it has some effect. Unfortunately, no matter what mistakes SOE makes, I'm still under orders from them. Both of us are."

"Yeah, we know," Odin said coolly, pulling on his parka. "I'll send your message tonight and come back to you with their reply. Just stay out of sight." With that, he stepped outside, and Birgit locked the door behind him.

Without further discussion, Birgit crossed the room toward the door to the café. "It's been a long, hard day for all of us. You know where the blankets are. Make camp with them, and I'll bring you what's left from today's kitchen." Birgit had never been welcoming, but now her tone was icy. If the Norwegian resistance felt any sense of solidarity, it was clear they were at its periphery.

Kirsten and Maarit rolled out their own deerskins onto the concrete floor and laid the cushions and blankets over them. By the time they'd prepared their usual nest, Birgit returned with bowls that smelled of beans in gravy, setting them on the table beside the stove. "I'll wake you tomorrow at first light," she said over her shoulder and closed the door behind her without waiting for a reply.

Their supper finished, they sat down on their nest to remove their boots. Kirsten turned the kerosene lantern down to a tiny flame that left most of the storeroom in a dull-brown semi-darkness, but created a sphere of soft orange light around them. They lay back under the common blanket, each one clasping her own hands chastely across her chest.

"It feels a little like we've just crashed, doesn't it? We thought we'd get a hero's welcome, but instead we have to suffer the blame for a bombardment that went wrong."

"Yes. It's depressing. And confusing. Should we have done nothing and let the Germans have their way in all things? That would have been cowardice."

"But what about the reprisals? The killing of innocents?" Maarit asked into the air.

"I don't know. But war's a strange thing. People higher than us declare it, plan it, and execute it, and when one side surrenders, people higher than us arrange the terms. The point is, we're foot soldiers, and we shouldn't accept the guilt for the bombing no matter how badly it went wrong."

"Foot soldiers. Yes. I like that."

They lay a few moments in silence, neither one yet ready to sleep.

"Are you warm enough?" Kirsten asked. "It's not the same as having your feet to the goahti fire, is it?"

"I'm fine. It's always warmer with two people under a blanket."

"We've slept together so many nights. I can't imagine sleeping alone anymore."

"Mmm." Maarit agreed neutrally. "Family sleeping. The Sami way of keeping warm."

"I like to think I'm more to you than Alof or Jova." Kirsten still stared at the ceiling.

"How do you mean?"

"I mean, you haven't kissed them the way you kissed me."

"That's true," Maarit said, her tone unchanged. "Under the aurora borealis."

Damn, this was not going to be easy, Kirsten thought. "But I feel like I know you almost intimately—your facial expressions, your mind, your thoughts, the quality of your spirit."

"That's more than most people know me."

"Yes, but I also want to know the physical part of you that I've never seen. Your legs, your...breasts."

Maarit chuckled softly. "I haven't seen my legs or my breasts for months myself. But it pleases me to know you want to."

"Don't you want to know what I look like, too?"

"I suppose so. I haven't thought about it much." She paused a beat. "Well, that's not true. I've thought about it quite a lot."

Another long silence followed, and they both still stared upward. "Do you think about making love with me?"

Maarit seemed to consider the question. "To be honest, I'm not sure what 'making love' is. Love in a goahti isn't terribly romantic, and most Sami make short work of it."

"You've lived in a city, even gone to a university. You were never involved with anyone? With a boy or a girl? Your grandmother said you planned to marry."

"In Trondheim, I lived in a rented room with three other girls, but no one ever got into my bed." She turned on her side, facing Kirsten, and rested her cheek on her hand. "But after I left and came back to my mother's people, she tried to marry me off to my cousin Niilas. It was understood that we'd marry after the autumn migration."

Kirsten let her eyes wander everywhere but Maarit's face. "Were you...um...intimate with him?" She asked lightly, as if to inquire if she'd ever eaten fish and chips.

"Once. He came to visit me when I was alone. I expect the family made a point of not being around that day to give him the opportunity. Anyhow, it was late summer, so clothing wasn't an obstacle, and he gave me an idea of what it would be like to be his wife. The whole thing went rather quickly. If we'd married, I suppose I'd have gotten to like it. But I had second thoughts and put him off. He ended up accepting a job transporting reindeer meat down along the coast and earning more than he'd done as a herder. He was just outside the corral during the slaughter last week, but you were probably too busy to notice him."

"I'm glad you didn't marry him. Sex shouldn't be something you have to learn to like. It should be so wonderful the first time that you want to do it again and again for the rest of your life."

"Is it that way between women?"

Kirsten was taken aback by the question, which cast her as an expert. But compared to Niilas, perhaps she was.

"There's a better chance of it. After all, women know what other women like. Generally, they're not in a hurry, and a woman can't take selfish pleasure on another woman's body. She can only give it."

"That sounds quite nice. Why don't all women do that?"

Kirsten snickered. "I ask myself that all the time. Maybe because they don't know about it. Parents all seem in a hurry to marry their daughters to some successful man. The poor girls never find out about the alternative until someone comes along to show them."

Maarit laughed softly as well. "Or they find someone in a snowdrift and bring them home to recover."

Kirsten caressed her cheek with the back of her forefinger. "Exactly."

"So, does that mean you're making promises of some sort? For unselfish pleasure?"

"Yes. I promise you that one day, when we are warm, and washed, and safe, and naked, we will share an experience that will be far better than your little hour with Cousin Niilas."

"An hour? I can assure you, it didn't last that long. He's a good man, strong, kind. But his kisses are kind of sloppy. Are your kisses better?"

"That's for you to decide." Kirsten rose to rest on one elbow. Her hand that had been stroking Maarit's hair found its way to her neck as she bent over her. She brushed her lips lightly over the corner of Maarit's mouth and swept them playfully across her mouth, chin, throat.

Maarit responded in the same way, and they played a little back and forth, a sort of game of tag, until finally their mouths rested together.

They embraced more fervently, but their heavy trousers and sweaters were between them. Kirsten ached for more; the swelling in her sex was almost painful, at once demanding continuation and relief.

"Your kisses are so sweet, I want to do them forever," Maarit murmured, and Kirsten suddenly thought of Niilas, who couldn't kiss. She stopped, and let her breathing slow. This was not what she wanted, to fumble through layers of clothing and grime. Maarit's first sexual experience had been brief, emotionless, as the passive object of someone else's gratification, even if he had been kind. Kirsten wanted their first joining to be ecstatic, not just all right.

"What is it?" Maarit sounded anxious. "Did I do something wrong?"

"No. Not at all. I'm the one who started something we couldn't finish. In a cold place, on a stone floor, where we can't even touch each other. I want us to have something wonderful and luxurious."

"How do you imagine that ever happening? And where?"

"I don't know, but I promise you, there will be a time and a place. I want us to wait for that day, and in the meantime, I promised Jova I'd take care of you."

Her face still against Maarit's neck, Kirsten felt her head nod gently. "Yes. I like that idea. To care for each other until the war is over and we both know what to do with our lives. Why don't we exchange something in the meantime? Like making a pledge."

Kirsten sat up. "Exchange what? Almost everything I have is from the Sami anyhow."

"How about our amulets? I'll give you my fox, and I'll wear your reindeer. If Gaiju gave you the piece to carve on, it's probably made from the same antler as mine anyhow." She sat up as well, lifted the cord over her head, and presented it to Kirsten.

"And here's my reindeer." Kirsten handed over her own amulet. "We're connected now through the antler. Do you believe in magic?"

"Absolutely not."

"Me neither. But I believe in you, and in us. And in sentimentality."

"Sentiment, yes. I believe in that, too. Now kiss me again, and hold me in your arms until we sleep."

CHAPTER TWELVE

The sound of voices in the café woke them, and a moment later Birgit gave a warning rap and then entered. "Odin just came by to say he's heard from London."

"Really? What did they say? Why didn't he tell us directly?" Kirsten was already on her feet.

"Because there wasn't much of a message. London simply signaled, 'Waiting for more information. Stand by.' As for our complaint about Norwegian fatalities, all they said was 'so sorry.'" She made an about-face, obviously still upset, and returned to the café.

Maarit frowned. "'Stand by.' What does that mean? Wait a few hours, a few days, a few weeks? Birgit has made it clear we can't hide out here."

"What alternative do we have?"

"To go back to the Sami. They always need more hands, and we might as well be working while London makes up its mind what to do. We could come back in ten days or so to ask again."

"But we just got here, after two hard days of skiing. What if they set some plan in motion the day after tomorrow, and we're up on the tundra with your reindeer?"

Maarit shrugged. "You're the one with relatives in the resistance. Can't those people suggest a place in the valley for us to live?"

"You're right. I'll ask Odin to send another message to SOE. Something like, 'Cannot remain at current location. Please suggest alternative. Otherwise forced to return north and out of range of communication.'"

They peered through the storeroom door into the café, which had not opened yet and was empty of customers. Birgit stood in the kitchen behind the counter, making coffee. She set out two cups and a plate of dark-bread slices when they approached. "So what's your plan now?" she asked, neutrally, though Kirsten sensed "to stay here" would not be an acceptable answer.

Kirsten took a sip of the scalding ersatz. "I'd like to send another message through Odin, to be forwarded to my father, saying we need housing. Otherwise we have to return to the *vidda* and be unavailable for a few weeks."

Birgit seemed relieved. "Good idea. If London wants you working for them, they have to protect you better. You can find Odin in the town garage. Go to the end of the street and turn left for about two hundred meters. You'll see the garage behind the stable. You should head down there now. Meanwhile, Maarit can help me bring in the day's wood for the stove."

"Fair enough." With the other half of the bread in her teeth, she went back for her coat. Cheered by what seemed to be a step forward, she laced up her boots and stepped out into the frigid February morning.

She'd gotten nearly to the end of the street and was already composing the message she'd send. Brief and to the point.

Milorg has no role for us and no housing. Pls suggest alternative or we must return to plateau and out of range.

But something caught her attention. At the corner, two policemen were shouting at a Sami man. She seemed to recall him from the separation corral. Yes, it was Miko, from the Tuovo family, the one who helped her to her feet when the reindeer had thrown her to the ground. He caught sight of her and seemed to recognize her, then returned his attention to the policemen. His dog must have snarled, for suddenly one of them kicked it, and it yelped.

Everything in her warned not to go near them, but she slowed her pace, indecisive. Miko knew her and would expect help. Worse, the confrontation seemed to escalate as the soldier drew his pistol and pointed it at the poor beast. Spontaneously, she hurried toward them.

"Stop it!" she called out, reaching toward the abuser's arm.

Surprised, he swung the gun toward her, and she knew in an instant she'd made a terrible mistake. Even Miko looked at her incredulously.

The second policeman, gaunt and buck-toothed, unhooked his rifle from his shoulder and pointed it at her as well. "You better come with us," he ordered. This would not end well.

In the same instant, Miko unsnapped his leash and shouted something at the dog that caused it to run back up the street where she had just come. Mercifully, the soldiers didn't fire at it. "Move!" The first one shoved Miko by his shoulder.

Kirsten fell into step next to him, trying to formulate an explanation to give whomever was about to interrogate them.

She had a cover story, a simple Norwegian woman, returning to the town of her birth for sentimental reasons. Would Miko pretend to not know her or let something slip?

But Miko was furious. "Why did you interfere?" he snarled under his breath.

"They were going to shoot your dog. What should I have done?"

"Now they're going to shoot us."

"Shut up, the two of you!" one of the policemen barked, and they fell silent. Just then they passed the garage, where, if she'd minded her own business, she would be passing a message to Odin. Now she'd thrown away that opportunity. Was he at that moment witnessing their arrest?

A dozen thoughts ran through her mind. How stupid she'd been, ignoring months of training with SOE to not be distracted. How worried Maarit would be at her disappearance. How convincing would her cover story be?

She was jarred from her thoughts when they reached what she recalled was the police station. The arresting officers prodded them through the doorway into a reception area with a counter and window similar to a railroad-ticket office, but barred and reinforced. The man behind the window slid a clipboard through the window, presumably for the officer to write his report.

Her hopes were raised. Perhaps they could still get away with being charged with a minor disturbance. Whatever Miko was arguing about, she was an innocent bystander who loved dogs.

An interior door opened again, and another officer entered. Once again, she stared at a familiar face, struggling to recall a name and connection. But this time it was a disaster.

It was Niels Halvorson, and she'd known him—all too well—at

Oslo University. He was heavier than when she'd last seen him, and his hair, slicked back from his forehead, was thinner. But his cold, puckering mouth hadn't changed. He stared at her for a long moment, and then recognition brightened his face.

"Kirsten Brun. It's you, isn't it? Well, well. What a surprise to see you here. What's going on?"

The policeman who'd brought them in showed him the report he was filling out. Niels's eyebrows went up. "You attacked them on patrol? You and this man's dog." He glanced briefly toward Miko's feet and puckered in confusion at the absence of a dog.

"The dog ran away and was just defending his master anyhow. These men were threatening him, a simple Sami, going about his business. I intervened because they pulled a gun to shoot the dog." Suddenly outrage gripped her. "Why are you arresting innocent people, anyhow?"

His voice was cool, authoritative. "You know full well that Norwegian law enforcement is fully coordinated with the German administration, and vagrant Sami are designated a nuisance."

"Coordinated. What a cowardly word that is. You're quisling lackeys to the occupation."

Niels's face grew cold. "You'd do well not to insult your captors."

"Captor. For the Germans. That's what you are now? Where's your patriotism?"

"I'm doing more for the Norwegian people than you are. And why are you wearing a British coat?"

"It's not British," she insisted, glancing down at where the insignia had once been. "It's just a coat. I've had it for years."

"I know a British man's coat when I see one. Ah, yes, I remember now. Your mother was British. And your father is a traitor who worked up at Vemork before he fled."

He frowned, repeating "Vemork" under his breath, and she could almost hear the pins falling into place. "Is that what you're doing back here? Working with the saboteurs that attacked the plant?"

"I don't know what you're talking about," Kirsten spat, and her response sounded pathetic even to her. Every common thief she'd ever read about or seen in films said that before being forced to confess. Her mind raced. She had to come up with a story that was true enough to convince him and endanger no one. And she had to start with Miko.

"Look, this man really has no idea what's going on. Let him go chase down his dog, and I'll tell you what you want to hear."

He stared, squinting at her for a long moment, calculating the losses or gains from making the deal, and then agreed. "All right, he goes, and you talk." He shoved Miko by the shoulder toward the door.

Miko stepped out into the cold air with only the briefest glance over his shoulder, and she knew that word would get back of what had happened.

Now she struggled to choose bits of information she could give him that would harm no one. The Germans already knew about the Vemork attack, and the saboteurs were mostly in Sweden anyhow. But she had, above all, to protect Birgit and Maarit, and the radio connection they had through Odin.

Without further discussion, he led her along a corridor to a narrow steel door. Opened, it revealed a cell some four meters wide and five meters deep. At the far end, a tiny window emitted the dim, sunless light of late afternoon. It held a single narrow bunk, and when he pointed toward it, she sat down.

"So. Now let's have a little talk, two adults getting to know each other again," he said, standing over her. A wave of revulsion went through her as she recalled the last time he'd said nearly those same words to her. It all came back to her.

The last student party at school, before the auditorium fire and the closing of the university. A summer party outdoors, of some fifteen boys and a similar number of girls, full of vitality and easily excited. Some of the students had paired off, but she stayed in the larger circle. Niels had been hovering around her for weeks, admiring her hair, making little presents, but she'd rebuffed him. He would not be put off and, after a few beers, had drawn her aside, away from the others. "We're two adults. Let's get to know each other better." He'd grabbed her breast, though only for a second before she slapped him and fled back to the others by the campfire.

Niels's cold squint told her he remembered the incident as well. Would he bring it up?

But all he said was, "The attack on the hydro plant. I want names of all participants." He handed over a block of paper and a pencil. "Most importantly, the names in your organization."

She took a long breath. "Does this mean you'll release me?"

He snorted. "Of course not. But I think you'll prefer being arrested to being shot, which is generally required for spies and saboteurs." He sat down across from her and lit a cigarette. "I'll wait."

Maybe he didn't remember the slap after all. So many more dramatic things had happened in the following months: the auditorium fire, the closing of the university, the shipping of hundreds of students to Germany for indoctrination. He could easily have forgotten. Maybe she could negotiate herself out of this crisis after all.

Besides, having to write rather than reply gave her an advantage—time to think. She could structure the confession, control the narrative to an extent. A nice list of a dozen names would please him, make him think he'd gained something, and it would take him a while to realize she'd given him nothing new.

She started by listing the dead men on the gliders, and those they'd already captured and killed. She followed by adding one or two names of the Norwegians in charge of the operations at SOE, names he almost certainly knew. The rest of the names she listed were pure fiction—Pedersen, Sørensen, Lindberg, though for authenticity, she finished by writing the name of her own father, Jomar Brun, safely arrived in Scotland. Not a single authentic local name. She handed the paper to him.

He read through it quickly, then glanced up with cold suspicion. "Who are your local contacts?"

"I don't have any. That was my problem. I worked with Sørensen and Lindberg on the Vemork mission, and then all three of us went our own ways. I don't know where the others ended up, but I fled westward and got caught in a snowstorm. By sheer luck, the Sami discovered me, and they didn't ask questions. As long as I made myself useful, I could stay."

He stubbed out his cigarette. "You can't seriously expect me to believe you committed a major act of sabotage with only two associates, then went to live on the Hardanger for a month. What involvement did you have with the recent bombardment?"

"None at all. I didn't even know about it until I came into Rjuken hoping to hide."

"You are trying my patience, Kirsten. You had to at least have access to a radio to coordinate with the others."

She had a cover for this, too. "Yes, of course we did, before the attack, at a cabin near Lake Langesya. After we succeeded in shutting down the facility, I don't know what they did with it. My only concern was hiding out for a few weeks, then trying to get help to escape Norway."

"You mean to tell me you had no contact with resistance people in Rjuken? That beggars belief."

"Why would I have anything to do with the local resistance? All the planning was done outside, and the sabotage by myself and the men I've told you about."

He dropped his eyes in quiet exasperation. He drew out a cigarette, slowly, methodically, and lit it with a silver lighter from his chest pocket. He took a long inhalation and studied her. She hated being at his mercy and tried another tack. Nostalgia.

"We were fellow students in Oslo, Niels. All of us were patriots, courageous and bursting with ideals. Then Terboven shut down the university and arrested a few hundred of the best of us. I never saw you again after that. About half of us were released, and the rest carted off to Germany. What happened to you?"

He flicked the ash of his cigarette onto the concrete floor. "I was one of those people 'carted off,' as you call it. But it was the best thing that ever happened to me. The Germans gave us a chance to be re-educated, to join forces with them, and become leaders in the New Norway."

"To become one of the master race. Is that it?"

He took another puff and blew smoke straight upward, as if offering it to some higher being. "You say that with such contempt, but you're wrong. The only people more Aryan than the Germans are the Norwegians, and they're offering us the chance to take advantage of our superiority. Why anyone, especially someone who looks like you, would refuse that offer, is beyond me."

"Why didn't you join the SS? I understand they have a Norwegian division."

"You mean Den Norske Legion? I tried. But I was a few centimeters too short. A shame, because it's obvious, my blood is pure Aryan. Yours, too. We'd have made a good couple, you and I."

"I don't think so," she said softly, her skin crawling with the memory of his hand on her breast.

He took a final puff, then dropped the butt on the floor and crushed it with his foot. He smiled gently as he stood up and strode toward her.

"You haven't changed a bit, Kirsten. You're still that deceitful little vixen you were in Oslo." He squinted again, apparently recalling old resentments. "You women think you can control us, toy with us. You use your bodies to make us chase you, and then you humiliate us."

He stood directly in front of her now and yanked her up by one arm to face him. "But now the tables are turned, aren't they? Now you need me on your side."

"We're both Norwegians. You should already be on my side." He was so close, she could smell his cigarette on his breath.

He ignored her remark. "I can release you, you know, destroy your report and simply say it was a misunderstanding. If you cooperate." He stroked her breast. "I know what women like. I like it, too." He slid an arm around her waist.

She leaned back, away from him. "You really think I'd let you maul me to get out of here?"

"Maul you? Don't be dramatic. It would just be an hour of pleasure for both of us, and then you could go home." He pressed his pelvis against her, and she felt his erection. It was reckless to refuse him, even worse to insult him, but she lost control.

She slapped him, recalling that she'd done it once before.

He recoiled, his expression ice cold, and struck her back, so hard her ears rang.

"You're going to regret that slap, and the one before. I neglected to mention that Reichskommisar Josef Terboven is due to inspect the Rjukan facilities in a few days. I'm sure he'll be delighted to know we have the daughter of Jomar Brun in custody. And while he's interrogating you, which may turn out to be extremely unpleasant, you should remember that you could have spared yourself the whole mess."

He turned abruptly and left, slamming the steel door closed behind him.

She dropped back onto the cell cot and stared, stupefied, at the cell walls. The dark window revealed that night had fallen, and as she lay down, all her fears invaded her like a string of phantoms.

The faces of those who depended on her silence flashed by: her SOE comrades, Paulsson, Skinnarland; then Jova, Alof, and Gaiju, whose political innocence she'd destroyed; Birgit and Odin, whose courage she admired; and Maarit, whom she loved.

The final thought caught her up short, and she turned it around in her mind. Suddenly she seemed to have an anchor and a resolve. She'd try to protect all the others, but for Maarit, she would endure the most. For Maarit she would keep silent, no matter what.

The glaring overhead light and the activity in the corridor outside her cell kept her from sleeping. She ached, and her feet were painfully cold, so she stood up and moved around, trying to warm herself and drive off anxiety. Had word of her arrest gotten back to Birgit and Milorg. Or had Miko simply fled? Were Maarit and Birgit still safe? What had they done after she disappeared?

Defeated, she cocooned herself again in her single blanket and was trying to sleep when she heard a voice. Startled, she sat upright but could see no one.

"Psst," the voice said again. "You, in the next cell!"

She tumbled out of the cot and pressed her ear against the wall for the voice, finally locating the sound coming through the ventilation hole near her feet. She knelt down and spoke into it. "Who are you?"

"What's your name?" the voice asked.

She hesitated. Should she risk telling her name to an unknown person? But the police already knew it. It could scarcely hurt if a fellow prisoner knew it as well. And possibility of communication instantly relieved the grimness of the cell.

"Kirsten Brun. What's yours?"

"Dag. You just arrived? I've been here a week. Nice to have a neighbor. Do you know why they arrested you?"

She debated how much to tell him. It was not impossible that he was an informer, getting information in the guise of a prisoner. But it would be safe to tell him what her captors already knew. "They suspect me of resistance activity."

"If you're related to Jomar Brun, I hope you are. With me, it's no secret. They shot my wife for hiding fugitives. They'd have shot me, too, but I was at work. They arrested me later, and now I wish I'd done something more to deserve it, some kind of sabotage. Then jailing would make some sense. Anyhow, I want to rest now. We can talk more tomorrow."

She returned to her cot and tried to sleep again, consoling herself that at least she had blown up a German chemical laboratory. She was an adversary, not a victim.

❖

Kirsten had no way to know how much time had passed, but she must have dozed after all, since when a sound awoke her, she recalled her dream of trying to flee, paralyzed, through snow.

It was a jailor bringing some warm liquid that was neither tea nor coffee, but she drank it, grateful.

An hour later he came again, to lead her wordlessly to another room. Two chairs, the sole furniture in the room, lit by a single bulb hanging overhead, revealed it was for interrogation.

Nonetheless, her captors seemed to be in no hurry to question her, for she waited, it seemed, endlessly, passing from fear to nervous irritation, and then to somnolence. She was nodding off when the door finally opened again, and she jerked to wakefulness.

Halvorson entered first and stood off to one side, giving way to an officer who stopped directly in front of her. He held a piece of paper, which appeared to be her written confession. Presumably it was to intimidate her.

Reichskommisar Josef Terboven was immediately recognizable. His thin, bony face was rendered even more austere by wire-rimmed glasses. His hair, cut in the military style with close-shaven temples, was thin and greasy. The icy ambition that made Norwegians— even Norwegian Nazis—hate him was evident in his expression, which never seemed to change. He had ordered the shutdown of her university and the "reeducation" of hundreds of students just like Niels Halvorson. Although he had been traveling, his uniform was immaculate.

She gazed up at him, trying to show neither fear nor defiance. It was important to convince him she was cooperative but not craven. "Kirsten Brun, is it?" It was a rhetorical question. "I will be brief. We know what you've done at Vemork, and that alone is enough to have you executed. But it is impossible that you were unaided by Milorg criminals in Rjukan. Give us their names, and I'll spare your life."

Remarkably, he didn't threaten torture. Could she still talk her way out of this?

"I've given you all the names I can. We were directed completely from London and the British forces. The only local Norwegians involved were Pedersen, Sørensen and Lindberg. I don't know what happened to them after we separated. They were supposed to try to get to Sweden, and I was headed south for Oslo but got lost in a snowstorm. The Sami saved my life, but it took weeks for me to recover from frostbite. When I finally recovered, I came into Rjukan hoping to locate someone in Milorg with a radio. I might have found someone if your men hadn't arrested me for trying to stop them from abusing a Sami and his dog."

"A very nice tale, which I understood you've already told Deputy Chief Halvorson. You'll have to do better than that."

"I told him everything I could. I swear. London deliberately avoids contact with local resistance to prevent reprisals. I looked for local help only because I missed my contact in Oslo."

"Who was the Oslo contact?"

"Sonderberg," she answered, knowing he, too, had fled Norway.

"How exactly did you expect to contact traitors in Rjukan? What was your signal to them?"

"I…I planned to mention Vemork, ask if people knew anyone at the plant. If they were happy about the raid, I knew I could trust them. But no one claimed to know anything about it. Or if they did, they said it was a bad idea. If Milorg is in Rjukan, I never did find it."

"Where's Jomar Brun?" He looked into empty space, as if he found the entire conversation boring.

She stifled a smile, answering that one. "London by now, I think."

"Who at the plant is working with you?"

"No one, now. We didn't need anyone. My father sent plant details so we could find our way rapidly to the heavy-water laboratory. It went very quickly, and we were amazed that the searchlights never came on."

"Who did you report to in Rjukan?" He was trying to trick her; she'd already told him she knew no one.

"I told you. London specifically set the raid up as an independent action."

"Why did you go to Rjukan?" He was repeating himself, obviously hoping she'd forget the details of her story.

"I knew it from my childhood. I was looking for a place to stay while I searched for someone with a radio, and I thought I'd have a better chance here. But no one would talk to me."

Terboven sighed, and Kirsten was certain she'd be tortured. But all he did was turn on his heel. "Put her on the transfer list," he ordered, then marched from the room.

Left alone with his captive, Halvorson finally spoke. "This is your lucky day. I never would have guessed it. I'd have shot you in a minute, but I guess it pays to be the daughter of someone important. He's putting you 'in storage' in Germany for future use."

"I'm being shipped to Germany?"

"Yes, to one of their camps, where your 'nonexistent' Milorg friends can't help you." He stepped toward her, where she still sat, and gazed down at her breasts. "What a fool you are. You could have avoided all this, and a lot worse to come." Then he, too, strode from the room.

Back in her cell Kirsten felt the urgent need to talk to someone. She listened for the jailor to lock her cell door and walk away, then waited a few cautious minutes before dropping to the floor to the ventilation hole.

"Dag, are you there?" she whispered.

After a few moments, his voice came back through the hole. "I'm here. What happened? Did they hurt you?"

"No, astonishingly. Terboven himself interrogated me, and he just put me on a list for transport. To Germany, I guess."

"Sounds like they decided you were more valuable to them alive."

"You think so?"

"It's a good strategy. You know, since they were wiped out in Stalingrad, they've been more or less retreating from the eastern front. Maybe they're using people like you as an insurance policy for future negotiations in case their glorious *Reich* doesn't succeed after all. You can be exchanged for someone."

"You really think they're planning that far ahead?"

"They must be. Why else would they be transporting so many of us to Germany? They ship us by the thousands, when they could just as easily execute us here."

"Strange. And sad. I also wonder, if we're so many, why do we turn into sheep? Why don't we attack them? After a few fatalities, we'd overcome them."

"Because no one wants to be the first man to strike. He's always shot. Everyone's willing to rebel later on, after the guns have been taken away."

"I see the problem, but I hate it. I think—"

Angry male voices came through the ventilation hole, as did the sound of scuffling. Dag had been caught talking to her and was being beaten. She retreated to her cot and curled up, anxious and uncertain.

Another day passed, and no voice came through the little hole. When she lay on the floor to listen, she heard nothing. Presumably he'd been taken to another cell, and she felt another layer of guilt. He was being punished for helping her. She was left largely alone, though she received mugs of the warm but unidentifiable drink twice a day and heavy saw-dusty bread in the evening. By the third day, she was weak with hunger, but as she was drifting into a torpor, the cell door suddenly sprang open. Apparently, it was transport day.

Chapter Thirteen

In Rjukan, Maarit sat with Birgit, Odin, and Rolf Sørlie, at a table in the kitchen belonging to someone called "Red," though he had not a single red hair on his head. Clever, actually, to separate code name from appearance.

Maarit got to the point. "Can't we do anything for her?" She glanced toward Birgit for support but found none.

"Not at the moment. Remember, by now she's probably been interrogated, and we can't know what she's told them. It's likely they'll get our names from her. We have to reckon with that."

Red packed some sort of tobacco into his pipe. "Birgit's in the most danger, because of the café, but your friend also might have talked about Odin's garage. That's why we should stop meeting there."

Maarit returned to her question. "Can we get a note back to her, to let her know we haven't abandoned her?"

Birgit shook her head. "That would be reckless. And in any case, we have no contacts in the local jail. We know what's going on because the asshole of a deputy chief of police boasts about it in public. It's a way to keep everyone in line."

"Do we know anything about the process? I mean, what are her chances?"

Red set aside his pipe for a moment. "That depends on what they've gotten out of her. If they find out she's a spy, they're not good."

Sørlie tilted his head skeptically. "On the other hand, if they find out she's Jomar Brun's daughter, she might be more useful to them as a hostage. In that case, they might transport her to a German camp and hold her until the last minute."

Maarit felt a surge of horror. "Germany! But couldn't we rescue her somehow?"

"Maybe. But that's at the end of a long string of uncertainties, so you mustn't get your hopes up. We have limited resources and other, more urgent actions."

Maarit slumped in her chair and listened dully as the men discussed moving the radio, obtaining arms, spotting quislings. How depressing to think she had joined the resistance only to learn the resistance had not joined her.

❖

After the meeting, Maarit paused a moment at the doorway into Birgit's storeroom that had taken on a sort of familiarity. It had been the scene of her first embrace with Kirsten, of the first hints of what might be possible between them. Now, under the light of a single overhead lamp, it was desolate.

Morose, she entered and knelt by her meager belongings, their tarp, four reindeer skins for sleeping, her skis, and a leather rucksack for provisions. As she began to roll up the skins, Birgit came in behind her holding two cups.

"Here. Have some coffee before you leave." With one foot she slid an empty crate toward Maarit and sat down on it. She handed over one of the cups.

Sullen, Maarit held the cup to her chest, absorbing the warmth while staring at her feet.

"I'm sorry it's turned out this way," Birgit said. "I've grown fond of having the two of you pop in and out of the café."

Maarit glanced up, astonished. "Really? I had the impression you didn't much like us."

"Strange you should think that. It was quite the opposite. I tried to keep you away because the café is so central to Milorg, and we were always careful to look ordinary, non-political. New faces, strangers, always aroused suspicion. But I knew you were making your own sacrifices, and after a while, you seemed a bit like daughters." She snorted softly. "Though I suppose I don't come across as terribly maternal."

"Like daughters?" Maarit couldn't keep the surprise out of her voice. "What a nice thing to say. You don't have children?"

Birgit looked into the distance and ran her hand over her tightly bound hair. "I had a son. Killed in the Norwegian campaign in the mountains around Narvik."

"Narvik? Really? So was my father."

Birgit brightened. "Ah. Perhaps they knew each other. I had no idea that Sami fought in that battle."

"I don't think they did. My father was Norwegian. It's my mother who was Sami."

Birgit's expression softened, revealing a side Maarit hadn't seen before. "He'd be proud of you and your courage, I'm sure."

"Oh, but my mother was courageous, too. She died trying to rescue my brother. A very strong woman. Her mother, too, tough as nails, who still keeps the herd with her husband. I get it from them."

Birgit rubbed fatigued eyes. "They all sound like good people. I wish I knew more of you. We Norwegians have a lot to answer for regarding the Sami. Maybe one day we'll rectify our mistreatment of them. What made you leave?"

Maarit took a long drink of the cooling coffee and decided she liked this woman after all. "Kirsten did. My family found her injured along the migration route. I helped her recover her health, and she helped me recover my conscience. I'd like to say I'm with the resistance because I want freedom and justice for Norway, but in fact, I'm here because I wanted to be with her."

"You really care about her, then."

"Yes, I do. And if she's lost to Germany, I don't know what I'll do. Go back home again, I suppose, to fight another day on another front."

Birgit shook her head. "It would be terrible to lose both of you, especially after you've proven yourselves at Vemork. Let me talk to the men again and try to convince them of your value and hers. I don't know what our group can do with so little information, but at least I can get them to move her up higher on our crises list. Considering I'm the only one who can't run and hide, I can make a strong case for us to get her away from the Germans before they pry my name out of her."

Maarit leaned forward and hugged her warmly. "Thank you, Birgit. I won't forget you for this."

"Now don't make a fuss." Birgit backed out of the embrace. "Just get on over to Red's place while they're still waiting for you. You might even get some supper."

Chapter Fourteen

Another day passed while Kirsten waited to be transported. Another day of failed hopes, of anxiety, and of simple hunger. The meals in the Rjukan jail consisted of little more than damp bread and a tiny portion of pickled fish once a day. She was ravenous and imagined it was even worse for the men.

On the third day, she received no breakfast at all, only the coat in which she was arrested and the notification that transport would take place that day.

By midday, the guard returned to lead her out of her cell and into a courtyard to wait for the transport bus. Dag was led out just behind her, and she was surprised at his appearance. The voice she'd heard through the ventilation hole had always been firm and clear, in spite of his depression at losing his family. Now she saw for the first time how small and frail he was. His face was skeletal, with sunken cheeks and a spotty two-week beard. He was clearly starved and abused, and if she had hoped to lean on his masculine strength during the move, it was clear the opposite would be the case. They seemed to be the only passengers to come from the Rjukan police station.

Finally, the bus pulled up. The door swung open, and under the cool glare of Deputy Chief Halvorson, a policeman urged them inside.

The bus was full, and in the rear some half dozen prisoners already sat on the floor. As the last to be added, she and Dag took their places in the aisle at the front.

In control were three SS men: two guards sitting at the front and the driver. She'd fantasized about escape while in transit but saw now how difficult it would be. Packed in as they all were, someone at the front would have to take the initiative to rush the guards and overpower the driver. Sitting directly in front of her, Dag coughed, and she wondered if he also saw the problem. They could overcome the two guards only if someone was willing to be shot. She glanced around, and the gray, sullen faces of the prisoners told her that no one was.

The guards, too, seemed to sense the docility of their prisoners and casually lit up cigarettes. It seemed an additional cruelty to smoke in a bus full of tobacco-starved prisoners, and she was relieved she didn't have that craving. She listened to the soldiers talking openly, obviously not caring if anyone understood German.

One of them, plump and swarthy, blew out smoke. "You made this run before?" he asked his comrade. Bored soldier talk.

The other, pale and blond, who sniffed constantly as if to clear his sinuses, nodded. "Yeah, a few months ago. Pretty straightforward. Breaks the monotony."

"They ever give you any trouble?"

Blondie snorted, temporarily reversing the direction of mucous in his troubled nostrils. "Never. Not a decent man in the pack of them. We slap them around, kick them like dogs, and they just take it."

Swarthy man shook his head. "Mmm. Norwegians. Supposed to be as good as us, but in the end, they're pathetic. What happens after we drop 'em off at Lysaker Station?"

"Train takes 'em down to Akershus, where the local police load them onto one of the troop ships—the *ISAR*, I think. I'm going along myself this time. I've got a two-week furlough, and my family's in Potsdam. Maybe I can get rid of this damned cold." He sniffed again, as if to make his point.

Swarthy man glanced sideways at his colleague. "Lucky bastard. I had no idea they moved troops along with the prisoners. Big boats, eh?"

Blondie picked tobacco from the tip of his tongue. "Oh, yeah. This lot is just a part of the crowd they're collecting at Akershus. Be a couple hundred in a few days. When the brass gives the order, we march 'em to the harbor and onto the ship, where they go into lockdown in the hold. Transport's pretty quick, down the Skagerrak strait past Denmark to Kiel, where we load 'em out again into trains to the camps."

Akershus. At some point, they'd have to be moved from the bus to a train, and from the train to Akershus. Two chances for escape.

They traveled in silence for some time, and the close, smoke-filled air made her drowsy. She rested her head on the side of one of the bus seats and began to doze.

A sudden bang startled her. Gunshot. A second bang, then a third. The bus fishtailed, careening wildly as the driver slumped over the wheel, blood streaming from his head. It skidded sideways toward a ravine and toppled onto its right side, blocking the exit door.

Kirsten tumbled back and forth among flailing arms and legs, anchoring herself on one of the seat legs.

"DON'T MOVE, ANYONE." Braced against the front window of the bus, the swarthy guard shouted absurdly, as if the thrashing prisoners could do anything other than try to struggle upright. Both guards swept their rifles back and forth, holding them all at bay. Kirsten stayed on her knees, waiting for an opening. Perhaps she could bolt.

A shape shot up in front of her.

Dag threw himself with outspread arms at both guards. Startled, the swarthy guard fired. Grunting as the bullet tore into his chest, Dag dropped onto him, pinning him down. Still standing, Blondie now swung his rifle in a small arc, covering the remaining prisoners and repeated, "NOBODY MOVE," while his colleague struggled out from under the dead man.

The standoff was agonizing, as a busload of trapped men waited for someone else to throw himself at the cornered guard. No one wanted to die, not even Blondie, who was about to be on furlough. He was wide-eyed with fear, clearly seeing the odds and grasping that the docility of the "pathetic Norwegians" was broken.

Glass shattered just over her head, and the rifle swung upward toward the sound. The rifle shot and the sudden blast of cold air caused her to jerk backward as a rifle barrel jutted downward through the broken window and fired twice. Blondie dropped forward, his furlough indefinitely postponed, and swarthy guard, still halfway covered by Dag, caught the next bullet.

Shards of glass dropped onto her shoulders, and the men sitting nearest the smashed window lurched upward through the jagged opening. Kirsten struggled against the arms and legs of the men climbing over her and was pushed forward by the panicked prisoners behind her.

As her head rose past the broken glass, Maarit's face came into focus, then Sørlie, and someone's hands hauled her by her coat up into the air. Vaguely aware of the men clambering from the crashed bus and fleeing in all directions, she labored to run alongside her rescuers. Maarit and Sørlie took hold of her arms and dragged her stumbling toward a woods.

"How did you…?" she asked into the air. No one answered. A few moments later, as they slowed, she asked, breathless, "Where are we?"

"A few kilometers outside Lysaker Station," Sørlie said. "We have people in the next town who'll hide you, but we have to get there before the Lysaker detachment notices the bus is late."

They stumbled on to a thicket, where her rescuers abruptly stopped. Brushing away snow and rubble, Maarit uncovered three sets of skis. Each one buckled on a set without comment, and Maarit leaned toward Kirsten. "How are you holding up? Can you ski?"

Freedom. Kirsten was elated. *Freedom and Maarit.* "Yes, of course I can."

They covered the three kilometers to the settlement in good time and skirted around the periphery to a small house at the edge. Kirsten smelled livestock, heard the mooing of cows, and the row of tall cans along the outside wall told her it was a dairy farm.

Sørlie signaled them to remove their skis and follow him into the barn. A double knock, followed by a triple one, obviously a signal, caused the door between the barn and the house to open. A woman stood in the doorway with a lantern and blankets over one arm.

"Under there," she said, pointing toward the spot where a boy was already brushing away straw with his foot. A trap door came into view, which he raised, exposing a ladder into a chamber of some twelve square meters. Maarit took the lantern from her hand and led them to the edge of the pit.

They stepped down into the hole and sat on the ground with their knees drawn up as the trapdoor over their heads dropped, raining grit and straw dust on them.

Kirsten found the sudden darkness frightening, but Maarit took her hand, and Sørlie's voice came as a comfort.

"By now the Germans will have sent out troops to round up the escapees, and we're still pretty close. But it'll take them days to examine every house and barn. When it's dark, our friends will tell us so we can start the next leg, the twelve kilometers to Skilling."

Kirsten needed to keep talking, to dispel the sense of suffocation in the pitch-black space. "Do I need to say it? Thank you for rescuing me."

Sørlie answered. "You're welcome. You weren't our first choice, but Birgit convinced us to get you out, and Tronstad backed her up. I guess he didn't want the Germans to boast they'd captured Jomar Brun's daughter."

"How'd you know where I'd be?"

Maarit's voice right next to her in the dark was reassuring. "Miko reported what happened, so we knew the police had you. Even though we couldn't get a message to you, we monitored the station. One of our Oslo connections informed us that Terboven had ordered a bus to round up certain prisoners for transport, and since one of the stops was the Rjukan police station, we knew we had a good chance of getting you. Even if we'd miscalculated, we'd still have liberated a lot of prisoners."

"What *about* the others? What will happen to them?" She thought of Dag, the only fatality, for being the first.

She felt Sørle shrug next to her. "They weren't part of our orders, so they're on their own. But they're Norwegians, after all. Most will be able to blend into the terrain."

"Where are we headed? Obviously not back to Rjukan."

"No. Of course not." It was Sørlie's voice. "We go through Skilling, by boat over to Vikersund, and then the sixty-five kilometers to Laufhøgdi, where we have a radio and can contact London. At that point, I'll return to Rjukan."

"Maarit and I, where do we go after that?"

Maarit leaned against her again from the other side. "That's up to Tronstad, apparently. He'll decide whether you return to Britain or stay in Norway."

"I see." Kirsten gripped Maarit's hand and was ready to sink into the comfort of rescue when she realized that another question hovered in the darkness and only she could answer it.

"I didn't tell them anything. Nothing at all."

Maarit's grip tightened. "I knew you wouldn't."

CHAPTER FIFTEEN

Once rested, they continued through Skilling and, in the still-long February night, were able to cover most of the sixty-five kilometers to Lauvhøgdi before daybreak. Even after the sun rose, an overcast sky and fog permitted them to risk the remaining distance.

At Lauvhøgdi they bypassed the scattering of houses and family farms, then climbed up to an isolated hunting cabin, as anonymous-looking as dozens of others that spotted the snowy hills. They thrust their skis into the snow and banged on the door.

The cabin door opened, and Einar Skinnarland stood in front of them, grinning. "Nice to see you again," he said, grasping Kirsten's hand.

"Nice to see you, too," she answered, letting herself be pulled in. It *was* nice, for both the circumstances and Skinnarland himself had changed. He was still blond and square-faced, but he sported a beard a shade darker than his hair, which softened his image, made him look hardier and less glamorous.

He gestured for them to sit on the various stools and crates while he collected cups from a shelf over the stove. "As soon as everyone's warmed up, I'll send out a message that you've arrived safely."

Moments later, he handed around the four hot cups, then sat down in front of his radio. "Anything you'd like to add?"

Kirsten held her cup under her chin, letting the steam warm her badly chilled face. "No. Just keep it short. Something like 'Chemist and Reindeer arrived safe. Await orders.'"

Skinnarland encrypted the brief message, then set on his

earphones and tapped it out in Morse. As always, he disconnected again immediately to avoid detection.

"What's the latest on Vemork?" Kirsten asked.

"Nothing specific. Our man there reported that the Germans have figured out the attacks will never stop, so are planning to move production. That'll require a whole different strategy, of course, and London is working on that."

Sørlie emptied his cup and wiped the back of his hand across his mouth. "More to the present, what's that wonderful smell coming from the stove? We've been traveling on reserves and would really appreciate some...of whatever it is."

It was the cheerful preliminary to the ritual of eating, pipe-smoking, and picking out places in the cabin to sleep.

The next morning, before sunrise, after handshakes and well-wishes, Sørlie departed for the trip southwest back to Rjukan, and an hour later, a radio message came in from Tronstad.

Glad you're safe. Intel is Germans will move current juice to Ger. date unknown. Await details to plan next steps in some weeks. Stand down until then. Ch and R. will receive commend from King.

"Well done," Skinnarland said. "You've both received royal commendations, along with the other Vemork saboteurs."

"Glad to hear it. But what does it mean to 'stand down' anyhow? How am I supposed to do that? I've just escaped from prison, and I'm a wanted person."

Maarit laid a hand on her arm. "Come back with me to Udsek. We were headed there anyhow, before you were arrested. In a couple of weeks, we'll check in with London again."

"Isn't everyone on the migration?"

"Alof, Jova, and Gaiju will be with the reindeer, but the village is never empty. We'll have the goahti all to ourselves."

The solution was reasonable, even obvious. "How far is Udsek from here?"

"About half the distance to Sweden, and I know every bit of the terrain. With the right equipment, we can camp on the plateau and never need to worry about being seen."

"I can give you some of the deer meat I have frozen, enough for a few days, some wood for a fire, and a tarp. Just promise to report back here in a couple of weeks. I'll radio the update in to Tronstad, and you can return my tarp."

"I guess it's decided, then. Udsek it is."

❖

The Hardangervidda, in winter a vast region of snow broken only by rocks and crevasses, no longer frightened her. They'd skied at a moderate pace since dawn, circumventing the dry ground, and when Maarit judged that Kirsten was fading, she called for a rest halt.

The sun was high, and Kirsten gazed out over the white expanse toward the distant mountains. Clouds covered their peaks as a harmless slash of dusty gray, dark clusters of hardy small fir or spruce on their flanks. The wind was mild and soundless, stirring up particles of ice that sparkled in the air. She squinted at the swirling specks of light that seemed like minute creatures. The vidda was being kind today.

They started off again, setting a rhythm of two hours skiing and fifteen minutes resting, and managed to cover some two-thirds of the way before Maarit called a halt. Though it was night, the snow radiated back the moonlight, creating a vast blue landscape and providing ample light to set up camp.

"Camp," as before, was a shallow pit and a low wall that curved slightly over them. The tarp isolated them from the wet snow, and their deerskins, under and over them, as well as their winter coats, kept them from freezing. Automatically, they slipped into an embrace, back to front, with the exhausted Kirsten lying in Maarit's arms.

"I see what it is you love on the vidda," Kirsten said.

"Yes, its purity. It was here before the Germans, before the Norwegians and the Sami, too. It knows no evil."

"It's heartless, though. It kills you innocently while the Germans do so malevolently. Either way, you're still dead."

Maarit chuckled, and Kirsten felt her warm breath on her neck. "Probably why the Sami have their religion—Hahtezan, the winter night, and Njavezan, the fae of warmth and light, fighting for our souls. And don't forget Aigi, the crippled boy who fights the darkness and takes back the magic waters."

"I haven't forgotten him. Poor little guy. His facing Stallu the child-eater makes me appreciate how easy I have it. I have only Germans to worry about."

"The Sami would say a little bit of Aigi and his fox lives in you." Maarit tugged her tighter.

"Nice to know you see Sami virtues in me. Since your family took care of me, I've felt part of them…of you. Of the reindeer, too."

"Reindeer. That would be me." Maarit snickered and kissed the back of Kirsten's head. "Now let's try to sleep. We have another eight hours of travel tomorrow."

❖

Eight hours was a good estimate, for after seven, Maarit halted. "There it is, Udsek," she announced, pointing with her chin toward the east, where a few black dots were just visible in the distance.

"You've got an awfully good eye. I never would have spotted it."

"I know it because we passed a frozen stream a while back, the one we use in summer, and I recognize those rocks over there toward the north. If you look closer, you can see a few lines of smoke. The people will be keeping by their fires."

They skied on for a while as the sky darkened, and Kirsten half expected to be met, if not by one of the villagers, at least by barking dogs. But all was silent, and the first goahti they passed was empty. So were the next two, and only when they reached what was more or less the middle of the settlement did someone step out in front of them.

She recognized Aibmu, an elderly man who owned no reindeer but served the community by building sleds and traps. He held a lantern up in front of them to identify them.

"Maarit," he exclaimed. "And Kirsa." He used his own variation of her name.

"We're here only for a couple of weeks. And if the herd isn't too far, we might join Alof and Jova."

Aibmu dropped his glance. He spoke in Sami, but his gesture was clear to Kirsten. They were to follow him.

Maarit held back and pointed toward her own goahti, but Aibmu took her by the arm and shook his head ominously. Something was wrong, she translated to Kirsten.

"He says his wife will make us coffee, and he has news to tell." Her tone suggested she was ill at ease, too. Removing their skis and dropping their packs outside, they stepped inside the hut after him.

He spoke to his wife, whom Kirsten knew as Livli, and Kirsten recognized the words for coffee and bread.

Livli's expression changed rapidly from cheerful surprise to solemnity, and Kirsten was suddenly filled with dread.

They sat on the left side of the fire while Aibmu took up his proper place on the right, and Livli set a tiny battered pot on the fire. No one spoke, which added to Kirsten's fear, and she let Maarit take the lead in finding out what was wrong.

They sipped their bitter coffee and stopped the rumbling in their stomachs with bread dipped into the salty brew. After what Maarit obviously judged to be a polite length of time, she spoke.

"Alof and Jova are with the herd? Is Gaiju with them?" They were all phrases Kirsten understood.

Aibmu dropped his glance again. "Gaiju lives," he began. "He was not here when they came."

His answer made no sense. "When who came?"

"The Germans, because of the dead soldiers."

"Alof and Jova." Maarit insisted, her voice dull with dread. "What happened to them?"

Aibmu narrated slowly, gesticulating and shaking his head.

Ashen, Maarit explained in Norwegian. "He said the Germans came, looking for their two men. They threatened to burn down everything if no one talked. So someone, he didn't say who, told them what Jova had done. The soldiers shot Jova and Alof too, then went with their machine guns and killed all the deer that were anywhere near. About fifty. When Gaiju returned the next day, the people buried Alof and Jova, then started the migration early. They were afraid the Germans would come back to shoot the rest of the deer."

"How could Gaiju leave that way after losing his family, as if nothing had happened?" Kirsten asked.

"How could he not leave? The deer are all he has left, and he wouldn't have known we were coming back."

Aibmu was speaking again, and it appeared he was offering to shelter and feed them both as long as they needed. Livli nodded, her expression full of concern.

To Kirsten's relief, Maarit shook her head and made some explanations as to why they couldn't accept. She set down her cup, and Kirsten followed suit, leaving the expressions of sympathy and bereavement to the Sami.

Aibmu handed her the block of desiccated reindeer meat that hung from a hook near his shoulder, and Livli added a bundle of roots for firewood.

Maarit accepted the gifts, and murmuring thanks, she stepped through the door with the bundles cradled in her arm. Stunned, Kirsten repeated the thanks and followed her out.

Their goahti was at the other end of the village, and they trudged toward it without speaking. Once inside, they found a reserve of firewood to supplement the gift from Livli and began the practical tasks of starting a fire. They still carried food from Skinnarland, but neither one was hungry enough to prepare a meal. They sat, side by side, staring at the low flames.

"All this..." She swept her hand across the bread stone, the pots, the utensils. "These belong to Jova. She should be making bread here. And look, there's Alof's pipe and tobacco pouch. He should be sitting here, smoking, telling his stories." Her lips began to tremble.

Kirsten could think of no words of comfort and simply leaned against her shoulder.

Maarit's voice was tight. "I want revenge for this. Simple revenge, even if I do it alone."

"You're not alone. Do you understand? I'm your family now." She brushed back a strand of Maarit's hair. "We'll have revenge by staying with the resistance, through Milorg or SOE. It makes no difference."

Maarit nodded. "Yes. To force the Germans out of Norway. But it won't bring anyone back. We've lost so much." She stared into the middle distance.

"We'll start over. Together."

"Start over. I'm not sure what that means, now. I don't know how many reindeer I have left, but I certainly can't make a living from them. And I can't see being a full-time herder, anyhow."

"Then stay with me. I want you to live with me instead of a Sami husband. What was his name?"

"Niilas. Stop worrying about him. He's a decent man with a trade and doesn't have a herd to care for. I wouldn't consider being with him as long as I have you."

"I understand. We have so many things to work out, but those decisions will have to wait until the end of the war. The important thing is that we have each other."

Maarit lay down and pulled Kirsten close to her in the way they were used to sleeping. "Promise me you'll stay?"

"Yes. I promise. With all my heart."

❖

Still half asleep, Kirsten sensed Maarit sliding out from under the covering and drawing off the tattered Norwegian sweater Poulsson had given her. Fully awake, she turned on her side to gaze at her. Half dressed, Maarit began to rummage through a battered chest at the rear of the hut.

"What are you doing?"

"Looking for something to put on that doesn't stink. Ah, this will do." She drew on a gray sweater. "This was Jova's from years ago. It's had plenty of time to air out."

"Anything there for me?" Kirsten sat up, drawing the blanket around her shoulders.

"Let's see." Maarit's hands were busy inside the chest. "Yes. Try this on." She tossed over a blue gakti Kirsten hadn't seen before. Embroidered bands in red and yellow ran along the yoke and around the bottom of the sleeves. Best of all, it was unstained by soil or the various reindeer excretions that covered the herders' work clothes.

"Was this Jova's, too?"

"No. Alof's. His wedding gakti. Looks like they never threw out anything."

Kirsten drew it over her head. The shoulder seams hung low, and the sleeves were a bit too long, but Alof wasn't a big man, so the fit was tolerable. "It's very handsome," she said. "I feel a little guilty expropriating it." She stood up and slid her legs into her trousers.

"Don't. Alof liked you. He might be a little shocked that it would go to a woman, but in the end, he'd be glad it stayed in the family. Anyhow, it means we can wash our undershirts and hang them out. The weather's good, so they'll dry without freezing. And when we return to what you call duty, we'll change back into the other things so as not to attract attention."

"So, we're setting up household?" Kirsten knelt down again beside her and examined the other objects in the kitchen area. It had always been Jova's domain, and without her death, they never would have dared to investigate what it held. Now she saw the iron pans, a stack of carved wooden bowls, a can holding utensils both modern and traditional. "Remember, we promised to report back shortly."

"Don't worry. I wanted to check in for news of my family and the herd, but now that I have no family, we don't have much reason to stay. As for the herd, I won't even know how many reindeer are left until Gaiju returns in the fall. After we've rested a few days, we might as well go back to Skinnarland and radio to London that we're reporting in for duty. And if your SOE has no work for us, we'll join Birgit and the Rjukan resisitance."

"Fine with me. So, what should we do in the meantime?"

Maarit glanced around them, as if searching for tasks that would be purposeful. "Well, obviously the goahti could use some repair, and that will take a few days. And of course, we'll need another to wash and mend our other clothing."

Idly, she rummaged through the contents of Jova's storage chest, and as she held up a leather sack full of flour, her face brightened. "Why don't we make bread? Jova would be pleased."

The bread, though not up to Jova's standards, was satisfactory as a supplement to the dried meat Livli had sent back with them. Kirsten ate, pensive and adrift, and it seemed to Kirsten that Maarit felt the same way. They had both ached for a homecoming of some sort, after their life-threatening struggle, and had come home to a vacuum. The whole trip back to Udsek had been a waste. The lack of closure to the events of the past weeks was soul-killing.

Kirsten lay back in Maarit's arms and said what she was sure Maarit was thinking as well. "If only we could have said good-bye to them."

Before Maarit could respond, they heard a voice outside the goahti door. "It's Aibmu. Can I come in?"

They both sat up. "Yes, of course," Maarit said.

He stepped inside but remained standing. He spoke Sami, but Kirsten recognized the names and the sense. "Some of the elders are sitting at my fire. Old Tuovo and Paavik and their wives. Will you come?"

Puzzled, Maarit agreed, and they followed him across the largely abandoned settlement to his place.

Entering his goahti, they found a circle of neighbors sitting shoulder to shoulder around the fire. Most were elderly or otherwise unable to join the migration. Nodding greetings to everyone, they sat down, and Kirsten studied the somber faces, wondering what the occasion was.

Old Tuovo, the senior member of the village, spoke. "We want to *joik*. For Alof and Jova," he said in Norwegian, presumably for Kirsten's benefit.

"Joik?" She turned to Maarit. "To honor them?" She knew only that it was a Sami way of chanting, but its purpose was a mystery to her.

"Yes, but also to summon them, to bring them back to our minds. It's a sort of ritual magic." Maarit gazed around at the gathering, obviously pleased.

Tuovo added, "Our tradition tells us the fairies and elves gave the Sami the power of joiking in a time past remembering."

Maarit elaborated. "When the Norwegians Christianized the Sami, they said joiking was savage and a sin. They associated it with the shamans and their magic spells. In a way, they were right, about the magic, I mean."

"Are they supposed to summon people who have died?"

Tuovo tapped the cinders out of his pipe. "No. They can also summon to mind a living person, or an animal, or a sacred place. But tonight, we want to bring Alof and Jova."

After a few moments, in which the only sound was the crackling of the fire, Aibmu began. He chanted in Sami, but Kirsten heard the name Alof, and between chants of *lo...lo* and a sort of tuneful mumbling, she seemed to hear the replication of Alof's chuckle and his cough, and recognized a few words that seemed to describe him. To her surprise, when she closed her eyes, she could even visualize him, with his pipe and his piercing, intelligent glance.

The joik came to an end but was immediately taken up by Livli, and it was soon clear that she joiked now for Jova. Words came through for "bread" and "hands," and in the middle of what seemed meaningless luuling and laaaling, she heard the unmistakable replication of Jova's infectious cackle. For a brief moment, and with closed eyes, Kirsten could imagine her close by, making bread.

It seemed the chanting was over, and Kirsten watched Maarit for a signal that they should leave, but to her surprise, Maarit, too, began to hum. Kirsten recognized none of the features she imitated and only a few words, such as "brave" and "steadfast," and it wasn't until the end, when Maarit's eyes glistened and her voice broke, that it became clear she joiked for her mother and brother.

Kirsten's eyes also filled. No valediction or eulogy could have been as moving as those three solemn joiks, to call back the souls of four brave and good Sami who had fallen to war.

❖

Five days later, they rose just before dawn and set out from Udsek, just as the winter sun rose for its brief appearance on the horizon. The cabin at Lauvhøgdi was over a hundred kilometers away, and they wanted to make good use of the light. They carried deerskins and Skinnarland's tarp, and so made the distance in two days, with a single sleep-stop midway.

They arrived at the cabin in the late afternoon, pleased to see smoke trickling from the chimney. When they thrust their skis into the snow and pounded on the door, Skinnarland opened it, appearing surprised but obviously preoccupied.

When they were all inside, they saw a new man on a stool warming himself at the stove.

Skinnarland pointed with his chin toward the stranger. "This is Terje Martinson, head of the local Milorg." He turned to address Martinson. "These stalwart fighters are Kirsten Brun and Maarit. Sorry, Maarit. I don't know your last name."

"Quite all right. We'd prefer to be known as Chemist and Reindeer anyhow."

The three of them shook hands, and Skinnarland fed another few sticks into the stove. "I'm surprised to see you again so soon. No one would have thought badly of you if you'd stayed on with the Sami or gone onto Sweden."

Kirsten sat down. "We've no reason to stay at Udsek. We wanted to report back for duty."

"That's fortuitous, since the planning's been moved up, and we were just discussing how to structure the newest action."

"Ah, so there *is* a new action."

"Yes. Our sources tell us that production of heavy water is up, but since the Germans assume we'll attack the plant again, they've decided to move its remaining supply to Germany. In fact, movement seems imminent. But we're getting ahead of ourselves. Let me radio Tronstad and let him know you're here reporting for duty."

He took up his notepad to compose the shortest possible phrasing, checked his code book for encryption, then set on his earphones. As he turned on his short-wave radio and fiddled with the dials, everyone else withdrew to the back of the cabin so as not to disturb him.

Kirsten turned her attention to Martinson. He had a pleasant, boyish look. With a narrow head, rendered all the more elongated by a high forehead and blond hair that stood up high and was combed straight back, he reminded her of Reggie. The resemblance increased when he smiled at her, spontaneously and without reason. He seemed easy to talk to.

"From what I recall of the plant, it won't be easy to transfer all that liquid," she said. "They'll need specially made barrels and a lot of troops to guard the route. And speaking of that, do we know the likely route?"

He crossed his arms and stared up at the ceiling. "For the moment, we can only guess. But the British bombed the suspension bridge, so that eliminates truck travel, which would be impractical for large cargoes anyhow. I think they'll have to move everything by rail line. The Allies bombarded it, but they repaired it pretty quickly. The question will be, where to intercept."

Kirsten nodded. "Rail. That's what I would have concluded also. Assuming they let us in on this operation, who would we be working with?"

"I'll be coordinating other sabotage near Oslo in the next weeks, but Rolf Sørlie and Knut Haugland will be involved. I believe you know them."

"Yes. Sørlie helped me escape from Rjukan, and I know Haugland from Operation Gunnerside."

Terje Martinson's eyebrows rose perceptibly. "I heard you were part of Gunnerside. You have my admiration. We heard about the operation afterward, by radio."

Skinnarland had laid aside his headset and joined them. "London gave me authority to include you and fill you in on the details as they exist at the moment. We know, for example, that the plan is to transport the barrels of heavy water by rail across Lake Tinn on 20 February."

Maarit frowned skepticism. "Doesn't Lake Tinn sometimes have ice at that time?"

Martinson raised a hand slightly to indicate authority. "We've been monitoring the lake the last few days. It's almost all broken up now, and ferry traffic is ongoing."

"February 20 gives us five days. Any other details?"

"Quite a few, in fact. Our intelligence tells us that the train with forty drums of heavy water labeled POTASH LYE will travel down to the ferry station at Mael. They'll roll the railcars onto the ferry and, after the crossing, will load them again onto the train to Notodden. From there it's a short trip to Menstad and a ship bound for Germany."

"So, where along that route are we going to strike? At Vemork, along the line to Mael, at Notodden?"

Martinson sat down at the table and took off one boot. He seemed to be stalling, until he shook the boot and knocked out a tiny pebble. "Sorry. That's been killing me for hours. Anyhow, Sørlie, Haugland, and I hashed that out a few days ago. Striking at Vemork would be impossible now. It's too heavily guarded, and blowing up the train as it passed would kill the guards riding along."

Maarit frowned. "Which would bring more reprisals."

"Agreed. So that leaves the ferry port at Mael."

"Isn't that just as risky?"

"No, not at the port. In fact, that's the most vulnerable point in the transfer. It has lots of advantages for us. It's only about three kilometers south of here, easily reachable in a short time. From there we can plant a bomb to blow up the ferry in the deepest part of the lake, where they can't dredge it up again."

"And the ferry passengers? Won't they be mostly Norwegian?"

He glanced away for a moment, then replied with a noticeable lack of conviction. "We're assuming that once the ferry starts sinking, they'll be able to jump overboard. We expect the fishing boats around at that time can pick them up."

Kirsten fell silent. The water would be icy cold, and the passengers would be dressed in heavy winter clothing and boots. "I see," she said quietly.

"I know what you're thinking. Yes, there will be fatalities, but think of how many fatalities a radioactive bomb would cause. That's what's behind the whole program, after all, the Allies' belief that heavy water is used to develop a fission bomb."

"I'm a chemist, and I understand the process you're talking about. Heavy water can be used as a moderator in experiments with radioactivity. It just seems so…unlikely that the Germans are anywhere near creating a bomb. The deaths right now are what bother me, not the potential ones from some vague super-bomb that doesn't even exist yet."

Martinson nodded, obviously pained. "I know what you mean. But we're soldiers in a war, and if our side is to win, we have to trust that such decisions are made in good faith and follow the orders that come from them."

Skinnarland ended the discussion. "I've also radioed to Rjukan. Sørlie and Haugland are on their way here."

❖

An hour after Martinson had left to return to his own headquarters, Sørlie and Haugland arrived. All knew each other, so greetings were brief, and Skinnarland hastened to roll out a map of the land between themselves and Lake Tinn.

"I've laid out the areas of responsibility. Kirsten, I'd like you and Maarit to travel down to Mael and find out which ferries will be running on 20 February. You'll cause less suspicion than one of us."

"We'll leave immediately, but I know already that 20 February is a Sunday and only one ferry will be running. Why do we need to know which of the two it is?"

"Because the two are a little different, and we need to know where to place the explosives. Consequently, you also have to go on board and locate a place under the bow. We can't waste time doing that on the day of the action."

"Yes, sir." Kirsten exchanged glances with Maarit, who also seemed pleased to have a specific task in the operation.

Skinnarland continued. "Sørlie will fetch the detonator from our source, and Haugland is responsible for obtaining the explosive. After you've identified the best location and we've assembled the bomb, they'll go on board the night before to mount it. Any questions?"

"Do you think someone will recognize Kirsten?" Maarit asked. "She's a fugitive, after all. And easy to remember with that red hair."

"It's simple enough to keep her hair covered, and we'll give her a new identity card." He rummaged among items in the table drawer. "Here. This one looks a little like you." He handed her a battered card with grease spots that covered part of the photo. "It's unlikely anyone will ask you to show it. Just keep it, in case. We'll also issue you some money."

Kirsten studied the grimy card. "So I'm Britta Nielson, age forty-six. Nice," she added with faint sarcasm.

❖

On 18 February, two days before the transport, they made the leisurely two-hour ski trip to Mael. At the agreed-upon spot, they hid their skis and hiked the last half kilometer to the ferry terminal. Amazingly, they found virtually no guard. Bundled in their coats, they looked like two farm women, and no one glanced their way when they entered the terminal to check the posted schedule.

"There it is." Maarit tapped it with a finger. "February 20, nine o'clock departure, on the S/F *Hydro*."

"It's the ferry that's outside right now. What luck. We can simply go on board as passengers."

They pivoted around to the ticket window and purchased tickets. While they waited to join the line of passengers, Kirsten studied the steam ferry *Hydro*. It was larger than she expected, and uglier. Nothing about it was boat-like. It was flat-bottomed, with a wide, heavy bow that could break ice. Each side held railroad tracks, revealing its primary purpose was to transport materials on railcars in both directions across the lake. A disagreeable odor that hovered around it suggested one of those materials was chemical fertilizer. The tracks merged at the front, to allow movement of railcars to or from a single track on land. Tall black funnels stood on both sides of the bridge, making the whole vessel look more like a factory than a boat.

As they watched, some railcars slid onto the ferry and were bolted in place. Presumably they carried fertilizer, which the plant still produced. After the railcars were loaded, Kirsten and Maarit joined the line of people shuffling past a Norwegian policeman, marveling that the German forces in charge of the Vemork transfer had not yet installed their troops at Mael. Perhaps the war had robbed the occupying force of its best officers.

As they passed the gate, they had only to show their tickets, with no identification. The crowd moved down into the passenger section below deck, and Kirsten checked her watch. Right on time. According to the schedule, the crossing would take two hours.

Once they were underway, Maarit remained on deck, while Kirsten sought out a seaman and apologized for bothering him. The young man, with grease on his well-muscled hands, looked surprised to be spoken to. Apparently flattered at her attention, he smiled broadly and asked how he could help.

Casually, she removed her thick hat and ran her fingers through her striking red hair, fluffing it slightly. "You might not believe it, but I'm studying commercial naval engineering at Oslo. Really, I am. My father was a port captain before the war and wants me to follow in his footsteps."

The young seaman blinked, captivated by her interest in him, and most likely also her hair, waiting for her to tell him what she needed.

"Well, you may think I'm crazy, but I'd love to see the engine room. Would that be allowed? I just want to see what it looks like in person."

"Gosh. No woman's ever asked me that. Besides, it's pretty nasty down there. Aren't you worried you might get dirty, or even hurt?"

"Oh, I promise not to touch anything. I just want to look around. She slid a notebook and pencil from her pocket, to show how serious she was. "A vessel as big as this one must have a very powerful engine." She emphasized the word powerful.

He seemed nonplussed but eager to please. "Uh, I guess so. But stay close to me, and don't touch anything."

"Of course. I'll be right next to you. Is it okay if I make a few drawings?"

"That's fine. We have a lot of very complicated machines down here." His expression was a boyish mix of flirtation and pride. "I'll try to explain what each one does, and you can ask me questions if you want."

He led her deeper into the engine room, pointing out pieces of equipment as they walked. Replying with exclamations of girlish awe, she sketched out the layout of the room, the two large boilers and the coal-fed fireboxes that heated them. The machinery was indeed complicated, built close together, and half a dozen seamen were monitoring, oiling, or stoking the fire with coal, but that wasn't what worried her. With so many men moving about the engine room, it seemed impossible to plant an explosive that would remain undetected.

She would have to locate a place that was out of sight.

"Where is the bilge chamber" she asked suddenly.

"The bilge chamber?" He seemed astonished. "You don't want to see that. It's a dark, filthy place and stinks of rot and oil. Why would you want to go there?"

The more she thought about it, the more reasonable it seemed. "I know, but it's all part of the way a boat runs, isn't it? As important as the grease on the engine. So, I'd at least like to have a look at it, to compare it with the others I've seen. It will really impress my teachers. They think women don't want to get their hands dirty."

"All right." He agreed, reluctantly, and pointed toward a spot they'd just passed. At the center of the engine room, midway between the two boilers, he knelt and tugged on a metal ring. A wide metal plate, hinged at one side, came up in his hand. On the side opposite the hinge, a metal ladder dropped into darkness. He was right. It stank of oil and rot.

"Can I take a look inside?"

He shrugged. "Sure. If you insist." He stepped out of the way, and she knelt to peer into the pit.

It was perfect. By the indirect light of the engine room, she could see that a support beam ran horizontally across the chamber. She could just make out the bilge pump on the bow side, though it was irrelevant to her needs. It was easy to memorize the layout of things, and she could make a sketch later. She stood up again.

"Well, thank you for that revelation. It's certainly a well-built boat, and you obviously have your hands full to keep it running." She gave him a look of glowing admiration.

He beamed. "Yes, ma'am, we do our best. Unfortunately, I've got to work now, so you'll have to go back upstairs."

"Yes, of course. Sorry to keep you from your duties." She smiled warmly and patted his sleeve as she passed him. A sweet man. She'd been lucky to encounter him. She climbed the first ladder to the passenger level, and only as she stepped onto the second ladder up to the deck did it occur to her she was condemning him to death.

Chapter Sixteen

A day later at the cabin at Lauvhøgdi, the five of them sat around Skinnarland's table. "So, that's the detonator." Kirsten leaned forward on her elbows to study it.

Haugland shoved the apparatus to the center of the table. "Simplicity itself. Just two alarm clocks with the alarm bells removed." He tapped the place where they had been removed and replaced with copper and Bakelite plates. "These wires welded to the copper connect the clocks to the detonator caps. An electrical current will set them off."

Maarit leaned close, interested. "Where does the charge come from?"

"From these." Sørlie held up four large flashlight batteries.

"Very nice. Elegant, one might say."

"And everything attaches to these babies." Haugland opened a canvas sack to reveal two large rust-colored sausages.

"Nobel 808?" Kirsten asked. "It looks like the stuff we used at Vemork."

"Yes, but in a single big load instead of a series of small blasts. We calculate this will blow a hole about ten or eleven square feet in the hull."

Maarit frowned. "That's going to bring in a lot of water fast."

"That's the idea. Once it detonates, we don't want the ferry to limp toward shore and then sink in shallow water, where the Germans could retrieve their barrels. We'd be back where we started."

"It's also why we want to plant it under the bow," Sørlie added. "That way the ferry will go down bow first, raising the propellers up out of the water so they can't move any farther. We figure it will take four to five minutes to sink completely."

Maarit looked glum. "Four or five minutes. Not enough time for all the passengers to escape."

Skinnarland appeared pained. "Do you imagine we haven't already thought about that? We know we'll probably lose a few. We won't always have the luck we had at Vemork. But five minutes will allow most of the passengers to get into lifeboats or, if they're able-bodied, to stay afloat until one of the fishing boats picks them up."

"In near-freezing water," Maarit added in a monotone.

"What more can I say? We're doing our best to minimize civilian casualties. If this doesn't succeed, you can be sure London will send bombers to take out the cargo in port, and that will cost a lot more Norwegian lives."

Maarit nodded sullen agreement.

"All right." Sørlie redirected the conversation. "Tomorrow's the day, so we have to plant the explosive tonight. Do you have the diagram?"

Kirsten drew the sketches from her pocket and unfolded them on the table. "The engine room is no good. It'll be crawling with seamen even when they're docked, and I didn't see any place to hide the explosive. But the bilge compartment, just underneath, is perfect." She ran her finger along the horizontal beam she had drawn between the two bulkheads. "This is the ideal place to tape the whole apparatus. During the trip, no one has any reason to go down there, and the noise in the engine room will muffle the sound of the ticking."

"All right, then. We do a night ski to the Mael Terminal. Sometime after midnight, when the guard is bored and drowsy, we can slip aboard."

"I think you should also have some plan, in case the guard is increased," Skinnarland said.

The four of them exchanged glances, and Kirsten spoke. "Judging by their conspicuous absence yesterday, I'd say the Germans are focused on guarding the railcars and have completely overlooked any vulnerability on the ferry. Unfathomable."

Haugland snorted. "No wonder they're losing the war."

"One last question." Maarit raised her hand. "Are we absolutely certain the railcars with the heavy water will be on that particular ferry? Is there any possibility they'll be held up?"

"There's always a small chance, but it's unlikely. The train's scheduled to arrive tonight, and the railcars go out tomorrow morning. None of our contacts suggest a delay. Why do you ask?"

She chewed her lip. "I was just thinking that it's bad enough to sink a boat with dozens of civilians on it if it hurts the enemy. It would be appalling to do it for nothing."

Haugland snorted, obviously weary of the discussion.

Maarit still scowled, and the mood of the group changed. Skinnarland replied wearily, "Your reservations have been noted, but there's nothing we can do."

"Yes, there is. No one's looking for me. I can blend into the crowd of passengers, even buy a ticket. Once the railcars are loaded, I'll leave, and the operation will go forward. But if something prevents the transfer, if the Germans suddenly have a change of plan, or grow suspicious, I volunteer to go aboard and defuse the bomb."

"You can't do that without being captured. How would you explain, as a passenger, going down into the bilge compartment?"

"I wouldn't explain anything. I'd just do it. I could just say I heard rumors of someone planting a bomb. I'd be a hero, not a saboteur."

"I don't like it," Haugland said. "They're bound to suspect you, and besides, if the bomb is revealed, that ruins our chance of doing the same thing later."

"But you just said the transfer was almost certain. I'll just be the life-insurance policy—for the lives of the passengers."

Skinnarland had rested his chin on his clasped hands, his eyes darting back and forth between the two as they quarreled. Finally, he turned to Maarit.

"Look, I respect your humanitarian instincts, and since there's practically no chance the transfer will be halted, you can go ahead and join the crowd. Just stay on the edges, and as soon as the railcars roll onto the ferry, get the hell out of there. If, for some reason, they don't, you're authorized to tell one of the seamen you'd heard a bomb was on board and then disappear. If you're arrested, you'll be a major liability for all of us."

"I understand."

Kirsten studied Maarit's face, which, in spite of her moral victory, was still somber. Understandably, she wanted revenge for the murders of her family, but they both knew that blowing up a Norwegian ferry for a few barrels of water was a far cry from punishing the murderers.

❖

At seven o'clock Sunday morning, Kirsten and Maarit stood together at the periphery of the crowd of passengers on the dock at Mael. The saboteurs had done their work in the predawn hours, when the crew still slept and the seaman on watch waved them on board among the handful of early passengers who'd come from long distances and had no place to shelter before departure. Sørlie had assured them that the explosive was under the bilge water; only the clocks and detonator were visible, but only to someone who stepped halfway down the ladder.

Maarit bumped shoulders with Kirsten. "Look, the train from Vemork's pulling in. Seems like everything's on schedule. But, just to be sure, let's wait until the railcars are actually on the ferry before we leave."

Kirsten sighed and swept her gaze around the gathering crowd. The sight of the railcars rolling from the single land track onto one of the two tracks on the ferry had caught the attention of the passengers, not least because of the shouting and arm-waving of the dozen or so soldiers assigned to guard them.

But for some reason, after two railcars had rumbled onto the deck, the whole process came to a halt. Her stomach sank. What was wrong? Had someone discovered the detonator? Even worse, had something gone wrong in the transfer process itself?

"I don't like this," Kirsten muttered. "It's set to go off at ten o'clock exactly. If they delay too long, it'll blow up right in front of them, killing civilians while the railcars are undamaged." She waited another five minutes, then walked toward an old man leaning against the administrative building. "Did they announce why they stopped loading?"

"Nothing that I heard." He scratched his throat under his beard.

"Kirsten? Is that you?" A female voice startled her, and she turned. A woman approached her, carrying an infant partially buttoned inside her coat. Shocked and slightly panicked at being recognized, Kirsten squinted, trying to identify her.

"Don't you remember me? It's Sigrid Thorwald. We were in school together. Dear Lord. So many years ago. But I'd recognize that red hair of yours anywhere." She pointed toward the few strands that were visible. Grinning at her good luck, she stepped toward Kirsten and embraced her awkwardly, the baby pressed between them.

Kirsten pulled her scarf back up to her forehead, horrified that she'd allowed her hair to show. Such an amateurish mistake. At the same time, a sudden wave of memory washed over her. Sigrid, at thirteen, a year older than Kirsten, the most beautiful girl in her class. Long, thick, blond hair, ice-blue eyes, and the beginning of a bosom. Every boy in the class was smitten, and so was Kirsten. Her infatuation went so far as to produce an impetuous kiss in the winter darkness on the way home from school. The timid flirtation might have blossomed into something else, but Kirsten's emigration to Britain a few months later had prevented it.

"Oh, yes. Of course. You look wonderful!" She swept her glance over the two children and the baby curved over Sigrid's ample chest. Concealing her alarm, she feigned delight. "Motherhood becomes you."

"Well, I have gained a few pounds having these guys." She glanced down first at the infant and then at the two older children at her side. "This is Torsten, my oldest."

A child of perhaps five stared up with interest at Kirsten and Maarit, as if deciding whether he trusted them. The younger boy, who gripped his mother's coat, glanced up as well, with anxious eyes. Straw-blond, bright-blue-eyed, and angelic, he was the image of his mother. He clung to her coat and pressed his face against her leg.

"Arno is three, and the baby is Fredrika. We're just on our way to Tinnoset to visit my parents. They haven't yet seen their newest grandchild."

At that moment, the train started again, and the third railcar crept up the ramp onto the right track behind the two others. Once it was fully on board, an engineer detached it, and the remaining cars backed down momentarily. After clearing the right track, the rest of the railcars moved forward once again, pushed from behind by a locomotive, onto the left track. All the while, Sigrid kept up a running narrative of what she'd been doing since leaving school, pausing occasionally to ask Kirsten about her life since that time.

"Attention" came from the loudspeaker. "All passengers are requested to come on board. Departure in five minutes."

Kirsten was briefly relieved. The delay had been slight. The bomb would go off only slightly short of the deepest part of the lake.

The bomb. Just then the infant began to cry, and Kirsten had to glance away. A newborn infant had no chance in the freezing lake.

"Sigrid, are you sure you want to take these babies out on the lake in this cold? It can't be good for them. A cousin of mine works for this line and told me this ferry is barely seaworthy. The engine room is held together with spit and string. Besides, you and I have so many things to talk about. Why don't you come back with me to Rjukan and catch the ferry tomorrow? I really want to spend time with you. I'll even pay for your ticket."

"Oh, you're so sweet, Kirsten. That would be nice, but I can't. My parents are waiting for us at the terminal across the lake. Their new grandchild is the first girl in the family. It's also my mother's birthday. We'll have to meet another time. Give me your address when we're on board."

Kirsten cringed inwardly, already imagining the sinking ferry, with passengers struggling toward a lifeboat, of Sigrid in the icy water with three drowning children. She was sick to her stomach.

"Final call," the loudspeaker crackled at them. "All passengers must be on board. Departure in two minutes!"

"I'll sit with you," she said abruptly, drawing her ticket from the previous day out of her pocket.

Maarit seized her by the arm, pulling her aside. "What the hell are you doing?!" she whispered.

"I have to go," Kirsten said. "I'll stand near a lifeboat until the explosion. I have to get at least one of them on it."

Maarit snorted exasperation. "Look. Half a dozen fishing boats are on the lake. Someone will fish them out."

"Only those who can stay afloat for God knows how long. The icy water will kill the children. Don't try to stop me."

Maarit closed her eyes for a beat, then nodded. "All right, then. I'm going with you so we can save two. If we can get on board." Together they shuffled forward in the middle of the crowd that pressed toward the entry gate.

In the hurry to urge passengers on board and make up for lost time, the seaman at the gate barely glanced at the ticket each person held up and waved them all through. The air over the ferry blew icy cold, and to escape the wind, all the passengers filed along the passageway down the ladder to the lower deck.

The ferry embarked immediately. In spite of her nervous excitement and fear, Kirsten knew this meant they'd probably be over deep water more or less according to plan. She checked her watch. Nine twenty. She had forty minutes to convince Sigrid to come up on deck, if she and her children would have any chance of surviving.

She sat down next to Sigrid in the passenger hold, while Maarit remained standing and seemed to be trying to catch the eye of the oldest boy.

"I'm sorry," Sigrid said. "I was so busy babbling about myself and my family, I didn't ask very much about you. What have you been doing all these years? I seem to remember you left Norway before we finished school. To Britain, right?"

"Yes, in 1920, with my mother. But I came back to study chemistry at Oslo University, until Terboven closed it down. Oh, excuse me. This is my friend, Maarit."

"Chemistry. Oh, my! Well, you always were a smarty. We called you 'sticky brain' behind your back. Torsten, my oldest, is a bit like that. I'd be happy if he studied chemistry."

That seemed to be Maarit's signal. She bent toward the boy and caught his eye. "I bet you like ships, too. All the smart boys I know like ships. How about we go up on deck and look around this one? Then we can look at the fishing boats and see if you can name them." She threw a look toward Sigrid. "But only if Mama says you can."

Sigrid smiled, apparently relieved to have one less child to entertain. "It's all right. Just be careful."

"Don't worry. Lots of children in my family. I'm very good with them."

As they hurried toward the ladder leading up to the deck, Kirsten studied her watch, calculating how much time remained. Twenty minutes. Unconsciously, she tapped her foot.

"You seem nervous."

"Uh…yes, I am." She invented freely, as Maarit had just done.

"Someone's meeting me on the other bank also. A colleague, but neither one of us knows what the other one looks like. We're meeting some others as well, and it would be a bad beginning to arrive late."

Sigrid leaned sideways and whispered, "Someone in the resistance?"

Taken aback, Kirsten maintained a neutral expression. "That's not something I can answer, is it?"

Sigrid smiled conspiratorially. "Oh, I hope so. I hate it that the Germans control us and that so many Norwegians are quislings. If that's your reason for the crossing, then go with my blessing." She rocked her baby, Madonna-like.

Kirsten swallowed hard but gave no sign of agreement. If Sigrid survived the explosion, she would know who and what caused it, would guess that Kirsten was somehow involved. A dangerous knowledge. And if she lost one of her children, an excruciating one.

Arno tugged at his mother's sleeve. "Mama. Pippi," he mumbled, as if ashamed.

"Oh, dear. I was afraid of this. He went back at the station, but he obviously has to go again. And he's just now learning to tell me. I don't even know where the toilet is."

"It's over there, down the ladder to the second deck." Kirsten snatched a quick look at her watch. Ten minutes. "I'll hold the baby while you take him. But please hurry, before she wakes up and screams."

Smiling gratitude, Sigrid unbuttoned her coat and slid the sleeping infant into Kirsten's arms. With an expression of maternal resignation, she took her son by the hand. "We'll be back in a few minutes." She hurried off with the toddler stumbling beside her.

Four minutes passed, then five, then six, and Kirsten's heart pounded. How long did it take a little boy to pee? Though perhaps he had soiled himself, too, and had to be washed. Her mouth dry with anxiety, she edged toward the ladder leading up to the main deck. Two minutes left. She climbed the ladder to the deck and saw the lifeboat in its place. Why was there only one? It couldn't possibly accommodate all the passengers and crew. And where was Maarit?

She held the newborn close to her inside her jacket as Sigrid had done, while a small part of her consciousness registered that they had made up the lost time and were indeed midway across the lake. One minute left. Dear God. Where was Maarit? How had the operation turned out so badly? She paced across the deck past working seamen and a couple of German guards idly smoking. She peered down the starboard passageway. No one was moving.

Was there still time to call "fire" down to the lower deck to start the passengers running?

While she struggled with uncertainty she heard the dull thud of the bomb detonating. She startled violently, and inside her coat the infant began to wail against her chest.

The ferry continued to move forward for a few minutes, then stopped, and she felt the deck tilt as the bow began to drop. "The lifeboat," Kirsten shouted toward one of the seamen. "Lower the damned lifeboat!"

Another seaman appeared, and together they untied the boat, reeled it out over the water, then lowered it until its gunwale was even with that of the ferry. The bow continued to sink, and the entire ferry was listing toward starboard. A dull whirl behind her told her the screws were out of the water spinning uselessly. With the painful screech of metal against metal, the first of the railcars on the starboard side plunged into the water, dragging the others with it. Only the cars on the port side remained.

Passengers were streaming up from the lower deck shouting and screaming, but none of them was Sigrid. Or Maarit. Dear God, where was Maarit? Desperate, she took a few steps toward the port side, hoping to catch sight of her, but the starboard list increased, and the port railcars began rocking, threatening to crash down onto the deck. Kirsten felt horribly alone and guilty. Sigrid's infant wailed, as if in accusation.

"Women and children!" One of the officers had taken charge of the lifeboat. A seaman shoved her toward the boat, and with a last desperate look around, Kirsten obeyed.

A dozen other women and a few men crowded in with her, and when the lifeboat hit the water, two seamen rowed it away from the listing vessel. The ferry groaned for a moment, then slipped fully onto its starboard side. The port railcars separated from their tracks and toppled sideways, crushing the bridge and smokestack. A few remaining passengers who had managed to struggle up from below decks now slid or jumped into the surging water amidst the sinking railcars and debris.

All around the sinking ferry, heads bobbed in the water screaming, hands waved, and Kirsten searched among them for Maarit. In the distance, fishing boats were approaching, two, then three, but how long could the passengers stay afloat in boots and winter coats, their limbs slowly growing numb?

"Over there, a child," someone in the lifeboat called out, and Kirsten turned. It was Maarit, swimming on her back and grasping Torsten against her shoulder. The seamen stopped rowing, waiting for them to cross the last few meters.

Handing the still-wailing infant to her neighbor, Kirsten leaned over the side of the lifeboat and hauled the drenched Maarit and the child to safety. Maarit exhaled relief, but the little boy was unresponsive. "He's freezing." Kirsten stated the obvious as she yanked off his sodden little woolen jacket, then drew off her own dry coat and wrapped it around him.

The first fishing boat came close and began heaving people on board, those who had not sunk from the weight of their boots and coats, and who hadn't drowned from cold paralysis. Kirsten saw no more children; only the newborn Fredrika and the stunned five-year-old Torsten had made it.

"You all right?" she asked Maarit. "I thought I'd lost you."

"Don't worry about me," she said through chattering teeth. "I'm fine." Dazed, she stared at the bubbles surrounding the spot where the ferry had sunk. Her dull glance seemed to say, *We sank those goddam barrels. I hope to God London is finally satisfied.* Kirsten too thought of the sunken barrels of heavy water and found it impossible to feel victory. She could only think of one name, Sigrid. Sigrid and her beautiful, angelic boy, who looked just like her.

Kirsten leaned toward her neighbor and took the infant in her arms again. She had worn herself out crying and now only whimpered. Maarit nudged Torsten and showed him his little sister, to comfort him, but all he said, finally, was "Mama."

Very soon no more heads were visible in the water, and the rescued passengers sat in stunned silence. The only sound was the creaking of the oars as the seamen rowed them on toward the other side of the lake.

As they pulled up to the dock, a dozen or so people swarmed toward them along the pier, arms outstretched, ready to bring them in. Holding children, Kirsten and Maarit were among the first lifted to safety. Other passengers came immediately behind them, some staggering into the arms of relatives. Those, the lucky ones, walked together back up to the station. Others in the waiting crowd who didn't see their loved ones stared out toward the incoming fishing boats, obviously frantic and hopeful.

Kirsten stood for a moment, at a loss. How would they recognize Sigrid's parents? Then, as the crowd thinned out and only a dozen people remained, they appeared, unmistakable.

An elderly couple hurried toward them, obviously recognizing their grandson Torsten, and Kirsten felt tears welling. Sigrid's mother was her very image, an older version of the stunning blond woman Kirsten had once been smitten with. Now her face was strained with fear as she knelt and embraced the boy.

"My daughter. Have you seen my daughter?" she asked, looking up.

Kirsten shook her head, unable to speak. Maarit replied, "We didn't see her in the water. But…there's still a chance."

The man, gaunt, clean-shaven, and with a full head of white hair, bent over the infant in Kirsten's arms. "Is this…her baby?"

Kirsten placed the child in his arms and forced herself to speak. "Yes. She gave her to me to hold while she took Arno to…" She stopped, choked by the ludicrousness and horror of two cruel deaths, because a child had wet himself.

"This is your coat?" the man asked, indicating the jacket that was bundled around Torsten.

"Yes. He was freezing when he came out of the water. My friend swam with him to the lifeboat." She nodded toward Maarit, who was still drenched and shivered visibly.

"Go up to the station and get dry," he said. "You too, Hanne," he said to his wife. "I'll stay here and watch for her in the other rescue boats."

Without speaking, the three of them trudged with the two children along the dock to the station, where a cast-iron stove gave off some warmth. Other passengers were already huddled around it, but seeing how drenched Maarit was, they made room for her. She stripped off her coat and laid it over the back of a chair, then drew the chair up close to the stove to sit on it.

Obviously numb with fear, if not bereavement, Hanne still clutched her granddaughter to her chest and seemed unable to speak. Kirsten could have found nothing to say in any case.

The other passengers spoke in undertones to each other, thanking God for saving them and speculating about what had happened.

"I was near the ladder, so I got out. But I heard an explosion coming from the engine room."

His neighbor disagreed. "No, it was lower than that. Right under the hull, like from a mine."

"Who would mine the lake? Only Norwegians traveled across it, except for today."

"You think someone wanted to blow up the Germans? We had a dozen of them, guarding their train."

A third voice said, "Maybe they wanted to blow up the train."

"Why would they do that?"

"I think they were carrying something special. That's why they were guarding it."

"If they were after the train, then the explosion came from the resistance."

"Yes, the resistance, and they didn't care how many of us they killed. The bastards."

Kirsten cringed inwardly. The simple passengers crossing on the ferry had worked it out in short order. The Germans would have done so in even less time and would be searching for the saboteurs.

The crowd cursed among themselves, then fell silent, and Kirsten glanced toward Hanne, who stood clutching the children and sobbing softly. She drifted over to Maarit, who shivered on her chair, and laid a hand on her back.

Some ten minutes later, Hanne's husband came through the station door. Hanne glanced up, but his appalled expression told them there were no more survivors. She pressed her face against her granddaughter's blanket and groaned softly.

Her husband embraced her, pressing his cheek on her hair, then lifted the young Torsten into his arms. Then, seeming to hold back his own tears, he approached them as they huddled by the stove.

"I'm sorry. You saved two of my grandchildren, and I haven't asked your names."

"Kirsten." She deliberately omitted her family name. At no cost could she let him make the connection with Jomar Brun and the heavy water at Vemork.

Maarit also gave only her first name.

He forced a polite smile. "My name is Torsten. The same as our grandson. And my wife is Hanne. No one was here to meet you?" he asked. Kirsten shook her head but provided no explanation.

"Then why don't you come back with us? Our house is in Tinnoset, just a few kilometers from here. You can dry out properly and have something hot to drink."

Kirsten exchanged glances with Maarit. They hadn't planned on this, but it was clear that whatever they did next, they had to get away from the station, a place the Germans would surely investigate. Even if Maarit escaped scrutiny, Kirsten was still a fugitive.

"You'll never get dry here." Without waiting for an answer, Torsten nodded toward the station door. "Our wagon is just outside," he said and, with his free hand, drew Maarit up from her chair.

Kirsten helped Maarit into her still-damp coat, and they all filed out. The same February air they had endured in the lifeboat hit them again, more cruelly than before, after their few minutes by the fire.

They rode silently, for they had nothing to say, until the wagon arrived at the house of Hanne and Torsten, a two-story wooden structure with a porch. It was painted black but enlivened with a bright-red door and red window casings. The roof was covered with turf, though at the corners, she could see signs of slate tiles. On one side, the house extended to a low addition with a double door. When Torsten unhitched the mare and guided her to it, she could see it was a sort of barn.

While he saw to the horse, Hanne led them up the steps and into the house.

The interior was rustic and warm, with a floor of varnished pine planks. Only the area in front of the fireplace was brick. On one side, a staircase led upstairs, and on the other a tall wooden cabinet was painted pale blue and decorated with rose garlands. Shelves on both sides of the fireplace held books, pottery, and framed photos. Two wooden armchairs covered with knitted blankets in front of the fire obviously served as warming places.

Hanne marched directly to the stairs. "Excuse me, but the baby needs changing, and I must find something dry for Torsten. Please, go warm yourselves by the fire." Without waiting for a reply, she mounted the stairs, holding the baby against her chest and grasping the hand of her grandson.

Kirsten and Maarit stood awkwardly for a moment, then migrated toward the fireplace, where embers still gave off heat. A small pile of wood lay close by in a tin tub. Maarit drew a small log from the pile and laid it on the embers, stirring them until the new wood took flame.

"Oh, that feels so good." She drew off her coat and hung it on one of the iron hooks embedded in the mantelpiece for just such purpose. After a moment of hesitation, she slid off her trousers as well and hung them on the adjacent hook. Both garments gave off steam.

Kirsten grabbed one of the blankets from the chairs and wrapped it around her. "Here. I'm sure they won't mind."

Maarit warmed herself, pivoting in a small arc to bring heat to as much of her body as possible, then looked toward Kirsten. "What are we going to tell them?"

"Well, I was thinking—"

The sound of the opening front door interrupted her. The elder Torsten stepped in, panting slightly, and drew off his hat and heavy gloves. "Oh, good. You've stoked the fire. We'll be warm shortly. It's a good fireplace." He slid off his coat, hung it on the hook at the back of the door, and joined them in front of the flames.

"I'll have to leave again soon to go to the post office to use their phone. Sigrid's husband probably doesn't know about the explosion, and it will be my terrible duty to tell him."

"Yes, of course. We understand. We have to be on our way also, as soon as Maarit's clothes are dry."

He rubbed his hands and held them out over the fire. "I'm sorry we can't offer you a supper, but as you can see my wife is in no state to prepare food for guests. The children will demand her full attention, and I have to leave in a while as well. But we are deeply grateful to you for saving two of our grandchildren. I will make you some tea to warm you while you wait for your clothes to dry."

He strode toward what was presumably the kitchen.

"Tuddal," Kirsten whispered when he was gone. "We were on

our way to Tuddal. To visit your aunt." She squinted for a moment, then elaborated. "Aunt...Birgit," she invented freely. "A widow. No children, only you, the niece. She has gray hair and a cat, and reads Ibsen."

Maarit chuckled. "You're really good at making things up. You should write a novel."

Torsten reappeared with two mugs of steaming tea. "I added a little sugar. You deserve it."

He handed over the mugs, and they warmed their hands on the hot porcelain.

"Where are you headed, anyhow? Torsten asked.

"Tuddal," Maarit replied immediately. My aunt lives there, and she lost her husband last year. She has only me and the cat, so we'll be checking up on her."

He stood next to them, rubbing his hands. "Tuddal is about seven kilometers northwest of here. How did you plan to get there after the ferry?"

"Well, uh, by ski, of course. We're both good skiers, but they were lost, along with our luggage, when the ferry went down."

"I'm sorry to hear that." He stared into the flames for a moment, then took a breath and spoke as if he had made a decision. "We owe you so much, I'll be happy to give you skis. We have a pair from our son, old but still serviceable. He's in Sweden and will never touch them again." His glance swept over the two of them, acknowledging that one pair alone wouldn't suffice. "And we have our daughter's skis." His voice grew soft. "I'm sure she'd be happy to know you had them."

Kirsten nodded and glanced away, speechless. Maarit spoke for both of them. "You're very generous."

"Well, while you wait for your clothes to dry, I'll check on my wife and grandchildren. Please excuse me." He hurried away.

Maarit squeezed the arm of her coat. "Still damp," she murmured, then reversed coat and trousers to expose their other side to the heat.

Kirsten stood next to her with her eyes closed. "How I hate this war," she muttered, cringing at the banality of the sentiment. Everyone hated the war, and they were the ones who waged it.

They stood in excruciating silence, holding their outspread hands over the flames, Maarit adding wood as needed. Their alibi was established; they no longer needed to conspire, only to escape. Kirsten heard the wall clock ticking while they waited.

Torsten returned, just as Maarit was sliding on her newly dried trousers. "Oh, good," he said, and stepped forward to help her on with her coat. "If you're ready, we can go to the barn for the skis. Then I'll go down with you to the road, though we have to travel in opposite directions. You're going to Tuddal, you say?"

Kirsten avoided his glance. "Tuddal, yes."

As they entered the barn, the horse snorted, acknowledging them. Torsten patted its flank, then grasped the skis that leaned against the barn wall. Maarit took the older, heavier skis, and he handed the shinier ones to Kirsten. "The bindings on both are simple and should fit over your boots." He looked away as Kirsten tied them on, though it must have torn him apart to hand over his daughter's skis.

They skied outside and waited while he closed up the barn. A farewell of some sort was in order, but pleasantries seemed out of place. Instead, he shook hands with both of them, said merely "Thank you. God speed," and stepped off toward the post office and his grim task.

Still wordless, they began their trek northwest, not to Tuddal, but along the lake shore, then in a curve westward to avoid Mael, and ultimately back to the cabin at Lauvhøgdi.

They traveled through the night, until Maarit finally spoke up. "So, what are we going to tell Skinnarland? The others will have already reported back, and they probably think we're dead."

"They'll see we're not dead. And we'll tell him that we accomplished his filthy mission, at a sickening cost. If SOE doesn't care about killing Norwegian children, the king will care. Tronstad will care."

Maarit grunted agreement but declined to say *I told you so.*

They reached the cabin late the next morning. Even before they knocked, the door opened. Skinnarland's initial frown of confusion suddenly brightened. "You survived after all! Haugland and Sørlie saw you go on board, and we all thought you'd drowned."

"No, we didn't." They strode past him into the cabin and marched to the stove, where they removed their gloves. Kirsten was brusque. "A cup of coffee would be good right now. And do you have any food? We haven't eaten since yesterday."

Obviously taken aback by her abruptness, Skinnarland hesitated for a moment, then reached for the kettle. "Yes, of course." He spooned out coffee powder from a battered canister into the kettle and set it on the stove. "So, you're going to tell me what happened?" He removed a cloth from a loaf of dark bread and sliced off two large hunks.

Only after they had finished their breakfast did Kirsten begin. "It was my idea." She swallowed the last of her coffee. "I saw someone I knew among the passengers. She had three children, and one was a newborn."

Skinnarland rubbed his forehead wearily. "What did you expect to accomplish by joining them?" he asked softly.

"I hoped to save her and the children. We rescued two out of the four."

"And endangered the mission. What if you had been identified while boarding? They would have stopped the departure, and the bomb would have gone off anyhow. It was a reckless, sentimental act that could have undone months of planning. You know as well as anyone that removing the heavy water was critical to winning the war. Your impulsive behavior reminds me of why I don't like to use women in our operations."

You bastard, Kirsten thought, but said nothing. To her surprise, Maarit struck back.

"Don't be an ass. If it were up to you, wars would be fought until annihilation and won by the last man standing."

Skinnarland blinked at the insult, then took a breath. "Look, I'm a Norwegian citizen too, but we can't all go around making up our own rules. Defense requires organization and trust in the leadership. No army could ever fight if every soldier applied his personal moral judgment, and neither could Milorg."

"Maybe that's the problem," Kirsten muttered, but as soon as she said it, she heard how naive she sounded.

Skinnarland set aside his cup and moved to the radio. "In any case, I was about to radio Tronstad, and now I can add the news that you're here. I'll also mention your personal misgivings."

He lifted his code book out from under the radio table and set about composing the message.

The all-night ski journey had left them both exhausted, so, having made their case, they both lay down on the two cots in the cabin. Sleep came quickly.

❖

Kirsten felt a hand pushing lightly on her shoulder. She sat up, stupefied, focusing on Skinnarland. "Was I out long?"

"Long enough. Both of you slept through a radio transmission and a windstorm."

She peered out the tiny cabin window to see a landscape of complete calm. The windstorm was old news. "Radio transmission? From London?"

"Yes, and most of it concerned you."

She shook Maarit, who sat up beside her. "News from London. About us." To Skinnarland, "What did he say?"

"He commended both of you for your service." He handed them both cups of coffee.

"Oh, that's nice," Kirsten said between sips. "Did you mention my objections?"

"I said you found the loss of life excessive."

"That was an understatement."

"It was enough. Torstad thinks you should return to the UK."

"Return? Because of my moral objections?"

"Partially. But there's something else."

"What's that?"

"Your mother's sick. Cancer of the pancreas." His voice softened. "I'm sorry to be the bearer of bad news."

She recoiled. "My mother? Cancer?" Her thoughts roiled. How to respond? What should she do? She glanced at Maarit but saw only puzzlement. Finally, she took recourse in the practical. "How am I supposed to get there?"

Skinnarland shrugged. "The same way you got there before. By fishing boat to the Shetlands."

"They're still in operation?"

"Most definitely. And as it happens, we need a courier to carry documents back to SOE headquarters. Aerial maps of the Norwegian coast, pinpointing German positions."

The surprise news caused her to veer away from her personal crisis. "You mean the Allies plan to invade Europe through Norway?"

"Nobody knows the answer to that. But they've asked for the maps, and we need to send them. You'd pick them up in Trondheim. Someone up there would determine when and where you will meet the Shetland carrier."

"Trondheim? That's over three hundred kilometers."

"Four hundred, in fact. The best route would be to trek the distance to Lillehammer and get on the train. They'll be checking identification, of course, but you have an invented card, and Lillehammer is far enough away from Oslo that they won't be so much on the lookout for you."

Kirsten was speechless. The degree of detail suggested people had already made plans for her departure.

Skinnarland stood up and pulled on his parka. "Now that you're awake, I have to try to find some meat for us."

He pulled his hood up over his handsome head, picked up his rifle from the corner of the cabin, and marched outside, leaving them in a tense silence behind him.

After a few moments, Maarit collected the empty coffee cups and took them to the sink. "So, you'll be leaving Norway," she said lightly, staring down at her hands as she washed them.

"I…I don't really want to. But…I'm not sure."

Maarit turned to face her. "You have to be with your mother now, in her last hours. If you don't go, it will haunt you for the rest of your life. I know."

Her eyes closed, Kirsten nodded morosely. "And if the invasion comes through Norway—it's what we've been hoping for. I can't refuse to be a part of that."

"No, you can't. It would be more important, even, than Vemork."

Kirsten came to her side and took her hand. "Will you travel north with me, to Trondheim?"

"Of course I will. I'll stay with you until the moment you climb aboard your fishing boat for the trip back to the Shetlands. I'll wave good-bye to you with a handkerchief."

Kirsten frowned at the image. "It won't be good-bye." She leaned forward, enfolding Maarit in her arms. "I'll come back. I promise," she said into her hair. "Do you believe me?"

They held the embrace for long moments, as if each kept the other standing. Then Maarit breathed, "I believe you *want* to come back."

"How could you imagine I would meet anyone like you again? Please trust me, the way I trust you to wait for me."

"Of course I'll wait, for the same reason." She snorted. "Do you think I'm suddenly going to fall for the next Sami herder who shows up at my goahti?"

"It could be a long wait. I may not be free to come back until the war's end. The Germans are losing on the eastern front, but it could be many months before they capitulate."

"I can wait. I have a lot to settle in Udsek anyhow, now that my family is reduced to Gaiju and who knows how many reindeer. When you return, I'll be easy to find. Besides, if the invasion is through Norway, they'll need you here, won't they?"

"They might, but I'm coming back anyhow, no matter what. After the war, my father will want to rush back to Norway, too. They'll need him for postwar reconstruction, and they'll be asking for chemists. So, you see, we'll be together, you and I, if we can just wait."

They both smiled at the pledge they'd made, and Maarit snickered. "How silly we are. This is the first time in days we've been alone in a warm place. Why haven't you kissed me yet?"

"Because you haven't stopped talking." Kirsten tightened her grasp around Maarit's waist and covered her mouth with a smile-kiss that tasted of coffee and stifled laughter. They had slept in an embrace many times, but they still had so much to learn about each other. Skinnarland's cabin wasn't the place to do it.

A gunshot outside the cabin startled them apart.

Alarmed, Kirsten bent toward the cabin's one window, then exhaled relief. "Relax. It's Skinnarland. Looks like he's caught something for lunch."

Maarit smiled, wan. "I'd have preferred a few more minutes with you, but lunch is good, too."

Moments later, he strode through the door holding the carcass of a snow hare. "Meat, my dears. And I have some frozen potatoes to make you a stew before your trip north."

So, it was decided. She'd never had a choice, so it was just as well she'd agreed.

Kirsten would have called Skinnarland a comrade, but not a friend, and the sharing of private feelings was simply not done. But they'd worked together a long time now, and while the three of them prepared the hare and potatoes and stoked the fire, a certain domestic tranquility settled over them.

"The circumstances are sad, of course, but at least you'll be going home to family," Skinnarland observed, peeling off the animal's skin. "Families are important, and our kind of work tends to tear them apart."

"I hadn't thought about it that way," Kirsten admitted. "I guess that happens to the men, too. Do any of them have wives and children?"

"They do. Haugland's wife is in Sweden, and he hasn't seen her in ages. Torstad, stuck in Britain, has been away from his wife and children since the war began. Me, I'm still single. I have…someone… but we won't marry until after the war. What's the point if you can't be together?"

Maarit frowned. "Of course, our kind of work keeps us separated. But while you're out in the field, or in prison, for that matter, knowing someone you love is waiting for you keeps you going. In wartime, above all, you need someone to anchor you, someone to give you a reason to endure, even if they're far away. Otherwise, if we have no family, no…lovers, what are we fighting for?"

Kirsten studied her earnest expression and took it as a declaration of love.

CHAPTER SEVENTEEN

After the long trek from the cabin to Lillehammer, and a few tense moments as they purchased rail tickets under the watch of quisling policemen, they boarded the train, set their skis on the overhead rack, and tried to remain inconspicuous for the remainder of the journey.

Trondheim, at the end of February, was frigid and overcast, a glum atmosphere in which everyone hunched deep in their coats, sullen and anonymous. The city streets were unsuitable for skiing, so they continued on foot to the Norwegian Institute of Technology. As directed by Tronstad, they located the service entrance. Upon knocking, they were met by an elderly man with snow-white hair and a well-trimmed beard. Father Christmas, Kirsten thought, and might have smiled at the idea if she weren't so depressed.

"Hello. Welcome to Trondheim. I'm Iver." He seized first Kirsten's, then Maarit's hand and shook each firmly. "We heard what you did at Vemork, so it is an honor to meet you."

"Um, yes." Kirsten wondered how the news had spread and noted that he made no mention of the ferry sinking at Lake Tinn. Something to be less proud of. But she was cold and had no interest in social niceties. "We understand you have some documents for us."

He clasped his hands, a gesture that seemed almost jovial. "I do indeed. We'll see to it that you have them in hand when you depart. Everything is arranged. You'll be traveling on the *Hitra*. It's far offshore now, but before dawn it will anchor near the village of Trolla, some five kilometers north of here. It has only one dock, and someone will be waiting for you there with a rowboat between four and five o'clock tomorrow morning. If you don't make it on time, they'll leave without you."

"Between four and five," Kirsten repeated, glancing at the afternoon sky. "Good. That gives us a few hours to rest. Can you accommodate us in the meantime?"

"Of course. Any number of our people would be happy to put you up for these few hours, but it's probably best if we get you out of sight immediately. In fact, it's safest if you pass the time here in the institute."

"That'll be fine. It's not long."

Her voice must have conveyed their fatigue, for he bent forward solicitously. "You've come a long way, and I'm sure you don't want to stand around chatting. I'll take you to a place where you can rest, even have a little sleep before leaving."

He turned abruptly and guided them to the back of the institute's main building. Stopping at one of the doors, he drew out a key and unlocked it, turning the light switch as they entered.

"I apologize for having to put you a storage room. We weren't sure when you'd arrive, or how long you'd have to wait for the *Hitra* to come in. We've left a bit of food for you, along with some blankets." He gestured toward the rear of the room. "Once again, I'm happy to meet you and hope all goes well with the departure. When you leave, simply pull the door closed, and it'll lock by itself." After two more vigorous handshakes, he was gone.

It was a dusty place, filled with stacks of chairs, empty bookshelves, and a wall of cardboard boxes. It smelled sour, like badly washed clothing that had dried too slowly. Atop one of the boxes lay several coarse mats, presumably used for packing. They served quite well as bedding over the concrete floor. The promised blankets were also there, along with a box of dried cheese, crisp bread, and a bottle of local beer. As a shelter, it was a variation on Birgit's storeroom in Rjukan.

The cold supper did little to dispel the glumness, but after eating, they laid out the mats and blankets and rolled up their coats as pillows. As they had in so many back rooms, barns, goahtis, and snow caves, they lay in each other's arms, always with Kirsten on the inside of the embrace.

They had slept this way for months, their intimacy evolving from practicality to something more tender and romantic. But always the cold, squalor, and discomfort had kept sexual desire inchoate. And yet it grew, at least for Kirsten, until it seemed to fill her, crouching inside her like another creature. Now, on the eve of their separation, it moaned to be released.

Kirsten twisted around to face Maarit and ran trembling fingertips along her cheek and lips. "Surely you know that I want you."

Maarit closed her eyes for a moment, allowing the touch. "What does it mean, that you 'want me'?"

"You know what I mean. You just want to make me say it."

"Yes. Say it." She blinked slowly, and her dark eyes seemed to smolder.

"I want more than kisses. I want to touch you and thrill you with my fingers, to make you crave more and beg me not to stop. I want you to belong to me and become excited when you think of me."

"You could have told me sooner. I was always here, right next to you."

"I just was waiting for a bath and a clean bed. I wanted it to be perfect, and thrilling, not something you simply agreed to, like with Niilas."

Maarit kissed the tip of her nose. "It could never be like that. Ordinary. With you it's like we're outlaws."

Kirsten laughed softly into her neck. "That's what we are. Fugitives, bandits. Living on the fringes, hiding in storerooms and on the vidda, with no bath in sight." She kissed Maarit's throat, sensing the pulse against her lips. Unhurried, she undid the belt around Maarit's sweater, slipping her hands underneath the rough wool. She let her hands warm for a moment on the soft flesh, then inched farther along to caress Maarit's breasts. Such wonderful breasts, which she had never seen. Firm and youthful, they seemed to swell against her hand as she brushed her fingers over them.

She tilted her head back, searching for Maarit's mouth, found it, and pressed a long, soft kiss, exhaling a sound of longing. Maarit responded, and the kiss became a back-and-forth of lips and tongue and teeth, each movement increasing the ardor of the other.

Outlaws. Lawless creatures, without rules or expectations, witnesses or judge. Just the two of them in a vacuum, with no before or after, and nothing was illicit. She slid her hand downward inside Maarit's trousers and felt her startle slightly, then surrender to the intimate touch. Her fingers, too, were bandits, which crept along the warm belly to do what wasn't allowed or even spoken of, at the place that waited.

But the innocent place was already welcoming and wet to the outlaw touch.

"Yes, oh, yes," Maarit breathed. "Don't stop."

Kirsten didn't stop.

❖

They had scarcely fallen asleep when loud knocking awakened them. As expected, it was Iver, who carried a leather briefcase that had obviously seen many years of service. "Everything that needs delivering is here. The people at the other end will know what to do with it."

Kirsten accepted the briefcase, noting it was locked. "I'm to carry this to London, to Lief Tronstad?"

"To him or to Mr. Wilson. I've let you sleep as long as possible, but you really must leave now if you're to cover the distance by ski in time. Thank you again for this service." He shook their hands again with the same vigor as before and directed them toward the coastal road.

After wolfing down the last scraps of cheese and now-stale bread, they set out from the institute. Outside the town, where the snow was smooth, they buckled on their skis and made the five-kilometer hike northward along the coast to the village of Trolla. Arriving at the main dock, they checked their watches and determined it was shortly after four thirty.

To their disappointment, the glamorous sub-chaser that promised a speedy and luxurious trip across the North Sea wasn't visible. The *Hitra* obviously still waited offshore in the darkness, for only a rowboat was present. One man sat in the boat, and a second approached them on the dock. He was short and burly, with more bulk than she was used to seeing on the men around her. He must have enjoyed better rations than the average Norwegian. With a wide beard and dense head of hair, he wasn't someone she would ever want an altercation with.

"What are you looking for here at this hour?" he asked brusquely.

Kirsten gave the required response. "We were told fishermen went out at night, and we were hoping to buy some of the catch."

He scratched his beard, clearly suspicious. "They said there'd only be one of you."

"Yes. That's me. My friend will be staying." She turned to Maarit. "Here. Take the rest of our money. I meant to give it to you earlier." She slid a handful of kroner from her pocket and dropped it into Maarit's hand. Then she slipped out of her skis and kicked them aside.

Burly bearded man obviously decided all was correct and was already climbing down onto the rowboat. Now men both waited impatiently.

She embraced Maarit quickly. "Please don't forget me," she whispered in Maarit's ear.

"Please come back to me," Maarit whispered back.

Kirsten tightened her hold. "I will. In six months, I promise. If I'm alive, I'll find a way back. I love you." Then she turned abruptly and stepped onto the ladder to the rowboat.

❖

Holding back tears, Maarit watched until the rowboat disappeared from sight. She trusted Kirsten's declaration but was no fool. A war was on, and a hundred things could happen, starting from that very night, that could prevent her return. She shook her head. It was torture to think about them, so she picked up Kirsten's discarded skis and began the trip back to Trondheim.

What to do next? Months lay ahead of her now, before Kirsten returned and they could plan together. Thoughts and half-formed ideas swirled in her mind.

Her whole future at Udsek was now in question. She had matters to settle with Gaiju and the others regarding the family herd, not to mention decisions to make about staying alone, unmarried, and essentially without family among the Sami. But with Kirsten gone, she felt a sudden vacuum around her and the craving to belong to someone, somewhere. If she remained with the Sami, she could call on old friends: the Tuovo family, Aibmu, and perhaps even the wandering Niilas. He was a good man.

But she could postpone those decisions. The reindeer were currently scattered over the Hardangervidda and wouldn't begin to migrate until about April. They usually moved in a wide arc northwestward. Sometimes their trajectory brought them almost to the coast, but that wouldn't be until June.

For now, she felt more driven by her desire to stay connected, however thinly, with Kirsten. That meant, simply, to remain with Milorg. She enjoyed a certain prestige now since Vemork.

"I damn well better," she said out loud into the darkness as she skied. "They'd be crazy not to take me." What was the institute man's name again? Ah, right. Iver. She rehearsed in her mind what she'd say to him.

I know the terrain, the best routes to and from Trondheim, and if you need someone to guide people from the vidda—or from anywhere, for that matter—to the Shetland boat, no one could do it better than a Sami.

Skiing in the darkness, she relaxed slightly. She had a plan. Work with Milorg until spring and then return to the Sami. She recalled that Niilas made a living delivering reindeer meat to a dozen towns, including Trondheim. It would be no surprise if they ran into each other one day. That would be amusing. She wondered if he still had a soft spot for her.

CHAPTER EIGHTEEN

As Maarit disappeared in the darkness on the dock behind her, Kirsten felt conflicting emotions. Most strongly, a residue of euphoria after a night of lovemaking and an immediate longing to return, followed by fear of what could happen to them in the long months of separation, and finally, resentment that she'd been summoned to Britain at all. She gripped the leather case that hung at her side. Any number of other agents could just as well have delivered the maps.

But her mother lay dying, and she had that duty to fulfill as well. Huddled in her coat against the wind and spray, she thought about Eleanor Wallace, who had remarried three years after the divorce. They'd been close enough through Kirsten's childhood, especially during the first years after their return to Britain, but the arrival of a stepfather had broken the tie and made her resentful. A certain sullenness had replaced the easy affection of childhood. She felt a certain guilt at that memory, but perhaps she could rectify the negligence before it was too late.

The sight of the *Hitra* looming up in front of them interrupted her brooding, and her jaw dropped slightly. The craft was more than twice as long as the fishing boat she'd crossed in the year before.

"She's a beauty, ain't she," the bearded one said. "Submarine chaser from the Americans. Navy gave it to us. Cruises at seventeen knots and can go as fast as twenty-two. It'll really spoil you."

She climbed aboard, and the seaman who met her led her to her compartment, which had, to her astonishment, a cubicle with a hot shower. Warm pipes along the bulkhead told her the vessel had central heating, and she shed her tattered coat to enjoy it.

A few moments later, the seaman returned with something bulky over his arm. "You might find one of these useful. Courtesy of the US Navy." He held out a thick, fur-lined coat, and she slipped her arms into it. "A bit large," she observed, "but I'll take it. What luxury."

"Oh, there's plenty more where that came from. Come on down to the galley for supper. You'll be amazed. We have an oil stove, refrigerator, water fountain, wine lockers, even an electric toaster."

The last item reminded her of how hungry she was, and laying her new coat across the bunk, she followed him to the galley, a bit dazed. It was all so sudden. After a year of cold, pain, subsistence rations, and deprivation, she'd stepped into a world of comfort and hot meals.

If only Maarit could have come, too.

Scalloway, Shetland, seemed even less hospitable in March than the shores of Norway had been. A scattering of huts along the low, brownish hills showed no sign of life or beauty, for they lacked the dark-green patches of fir forests that alleviated the Norwegian winter. Only the remains of Scalloway Castle gave the landscape a touch of interest.

"Welcome back." A uniformed man, a sergeant, she thought, met her as she stepped out onto the dock. They exchanged pleasantries, and he led her away from the harbor. "We understand that ISO is awaiting your report in London, so I'm to drive you directly to Sumburgh Airport."

"Very good," she said blandly, and followed him to his vehicle.

"I hope they took good care of you on the *Hitra*," he said as he started the motor. "In the old days, people used to arrive starving, half-frozen, and exhausted from the crossover."

"I was one of those people in the 'old days,' and I can tell you, it's much better now. Thank you for asking. Scalloway Base has changed a bit as well."

"Yes. We're getting quite good at this sort of thing," he said, and provided a lengthy description of the benefits of the new site over the original base at Lunna.

Kirsten nodded, encouraging his narrative so as not to have to talk herself, and in short order they arrived at the airport. An RAF plane waited, and once aboard, she allowed herself to doze. When she awoke, they were at RAF Croydon, London.

❖

As Kirsten entered the SOE Norwegian Section office, Lief Tronstad, Jack Wilson, and Jomar Brun all stood up. "Welcome back, dear." Brun embraced her lightly. She shook hands with the others, and Tronstad directed her toward a chair. "Please take a seat. We're looking forward to your filling us in on events."

"First of all, here are your maps." She handed over the leather sack that had hung over her shoulder most of the way. "I hope this means you're planning the invasion through Norway."

Wilson crossed his legs and looked very British as he lit the cigarette jutting from a dark wooden holder. "We'll talk about that later, but first tell us about Operation Hydro."

She shrugged, concealing her regrets. "There's not much to tell that you don't already know. Skinnarland, Haugland, and Sørlie did their jobs perfectly. They put together the timer and plastic explosive and planted it under the bow. For some reason departure was delayed, but the crew made up for the lost time, and we were almost mid-lake when it blew. So, all went according to plan."

Wilson nodded approval, then added coolly, "As we understand it, you were on board the *Hydro* at that moment. Why was that?"

Kirsten met his glance. "Because it turned out that a person I knew was one of the passengers, and I wanted to save her after the bomb detonated."

He blew out smoke through his nose. "That was reckless and a violation of protocol, as you must have known. Did you succeed?"

"No. She drowned, along with her three-year-old son." She paused, undecided whether additional information was necessary. "But we saved her infant and the oldest child."

"Very touching. But your humanitarian urges endangered the whole operation. If you'd been caught, you would have jeopardized all your colleagues as well." Wilson paused and looked toward Tronstad for support.

But Tronstad was more conciliatory. "Nonetheless, the mission was a success, and as we informed you, the King has issued commendations for you and your comrades. The loss of life was regrettable, but as we understand it, there have been no reprisals. It does appear that the Germans have ended their heavy-water production, which was the whole point."

Jomar sighed. "A pity though. We Norwegians set up the installation, years ago, to separate out deuterium and had no idea it could be used to develop a weapon. But now the technology exists, so perhaps after the war, we can use it for civilian purposes."

Kirsten was keen to change the subject. "Can we talk about the invasion of Norway? I understand that invasion plans are top secret. I'd only like to know if my delivery of the maps means it's a real possibility."

Tronstad shook his head. "There's no plan, though Churchill has been pushing his Operation Jupiter since May of 1942. He insists that grabbing Norwegian airfields would keep open the sea route to Russia and open a second front. He has a fantasy of our squadrons advancing southward, as he said, 'to unroll the map of Nazi-controlled Europe.'"

"But no one was convinced," Jomar added. "And the plan variations became more and more outlandish."

"Outlandish? What do you mean?" Kirsten's disappointment was mixed with curiosity.

"I mean that someone even suggested using a giant aircraft carrier made of ice that could carry planes to provide air cover. Don't laugh. They concocted a product called pykrete, a mix of ice and wood pulp. Of course, nothing came of it."

Kirsten tried to imagine a war vessel made of ice. She shook her head and returned to the point. "So, the invasion-in-Norway idea was scrapped."

"Essentially, yes. But the Allied leaders want to implement part of it as a diversion and create the impression that our troops in Scotland are preparing to invade Norway, while they build up forces for an actual invasion through France."

Kirsten glanced down at the battered briefcase she had been guarding so carefully. "You didn't need the maps after all? Or were you hoping they'd be intercepted?"

"Oh, no. The maps are still quite valuable. They will be marked with spots showing Milorg bases and other significant locations. Someone needed to deliver them."

"I see. What now?"

Wilson inserted another cigarette into his handsome holder. "Now, you're going on furlough."

"Furlough? Because of my breaking the rules on Operation Hydro?"

He lit the cigarette with a Zippo lighter, which he then clicked shut with a flourish and slid back into his shirt pocket. "You've been in the thick of it for too long." He took a puff and breathed out smoke as he spoke. "Battle fatigue and all that. So we're taking you out for a while." Wilson crossed his legs in the other direction and turned toward Tronstad, ending the discussion.

"You're taking me out? I respectfully object."

Brun stepped toward her and laid a hand on her shoulder. "Don't object, Kirsten. You've made heroic contributions. You were involved in three operations, one of which was a disaster, then spent time in a German jail before succeeding in a major sabotage. It's way beyond what anyone would have expected of you. Consider the furlough a reward. You'll want to spend time with your mother, anyhow. She needs you now, more than we do."

Kirsten suddenly felt tired, defeated. Her own father had played the final and strongest card. "Yes, of course. A furlough of a few weeks."

"Or months. But don't worry. The war won't go away while you're absent." With that, he gently guided her to the door.

❖

The London Hospital in Whitechapel, with a series of archways surmounted by a row of pilasters, had the tired dignity of an architectural style from an earlier century. Its sooty, gray-brown main entrance was depressing, however, as Kirsten passed through it knowing she was about to begin a death watch.

She strode along the corridor, noting that the wards were all full. Undernourished people were slow to recover from sickness or air-raid wounds, and some, no doubt, had no home to return to anyhow.

Eleanor Wallace was in a smaller room of six beds, no doubt

due to her approaching death. Glancing around at the other five beds, Kirsten concluded that those patients, too, were moribund. The room smelled of bleach.

She drew up a stool that stood by her mother's bed and sat down, horrified. The emaciated woman lying in front of her was barely recognizable.

At the touch of Kirsten's hand, Eleanor awakened and turned her head. She seemed bewildered for a moment, and when she finally spoke, her speech was slurred. "Oh, it's you. How nice," she managed to say. "I was wondering if you'd make it."

The white of her eyes was faintly yellow with jaundice, typical of advanced pancreatic cancer. "Yes, here I am. How do you feel?"

"The way I look, I suppose. Bloody fucking awful." She licked dry lips after the effort of speaking. "Hurts like hell, too, but they give me morphine. Where've you been?"

Kirsten entwined her fingers into her mother's. "You know. On duty. The war."

"So Jomar's got you into his intrigue."

"Let's not talk about my father. You divorced him ages ago, and it's not worth getting annoyed about. But yes, I've just come in from Norway."

Eleanor took a breath. "I lost track. First Oslo University, then you worked at Jomar's plant, and then he showed up here. Said you were fine, but that's all. No way to contact you."

"A lot has happened in the last year, and I wasn't always reachable. How's Harry?" she asked, changing the subject to Eleanor's second husband. "Has he been to visit?"

"On duty in Italy. A colonel now, so awfully busy. So far, no sign of him. Awfully busy. The war…"

The sonofabitch. Kirsten had never much liked Harold Wallace, from the time they married when Kirsten was fifteen. She found him controlling and a bit of a martinet but didn't begrudge her mother her happiness. Even that didn't last long. After a few years, he grew detached and was obviously more interested in his military career than his wife. Now she was dying, and he had apparently not even bothered to request a few days of emergency leave. The bastard.

Eleanor squeezed her hand weakly. "What have *you* been doing? Nothing dangerous, I hope."

"Oh, Mother. It's just as dangerous being in London with all the raids. I was tromping through a lot of snow, helping people."

"Oh, yes. I remember the winters in Rjukan. Worst decision I ever made was to marry a Norwegian. You look just like him, you know. Except for your hair." She reached up to touch a strand of Kirsten's red-blond hair, then seemed to remember her first question. "Where were you, exactly?"

"All over. The Hardangervidda, then Rjukan, then near Oslo, and finally northward to Trondheim. A busy year."

"The Hardangervidda. Oh, my. In winter! Appalling place."

"Well, challenging. But part of the time I stayed with some Sami. Very nice people."

"Sami? Those primitives who sleep in dirt houses and live with reindeer? Blimey."

"Mother, they saved my life. I was injured and almost died in the snow. They found me and took care of me. Besides, their houses are made with wood and turf, not dirt, and much more comfortable than you think."

"If you say so." Eleanor's head dropped back on her pillow, and she closed her eyes, drawing an end to the conversation.

A nurse approached the bed. "This is as much talking as she's done in days, but I think you've worn her out. Perhaps you can come back again tomorrow?"

❖

Housing was scarce in war-torn London, but Harry Wallace, upper class and an officer in His Majesty's Army, had enough money to keep a decent apartment in Brixton on one of the few streets that hadn't suffered air-raid damage. His absence kept him from having anything to say about his stepdaughter moving into it. She had no more luggage than she'd carried with her in a single rucksack on the crossing to Shetland, but a search of her mother's closet had unearthed a cardboard box of her own clothing. Obviously, someone had packed them after her departure from Britain, at the age of twenty-five. She was now thirty-four, but the deprivations of Norway had kept her thin, and most of the articles still fit. She also had her mother's various jumpers to borrow, so she had to purchase only underwear and woolen stockings.

In the evenings, she listened to war reports on the radio and wrote letters to Maarit. She couldn't send them, but they gave her a sense of Maarit's presence, and she might present them altogether when they were finally reunited.

The following day, and each day thereafter, she arrived at the hospital at ten and took her place on the bedside stool. Eleanor's cancer had spread to her lungs, and her obvious deterioration was rapid. After a week, she did little more than sleep, though she rallied for a few moments of consciousness each time Kirsten kissed her and took her hand.

At the end of April, Kirsten knew she had only days left, and Eleanor seemed to know it, too. They both seemed to intuit the time was past for small talk and half-truths, of talking around subjects.

Eleanor seemed to force her eyes open and to focus them on her. She took a breath and wheezed out a question. "Are you happy, darling?"

"Not while I'm losing you, no. But if you mean in general, yes. I think so."

"Not lonely?" Breath. "No man…in your life?"

"Mother. You must have noticed. I've never had a man in my life."

"What, then?" Breath. "Need…someone." Breath. "Hate to think of you alone."

"I'm not alone, Mother. I met someone in Norway. We both wear these." She reached inside her shirt for her fox amulet, drew it over her head, and laid it in her mother's hand.

Eleanor closed her fingers around it weakly "Um. What's…his name?"

"*Her* name. It's a woman. She's named Maarit. She was the one who saved me when I collapsed in the snow on the Hardanger. Well, she and her family." Eleanor's eyes widened, suggesting a brief surge of lucidity, and her face radiated genuine interest. She seemed present as she had not been for many days, and filled with emotion, Kirsten wanted to tell her everything before she lost her again. A floodgate opened, and she poured out every detail she could recall.

"The reindeer found me first, but then she came with her family, and they dug me out." She was rambling. "I was injured, and I couldn't walk, so they put me on a sled, where I ended up sleeping with a reindeer calf. Cutest thing. White. I named her Lykke, for happiness and luck.

That's what this is all about." She tapped the amulet. "Anyhow, I stayed with the reindeer herd until I was better, and then Maarit and I both traveled back to Rjukan."

Eleanor was still holding a soft smile, so Kirsten didn't stop talking. She had so much to tell, and she wanted to fill her mother with lovely images. She wanted to describe the salty coffee, sleeping by a fire every night, joiking, and the sphere of white mist the circling herd sent up in the corral. Most of all, she wanted to talk about being in love.

"We worked together in the resistance, and it was so good to have her with me. After the war, or maybe even before, I'll go back to her. She has reindeer, but she's studying to become a doctor, which the Sami need. So, you see, I'm not lonely at all."

Eleanor's open eyes closed to a squint, as she seemed to focus on only one word of the entire tale.

"Sami? She's a Sami?"

"Half Sami. And so smart, and capable, and beautiful. I know you'd love her."

"Sami?" Eleanor repeated, barely audibly. "Blimey," she muttered, then quietly passed from life.

❖

Without a funeral service, and in the presence of both her first and her second husband, Eleanor Wallace was cremated on April 2, 1944. The next day, Kirsten reported back to Wilson and Tronstad, requesting to return to Norway.

"Sorry, Kirsten. We need you here for the moment. All SOE forces are focused on Operation Overlord, which has the highest priority."

"You're calling it Overlord? So, the plans for the invasion are in."

"Yes, and of course it's critical to keep the Germans guessing where it will be. What part of France or even Norway. That's where you come in."

"Yes. I'm listening."

Wilson lit a cigarette, which he always seemed to do for dramatic effect and to command full attention. He exhaled smoke slowly, forcing her to wait for more explanation. "Using the maps you brought us, as well as your knowledge of the coastal areas, we'll work with you to create false projections of deployment of men and materials. The German commanders aren't stupid, and they may have locals working with them anyhow. They're sure to detect impossible scenarios, so we need to create realistic possible ones. Then, after consultation with the war department, we'll draw up phony plans for ship embarkations, troop deployments, airdrops, all that sort of thing. You'll be the one to compose the cables in Norwegian, which our code people will then encrypt and radio to certain recipients who will know they're fake."

"Why encrypt them if you want the enemy to detect them?"

"The Germans are aware we'd never radio anything as important as invasion information in open Norwegian. But we'll use one of our old code systems, which we know they've broken," Tronstad explained.

"Are you sure I can't do any of this from the Norwegian side?"

Wilson's tone revealed he was losing his patience. "Out of the question. You're here, and this is where you're needed." He tapped off the long ash of his cigarette as a sort of punctuation. "What's your decision?"

She cringed inwardly at the thought that she would miss the "return in six months" she had promised and had no way to contact Maarit to explain. But the alternative was to do nothing and still be blocked from return.

"Yes. I could do that."

❖

A month passed, and judging by the movement of German forces into Norway, Operation Jupiter Deception had succeeded. Meanwhile, plans for an actual invasion somewhere in France developed apace. The Allied leaders declined to announce a date of departure, but southern England filled with Americans, Australians, Canadians.

British civilians now found their cities awash with fighting men, British and Commonwealth, as well as American, and growing anticipation filled the drizzly, late-winter air. War materiél—jeeps, troop trucks, and armored vehicles—moved through the streets. Even small airplanes were towed from their factories or from docks where they'd arrived from America.

Kirsten worked as many hours as she was physically able, having nothing to go home to, and home itself was a single room her stepfather grudgingly granted her in his Brixton apartment. Even he was mostly absent, for which she was grateful.

Her social life consisted of an occasional after-work tea with colleagues and one depressing visit to a bar. She would not be cajoled into dancing with any of the Tommies or GIs, and seeing them with their "girls" only worsened her loneliness.

She longed to send a message to Maarit, but even if she were permitted to, and had any idea where to send it, what could she write? That the Allies were coming? Not to Norway, by the way, but somewhere in France?

At the beginning of June it was evident to all that mobilization was imminent. The entire nation seemed to be drumming its fingers. When the troops were confined to their ships, everyone knew it was a matter of days. People bet on what day would be D-day, and the odds were for June fourth.

But a rainstorm arrived on the fourth and continued until the fifth, and all bets were off.

Then, just before dawn, Kirsten awoke to the sound of a tidal wave. She opened her window and peered upward to see scattered formations of planes of all varieties. She knew what she saw was only a tiny part of the wave of aircraft setting out at that moment over the Channel.

She splashed water on her face, dressed, and reported for work. The invasion had begun.

❖

Kirsten worked throughout the summer and September, but increasingly, all her labors felt mechanical. Like everyone else, she followed the advances of the Allied troops as they were announced on the evening radio, but SOE, and the Allies in general, had little to say about Norway. It was no longer relevant. If the Norwegians were going to be liberated from the Germans, it would not be by the British and Americans.

In September, Finland—which had been fighting in desultory fashion against the Soviets for over three years and thus vaguely allied with Germany—negotiated a peace, and the German *Gebirgsjäger* set about evacuating troops and supplies from Finland to northern Norway.

On the third of October, word came that the Russians had crossed over into Norway, and British interest seemed to be renewed. The next day, the radio reported that British aircraft had bombed the U-boat bunker and docks in Bergen Harbor. No mention was made of how many Norwegians had been killed in the operation.

But the Germans were in retreat in the north, and as they withdrew, they left a wasteland behind them. They set buildings ablaze and butchered people and their livestock, to leave nothing for the advancing Soviet troops. So much for the Norwegians being part of the chosen Aryan people.

British interest in Norway was desultory. They again attempted to bomb the submarine pens west of Bergen. No account was given of any damage to the submarines, but Milorg radioed an immediate communication protesting the fifty-some civilian deaths. Stray bombs had apparently destroyed a school.

In October, the Red Army liberated Kirkenes, in northern Norway, but they arrived to find its port destroyed and its houses and commercial buildings blown up or booby-trapped. No reports came in about the many Sami villages and settlements Kirsten knew were along the retreat route. But then the Soviets halted pursuit. To the Soviets, too, Norway had become irrelevant.

At the last report, something inside Kirsten broke. She stood up from her desk and marched along the corridor and up to the third floor, to Leif Tronstad's office.

She knocked and heard, "Come in." As she entered, he stood at the window, and he turned around.

"I'm sorry to disturb you, Major, but I respectfully request to return to Norway. My assignment, to create a feigned invasion through Bergen, is now obsolete, so I see no reason to remain any longer. Let me rephrase that. I beg you to let me go back."

"Have you discussed this request with your father?"

"No, sir. But we have different goals. His wife is here, and they can wait until the end of the war to help rebuild. I have reasons to be in Norway. Do you have any mission that would allow me to return? Anything?"

"Interesting that you should make that request just now, though I suppose you've been listening to the same dreadful reports I have. What the Germans are doing in the north is quite appalling. Some of us want to protect Norway against that sort of barbarism."

"Yes, sir. That was my thought."

"Well, if you want to get back into the fight, you're in luck. General Wilson and I have just been discussing Operation Sunshine."

"Yes, sir?" Her heart fluttered. He was going to offer her a way back.

"It is an anti-demolition operation that will take place largely in the south. Specifically, it would aim to protect power stations, industrial buildings, and the like around Rjukan, Notodden, Kongsberg, and Nore. A few of your old comrades have already signed on—Jens Poulsson and Claus Helberg, who are here, and Einar Skinnarland, still in Norway. Would you like to come along?"

"Oh, yes, sir. With all my heart."

"Do you know how to use a parachute?"

"I do, sir. They taught me that back in training for Operation Freshman." Mention of the failed mission brought a moment of embarrassed silence, but then Tronstad said, "Well, then, pack your kit, and prepare to be dropped by airplane over northern Norway."

"Yes, sir!" She saluted, unnecessarily, since she wasn't in the military, and marched from the room. Suddenly she had new purpose and energy.

❖

Five of them sat together in the modified Halifax BB 378 on their way over the North Sea: Kirsten, Leif Tronstad, Jens Poulsson, Claus Helberg, and a new man, Gunnar something.

Tronstad bent toward Kirsten and shouted over the roar of the engines. "Here's how it'll go. We'll be dropped over the Hardangervidda. Einar Skinnarland will join us after we've arrived as our radio operator, the same role he played in the Vemork operation. Jens Poulsson here is my second in command." He indicated with his chin the man sitting across from him with an unlit pipe clenched in his teeth.

"What about the materiél? Weaponry? Provisions?" Kirsten asked.

Poulsson removed his pipe for a moment and joined the shouting match. "Allied airdrops. Can't rely on local supplies. Germans burning everything."

Kirsten thought of Birgit and her fish soups. Would she ever see her again? "What's the first step?"

"Skinnarland's cabin, to start. Link up with Milorg people. Now that the Germans are running, more Norwegians will volunteer."

She had other questions to ask: whether the British military was acting directly anywhere, whether there was any liaison with the Russians in the north, or if they were acting in a vacuum, but conversation by screaming was simply too strenuous. They could discuss details later, on the ground.

"We're nearing the drop zone," the navigator reported, and Kirsten did a final check of her parachute. They were roughly over the vicinity where her glider had crashed a year before, and the recollection brought a sudden ghost twinge to her once-injured foot. She brushed the ominous thought from her mind.

At the pilot's order, the bomb bay doors opened, and the team dropped out of the plane in close succession. November cold had covered the ground below with a thick coating of snow, which promised a soft touchdown. Their luck held, and so did the weather. No snow fell at that moment, the wind was minimal, and in the clear air, the pilot could see the lights Skinnarland had set out to signal the location of his cabin.

The drop was timed to occur just before sunset, so that although the five of them would land some distance from one another, they could spot each other and the cylinder carrying their skis, weapons, and emergency provisions. If not, in the increasing darkness, they could signal with their torches.

The plan worked perfectly, and two and a half hours later, the team was crowded together once again in the cabin. In the year since she'd seen him, Skinnarland had aged. His usually handsome square face was lined, his eyes circled in gray, and his beard wild. In fact, she found him more sympathetic as a weathered warrior than as a glamor boy.

He passed around coffee. "Glad you all made it. I was getting bored here. So, talk to me about this defensive force you want to build."

Tronstad held his cup to his cheek for warmth. "Here's the plan so far. We'll divide into three sections. One will protect Nore Hydroelectric Power Station and surrounding substations. The second will cover Notodden and the power stations along the Tinn River. The third, which I'll be directing, is responsible for the dam at Møsvatn, the factories around Rjukan, Vemork, and the ferries on Lake Tinn."

"All that for six people?"

"Of course not. We'll be coordinating with Milorg groups and recruiting contacts through them in all cases."

"What irony," Kirsten said, shaking her head.

"What do you mean?" Poulsson set aside his cup and lit his pipe.

"I'll be guarding Vemork and the Lake Tinn ferries. Last year, I was trying to destroy them."

Tronstad's ironic expression showed he agreed. "Yeah. Strange how that works out. In any case, we start with recruiting. Once we have a sizeable force, SOE will drop weapons, ammunition, uniforms, and food. We'll train, as necessary, and then most of our fighters will carry on with their normal work, waiting for a signal to engage. A smaller group will be battle-ready and housed in cabins like this one, scattered all over the mountains."

"Sounds ambitious," Kirsten said.

"Ambitious, indeed. Let it never be said we were anything less."

Chapter Nineteen

Maarit sat in the vestry of Løkken Church in Meldal waiting for her pickup. If she wasn't mistaken, he'd be her twenty-fifth rescue that year, though that included the groups of two or three refugees collected together. This one, unlike most of the others, was British. She knew their first names, but nothing else, though she always assumed they were resistors or SOE agents who'd been called back for some reason.

Løkken Church, served by a pastor with ties to Milorg, was a frequent meeting place, and he'd even left a bit of food for her in the vestry.

Her rescue was called Will. Before headquarters had sent her out, they'd given her his name, the location of the meeting place, and the coordinates of the Shetland pickup boat, in this case at Hovde at the inland end of Vinjefjord. Will, they said, had managed to escape from Grini concentration camp, and that was a story she wanted to hear. But she'd been waiting for a day, and he hadn't shown up. If he delayed much longer, the pickup boat would be forced to leave, and she'd have to hide him someplace—if he came at all.

The vestry at least had a cushioned chair, but that was small comfort. It was October, the first snows had fallen, and the church was unheated. Worse, for fear that light would attract attention, she sat in darkness, which stirred old fears and anxieties around the subject that haunted her the most.

Kirsten.

No word or sign, after nine months, and she'd promised to return in six, at the most. Maarit rubbed her forehead, as if to relieve the dread. The end of the war was in sight, but she had made her plans for life after the war, murky as they were, with the assumption that Kirsten would return. Now her mind swirled with conflicting drives, questions, longings. What would it mean if Kirsten didn't reappear? That she was lost at sea? Or simply had second thoughts and decided to stay in Britain? In that case, wouldn't it be better to return to Udsek?

Even after the loss of almost her entire family, she felt drawn to the Sami and knew they would accept her unconditionally. When she'd shown up after her mother's death, Jova had made her a new gakti, and Alof had led her to the corral and shown her the reindeer she would inherit. They should have been Karrol's, but he was gone, and the community had closed, lovingly, around her as the last of the family.

She also knew the goahti and the herding life was too small for her ambitions. She had seen too much, done too much, was too much drawn to city life. Yet she was unwelcome among the Norwegians who had forced her out of her medical studies and back to the vidda.

Another voice she hadn't heard in years, that of her father, reminded her that he'd given his life for Norway and she was as much his child as her mother's. Both parents had died courageously, her mother trying to rescue her son and her father trying to save Norway, and she owed it to them to stand her ground. But what ground was that?

She felt a wave of love and loyalty to them both and recalled the joik she had sung for her mother and brother with Kirsten at her side.

Kirsten. Who'd changed everything. But where the hell was she?

Nine months.

Male voices in the church sanctuary made her snap to attention. Two voices? She'd been told to expect only one. Alarmed, she stood up just as the men entered the vestry. One was obviously wounded, for he leaned against the other man and dropped heavily onto the chair she'd been sitting in.

"Which one of you is Will?" she asked.

"That's him." The healthy man nodded toward the wounded one. "I'm Lars."

Maarit bent toward Will, gripping his shoulder. "What happened?"

"A wolf, apparently," Lars answered for him. "He showed up at my door yesterday with his leg ripped open. I offered to call for a doctor, but he said he couldn't take the risk, so I patched him up as well as possible. Then he asked me to help him get here."

Maarit didn't like either development, a wounded man and a stranger. Could the latter be trusted? How much did he know?

"What did you say, exactly?" she asked Will.

Will hesitated. "I…uh…I told him two wolves attacked me while I was sleeping in the woods. I managed to shoot them, but only after they ripped open my leg. I needed help, so I went to the nearest village and knocked on the first door. Fortunately, Lars answered and took me in and bandaged me up. He saved my life."

Maarit spoke slowly in a low voice. "What…did…you…tell…him?"

Will winced. "The truth. I had no choice." He whimpered. "What else was I supposed to do? I told him I had to get to Løkken Church in Meldal, and quickly, because someone was going to get me on board a boat to Scotland. He brought me here. I wouldn't have made it without him."

Lars raised a hand, dismissively. "Don't worry. The information is safe with me. I'm on your side and can help you take him to your boat."

His assurances did little to alleviate her suspicions. Lars might be patriotic, but she couldn't be sure. That he'd bandaged the fugitive rather than report him was a good sign, but in that case, only one man's life was at stake. If Lars was a quisling and traveled the rest of the way with them to Hovde, he could denounce her and the crew, and cripple the whole Shetland transport operation.

Forcing a smile of gratitude, she faced Will's rescuer. "Thank you for all you've done, Lars. But I'll carry on from here. You're free to go home now."

"Are you sure that's a good idea?" Lars leaned solicitously toward the wounded man and laid a hand on his back. "He's very weak. You'll be much better off with a strong man to help out. How far are you going, anyhow? North or south? Do we have to get him all the way to the coast or just somewhere along the fjord?"

She shook off his questions. "Just help me get him on his feet. If we can get him as far as Vinjeøra, you can leave us."

"Vinjeøra. Is that where he's being picked up? Is that where they're always picked up? Who's doing it? Norwegians? British? I'd like to meet those heroes."

"You don't need to know any of those things."

He stiffened. "You insult me. I've helped your man all this way and risked my life for him. What are you afraid of, that I'll denounce you? The resistance knows me. I've helped them a lot."

Them. Strange way to refer to fellow patriots.

"Who have you worked with? The person in charge around here is Kjell Langstrøm, and he never mentioned you." She invented the name. No one was in charge of the Meldal area, and there was no such person as Kjell Langstrøm.

"Of course he hasn't. He's a good friend and knows he'd endanger me. That doesn't mean he doesn't call on me when he needs a favor."

She drew her revolver from inside her coat and pointed it at him. "Kjell Langstrøm doesn't exist."

"What's going on?" Will stood up, unsteady, then started to back away from them. Lars lurched toward him and grasped him around the neck from behind. With the wounded man as a shield, he drew his own gun from somewhere inside his jacket.

"You stupid woman. We could have had a nice friendly trip to your pickup location. I'd have made a little telephone call to have you intercepted and would have gotten a nice reward. No one would have been hurt. I'm not a murderer, just a man looking after his interests."

Maarit stood paralyzed with uncertainty, still pointing her gun. How to back down from this, keep it from ending in someone's death, maybe her own?

"I'll make you a counteroffer."

Lars snorted. "What do you have in mind?"

"I have about two hundred kroner in my pocket. Just leave us and walk away, and you can have it. It's not much but will make your trip worthwhile. And, after the war, you won't be accused of collaborating with the Germans."

He laughed. "I'll take my chances with that, and I'll take your two hundred kroner, too."

At that moment, Will seemed to have lost patience with the whole standoff and pivoted around, apparently trying to throw his captor off balance. Lars fired, striking Maarit in the shoulder. As she fell back, stunned, she heard a second gunshot and saw Will crumple onto the floor.

As if shocked himself, Lars stood for a moment, dazed, his gun still pointing at the man at his feet. Maarit felt the air around her start to buzz and drain of color, and with her last moment of consciousness, she fired at him. Then she blacked out.

She came to, though she couldn't tell how long she'd been out. Her entire right side hurt, and even the slightest motion caused waves of white-hot lava to radiate from her shoulder. She heard moaning and turned her head. Lying on his side, Will seemed to gaze at her through half-opened eyes.

"Will? Can you hear me?"

"Can't feel anything," he said weakly. "Don't think I'll make it this time. Tell my wife I love her."

"Sure you will," she replied, hearing her own hoarse voice. "Someone will come and get us. I know it. Just hang on."

"What a waste," a third voice said. Obviously, Lars was also still alive, slumped up against a wall. Like her, he still held his gun, though now, with nothing left to negotiate, both their weapons were useless.

"Now look at what you've done," Lars said, his voice strained. "Your stupid, false patriotism has gotten us all killed."

Maarit tried to turn toward him, but movement was too painful, so she spoke into the air. "No. It was your greed. You could have had a little money in your pocket, and we'd all be able to go home. But you wanted more."

Lars snickered. "What are you fighting for, anyhow? It's between the Germans and the Brits. I don't care who rules Norway. Why do you?"

"But you chose the German side. Bloody coward. Now you're going to…" Will took a shallow breath and then fell silent.

"It's just us now, eh?" Lars snickered, though his voice gurgled slightly, as if he breathed through a layer of blood. He coughed. "So what's your story? Why are you working for the enemy? You Jewish or something?"

"In fact, I'm Sami." The minute she spoke, she was sorry. It was as if she'd offered her identity to him for abuse, and it wasn't long in coming.

"Oh, that's a good one. I thought you all squatted around your fires eating raw meat and shitting on the ground." He chuckled, though it was more of a croak, and coughed again. "I've seen the Germans shoot a couple of your sort, and good riddance. I hope you savages all die out." His voice was weak now, but he managed to growl, "Norway's for Norwegians."

She couldn't bear the thought that she and Will would die and that bastard would live, then realized she still had her pistol in her hand, but it was on the side where she was shot. All she had to do was pull the trigger and rid the world of one more quisling. She strained to raise her head to fire, but lifting it made her dizzy, and everything quickly grew dark. She couldn't tell whether the dull bang she heard was her gunfire or the impact of her head on the floor.

❖

The sensation of being lifted awakened her, and she jerked in reflex against the hands that held her.

"It's all right. No one will hurt you. We heard the shooting and knew something terrible had happened."

"Who…are you?" She groaned, in a stupor of pain as he touched her shoulder.

"Pastor Angeltveit. This is my church. Don't worry. We'll take care of you."

Befuddled, all she could say was, "What? Be careful…the others…"

"They're dead, and my men will bury them outside so no one finds them. You're in pretty bad shape, so we've called a doctor."

"No. Too dangerous. Have to contact Iver…" she muttered and lost consciousness again.

She awakened a second time on a cot in the church basement, with a circle of men around her. One of them, presumably a doctor, was just finishing a bandage around her arm and shoulder. "Ah, you're awake. I've stopped the bleeding and tried to clean the wound, but you need a surgeon to remove the bullet."

It was a slight comfort to know she was still alive, but the pain hadn't subsided, and she was too weak to sit up. "Can't stay here," she muttered. "Have to get back to Trondheim."

"Yes, we know," the man standing behind the doctor said. It seemed to be the same one who'd said he was the pastor. "One of our people will take you to the hospital there. A woman who's been shot will arouse suspicion on the road, so you have to travel hidden. He's a carpenter who has a pass to travel, so no one should inspect his wagon, but you'll have to lie in his saw box."

"A box? No...no. Please." She was conscious enough to refuse. She had no fear of small spaces, but the thought of lying in a sort of coffin that she would be too weak to climb out of horrified her.

"It'll only be for about two hours. We'll wrap you up warmly, and the box has holes in it for air. It's the only safe way to get you to Trondheim."

She neither consented nor refused, but simply went limp as they slid her good arm back into her coat and lifted her from the bed. As they carried her outside, it was full night, but she could see the wagon by the dull light emanating from the church.

She moaned in fear as they laid her in the wooden chest and draped burlap over her.

"Don't worry. It's only a couple of hours," the carpenter repeated as he lowered the lid of the box and cast her into complete darkness.

Immediately she drew her good hand out from under the burlap to feel around her. She hit the wood cover a few inches from her face and pushed against it, relieved to find she could raise it if necessary. Even better, her fingers detected several holes that someone had drilled to let in air.

The wagon started immediately, and a wave of panic made her forget the pain in her side. She had to have something to fill her mind to keep from going mad from terror. Two hours, they'd said. How much better it would be if she could pass out again, but the pounding of her heart kept her alert and in torment.

All right. She'd count it out. Sixty beats to each minute, each minute noted until she'd reached an hour. Then she'd begin again. She tested the lid once more to reassure herself she could still raise it.

The system calmed her as the wagon bumped and rattled along the road. Once or twice she lost count but then backtracked deliberately. It would be a pleasant surprise to arrive before she reached 120 minutes.

Diligently, she drummed out sixty beats with one finger, then whispered "one" and began the next count, slowly accumulating minutes. She lost track somewhere in the middle forties but started again at forty-one. By the time she reached sixty minutes, the satisfaction of reaching the halfway mark had mitigated her fear somewhat. All she had to do was repeat the process, and the journey would all be over.

At ten minutes into the next hour, the wagon stopped. What did that mean? Men's voices, aggressive and loud, then the thump of boots on the wagon floor. Her box rocked as someone kicked it. Was it a guard demanding inspection? She braced herself for exposure and violent seizure. But instead, she felt the dull thuds of additional boxes piled on top of her.

Dear God. Now she was helpless. Blind, bleeding, and helpless. She wanted to cry but was too weak. If only she knew what was happening outside over her head.

The wagon started again, and the added weight on the saw box caused it to creak as it rocked from side to side. If that had been an inspection, it appeared they had passed it, and even though she was trapped, she had only to hold out another hour. She began counting again.

But some thirty minutes later, by her reckoning, the wagon stopped once more. Worse than the sound of men climbing on the wagon was the silence that followed. What had happened? Were they stopped again? The driver arrested? Would he reveal his human freight, or would he abandon her, sealed in a box?

Even worse, she had to take ever deeper breaths to get enough air, and she realized the additional crates that imprisoned her also covered the holes above her head. How much air did she have left? Panic set in again, and she began to sob, then call out in German and Norwegian. It didn't matter who heard her. She preferred dying quickly in the open air to slowly suffocating in darkness.

"Please. Help me. Help me," she called.

A thud on the side of the box startled her. Someone had kicked her, signaling that she wasn't abandoned. A German guard would have opened the crate, so it had to be one of the carpenters. But did he know her air was cut off?

She was dizzy now from the lack of oxygen and tapped out a rhythm. Three quick knocks—three slow ones, three quick ones. Would he realize she was tapping out SOS? Would he care?

All he did was kick her again. It must have been a trap to kill her after all. Dear God, she didn't want to die, not this way. She began to sob again. The lack of air and the loss of blood together drained all her strength, and she began fading out. She fought to stay awake, knowing that once she succumbed, she would never awaken again, but now even her pounding heart couldn't bring her enough oxygen. With a final sob, she lost consciousness.

❖

A rush of cold air revived her, though she gasped and struggled to waken from her stupor as she was lifted out of the box and laid on a stretcher. She swam in semiconsciousness while she was jostled from darkness into light, and around corners, and finally laid onto a gurney.

She awakened fully in a brightly lit room, hearing the low hum of activity, and turned her head. A ward, obviously, with beds on all sides of her. It was difficult to breathe, and her whole left side hurt, but it wasn't the hellish pain she'd felt before. A careful touch with her hand told her she was bandaged tightly. Someone had tended to her wound. She glanced around again, recognizing the room. Trondheim hospital.

Her outer clothing had been removed, and she wore a cotton hospital smock. A single blanket covered her, though in the cold room, it wasn't sufficient to warm her feet. Where were her shoes?

With increasing clarity came a new anxiety. This was the hospital where she'd been expelled two years before. Did anyone recognize her? Had someone reported her and her suspicious gunshot wound to the Gestapo? It almost didn't matter, as long as she was out of that coffin. They could do with her what they wished. She was too weak to fight any longer.

"Ah, you're awake," a friendly voice said. She turned her head in the other direction to see a young man in a white smock. He was slender and blond, very blond, even his eyebrows, the sort of look the Germans seemed to love. Almost certainly a new staff member, for she didn't recognize him, and more importantly, he didn't seem to recognize her.

"How are you feeling? And while you're at it, you might tell me who you are. Some men in a wagon dropped you off, but as soon as we brought you inside, they disappeared. Odd behavior, but then, these days, nothing's normal."

She stalled for time. "Sorry. I don't remember much myself. I was walking along and was suddenly shot. Hunters, I guess. But it looks like someone treated my…uh…injury?"

"Two injuries. You had a concussion, which would account for your being unconscious when we brought you in, but also the surgeon removed a bullet lodged in your scapula. You were lucky it struck high enough to miss your lung. In any case, we're supposed to inform the authorities of injuries of that sort, but we've held off until we learned your name."

Name. Any name. The first one that came to mind. "Kirsten," she said. "Kirsten Johannsen." It was the most common family name she could think of.

"Well, Kirsten Johannsen, we've patched you up, and we can keep you a few days, but we're swamped and understaffed since the war. Can your family take care of you while you recover?"

Her mind raced, desperate. She had no one. Iver might know one of the Milorg people in Trondheim who could take her in. But that wasn't so easy to organize. How could she even contact him without exposing him?

"My family is…uh…well, I just have an aunt. In Tuddal. She lives alone, with a cat." She knew she was babbling, but she had to gain time until she could get back on her feet. "You said I can stay a few days? That will give me time to get word to her."

"Yes. You can send out a note as soon as you're able. In the meantime, let me take a look here." He untied her sling and made a cursory exam of the bandage. "Everything seems normal," he said, and with a gentle pat on her hand, he moved to the next bed.

She glanced around the ward, nervous. Surprising that no one on the staff had recognized her, but it was just a matter of time. Once that happened, the quislings who had expelled her in the first place would rush to report her and her gunshot wound. She had to have an explanation or an escape plan.

The chill in her feet also told her she needed to find her socks and shoes. Holding her breath, she pulled herself up with her good arm to a sitting position, then swung her legs over the side. As she recalled, patient belongings were stored either in lockers or under their beds. Carefully, she bent forward and, to her relief, spotted a cardboard box under the foot of the bed.

With slow, painful movements, she knelt and managed to slide the box out to retrieve her footwear. The woolen socks were filthy but warmed her immediately, and with sock-covered feet, she nudged her shoes toward a spot where she could put them on quickly if she needed to.

When she lay back in the bed, she caught sight of a man watching her. He stood near the door with a mop and seemed to study her, and slowly it dawned on her that she knew him.

A simple, good-natured fellow, he'd been the janitor when she was a student at the hospital. She'd chatted once or twice with him, enough to know he was half-Sami, like her, though from a village in the far north she'd never heard of. He was stocky, with a Slavic face and bad teeth, and looked more Sami than she did. Nonetheless, he'd kept his job through the racial purge, she presumed because of its menial nature. She couldn't remember his name.

Catching her eye, he leaned his mop against the wall and approached. She cringed but then remembered their grumbling together about the quisling government. He wouldn't denounce her.

"Excuse me," he said, reaching the foot of her bed. "You're Maarit, aren't you? I'm sure I remember you. I'm Olet. Do you remember me?"

She beckoned him closer, to speak in an undertone. "Yes. I remember you. But please, don't tell anyone I'm here. You'll get me arrested, maybe killed."

"Oh, my gosh. Okay. How'd you get hurt? Oh, sorry, I guess I shouldn't ask."

His appearance was a straw in a flood, and she clutched at it. "Can you help me?"

"Um, how?" He was hesitant, and she knew she could push him only so far.

"Just get a message to someone. At the Institute of Technology. It's not even very far away. Get word to someone named Iver and tell him I'm here. That's all."

It was a lot to ask. Iver was surely a code name, and not known to his colleagues. "Ask for him, and if no one recognizes that name, leave immediately. Don't endanger yourself."

"Uh, all right. Tomorrow's my day off. I'll try then."

"Thank you. In the meantime, can you help me with my shoes? I need to go to the toilet, and it takes two hands to get them on."

"Of course." He knelt down and slid her feet into the boots and laced them up, then offered his arm to help her stand. Together they shuffled through the door into a long corridor. She recognized this wing of the hospital, with a spiral staircase at one end, a series of six-bed rooms along both sides of a corridor, and a twelve-bed ward at the opposite end. Midway along the corridor was a toilet for the use of ambulatory patients.

As they edged their way forward, he spoke soothingly. "Don't you have friends in Trondheim who can help you?"

She shook her head. "No one here. Only Iver, if you can locate him."

They arrived at the door of the toilet. "All right, then. I'll take your message to him tomorrow, if I can find him. I'll do my best and tell you what happened the next day, when I'm on duty again." He glanced back at the ward where he was supposed to be working. "Can you make it back to your bed without help?"

"Thank you. Yes. I'm sure I can." She squeezed his arm wearily, her hopes undermined by the pain in her shoulder, and staggered inside to relieve herself.

❖

Sunday passed without event, and she discovered that removing her boots with one hand was possible, though tying them was not. So she simply shuffled around in them unlaced.

The nice doctor stopped by to examine her bandages again, and a nurse brought her some of the fish broth the hospital provided as food. But until word came from Olet, she was in limbo, anguishing over the near certainty that he wouldn't be able to find Iver at the Institute. And if he couldn't, she was trapped.

Monday brought matters to a head. In the morning, an orderly had changed her bandage and sprinkled another dusting of sulfa powder on the wound, though Maarit noted it seemed no better. She lay back and stared at the ceiling, fervently willing Olet to walk into the ward.

Instead, a nurse arrived on some duty or other, and Maarit froze. The nurse was about to pass the foot of the bed, when she stopped. Her eyes narrowed for a moment before she pivoted around and strode to the bedside.

"Maarit Ragnar. Whatever are you doing here, and as a patient, no less?" Without waiting for a reply, she took up the board that hung on the foot rail of the bed and read. "Ballistic trauma: gunshot." She glanced up, scowling. "So you've been shot. While you were out wandering with your reindeer? I thought the Sami took care of their own."

It was not a real question, simply derision.

Maarit had no reply, so remained silent, which seemed to irritate the nurse more.

"Who shot you? Has the admitting doctor reported this gunshot to the authorities?"

"Of course he has," Maarit lied. "It was an accident."

The nurse inspected the bandage, as if doing so would provide damning information of some sort. When it didn't, she stepped back. "I didn't care for it when the likes of you took a study place away from a Norwegian, and I don't like it, when you lie there taking up space a sick Norwegian might need. I'm going to look into this." She marched back through the door, postponing whatever she had come to do in the first place.

Maarit instinctively sat up. But to what end? She still couldn't run—only shuffle. And no one ever escaped anything by shuffling. Beaten, she dropped back onto the bed and lay there, resigned.

She lay for a good two hours, and her nemesis didn't reappear. Perhaps she was bluffing, or realized the rule of the Germans over Norway had become precarious, and had decided to leave well enough alone. It was a faint hope.

Where the hell was Olet?

As if in response to her fervent thoughts, the familiar soft swish of a mop wafted toward her, and she turned to see him at the other side of the ward. He worked with concentration, mopping between the beds and along the center aisle, ignoring her while medics and nurses came and went. Just a normal workday. She glanced away from him as well, waiting for him to arrive on her side of the room.

Finally, he did and spoke in a low voice while he mopped under her bed. "Couldn't find your friend at the institute. No one knew the name."

She closed her eyes in despair and barely heard his next words.

"But I told a couple of my Sami friends that a Sami woman was in the hospital and needed a place to stay. You'd be surprised who knows who around here. I ended up meeting someone who could help."

"Who? I don't know any of the Sami in Trondheim," she whispered.

"Well, he knows you, and he promised to come." That was all Olet was able to say, for at that moment, one of the doctors came through the door. Keeping his head down, Olet proceeded to mop a path from her bed through the doorway to the corridor.

Nonplussed, she stared at the spot where he'd been. What should she do now? Wait some more, it seemed, until her mysterious savior appeared. And hope that he did before the Nazi nurse showed up with the police.

Another urge interrupted her mood of anger and anxiety, and once again, she struggled into her boots and set out. She shuffled slowly along the corridor, supporting herself with one hand on the wall. At the end, she entered the tiny room that smelled strongly of disinfectant and relieved herself. Ironic, she thought. The one place she was safe from discovery was the toilet.

Resigning herself to the return trip, she opened the door and stared down the long corridor. Then she saw them.

Police. Two of them, entering the ward. The quisling nurse had reported to them after all.

She backed up instinctively into the tiled washroom and tried to pull the door closed. But a hand held it and forced it open again.

Bewildered and alarmed, she stepped back as the doorway filled with a large male figure.

"Niilas! What are you...oh, you're the Sami friend he found!" The question and answer came out at the same time.

He stepped into the washroom and hugged her warmly. He seemed older and bulkier than she remembered him from four years before, but his appearance delighted her. After Gaiju, ex-fiancé Niilas was the closest thing she had to family.

"But the police are already here." She tilted her head toward the direction of the ward.

"I saw them and wondered who they'd come for. It's you?" he asked.

"I think so. Help me get out of here, please."

"Can you walk?"

"Not very well. I was shot and lost a lot of blood. It left me very weak." She glanced toward the ward. "My clothes are still back there, under my bed."

"I have a blanket in my wagon. But first, how do we get you away from here?"

"I...I don't know. The police will be looking here the minute they see the empty bed. We don't have time..."

The sound of men shouting curses caused them both to turn. Olet knelt in the doorway to the ward, his bucket of soapy water overturned next to him, flooding the entrance and blocking the way of the two Germans.

Bless him. He'd created a diversion.

"You idiot!" one of the policemen shouted. "Look at what you've done!"

Niilas seized her arm and dragged her along while the policemen berated Olet. How long would it take him to mop up the pool of water and clear their path?

Long enough, it seemed, for they managed to stagger down the staircase and out of the wing to Niilas's wagon without capture. He helped her into the rear, where she curled up under a heavy blanket.

A light flick of the whip urged the horse forward, and the silence behind them told them there was no pursuit. She felt a wave of gratitude and relief. Niilas Paaval, the only man who had ever intimately touched her, had saved her life.

CHAPTER TWENTY

November 1944

Kirsten skied alongside Leif Tronstad, relieved to be back in Norway and in action again, under the leadership of someone she deeply respected. They'd skied more or less silently for three hours when they reached a large rock outcropping, and he called for a rest. Grateful, Kirsten brushed snow from a convenient spot and managed to half sit on it.

"How are you holding up?" Tronstad asked. "Sitting in an office is no preparation for this, is it?"

"No, but I'll manage." She paused. Perhaps this was the moment to say what was on her mind. "I was wondering. After we've set everything up, you know, recruited the men you're looking for, could I take off a couple of weeks for private business? I'd come right back…"

She'd gotten to know Lief Tronstad as a soft-spoken, engaging man, who was loyal to his team and who received loyalty in return. He was not given to ultimatums.

But now, in his gentle voice, he gave one. "Kirsten, you've served Norway well, and we're aware of that fact. This operation is as important as the ones you've already carried out, and you've signed on to it, but we can't accept half measures. If you're not up to this new mission, wholly and completely, we'll understand. We're desperately short-handed and need you, but you hold no military rank and signed no contract, so if you want to leave and go home, you can do so today. SOE and I will release you." He held out his hand. "Thank you for your service."

Kirsten cringed as if he'd slapped her. As if she were a whining child who'd grown bored with a task and begged to be allowed to play while the adults carried on. She was suddenly ashamed.

"No, no! I'm with you for the duration. No matter what happens. I've just been separated from someone I care about for over a year now and wondered if I could make contact. But I see the problem, and I'm sorry I brought it up."

He shrugged slightly, his voice conciliatory. "We're all separated from the people we love, our wives and parents and partners. I have a wife and two children, and I haven't seen them since 1941. I can't even let them know I'm back in Norway. They have to know nothing in case the Germans interrogate them."

Three years' separation! Her own anxiety now seemed petty. "I understand. Shall we carry on?" Humbled, she stood up, ready to continue skiing, no matter how long or how far.

Eventually they descended into the gorge that brought them to Rjukan, and the sight of the town raised her spirits. "I was arrested here last year, as you know. Do you suppose anyone is still looking for me?"

"No more than they're looking for me, but at least it'll be dark when we arrive."

"Dark" in Rjukan in early November meant about four thirty p.m., and even before that, the town at the bottom of the gorge was already in a dusky half-light. They skied along back roads to the meeting place, which, she was delighted to learn, was still Birgit's café. They removed their skies and approached the familiar store-room entrance. When they stepped inside, she glanced for a moment toward the corner where she and Maarit had slept...and kissed. A lifetime ago.

Birgit's welcome was sincere, but hurried. It was risky for so many Milorg to gather where Germans could enter at any time, so they quickly sat down to business.

Kirsten recognized a handful of others: Odin and Terje Martinson, leader of the local Milorg, and the one they called Red. Two women also sat at one of the tables, but she never learned their names. The discussion started, Torstad directing his remarks to Martinson.

"Our first job is to recruit," he said. "We need numbers, and we need them fast. The Germans are retreating all along the northern front and burning everything they pass through. They know they're losing, but Norwegians know it, too, so it's up to us to organize them and put weapons in their hands."

"Where are those weapons going to come from?" one of the women asked.

"From the Allies by airdrop. Odin, you'll be in charge of distributing them. For the time being, we'll still keep to teams of three. In case anyone's captured, each member can name only two others, and of course, we have to hold out for twenty-four hours so those people can escape."

"Who's covering what installations?" Red asked.

"Group one is assigned to the Nore Power Station and substations. Group two, headed by Terje, will take Notodden and the power station. The third group, under my command, will take care of Rjukan, Vemork, and the ferries left on Lake Tinn. Each team leader will recruit for his own team. That is, find the fence-sitters, the ones who are loyal but a bit timid. If you put a rifle in their hands and tell them this is the moment to prove they're men, you can fire them up."

After the meeting closed, Kirsten made her way across the storeroom to Birgit, who had remained silent throughout.

"Have you heard anything from Maarit? We separated in Trondheim last February, when I left for Britain, and I'd like to track her down."

Birgit shrugged. "As far as I know, she was working with the people in Trondheim for a while, delivering refugees to the Shetland transport."

"Do you think she's still there?"

"Almost certainly not. Word was, she was wounded, spent some time in hospital, and returned to her people with a man."

"Wounded? Was it serious? And the man she left with, did they mention his name? Gaiju, perhaps? Or one of the Tuovo men?"

"Someone she'd been engaged to. People assumed she was going back to marry. I don't think the wound was life-threatening. She couldn't have left the hospital if it was. And we had no indication that she'd given up any names. Unfortunately, that's all I can tell you."

Marry. The word stood out as if Birgit had shouted it, and Kirsten suddenly felt nauseous. It was her own fault. She'd stayed away too long.

Birgit seemed to sense her despair. "Don't worry, dear. The war will be over in a few weeks. Then you can travel up north and find out yourself."

❖

Kirsten wasn't sure which was more devastating—losing Maarit to the war or to a husband. It was of course selfish to equate death with abandonment, and she would have never spoken it out loud, but both possibilities shattered her.

And to add to the agony, she'd have to wait to find out. "A few weeks," Birgit said. "What will a few weeks be after almost a year?"

Defeated, she worked with Tronstad, gaining the confidence of Rjukan residents. Her argument was always the same. The Germans were losing, and after they were driven out, who would want to admit they did nothing to protect the homeland? She called on her memory—and theirs—of King Haakon, quoting him, the soul and symbol of Norway.

Resistors were emerging all over Europe, she told them. The Germans had lured them into thinking Norway was safe, that Norwegians would be part of the rulers of Europe. But the destruction they were leaving all across the north proved that promise to be a lie. The true Norwegian protected his homeland against invasion. Period.

Her argument was helped enormously on November 10, when the BBC announced that three hundred Norwegian troops that had been training in Scotland had arrived in the north. And if anyone had any doubts about who would be the victor, on November 12, the report came that RAF Lancasters had sunk the German battleship *Tirpitz* anchored in a fjord at Tromsø.

Irrationally, Kirsten took each victory as a sign that she would find Maarit and all would be well. So, the weeks went by, with more and more Norwegians signing on for last-minute defense, and she soldiered on. Tronstad saw to the chain of supply of weapons, each man or woman had a specific task, and, miraculously, the various local German authorities didn't catch on. The man was a constant inspiration, and his long separation from his wife gave her the courage to endure her own.

But in March 1945, when the end of the war was already in sight, she attended a meeting of Tronstad's section leaders. One of them, Jon Landsverk, arrived breathless and late. As he sat down he swept back his wool hat and ran his fingers through his hair. "We have a problem."

Birgit frowned wearily. "What are you talking about?"

"Torgeir Lognvik, the flunky the Nazis put in place to keep an eye on things, has been asking questions. Someone must have seen one of the airdrops and reported it. I don't know how much he knows."

"Can we interrogate him? If he's a danger, we have to neutralize him."

"We can't touch him here in Rjukan. We have to lure him away from his office. Far away."

Tronstad scratched his chin. "What about getting him up to Syrebekk? The lodge there is closer than Skinnarland's cabin, and we can concoct some reason, tell him we've found weapons."

"I can do that." Landsverk volunteered. "I know the man. Not well, but enough that he'll probably trust me. I'll tell him I saw a drop and followed it to a hiding place. That should interest him. Then we can find out if he's a problem. If he is…" He ran his thumb on a line across his throat.

❖

Kirsten waited with Tronstad and the others in the Syrebekk lodge. "Do you think he'll fall for it?" she asked.

Gunnar Syverstad watched at the window. "I'm sure he will. After all, it's his job to ferret out the resistance. A report of an Allied weapons drop should bring him running."

"And just how are we going to find out what he knows?"

Skinnarland stirred the embers in the cabin stove. "We'll have a little chat. If it looks like he's onto us, we have to bring him over to our side or neutralize him."

"I really hate that word. What you mean is 'shoot him.'"

Tronstad puffed on his pipe. "I'm afraid so."

Syverstad turned from the window. "I see them. Landsverk in front and Lognvik right behind him."

Minutes later, the two men stood at the doorstep, and Syverstad opened the door. Seeing the five people waiting for him, Torgeir hesitated, but Landsverk yanked him inside.

"What the hell is this?" Torgeir asked.

"Just have a few questions," Skinnarland said, snatching Torgeir's sidearm out of his holster and pushing him down onto a chair. "Mainly why a man would let the Germans use him to control his own people."

Torgeir swept his gaze over the entire group, contempt forming on his face. "You bastards. You're the traitors, working with the Brits, killing honest Norwegians. To hell with all of you."

"You stupid fool." Tronstad shook his head. "The Germans have lost this war, and it's only a matter of time before they're forced out of Norway. What do you think the courts will say about collaborators like you? We're giving you a chance to come over onto the right side before it's too late."

"The right side?" Torgeir sneered. "It's your lot who are the fools. The Germans had a plan that would have freed us from the Russians."

The recriminations flew back and forth for several minutes, and all attention was focused on Torgeir sitting defiantly. Tronstad stood in front of him, and all but Kirsten had their back to the door.

By the time she registered the danger, it was too late. The door burst open, and a man standing in the opening fired immediately. Struck in the back, Syverstad collapsed on the floor.

Tronstad glanced down at Syverstad for a fraction of a second, then rushed at the intruder, who fired at him point-blank. Instinctively, Kirsten threw herself over him as he lay on the floor, then realized she too was a target.

But the shooting was over, and Torgeir had already lurched through the cabin door and escaped with his rescuer.

It had all happened in seconds. Stupified, the rest of them crouched over Tronstad and Syverstadl, looking for signs of life.

Skinnarland shook his head. "Dead, both. Who the hell was the man who shot them?"

Landsverk stood up, ashen. "Torgeir's brother. He must have followed our ski tracks."

Stunned, Kirsten still knelt over the body of Tronstad. The whole operation was now jeopardized. Then she remembered Tronstad's wife. The next time she heard about her husband would be to learn he was dead. Just as bleak was the thought that if she herself had been killed, the same would be true of Maarit.

❖

They buried Tronstad and Skinnarland, and Kirsten knew nothing more would be revealed about them until the war ended. The operation had enough momentum to continue even after the death of its founder. Jens Poulsson stepped into the leadership, and recruitment continued.

In April, Norwegian forces counted over three thousand men, and they swept the enemy southward. Tronstad's successful operation to protect Norwegian infrastructure from the ravages of the fleeing army was his legacy.

The Norwegian High Command declared that Finnmark was free. When Kirsten reported in to Rjukan in late April, Birgit passed on a radio message from Trondheim that confirmed the rumors she'd heard, that Maarit was wounded and taken back to "her people" by a young man called Niilas.

Kirsten nodded, trying to order her thoughts, develop a plan. "Don't you have an assignment that will send me back up north?" she asked Poulsson.

"The Germans are no longer a threat there, but they're still fighting to hang on down here. We need everyone at their post. You know yourself how easy it is to blow up something like a power plant. All you need is one fanatical Nazi to toss in a grenade before he marches out of the city on his way to Germany." Poulsson laid his hand on her shoulder. "But it will all be over soon enough."

"Yes, sir." She consoled herself. If Maarit was able to travel, her wound couldn't be life-threatening. But…Niilas, of all people. How would he have known where to find her? Had she felt so abandoned that she'd consented to marry him?

Dutifully, Kirsten stayed at her post, day and night, reporting on German detachments that came anywhere near the substation. To her relief, the scorched-earth policy in the north had not spread.

As it became clear the Germans had stopped patrolling, and were largely waiting for orders from headquarters, someone brought a radio into Birgit's storeroom, and anyone not actively standing guard came to listen to the reports.

Curiously, even after word came on the first of May that the Russians had entered Berlin and planted the Soviet flag on the Reichstag building, the Rjukan Germans did not withdraw. But neither did they attack. The following day, news arrived that Goebbels and his family were found dead in the bunker of the Chancellory, and a smoking fire pit suggested that Hitler was dead as well. Berlin had surrendered.

On May 4, German troops in Denmark and the Netherlands surrendered, and still the Germans in Norway were silent.

Not until the evening of May 8 did official word come from London that Germany had capitulated. The news seemed anticlimactic, but Poulsson called together the operation leaders.

"Are we relieved of duty yet?" Kirsten asked him. "Surely we have nothing left to guard."

"Almost. Milorg is in charge now, and London has ordered Terje Martinson to retake Akerhus Fortress for Norway. We have one last assignment—to assist him. He's sent a messenger to inform the commanding officer—one Major Nichterlein—that he'll be arriving to accept surrender. We all know the German troops outnumber us ten to one and are far better armed than we are, so we just have to hope that everything stays calm."

At two thirty in the afternoon, Martinson led a contingent of some hundred Milorg fighters, most in motley and with green arm bands, into the fortress at Akershus. Kirsten and her SOE comrades marched nervously behind them.

Major Nichterlein waited in the Akershus courtyard. Hundreds of German soldiers stood stone-faced behind him, holding their rifles across their chests and prepared for an order from the commander. It looked for all the world like a trap.

Martinson told his own men to halt, marched the final ten paces alone toward Nichterlein and his adjutant, and saluted.

The contrast between the uniforms of the two men was deeply ironic. The victor wore old-fashioned, almost comical knee pants and, below them, hand-knitted, patterned stockings. His head was bare, his jacket was civilian, and only his bandolier and holstered sidearm hinted he was a fighter.

The defeated Nichterlein was in polished boots and full uniform, peaked officer's cap, belted tunic with shoulder bars, and decorated with the Iron Cross and a row of other medals across his left pocket.

Wearing leather gloves, he saluted smartly. Martinson responded with his own salute.

After what seemed like a long, tense moment, but was probably only a few seconds, the major barked an order, and his men laid their rifles on the ground. Still in formation, they did an about-face and marched back to their quarters.

Martinson let another lengthy moment pass, as if to wait until the fortress courtyard was cleared of the taint of occupation, and when the only remaining sound was the fresh Norwegian breeze, he ordered his men to collect the weapons.

It was what Kirsten had waited for. She turned to Poulsson, saluted, and asked, pro forma, "Request permission to be released from duty, sir."

A smile broke through his somber expression. "Permission granted."

Chapter Twenty-one

News came over the radio of the victory celebrations all over Britain, but Kirsten's euphoria had quickly ebbed, and now she felt drained, just as almost everyone around her seemed to be. There would be a reckoning now, a bitter period of recriminations, as patriot accused quisling, and the courts would surely be full. Could one separate the genuine collaborators from the merely cowardly or lazy? She suspected it would be a similar problem in every country the Germans had occupied.

At least her family was not tainted in that way and would return home in honor. But how was she different from the quislings? In service to the Allies, she had killed dozens of Norwegians, two of them an old friend and her baby. The recollection sucked away any joy she might have had in victory.

Her one thought now was to find Maarit, who might be seriously or permanently injured. And married. Probably married. Oh, God.

After a final supper at Birgit's café, with Poulsson and the other survivors of Operation Sunshine who were preparing to return home, she announced her departure for Udsek.

Poulsson puffed on his eternal pipe. "What a relief, eh? Now that SOE has paid us, and the Germans are gone, we're free to travel any way we want, visible to the whole world."

"Mmm," Kirsten agreed, though with less enthusiasm. "The freedom's wonderful, but I still have to deal with getting there."

"Where's the settlement located?" Birgit asked.

"Just northeast of the vidda. About a day's hike, or ski, from Lake

Skrykken. Between Geilo and Dagali. I don't think the trains, even if they're operating again, come very close."

Birgit stood up. "We still have all the Milorg maps. Let's take a look." She unlocked a cabinet and withdrew a cardboard box marked "Flour" and fished a map from its interior. Blowing away flour dust, she spread it on the table and tapped a city to the east. "Just as I thought. There's a station at Geilo, so you can go much of the way by train, though you'll have to pick it up at Kongsberg. A lot of rail lines were damaged, and the service will be irregular, but you'll get there eventually."

"Good idea. Even if it takes most of my budget, it'll be worth it to ride most of the way."

"Now that's settled, let's have a round of drinks." Poulsson tapped the ashes out of his pipe into an ashtray. "Come on, Birgit. I know you've got some akvavit hidden away somewhere."

She snickered. "You're right. I've had it for months, and I wouldn't bring it out for anyone but your lot." She stepped toward the same cabinet that held the "Flour" box of maps and drew out another cardboard box labeled "Dried Fish." Gingerly, she unwrapped a bundle of crumpled newspaper and revealed a bottle of the precious liquor.

Fetching glasses from the same shelf, she poured out a double dose for each person.

"Skål," she said, raising her cup, and they echoed her before tossing back the scalding liquid in a single swallow.

❖

Months of travel and homelessness had reduced Kirsten's belongings to an absolute minimum, so packing went quickly. A change of socks, shirt, and underwear, and a sack of provender for at least the first day. Surrendering her skis to Birgit, she hiked out to the road leading westward and flagged down a cart.

At the end of May, the air was tolerably warm, and the rains that had been heavy in April had stopped. It felt strange to be traveling toward Udsek in a green landscape and on public transportation.

From Rjukan, she made her way southeastward toward Tinnoset, then directly eastward to Kongsberg, by farmers' carts, and once, briefly, in a motor vehicle. But most of the time, she walked, and though the spring landscape was cheering, she made significantly poorer time than she had always done skiing.

She chatted with strangers along the way, people who were resuming their lives after accommodating themselves, one way or another, to an occupation. They were poorer and hungrier than before but were certain that things would get better after king and government returned. A few refused to talk about the war at all, and she suspected they had compromised themselves. But who was she to condemn anyone?

She reached Kongsberg in the afternoon and, luckily, a train was leaving that evening. The station clock showed nearly ten when she boarded, but it was still twilight, and the sky was not fully dark until she changed trains in Hokksund. Finally, she settled in and stared out the window at moonlit, newly liberated Norway.

She dozed for a while and was jostled awake when the train stopped. Rubbing her face, she peered through the window. The station sign said NESBYEN. Good. Almost there.

Awake now, she planned what to do once she'd arrived. She slid her hand into her jacket pocket and fingered the kroner she still had. She'd be too exhausted upon arrival to start the long hike to Udsek, along a route she wasn't even sure of. She'd need at least one night of sleep in Geilo.

She struggled with the usual doubts. The plan to be reunited with the woman she loved had lost its joy long ago. Now she asked herself whether Maarit would even want to be reunited. The sort-of vow of fidelity they'd taken to each other was based on the expectation of six months, and Kirsten had stayed away fifteen. How could she possibly expect Maarit to still be waiting?

And then there was Niilas. The man who had been Maarit's betrothed had rescued her and taken her home. She had no other family now, and little inheritance, so would certainly need him. At least in the beginning, he could give her a stability Kirsten couldn't offer.

So, what was the point of barging in on them? She cringed at the thought of surprising them in their family goahti or, more likely, in a real house, since Maarit had implied that Niilas was a successful businessman. She imagined them sitting together by a fire, at an actual table, preparing supper, perhaps expecting a child, and the scene almost brought tears. Why should she subject herself to such an excruciating confrontation? Much better to reverse course and leave, holding on to a shred of dignity.

But what if she was wrong? Uncertainty made her feel like she was losing her mind. How to find out and save herself humiliation?

The answer was obvious. She would send a message that she was coming. Maarit could either reply "I'm married now" or simply ignore the announcement, and Kirsten would reverse course.

Once she had resolved what to do, she was relieved, and when the train picked up speed, she fell again into fitful sleep.

The train arrived at six the next morning, in full spring daylight, and when she stepped out of the tiny station, she paused to take the measure of the place. Her map told her Geilo was situated between two vast areas, the Hardangervidda, to the southwest, and the Hallingskarvet, to the north, but her initial perspective was of a scenic village in a valley surrounded by hills.

Mercifully, the retreating Germans had left it intact, if a little worn. It was colder than it had been in Rjukan, and though it was already mid-May, patches of frost and dirty snow lay here and there from overnight periods of freezing. With a long snow season, it would be a good place for vacation skiing, once people began doing that again. It even had a hotel, though her scant remaining cash would not permit her to enjoy it. But she'd already decided on the age-old traveler's bargain of shelter for work.

She strode along the main street, then turned left onto one of the side streets, where she spotted a cluster of houses with barns. Arbitrarily, she knocked at the first one. Someone must have seen her approach the house, for the door opened immediately. A gaunt man stood in front of her, frowning slightly in apparent puzzlement at the intrusion. He had a receding hairline and a wide gray mustache that curved around the sides of his mouth in the style of an earlier generation.

"Good morning. I need to stay a couple of days in Geilo, and I'm looking for room and board in exchange for work. Maybe I could cut some wood for you?" She could see by the sudden brightening of his expression that he was interested.

"A woman who cuts wood?" He scratched his cheek. "If that's true, you can sleep in our barn. My wife and I can barely manage it."

"It's true. I'll cut all you want. Does that include meals?"

"If you're not fancy, my wife will cook for you the same thing she cooks for me."

"Sounds fine. If you'll show me to my, uh, lodgings, I'll start right away."

"How many nights do you think?"

"I'm not sure. Three, maybe four. Oh, and my name is Kirsten."

"Very well. I'm Trygve Oleson. My wife is Ingar." He stepped outside and closed the door behind him. "So, come this way."

The barn was set back from the house, and once inside, she wondered why he kept one. It held two stalls, both of which were empty and in need of repair. She dropped her rucksack in a corner of what seemed the cleaner of the two.

"Used to have two cows," he explained. "But the Germans took one of them, and we sold the other when she stopped giving milk." He glanced around, assaying his own barn. "But things will get better. My son was in the Royal Norwegian Navy, so we had no one to do the heavy work. If you can do it, you can stay as long as you want."

As he exited, he patted the barn wall, as if to reassure it, then said over his shoulder, "There's clean hay in the loft. Help yourself."

❖

The war had obviously been hard on the Olesons, because Ingar was as bony as her husband. The midday meal, of boiled salt fish and potatoes, was the same basic fare Kirsten had eaten at Birgit's place, but with more potatoes and a lower grade of fish. All the more reason not to stay long.

"Are there businesses in town where I might find someone to deliver a message?"

"Well, we're not exactly Oslo, but we have a few businesses with things to sell. Back on the main street, turn left."

The meal warmed and fueled her for the walk, though the

"businesses," when she spotted them, could scarcely qualify as shops. Mostly they seemed to be houses with porches or garages containing a workshop.

The first garage was a stable, the second a carpenter's shop. Both were empty, but the third shop, where someone was banging out a metal pan on an anvil, was in business. Best of all, she spotted a Sami, who was apparently purchasing something. His gakti showed he wasn't from Udsek, but he still might know someone there.

After waiting for him to finish his purchase, she approached. "Good morning. I'm sorry to bother you, but do you know anyone in Udsek?"

He looked puzzled for a moment, and she was conscious how strange it must have been for him to have a Norwegian woman confront him in a public place.

"No. I don't. Why?"

"I have to get a letter to someone in Udsek and can't go myself. I was hoping to find someone to deliver it."

"Sorry. I can't help you."

Kirsten shrank inwardly. "Yes. All right. I understand. Thank you." She turned away.

"Maybe I can," a voice said behind her. It was the metalsmith.

The hope that shot through her was as palpable as warmth. "Can you? I'll pay." She hoped he wouldn't ask for much; she simply didn't have it.

"Udsek, you say? I deliver there sometimes. And I'm going out tomorrow. Not directly, unfortunately. It's toward the end of my route. Usually takes me two days, but I can deliver your letter."

"I'm very grateful. Here. I've already composed it." She fished it out of her pocket, recalling its neutral simplicity.

> *Forgive my silence, but they would not let me leave Britain. Not released from duty until now. So much to tell you. I wait in Geilo for word that you want to see me.*

"Deliver it to Maarit Ragnar, granddaughter of Jova and Alof, grandniece of Gaiju, the only one in the family still alive. I've written all their names at the top." She laid it on his open hand, and he slipped it into a pocket on his jacket.

"You don't have to pay me for delivery, though you might buy something, to show good faith." He smiled with feigned innocence.

She calculated how much money she still had. "I'll buy a coffee pot that you can deliver along with the letter. Will that be all right?"

"It's a deal. I have a nice one, not too expensive," he said, and named the price. Kirsten counted out the kroner, grateful for the hundredth time for the money SOE had supplied her over the last months for her work. But now it was almost gone. "Two days, you say?"

"A day to Udsek, then I go on to a couple of other places. So, I won't be back for three or maybe four days to tell you what happened. Are you sure you can't deliver it yourself?"

"I'm sure. I'll look for you here in four days. In the meantime, I'll be staying with the Olesons, so any message to me should be through them." She slid her hands that now seemed useless into her trouser pockets and strode from the metalsmith's shop.

❖

The next morning, for lack of other amusement, she watched the metalsmith load up his cart behind a sturdy fjord horse. Then, with a click of the tongue and a tap of the reins, he started off, her letter, she assumed, tucked inside his jacket.

How would Maarit and Niilas react? She shrugged inwardly. No matter what happened, it would still take four days before she'd know. Four long, empty days. She turned away and began a slow, brooding walk through the town.

Postwar Geilo was not a pretty place, but presumably it never had been. Sparsely populated and with little commerce, its main virtue was its proximity to the vidda on one side and the glacier on the other. Before the war, it had probably attracted hikers, and perhaps would do so again one day.

But spring was in the air, and green moss was appearing here and there between the patches of old snow and pools of meltwater.

The journey had been tiring, and she felt no desire to hike toward the sparkling glacier or to anyplace out of town. Nor was she much given to chatting with the residents or with passersby. She was, in short, morose.

She fulfilled her wood-cutting obligation to the Olesons, though it turned out to be more strenuous than she'd expected. Clearly, she had overestimated her strength. But the hard, physical labor provided a means to blunt her longing and the torment of uncertainty.

To prepare for the worst, of having to return south, shattered and alone, she began to make plans for life without Maarit. It wouldn't be much different from the way she'd always lived. With her mother gone, nothing called her back to Britain. On the other hand, her father, a distinguished resistor, would soon return to Norway, almost certainly to some position in the reconstruction of Norway's hydroelectric system. And he had all but promised her employment. She could make a good living as a chemist.

She swung the axe high and brought it down hard, splitting the log with a satisfying *CHOCK*!

And surely, she could find other interesting women in Norway.

Three days passed, then four, and no news came. The Olesons had enough wood to last them into the autumn, and Kirsten could barely lift her sore arms to dress in the morning. Although the light would linger for some three more hours, she had no desire to socialize, or even stay awake, and so withdrew to her nest in the barn. She lay for a long time, sleepless, gnawing her lip, fighting back tears. The deadline was reached. The pot-smith was due the next day to tell her either that the message couldn't be delivered, or that it was refused. Either way, she'd be heartbroken.

The confidence she'd felt swinging the axe had left her now, and as she lay with her arm thrown over her eyes, she could only murmur, "Damn, damn, damn…"

She must have fallen asleep after all, for she awoke befuddled at the sound of the barn door sliding open. It was just becoming dark, and she squinted at the play of light. High at the top of the opening, the sky was still a rich blue, enough to obscure the figure in the opening.

Figures, rather, for there were two of them, a tall one and a very short one.

Her first thought was that it was Trygve and Ingar Oleson, and she puzzled at their intrusion into her private space. But then the double figure broke apart, and she grasped that one was a reindeer and the other was… Her heart leapt at the realization. Maarit.

She stood up, still incredulous.

Leaving the mysterious reindeer at the door of the barn, Maarit marched toward her and embraced her tightly. "I waited so long for you," she murmured, half sobbing, into her hair.

Kirsten felt her mouth tremble as she held back her own tears. "I'm so sorry. They wouldn't let me come back." She pressed her forehead against Maarit's shoulder. "Forgive me."

"Of course I do." Maarit traced her fingers lightly over Kirsten's lips, then covered them with her own in a long, fervent kiss. They stood with closed eyes, breathing against each other, and it was for Kirsten as if a gaping wound had suddenly closed. She had expected euphoria, but instead felt serenity, rightness, wordless benediction.

After a moment, she drew back. "Are you all right? They said you were wounded. What happened?" She guided Maarit over to the corner of the pen and drew her down to the straw that had been her bed for four nights.

"A gunshot wound on my last mission, and I got an infection. It's healing, but very slowly. I just don't have much strength, yet."

"Shot by a German?"

"A quisling. He killed the man I was trying to save. Fortunately, help arrived in time to get me to the hospital. But what about you? What kept you so long in Britain?"

"The Normandy invasion."

"You were involved in that?"

Kirsten chuckled softly. "Not directly. I was one of the team creating radio messages to convince the Germans the Allies were landing in Norway so they'd keep a large army up here rather than in France."

"But Normandy was last June. A year ago."

"I know. But they had no job for me in Norway, so they refused to let me return. Only when Lief Tronstad formed a team to defend power plants against the German scorched-earth withdrawal could I find a way to come back here. I was with Tronstad and then Poulsson from October until the surrender. Then, finally, they released me to look for you. Birgit told me you'd been working for the Shetland transport operation until you were wounded."

"Yes, I was a guide for our friend Iver, bringing people to where they could meet one of the Shetland boats. Big things now, those boats, submarine chasers and the like."

"Yes, the *Hitra,* which took me back to Scotland, was one of those. A luxury liner compared to what I first traveled on. But we're getting away from you. What happened so that you ended up in Udsek?" She dropped her voice. "And married, I heard."

"Married? To whom?"

"Niilas. The one they said rescued you and took you back to Udsek."

"Niilas? He did help me, but he's already married."

"Not to you?

Maarit laughed brightly. "No. Not to me. And he has a son. Also not with me. Did you really think…?"

"I didn't know what to think. How did he know you needed help?"

"I told you Niilas gave up herding years ago. He's a driver who supplies deer meat to various towns. During the war, it was all black market, of course, but he made it work. When he passed through Trondheim, a local Sami who worked at the hospital told him a Sami woman was there under a false identity and needed help. When Niilas found out it was me, he dropped everything and showed up to get me out."

"Oh. I'm so relieved!" Kirsten held her at arm's length, studying the face she hadn't seen for more than a year. Then she danced away to pile up clean straw from the barn floor. She laid her coat over it to form a pillow and held out her hand. "Come. Sit next to me and tell me everything. I've missed you so much."

Maarit lowered herself onto the little straw nest and leaned forward to stroke Kirsten's cheek. "I've missed you too, darling. And I've been waiting for you the whole time." She embraced Kirsten again and lay for a while with her head on her shoulder.

"I'd made wonderful plans for us until it began to look like you weren't coming back."

"What plans? To go back to school?"

"I'd like to. I can make a better living from medicine than from reindeer. I'm just worried about whether the Trondheim hospital will let me in. Remember, the quislings there treated me like dirt."

"The collaborators will all be gone now, most of them to jail for treason, and the patriots will still be working. And remember, you have a commendation from the king!"

"That's right. At least it's good for that. But what about you? How can we stay together?"

"As well as that royal commendation, I also have a degree in chemistry, or almost. I was nearly finished when Terboven closed the university. It should take only a few months to get the degree. Best of all, my father is known in Trondheim, an important person in the industry. He's all but offered me a position, once I have credentials."

Kirsten brushed her lips over Maarit's hair, and as her glance wandered toward the barn door, she noticed the reindeer. It had tried to follow Maarit inside but was held back by its harness tied to something outside.

"You brought a reindeer? In June?"

"And a sled, too. Not that it did me much good. I still have trouble walking long distances. I get tired very quickly and could never have hiked all the way here from Udsek. That thing out there is a pulka sled, with a flat bottom, and it pulled me over the snowy and mossy patches. Rocks tear it up, of course, so half the time, I just walked alongside it like an old woman. Anyhow, I'm surprised you don't recognize the deer."

"What do you mean? How should I recognize a deer?"

"Go take a look. And while you're there, you can unharness her and bring in the sack with her fodder. Poor thing."

Puzzled, Kirsten stood up, brushed straw from her legs, and strode toward the door. The animal had been in silhouette against the early evening sky, but as Kirsten came close, she halted suddenly.

"It's the white one. Lykke!"

"Yes, the calf we saved."

"The one I slept with." Cooing endearments, Kirsten unbuckled the harness and led the deer into the barn. "She's really tame."

"She's really spoiled. Gaiju kept her out of the herd and fed her by hand. He knew she was my pet. Fortunately, she escaped being slaughtered by the Germans."

Kirsten led the reindeer into the stall where Maarit sat and tugged her down onto the straw with them. "Will she stay with us?"

"Poor girl has been dragging me overland for two days. Give her some of the moss, and she'll snuggle up as long as you wish."

"I wish it forever. With you and our reindeer. Can we, do you think? I mean, make it forever?"

"I never imagined it otherwise. So, let's get a good night's sleep, the three of us, and tomorrow we'll work on the details of our plan. It's peacetime. We can do anything we want."

"Even this." Kirsten slid her arm under Maarit's back, pressed her close, and began the lovemaking she had dreamed about for over a year. At the foot of the stall, Lykke curled into a deer doughnut and closed her eyes.

Postscript

During World War II, the British and Norwegians made three attempts to sabotage the German heavy-water program: Operation Freshman, Operation Gunnerside, and the Sinking of the *Hydro*. Freshman was a disaster, resulting in the deaths (from crashing, or in captivity) of all participants. Gunnerside was successful and commemorated in a 1965 film *The Heroes of Telemark*. The sinking of the *Hydro*, although it was the final blow to the program in Norway, remains morally questionable. The sinking caused many Norwegian casualties, and it is unlikely the heavy water it carried would have ever led to a German bomb. While women were active in both the SOE and in the Norwegian resistance, none were prominent in the three operations. Wikipedia lists the actual names of the large number of men involved.

Deuterium (D, or ^{2}H), also called heavy hydrogen, is an isotope of hydrogen with a nucleus of one proton and one neutron, while the nucleus of ordinary hydrogen has one proton. D_2O occurs naturally in minute quantities in ordinary water, H_2O.

Hardangervidda. Plateau (vidda) in central Norway that is particularly rugged and crisscrossed by ancient reindeer-migration trails. While barren and only marginally habitable during the period of the novel, it is now a national park enjoyed by hikers and campers in summer.

Heavy Water D_2O (water with heavy hydrogen) was useful as a moderator to slow neutrons in a nuclear reaction. As such, it was a valuable tool for atomic power research. Norwegian scientists at the hydroelectric plant at Rjukan initially undertook production, with a minute output. During the occupation, Germans expanded and controlled the program to supply the liquid for development of an atomic weapon, though there is no indication the German program advanced very far. The American program to develop an atomic weapon used other moderators.

Milorg *(Militær organisasjon).* Originally merely a list of names of patriots who would fight when called upon, it was largely unarmed, untrained, and unequipped, with little leadership. By 1942, it had become a country-wide guerilla organization hoping to support an Allied landing. Each district had its own unit and leader. From May 1944, local Milorg units worked with SOE to carry out overt sabotage to prevent (German) mobilization of Norwegian workers and assisted peripherally in some of the heavy-water sabotage.

Occupation Government: Josef Terboven. Reichskommissar of Norway and head of civilian affairs. Ruthless and petty, he was widely disliked, even by Germans. He planned several concentration camps, was responsible for the closing of Oslo University, and ordered the massacres in the village of Televåg and the Beisfjord prison camp. Upon Germany's surrender, he blew himself up in a bunker. **Vidkun Quisling.** Founder of the Norwegian fascist party and prime minister of the pro-Nazi puppet government, he was largely beholden to Terboven and the fascist party, thus participated in Germany's program of genocide. After the war, he was found guilty of murder and treason and executed by firing squad. The word quisling became a synonym for traitor and collaborator.

Royal Family. King Haakon 7th and Crown Prince Olav (along with the much of the government) fled Norway with the aid of the British Royal Navy in June 1940 and established a government in exile in London. During the war, King Haakon broadcast regularly from London, and although he had little to say about the SOE sabotage missions, he nonetheless became the symbolic head of Norwegian resistance.

Sami (Laplanders). Indigenous people of northern Norway, Sweden, Finland, and the Kola Peninsula. Largely reindeer herders, many also subsisted on fishing, trapping, or other trades. In all four countries, Sami were suppressed up to and through World War II. Their distinctive clothing varied according to their respective communities. Germans used Sami labor, e.g., for laying rail lines to transport troops across Sweden, and some acted as guides for the German mountain troops. The Norwegian resistance also paid them to help transport goods and fugitives. In December 1944, Swedish Sami ski troops fought in northern Norway. The retreating Germans' scorched-earth policy caused widespread devastation of settlements and ancient structures, while destruction of forests reduced reindeer herds. In 1990, Norway officially recognized the Sami as an indigenous people and thus entitled to special protection and rights. Sami currently have their own parliament (Sámediggi) and flag. Their traditional houses, of birch frame, birch-bark waterproofing, and turf insulation, were called **goahti.** Temporary, teepee-like shelters used during migrations were called **lavvus. Udsek** is fictional and based on general information about Sami life, customs, and artifacts.

Shetland transport ("Shetland Bus") (1941–end of war). Officially named Royal Norwegian Naval Special Unit, though it was under the direction of the British military. It consisted first of fishing boats, later of armed submarine chasers, *Vigra, Hessa, Hitra.* They crossed the North Sea without lights between Norway and the Shetland Islands (northernmost Scotland) during the winter darkness to avoid capture or bombardment. Their task was to transfer agents, weapons, radios, etc. in and out of Norway and bring out Norwegians who feared arrest.

SOE (Special Operations Executive). A secret British organization formed in July 1940 to conduct espionage, sabotage, and reconnaissance in occupied Europe and to aid local resistance. Head of the Norwegian section was Jack Wilson, who sent missions to Norway both with and without the cooperation (or even knowledge) of Milorg and the Norwegian government in exile. The organization employed more than 13,000 people, about 3,200 of whom were women.

Vemork Hydroelectric Plant (outside Rjukan, Norway). Using the flow of the Rjukan waterfall, the plant opened in 1911, primarily for the production of fertilizer. In the 1940s it began to produce heavy water, which the occupying Nazis wished to expand for use in atomic research. The plant closed in 1971 (becoming a museum), and a new plant opened behind it within the mountain. From 1929, the head chemical engineer was **Jomar Brun,** who sabotaged the Nazi production with castor oil, then passed diagrams and photos to the Allies before fleeing himself to Britain, where he helped plan the destructive operations. He was not married to an Englishwoman and (sadly) did not have a lesbian daughter. **Leif Tronstad.** Professor at the Institute of Technology, Trondheim, planned, designed, and supervised the plant until he fled to UK to become head of Section IV of the Norwegian High Command. He returned to Norway and was killed while defending local installations, as described in the novel.

About the Author

A recovering academic, Justine has thirteen novels under her literary belt, all setting lesbians in the historical landscape. Her tales immerse us in Ancient Egyptian theology and the Crusades, then move to Venice under the Inquisition and to Michelangelo's Rome. Religious iconoclast, she also created an LGBT version of Sodom and Gomorrah and later an homage to Dian Fossey and her mountain gorillas.

Saracen's last four thriller/romances deal with World War II, shining lights on that shattering event as seen from inside Germany, from the French and Belgian Resistance, from the cockpit of a fighter flown by a female Soviet pilot, and from the focus of a Soviet woman sniper. Her last, *Berlin Hungers*, treats love between victor and defeated during the postwar Berlin Airlift.

An adopted European, Saracen lives in Brussels where she has become very francofied, drinking wine, eating smelly cheese on baguettes, and enjoying the benefits of socialized medicine. In Covid-free times, she travels to Egypt to scuba dive, and to other exotic and dangerous locations like the United States.

Books Available From Bold Strokes Books

Best Practice by Carsen Taite. When attorney Grace Maldonado agrees to mentor her best friend's little sister, she's prepared to confront Perry's rebellious nature, but she isn't prepared to fall in love. Legal Affairs: one law firm, three best friends, three chances to fall in love. (978-1-63555-361-1)

Home by Kris Bryant. Natalie and Sarah discover that anything is possible when love takes the long way home. (978-1-63555-853-1)

Keeper by Sydney Quinne. With a new charge under her reluctant wing—feisty, highly intelligent math wizard Isabelle Templeton—Keeper Andy Bouchard has to prevent a murder or die trying. (978-1-63555-852-4)

One More Chance by Ali Vali. Harry Bastantes planned a future with Desi Thompson until the day Desi disappeared without a word, only to walk back into her life sixteen years later. (978-1-63555-536-3)

Renegade's War by Gun Brooke. Freedom fighter Aurelia DeCallum regrets saving the woman called Blue. She fears it will jeopardize her mission, and secretly, Blue might end up breaking Aurelia's heart. (978-1-63555-484-7)

The Other Women by Erin Zak. What happens in Vegas should stay in Vegas, but what do you do when the love you find in Vegas changes your life forever? (978-1-63555-741-1)

The Sea Within by Missouri Vaun. Time is running out for Dr. Elle Graham to convince Captain Jackson Drake that the only thing that can save future Earth resides in the past, and rescue her broken heart in the process. (978-1-63555-568-4)

To Sleep With Reindeer Justine Saracen. In Norway under Nazi occupation, Maarit, an Indigenous woman, and Kirsten, a Norwegian resister, join forces to stop the development of an atomic weapon. (978-1-63555-735-0)

Twice Shy by Aurora Rey. Having an ex with benefits isn't all it's cracked up to be. Will Amanda Russo learn that lesson in time to take a chance on love with Quinn Sullivan? (978-1-63555-737-4)

Z-Town by Eden Darry. Forced to work together to stay alive, Meg and Lane must find the centuries-old treasure before the zombies find them first. (978-1-63555-743-5)

Bet Against Me by Fiona Riley. In the high-stakes luxury real estate market, everything has a price, and as rival Realtors Trina Lee and Kendall Yates find out, that means their hearts and souls, too. (978-1-63555-729-9)

Broken Reign by Sam Ledel. Together on an epic journey in search of a mysterious cure, a princess and a village outcast must overcome life-threatening challenges and their own prejudice if they want to survive. (978-1-63555-739-8)

Just One Taste by CJ Birch. For Lauren, it only took one taste to start trusting in love again. (978-1-63555-772-5)

Lady of Stone by Barbara Ann Wright. Sparks fly as a magical emergency forces a noble embarrassed by her ability to submit to a low-born teacher who resents everything about her. (978-1-63555-607-0)

Last Resort by Angie Williams. Katie and Rhys are about to find out what happens when you meet the girl of your dreams but you aren't looking for a happily ever after. (978-1-63555-774-9)

Longing for You by Jenny Frame. When Debrek housekeeper Katie Brekman is attacked amid a burgeoning vampire-witch war, Alexis Villiers must go against everything her clan believes in to save her. (978-1-63555-658-2)

Money Creek by Anne Laughlin. Clare Lehane is a troubled lawyer from Chicago who tries to make her way in a rural town full of secrets and deceptions. (978-1-63555-795-4)

Passion's Sweet Surrender by Ronica Black. Cam and Blake are unable to deny their passion for each other, but surrendering to love is a whole different matter. (978-1-63555-703-9)

The Holiday Detour by Jane Kolven. It will take everything going wrong to make Dana and Charlie see how right they are for each other. (978-1-63555-720-6)

Too Hot to Ride by Andrews & Austin. World-famous cutting horse champion and industry legend Jane Barrow is knockdown sexy in the way she moves, talks, and rides, and Rae Starr is determined not to get involved with this womanizing gambler. (978-1-63555-776-3)

A Love that Leads to Home by Ronica Black. For Carla Sims and Janice Carpenter, home isn't about location, it's where your heart is. (978-1-63555-675-9)

Blades of Bluegrass by D. Jackson Leigh. A US Army occupational therapist must rehab a bitter veteran who is a ticking political time bomb the military is desperate to disarm. (978-1-63555-637-7)

Hopeless Romantic by Georgia Beers. Can a jaded wedding planner and an optimistic divorce attorney possibly find a future together? (978-1-63555-650-6)

Hopes and Dreams by PJ Trebelhorn. Movie theater manager Riley Warren is forced to face her high school crush and tormentor, wealthy socialite Victoria Thayer, at their twentieth reunion. (978-1-63555-670-4)

In the Cards by Kimberly Cooper Griffin. Daria and Phaedra are about to discover that love finds a way, especially when powers outside their control are at play. (978-1-63555-717-6)

Moon Fever by Ileandra Young. SPEAR agent Danika Karson must clear her werewolf friend of multiple false charges while teaching her vampire girlfriend to resist the blood mania brought on by a full moon. (978-1-63555-603-2)

Serenity by Jesse J. Thoma. For Kit Marsden, there are many things in life she cannot change. Serenity is in the acceptance. (978-1-63555-713-8)

Sylver and Gold by Michelle Larkin. Working feverishly to find a killer before he strikes again, Boston homicide detective Reid Sylver and rookie cop London Gold are blindsided by their chemistry and developing attraction. (978-1-63555-611-7)

9 781